THE HEARTS WE LEAVE BEHIND

The Hearts We Leave Behind

A NOVEL

BUCK TURNER

E
EMORILAND
PRESS

Formatted with Vellum

This book is dedicated to my grandparents, Betty and Fred Turner, with love.

Thank you for sharing with me your love of art, for afternoons spent laughing and playing board games, for Sunday dinners, and for chats in the Blue Room while sipping sweet tea.

Those memories will be with me always.

Thank you for purchasing this book

To receive the latest news and info, or to join Buck's team of beta readers, please go to:

www.buckturner.com

Prologue

Twas not my lips you kissed, but my soul
— Judy Garland

Chapter One

APRIL 1998

"Nora, thank God." Even through the phone, the caller's relief was palpable. "How was the trip? Did you run into traffic? Are you settled yet?"

She was like an automatic weapon, firing questions one after another.

Nora Dawson took a deep breath and answered her mother all at once. "The trip was smooth... No traffic... And I just got the last box into the house." She drew a hand across her forehead as beads of perspiration trickled out from beneath her bangs. "And in a shade under three hours, which isn't bad considering I did all the work myself."

A titter of laughter echoed from the other end of the line. "So what do you have planned for the rest of the day?"

A grumble reverberated in Nora's stomach, reminding her that the Egg McMuffin she'd eaten for breakfast had vanished hours ago. She opened the cupboard doors—nothing. A check of the fridge revealed the same. That meant the only food she had left other than a half-eaten pack of peanut M&M's was a box of saltines she'd stolen from her mom and dad's pantry before leaving home.

"It looks like I need to go grocery shopping," she said.

"Well, it sounds like you've got things under control." Kathleen's compliment filled Nora with an unfamiliar sense of accomplishment; she had been dependent on others most of her adult life, and here she was, for the first time in as long as she could remember, doing things on her own.

"Yes, I think I do," she said, which brought a smile to her face. "By the way, I wanted to tell you that I start work on Monday."

"This Monday? But I thought you said you'd have the week to familiarize yourself with the area."

"So did I, but the hospital called this afternoon and asked if I wouldn't mind starting a week early. Since I can use the extra money, I agreed to do it. Besides, I'm anxious to get started, and I can always go exploring next weekend."

"In that case, at least make a trip to the hospital tomorrow," Kathleen said. "Just to get a feel for the drive. I'd hate for you to be late on your first day."

"Already on it." Nora scanned the note fixed to the fridge with the pair of butterfly magnets Gran had given her for her tenth birthday. "That's first on my list."

Kathleen chuckled. "Dad and I taught you well. Oh, before I forget, he wanted me to remind you to lock your doors and windows at night." She added in a whisper, "You know how he worries."

"Tell him to relax. This is a nice neighborhood." And as she said it, through the kitchen window Nora observed a young couple pushing a stroller up the sidewalk, followed closely by a black miniature schnauzer.

"I still can't believe you won't be close by anymore. But I'm really rooting for you. We both are. And after everything you've been through..."

Nora traced a finger along the edge of the sink, her thoughts following in its wake, and wondered if everyone in their late twenties carried with them the same emotional baggage.

"Thanks, Mom." She drew in a breath. "Well, I guess I'll get back to it—lots of unpacking yet to do. Talk to you in a couple of days. Love ya. Bye."

Nora ended the conversation and continued her inventory of the kitchen. Pots, pans, cooking utensils, dishes, and silverware came with the house, basically everything she needed to prepare a meal except groceries. A search of the drawers revealed a few odds and ends—batteries, a can opener, and a corkscrew—but tucked away beneath a pack of rubber bands, she discovered a beautifully handwritten note from the previous occupant.

To whoever reads this letter...

You don't know me, but two years ago I arrived in Brentwood with my heart in pieces. After watching my mother lose her fight with cancer, I was broken but determined to start anew. Little did I know what blessings awaited. I don't know your story or what has brought you here, but rest assured, this is where you belong. It may not look like much, but this little home has magic in its walls, and if you take care of it–it will take care of you in return.

Good luck and God bless,

Leslie

Leslie's kind words spread a warmth through Nora's chest, giving her a spark of hope. It seemed like ages since she'd felt that way; the past few months had been one disaster after another, beginning with the end of her engagement to Jeremy. What was once the joyous prospect of marriage had, in the blink of an eye, turned into the heartbreak of being single and alone.

A look around the living room revealed empty boxes sprawled across the floor, their hollow echoes bouncing off the walls. With every unpacked item, Nora placed in this new home a little piece of herself. The process was slow and exhausting, but every hour brought her closer to something that resembled peace.

So this is what it feels like to start over.

The decision to relocate from her hometown of Trafford, Alabama, to Brentwood, Tennessee, hadn't been easy for Nora and had happened almost entirely by accident. A month earlier, while checking her email, an online ad for a nursing job had caught her attention, and she'd applied. Truthfully, she thought she'd receive one of those automatic replies informing her that after a thorough review of her skills and qualifications, there were other candidates better suited for the position.

To her astonishment, she received a call instead from a woman named Gail Murphy, the director of nursing at Belle Haven Center for Health and Rehabilitation. From Nora's research, Belle Haven had a stellar reputation as one of the best long-term facilities in the Southeast and a proving ground for nurses with ambitions of working in major hospitals like the Mayo Clinic or Cedars-Sinai. It was exactly the kind of place she needed to take her career to the next level.

Gail explained that despite her lack of experience, which

she'd assumed would be the nail in the coffin, Nora was precisely the kind of candidate Gail was looking for. *New blood* was how she put it. After completing an initial phone screening, Nora made the drive to Brentwood and met Gail in person. The formal interview included a tour of the facility, lunch, and a meeting with Pamela Cronan, the head of Human Resources. The whole thing took half a day, which might sound oppressive, but Nora was so enraptured with the place that she hardly noticed.

When the interview ended, Nora and Gail chatted briefly, and Gail asked her what she thought about the hospital and the grounds and whether she could see herself working there. As Nora told her parents later that evening over dinner, she knew as soon as she turned up the long drive that Belle Haven was a fit. And while she knew very little about the area, aside from Nashville being the country music capital of the world, Brentwood had a small-town feel that set her at ease.

After taking the evening to mull over the offer, Nora called Gail the next morning and informed her of her decision to take the job. Two weeks later, she packed her entire life—all twenty-seven years of it—in the back of a U-Haul and headed north.

After unpacking most of the boxes, Nora took a break and went to the grocery store, stocking up on the basics. On her way back she stopped at Shilohs, a local bar and grill, got a burger and fries to go, then returned home and scarfed down dinner while enjoying the peaceful evening from the comfort of her back porch.

When she'd finished her meal, Nora went inside and continued unpacking her clothes. She laid out her pants and shirts in neat piles before hanging them in the oversized walk-in closet. At first glance, it seemed almost too perfect—with its built-in shoe rack lined with multiple shelves, hooks for belts and purses, and velvet hangers—like an interior designer had been hard at work. No longer did she have to compete for space with Jeremy's suits and ties; this was all hers.

Being single has its perks.

With the closet organized, she filled the tub with steaming hot water, poured a glass of crisp white wine, and sank in with the latest issue of Cosmo. She read *Ten Ways to Have Better Sex After Ditching Your Ex* and couldn't help but smirk at the irony of it all.

When her skin started to prune, she climbed out of the bath, toweled off, and spent a few minutes examining herself in the mirror. Her eyes widened as she studied her reflection. Her hair was longer than when she'd been an undergrad but still the same color, and her stomach, while flat and toned, no longer held the washboard definition that came when she was running competitively.

The whole situation with Jeremy had done a number on Nora and caused her to question a lot of things, her looks being one of them. She'd often wondered if Jeremy had left her because of her appearance. She had to admit she wasn't as confident about her appearance as she used to be. The bags under her eyes had gotten darker, and her cheekbones protruded too much for her liking. Thankfully, she had her grandmother's timeless beauty, passed down through her mother. Nora's curves might not be as prominent as those of other women, but her petite frame was offset by striking blue-green eyes that glistened against caramel hair and olive skin.

Convinced that she had at least a few decent years left, she tugged on a pair of soft pajamas, climbed into bed, and went over the list that she'd made for her transition to Brentwood.

Grocery store? Check. Local watering hole? Check. A drive

to Belle Haven was on the agenda for the following morning. The task of finding a suitable Baptist church lingered in the air; she'd spotted two while driving into town. Clothing boutique? Given her dated wardrobe, that should be at the top of her list. At least she'd taken care of her hair; the color and cut had turned out quite nicely if she said so herself.

Overtaken by exhaustion, Nora turned off the lights and settled in for the night. In the dark, she smiled, knowing she'd survived the first day of the rest of her life.

Chapter Two

THE KITCHEN WAS AGLOW WITH MORNING SUNLIGHT streaming in through the open windows, and a gentle breeze filled the air with the scent of honeysuckle and freshly cut grass. Nora looked out at the street as a family dressed in their Sunday best loaded into an SUV, obviously heading to church. It was clear, despite what she had been told, she was still firmly in the Bible belt.

After finishing her coffee, Nora freshened up, determined that today she would *not* waste a single moment thinking about Jeremy. She changed into a white sundress, paired it with tan strappy sandals and aviator sunglasses, then pulled her hair into a loose ponytail before leaving the house.

She spent most of the morning driving around with the top down, letting the wind dry her hair as she drove by quaint neighborhoods and parks. Above her, little puffs of white clouds clung lazily to a cerulean sky, reminding her of spring afternoons she used to spend back home in Trafford.

After a quick stop at the convenience store, where she purchased a bottled water and a pack of peppermint gum, she drove to the hospital as her mom had suggested.

Less than a mile from the interstate, Belle Haven occupied fifty acres of rolling green pasture. The hospital itself sat at the end of a long, sweeping drive lined with towering poplars, vibrant oaks, and a smattering of delicate dogwoods. Part of what was once a sprawling plantation, Belle Haven consisted of three main buildings (all predating the Civil War), five ponds, two stables, and an apple orchard. In addition, a tiny stream meandered its way along the edge of the property, drawing a line between the lush fields of Indian grass and thick forests beyond.

At the gate, Nora adjusted her glasses, then looked up to see a security guard stepping out of a glass-enclosed booth. She smiled and waved, and after she introduced herself, the man thumbed through the employee registry, found her name, and unlocked the gate, granting her access to the ground.

"Have a great day now!" he said kindly, tipping his hat.

Nora smiled, thinking how happy her dad would be to hear about the added security measures.

When the gate opened, she proceeded up the drive, taking time to appreciate the beauty of her surroundings. At the top of the hill, a gurgling fountain greeted her, its clear water sparkling in the sunlight. She couldn't resist stopping to admire it for a moment before turning around and making her way back down the drive.

After stopping at the Opry Mills Mall, where she purchased a new pair of running shoes, Nora drove down Old Hickory Boulevard, where she discovered schools, churches with soaring steeples, and various restaurants ranging from classic American diners to sushi bars. Closer to home, she located several sprawling parks with plenty of green space where she could run and ride her bike. Everywhere she looked, all the amenities she could need were at her fingertips.

That afternoon Nora unpacked boxes of dishes and placed

them in the kitchen cabinets. In the living room, she arranged the furniture to create a cozy seating area, then hung art on the walls with precision and care. One after another, she brought each room to life with rugs, curtains, pictures, and other accessories that fit her modern-farmhouse style. When all was done, she stepped back to admire her work. The empty house she'd moved into just yesterday was starting to feel like home.

With the daylight quickly fading, she slipped into her new running shoes and stretched her legs on the porch. She took a deep breath of air and set off for a jog, feeling the rhythmic pounding of her feet against the pavement.

She pushed the last stretch of her run and collapsed onto a bench at the edge of the park. Sweat beaded down her forehead, her breath heavy in her chest. She checked her watch; she'd made it in just under six minutes. *Not bad*. Between interviews, packing, and adjusting to her new place, this was her first run in nearly two weeks. But with that weight lifted off her shoulders, she felt like she could do anything.

When the afternoon light began to change, Nora turned around and jogged home.

Rather than dine out again, she prepared a meal of spaghetti with meat sauce, and toasted a piece of garlic bread in the oven. While the sauce simmered, she opened the window and enjoyed the sweet sounds of spring: birds chirping, lawn mowers whirring in the distance, joyful screams from children playing tag in their front yards as their parents called them in for dinner.

After she ate, Nora sank into the living room couch and tried to focus on the game show playing in front of her, but after pushing the image away all day with activity after activity, now all she could think about was Jeremy's smug face. The way he had smiled and lied with such ease made her stomach turn. One day his lies and manipulations would catch up to him; a smile made its way onto Nora's face. Eventually Jeremy would get what he deserved.

The next morning Nora silenced the alarm clock, then put on her pressed navy uniform and went into the kitchen to prepare breakfast. After downing two scrambled eggs and a piece of buttered toast, she pulled her hair into a ponytail and applied just enough rouge to give her cheeks some color.

She arrived fifteen minutes early for work and parked in the employee lot. After a quick check in the rearview mirror, she took a deep breath and got out of the car.

"Morning," said the receptionist as Nora walked through the front door.

"Morning." She introduced herself and said that Gail was expecting her.

While she waited, Nora flipped through a magazine, scanning the pictures that adorned its pages. A few minutes later, Gail appeared with a welcoming smile on her face.

"I'm so glad you're here." She pulled Nora into a hug and complimented her hair. "I apologize for the change in schedule." Gail led Nora through the double doors. "And for sounding so cryptic over the phone. But Pamela—You remember her, don't you?"

Nora nodded, keeping in lockstep.

"She's going to be out the next two weeks on vacation. Her husband surprised her with a trip to Hawaii for their anniversary. I hope this didn't ruin your plans."

"Not at all. I was going to use this week to get settled, but honestly, I got more done this weekend than I anticipated, so..."

"What about the house—will you be comfortable there?"

"Yes." She tried to keep up with the conversation as they

navigated the labyrinth of hallways. “It’s the perfect size for me. Thank you, by the way, for recommending it.”

“My pleasure.” They turned the corner. “I’ve always loved that little cottage. There’s just something about it. I think everyone that’s worked here has stayed in that place at one time or another.”

That revelation prompted a question. “Who’s Leslie? I found a note from her in the kitchen, wishing me luck.”

Gail plowed ahead without skipping a beat. “Leslie was one of my favorites.” Her face lit up. “A little quirky at times, but one hell of a nurse. It doesn’t surprise me that she left you a note. She was always doing things like that.”

When Gail’s expression turned wistful, Nora asked, “Did something happen to her?”

“Yes, she got married.” They slid past a nurse pushing a medicine cart. “To a real nice young man from Murfreesboro. It broke her heart to leave, but her husband took a big corporate job with FedEx, so they packed up and moved to Memphis.” Gail lowered her voice. “Not to put any pressure on you, but the last three nurses who have stayed in your house all met their future husbands while living there.” She gave an exaggerated wink.

No pressure.

They arrived at their destination—a large common room, its walls painted a warm shade of yellow. Tables were scattered throughout the room, and at each sat elderly men and women, their eyes alive with conversation and laughter as they enjoyed their morning coffee. At the far end, several more residents sat basking in the morning sunlight in front of a row of windows that overlooked a sprawling garden.

“This is it,” Gail announced. She paused and glanced at her watch. “Breakfast isn’t for another half hour, but everyone comes here to start their day. We have a library down that hall”

—she pointed to the left—"and there's a computer lab for those that are technically inclined. Oh! I almost forgot about our theater, which shows movies now and then. It's just there. I think I covered most of this during your interview but thought you might appreciate a refresher."

"Yes, ma'am." Nora had forgotten about the theater.

Gail grabbed the medication log and signed off at the bottom. "We also have a pool on the lower level. But most of our group activities like painting, reading, and bingo take place here."

"What about meals?"

"Our fine dining center is at the end of the hall, through the double doors. I think you'll find that Belle Haven has the most modern facilities around, and we try our best to accommodate the needs of all our residents. Any questions so far?"

"Just one." Nora silently counted the residents again. "You mentioned last time that there were twenty-two residents, but I only see twenty-one."

Gail's eyebrows jumped in astonishment. "You're very observant, Miss Dawson. I like that. The truth is our newest resident, Fred Carlisle, is a bit—how shall I say this—antisocial. He spends most of his time in his room and only comes out occasionally to sit by the window alone."

Nora felt a tug at her heart. Her grandfather had spent his last few years in a place like Belle Haven and had also been reluctant to acclimate.

"There must be some way to get him involved," she mused.

Gail smiled kindly at her. "I'm glad to hear you say that, because that's where you come in."

"Me?"

"I probably should have mentioned it in the interview," said Gail in a whisper, "but Mr. Carlisle is the reason my last two nurses quit. It's a shame too. They were both very talented." She sighed regretfully.

That would have been nice to know.

"And why do you think things will be any different with me?" Nora suddenly felt her lack of experience acutely.

"Because, Miss Dawson." Gail patted Nora's shoulder and looked her in the eye. "I have faith in you."

Well, that makes one of us!

"Now come along. I'm anxious to introduce you to the team."

Nora followed her to the nurses' lounge, put away her personal effects, then joined Gail for introductions.

The nurses—five in all—were an eclectic mix of ages and backgrounds. Nervously, Nora took them in, finally settling on Nikki Simmons, postcard pretty with petite features, blond hair, and sparkling blue eyes. She smiled warmly, and Nora could tell Nikki had the kind of infectious enthusiasm that made patients feel instantly at ease.

Beside Nikki stood another young nurse—Whitney Sloan—who had only been in Nashville for a year but seemed to fit right in. Right away, Nora imagined the three of them being friends. The other three nurses weren't as young but appeared welcoming and willing to lend assistance, which was immensely reassuring.

When introductions concluded, Gail had Nora follow Nikki around for the first part of the day. Nora assisted with various duties, got to know some of the residents, and when it was time for lunch, they grabbed a tray from the cafeteria and settled down to eat.

"So what brings you to Brentwood?" Nikki asked. "Gail said you moved here from Georgia... or was it Alabama?"

"Alabama. Trafford, to be exact."

"Where's that?" Nikki asked with a Tennessee twang.

"Near Birmingham."

"Did you grow up there?"

"Born and raised. What about you—are you from Nashville?"

Nikki shook her head. "No. I grew up in Knoxville. But after I finished nursing school, I was looking for some place with a little more excitement. Fortunately, Gail had an opening on her team, so I took it."

Nora glanced at her hand and noticed she wasn't wearing a ring. Single? Divorced? *She's far too attractive not to at least have a boyfriend.* She took the last bite of her sandwich. "So how do you like it here?"

"At Belle Haven or Nashville?"

"Either... or both."

Nikki laughed. "I love it. Honestly, I couldn't ask for a better job. If you haven't noticed, Gail is wonderful. She's demanding, but she takes care of us. As far as Nashville goes, I love the area. I live in Belle Meade," she explained. "It's just a stone's throw from downtown, which is convenient since I spend a lot of time in the city when I'm not working. There are so many things to see and do, and there's always a party if you're into that sort of thing. Since you're from Alabama, I assume you like country music?"

It sounded more like an observation than a question. "Sure," Nora answered. "So long as it isn't too sappy. You mentioned downtown. Do you go there often?"

"Mostly on the weekends. Whitney, who you met earlier, she and I hang out quite a bit... And there's another girl, Annette, who's one of the physical therapists here. She tags along sometimes too. You could be our fourth."

Though Nora wasn't big on parties, she didn't want to pass up the chance at making friends, so she told Nikki it sounded like fun. Besides, now that she was on her own,

Nora wasn't sure who or what she wanted Nora Dawson 2.0 to be.

After lunch, Nikki handed Nora off to Olivia Marshall, the charge nurse. Olivia was the oldest of the nurses on staff, forty-seven, and had a strict demeanor that reminded Nora of her twelfth-grade English teacher. While Olivia herded everyone into the common room for painting class, Nora did a quick headcount—nineteen... twenty... twenty-one. And just like before, Mr. Carlisle was missing.

When the class got underway, Olivia joined Nora by the window. "You seem calm for your first day. What's your secret?"

"No secret," Nora confessed. "I guess I just have a good poker face."

Olivia smiled in response.

"Do you think I should ask Mr. Carlisle to join us?" Nora looked down the hall.

"Don't waste your breath. He hasn't attended a class since he's been here."

"But he has to come out of his room sometime, right?"

Olivia shrugged her shoulders as she picked at a scab on her left arm. "Not necessarily. We can't make him."

"How does he eat?"

"Gail has one of the orderlies bring his meals to him. With the white-glove treatment he gets, you'd think he was a guest at the Hermitage Hotel. What that man needs is a dose of tough love."

"I don't follow." Nora wondered if maybe tough love had driven him indoors in the first place.

"Stop providing room service! He isn't too good to sit in the cafeteria like everyone else. If Gail keeps pampering him, he'll never leave his room."

One of the residents held up a hand, and when Olivia went

to see if she could help, Nora seized the opportunity and tiptoed away.

Fred Carlisle lived at the end of the hall, in the last room on the left.

The door was ajar, so Nora peered inside. In a faded recliner near the window sat an elderly gentleman dressed in neatly pressed khakis and a short-sleeved, button-down shirt. His hands were folded in front of him as if he was waiting patiently for someone to arrive.

"Mr. Carlisle." Nora tapped lightly on the door. "Mr. Carlisle, my name is Nora Dawson. I don't mean to disturb you, sir, but I wanted to introduce myself. Today is my first day, and well... I just wanted to say hello and that if there's anything I can do for you, don't hesitate to ask."

She stood in silence for a moment, expecting some sort of reaction from him. When none came, she pushed ahead.

"I noticed you didn't come to painting class with the rest of the group, so I wanted to stop by and see if there was anything I could say or do to change your mind." Again she was met with silence. "Well, if you do change your mind, you know where to find us." She backed out into the hall. "Sorry for disturbing you."

As Nora walked back toward the common room, her curiosity grew stronger. Who was this man who had such an icy demeanor, and what had driven him to such resignation? When she explained to Olivia where she had been, her heart sank as Olivia told her about Mr. Carlisle's arrival at the hospital—how he'd looked so defeated as his daughters wheeled him in against his will. In that moment, despite not having known him, Nora made a silent vow to try to bring some joy into his life.

At the conclusion of Nora's shift, Gail pulled her aside and asked how the first day had gone.

She smiled wearily, her feet throbbing in her shoes. "As good as can be expected."

Gail gave a satisfied nod. "That's what I like to hear. Are you comfortable working with Nikki and Olivia for the rest of the week? They'll get you up to speed faster than anyone else."

"Yes, ma'am." She fished out her keys from the locker where she'd stowed away her purse.

Gail grabbed her bag and slung the strap over her shoulder. "Excellent! You can learn a lot from them. Nikki's still young but sharp as a tack, and everyone loves her. Olivia is older and seasoned, and of all my girls, she's the best I've got."

They said their goodbyes, and Nora stepped out into the cool evening air. When she got in the car, she breathed a sigh of relief. Though exhausted and sore, she had made it through her first day of work.

On the drive home, Nora considered a run, but after discovering a blister on the bottom of her foot, she nixed that idea. Instead, she turned on the TV and soaked in a tub of Epsom salts. After dinner, she rinsed the dishes in the sink, then called her mom and talked for an hour, replaying the day's events for her.

By ten o'clock, fatigue finally took its toll and Nora crawled beneath the covers. Fumbling for the remote, she flicked off the TV and closed her eyes. And as she drifted off, Nora realized that for the first time since the breakup, she'd made it through an entire day without once thinking of *him*.

Baby steps.

Chapter Three

By the end of the week, Nora had found her groove. Nikki and Olivia had helped her adjust to hospital life in no time, so Gail felt comfortable allowing her to take on tasks autonomously. As she discovered, mornings were always more hectic than afternoons, so when it came time for lunch, Nora was happy to pause and relax. Luckily, she and Nikki took lunch at the same time, and just as she had expected, they clicked immediately.

"You're much faster than the last girl," said Nikki as she spooned chili into a bowl. She added a sprinkle of cheese and a handful of crackers before making her way to an empty table. "Gail took almost a month before she let her loose."

Nora's heart was bursting with pride, but her cheeks stayed still. "I guess I'm a quick study. Besides, it's not too different from my work in Trafford at the home health facility."

"Yes, speaking of that"—Nikki locked eyes with Nora—"What brought you here, besides this job?"

The question sent chills up Nora's spine, filling her with fear and apprehension.

"Isn't that enough?" she answered, dodging the question.

"I suppose, but I'm pretty good at reading people, and something tells me there's more to it than that."

Nora opened her mouth to answer, but only a few words escaped before she clammed up. She had no intention of telling the whole story, instead opting for the cliff notes version.

"Well, you're not the only one at this table who has had their heart broken," Nikki reassured her. "God knows I've had my fair share of heartache. But maybe it's for the best. I mean, look at you—you've got your own place in one of Nashville's most desired neighborhoods, have an exciting new job, and best of all, you get to hang out with fun and exciting people like me." She teased her with a wink. "All in all, not a bad deal."

Nora smiled and said, "Well, when you put it that way..."

Although Nora had hit it off with Nikki right away, when it came to Mr. Carlisle, her luck hadn't been so kind. Despite her initial optimism, Nora still hadn't gotten anywhere with him. There was, however, an odd encounter on her second day. On her way to the nurse's lounge, Nora rounded the corner and saw Mr. Carlisle coming toward her. Their eyes met, and for one long moment they stood locked in a gaze. He looked startled and took a step back as if he was frightened by her presence. But at five four and a hundred and fifteen pounds, Nora was convinced it was her imagination at play.

Just before quitting time, Gail called Nora into her office with some welcome news—she had heard positive reports from all the staff. Nora breathed a sigh of relief. Then Gail handed her a thick manila folder and asked that she read through it over the weekend.

Nora sat down in the chair across from her. "What is it?" She felt the heft of the folder in her hands.

"The file on Mr. Carlisle. I've officially assigned you to his care, so you're allowed access. As you can see, there's a lot to go through, so take your time. Let's meet in my office Monday morning and discuss, shall we?"

Sensing there was something important Gail wanted her to glean from the pages inside, Nora felt a tingle of anticipation run up her spine. "Yes, I look forward to it." She rose from the chair. "Well, have a nice weekend."

On her way out, Nora bumped into Nikki.

"The girls and I are going out tonight," Nikki said as she opened the door. "Want to join us?"

"Thanks, but I'm beat," she replied, feeling like she'd just run a marathon. "Rain check?"

"Suit yourself." Nikki's smile faded away as she eased toward her SUV. "If you change your mind, you have my number."

When Nora got home, she went inside and turned on the lights. After throwing her bag on the couch, she checked her messages and found one from her best friend, Erin Ivey. It sounded urgent, so Nora called back right away.

"Nora, how are you? Thanks for calling."

Nora sank onto the couch and kicked off her shoes. "No problem. It's good to hear your voice. How are things? It feels like forever since we've talked."

"I know. Things are good. How's life? How's the new place?"

"Great. I just finished my first week of work, so I'm drained.

But other than that, I'm well." She removed the ponytail holder and ran a hand through her hair. "So are you still in Mobile?"

Erin hesitated. "Um, no. Actually, that's why I called. I just moved back home, believe it or not." She gave an uneasy laugh.

That threw Nora for a loop. "Home? Really? What happened? I thought you liked it in Mobile."

Erin took a deep breath and let out a heavy sigh before answering. "I did. I mean, I do. It's just... Well, I sorta met someone."

Nora's mind did somersaults. "You met someone? From Trafford? In Mobile?" She struggled to connect the dots. "What are the odds? Do I know him?"

"Umm..."

"Well, who is it?"

The silence felt longer than it actually was before Erin finally replied with one word. "Jeremy."

It took every ounce of strength Nora had not to scream into the phone. Jeremy! Her mind raced as it desperately tried to process that her best friend had fallen for her ex. "Jeremy? You mean *my Jeremy*?" Her voice quivered slightly as she spoke his name out loud. "You're joking, right?" Erin's silence was all the confirmation Nora needed. "Wow... you're not joking." Shock gave way to anger. "How could you do this to me? I thought you were my best friend."

"I am your best friend," she said, then added, "look, I know this is awkward, which is why I thought you'd appreciate hearing it from me rather than someone else."

Awkward? Seriously? Taking a deep breath and counting slowly backward from ten in her head, Nora tried as hard as she could to keep her composure before she spoke again. "I think this qualifies as a little more than awkward, don't you?"

"You're right—it's borderline insanity, I know. But it's been six months."

"Six months!" Nora jumped to her feet. "Six years would have been too short for something like this. And him? Of all the billions of guys in the world, you picked him? What's wrong with you?" Her hands tightened into fists around the phone until they started turning white. "You gave me your word that you were on my side."

"I was on your side... am on your side. I didn't mean for this to happen," Erin added apologetically.

"Really?" Nora shot back coldly. "So how did it happen? You two just happened to run into each other somewhere, got to talking, and magically all was forgiven? Or did he flash his money around or his fancy car, and you just couldn't help yourself? Or maybe," she continued, choosing her words carefully, "you were drunk. Yeah, that makes more sense, considering..."

Erin bristled at the accusation. "How dare you bring that up! You know I haven't had a drink since I got help!"

But Nora felt no remorse. In the silence that followed, she put two and two together. "Wait a minute... You're the one he was cheating on me with, aren't you? There wasn't any secretary. It was you this whole time, wasn't it?"

"No!" Erin shouted defensively. "That's not true, and you know it. I would never do something like that to you."

But after what Nora had just heard, she had a hard time believing it.

Erin sighed into the phone and said, "Look, Nora, I'm sure this is the last thing you expected to hear from me, and I know it's a lot to process, so I'm going to let you go before one of us says something we can't come back from."

"Too late!" Nora scoffed. "As far as I'm concerned, we're through." She slammed down the phone so hard that the pictures on the wall shook. She sat on the couch and tried to process what Erin had told her, but the betrayal was too much for her to comprehend.

Nora spent the next few minutes pacing the floor, taking turns crying and screaming obscenities at the wall. After surviving the breakup, the move, and starting this new job alone, she wasn't about to let this get her down, so she did the only thing she could think of—she picked up the phone and called Nikki.

Chapter Four

THE CAR SLOWED AS THEY REACHED THE EDGE OF downtown Nashville. Nikki was at the wheel with Whitney riding shotgun while Nora shared the back seat with Annette.

"What changed your mind about going out tonight?" Nikki asked casually from the front seat.

"It's a long story," said Nora, still seething mad. "And no, I don't want to talk about it."

Nikki pulled off the highway and parked in a dingy garage. Then they got out and continued on foot. When the light changed, they crossed the street and rounded the corner onto Broadway. All at once, Nora found herself awash in the glow of neon lights.

"It's something, isn't it?" Nikki asked as she surveyed the crowd.

"Yes, it is." Nora stood in awe of the sight before her.

From one end of Broadway to the other, people stood in line, waiting for their turn to be granted entrance to one of the many bars. Vehicles packed the street, and horns blared as merchants called out feverishly, peddling their wares to anyone willing to take a peek. The bustling scene left Nora feeling both exhilarated and overwhelmed.

Nikki took her hand and led her through the crowd as Whitney and Annette followed in their wake. They walked into Tootsie's Orchid Lounge and found an open table. It was a cozy, dimly lit place with multicolored lights hanging from the ceiling. A live band played country music in the background while waitresses weaved their way through the crowd carrying trays of drinks.

"So what do you think?" Nikki asked as she signaled for a waitress.

Nora took in her surroundings. The place was packed with men and women in cowboy hats, boots, and tight jeans, swigging back beers and laughing loudly. "This is quite the scene."

They ordered drinks and chatted about random things. As the buzz of alcohol crept into Nora, her anger gave way, and she started to relax.

"A word of advice." Annette leaned over and whispered in Nora's ear. "These guys look harmless, but trust me, they're not always what they seem."

You don't say.

Whitney rolled her eyes at Annette's warning. "Don't listen to her. She had one bad experience, and now she thinks every guy here is the devil incarnate."

At just that moment a young man in a cowboy hat approached the table and asked Nora to dance. After getting the okay from Annette, she took his hand and followed him through the crowd. As soon as they got onto the dance floor, he guided her through some line dancing steps while they moved under the flashing lights.

After a few dances, Nora returned to the table and wiped the sweat from her brow. "Where's Nikki?"

Annette motioned toward the dance floor, where Nikki

danced cheek to cheek with a tall, dark, and handsome man. "That's Rick," she explained. "Nikki's... friend with benefits. They have this on-again, off-again thing."

Nora took a closer look, watching as Nikki danced dangerously close to him. "They look pretty *on again* to me."

"She only calls him up when she wants some," Whitney said, watching them like a hawk.

When Nikki returned, she took a deep swig of beer, then looked at Nora and smiled. "Having fun?"

Nora nodded, trying to remember the last time she'd had a girl's night out.

"How's Rick?" Whitney asked, casting a glance in his direction as he ordered drinks at the bar.

"Fine. He just got back from Jacksonville. Apparently he didn't play well. Poor baby. But I've got something that will cheer him up."

"Well, at least one of us will get lucky tonight," Whitney muttered before downing another shot.

Ignoring Whitney, Nikki turned to Nora and asked if she could drive the others home at the end of the night.

"Sure, but what about you?"

"I'm gonna catch a ride with Rick," she answered and finished her beer.

When Nora agreed, Nikki handed her the keys. "Thanks. I owe you one." Then she disappeared back into the crowd.

When Nikki was gone, the conversation quickly turned to men, and somehow Dr. Kenner—the forty-five-year-old physician from Vanderbilt that made weekly rounds at Belle Haven—became the topic of discussion.

"He does have a nice ass," Annette commented as she swayed on her stool to the beat of the music. "But he's too old for me."

"Who cares?" Whitney refilled her glass with more tequila. "I'm only talking about having sex, not dating him."

"But he's married." Annette shot Whitney a look of disapproval.

"What about *him*?" Nora asked, eager to change the subject.

"Who?" Annette and Whitney said at the same time.

"There." Nora pointed to a tall figure sitting at the bar. "The guy with the jeans and rolled-up sleeves."

"Oh, you mean John," said Whitney.

"You know him?"

"Not really. I've seen him out a few times, but he always keeps to himself. I think his family is in sales or something."

"Politics," Annette said.

"Same thing," Whitney replied with a smirk.

Curious, Nora grabbed her purse and slid off the stool, weaving through the crowd toward him. A new energy surged through her as she stood next to him, waiting for him to look up from his drink. When he finally did, she cleared her throat and asked if the seat was taken. He smiled, introduced himself as John Patree, and pulled out the chair for her.

"I'm Nora." She shook his hand.

"Pleasure to meet you, Nora. Can I get you something to drink? Beer? Wine?"

She glanced at the drink in his hand. "I'll have whatever you're having."

John hailed the bartender and ordered another gin and tonic. "So are you a local or tourist?"

She had to think about it. "Local," she finally said.

His lips twitched into a smile. "Is that your final answer?"

"Sorry, I just moved here."

"Ah." He nodded, then took a drink. "How do you like it so far?"

"The jury's still out, but things are looking up." Her gaze lingered over him for a second before the bartender returned with her drink and placed it on a napkin in front of her.

"Cheers." John tapped the rim of his glass against hers.

Nora took a small sip. "This is... interesting."

"It's an acquired taste," he replied, taking a sip of his own.

She brushed the hair from her eyes, then scanned the crowd. "Is it like this most nights?"

"Yeah, but the weekends tend to be a bit... livelier."

She could feel his eyes on her as she checked on Whitney and Annette.

"I find most people come here for one of two reasons," he continued, staring into his drink. "Either to drink their troubles away, or to find someone to take home."

"Or both." She faced him again.

He raised an eyebrow.

"What about you?" she said. "You hardly seem troubled, and you don't exactly strike me as Mr. One-Night Stand."

He gave a crooked smile. "Thanks... I think. I'm part of a very rare breed that comes here to unwind. Normally, I'll have a drink or two, listen to the band, then go home. I've also been known to grace the dance floor on occasion." He glanced at the people swaying to the soulful sounds of the band, then back to Nora. "When the mood strikes me."

She finished her drink and hopped off the stool, taking John by the hand. "Come on. Show me what you've got."

Fortunately, the band played a slow song, so it wasn't as much dancing as it was swaying to the music in each other's arms.

"What do you do, John Patree?" Nora set her gaze upon him.

"A little of this and that." He smiled at her with his brown eyes.

"Okay." She changed tactics. "What do you do for work? In other words, how do you make your living?"

"Does it matter?"

"That depends."

"On what?" He seemed amused by her line of questioning.

"Well, if you're a hitman for the mob or something, I'd certainly like to know that."

He laughed. "So what you're saying is you're not so much interested in *what* I do, but rather if what I do is aboveboard?"

"Exactly."

"In that case, I work with local businesses to build inner city youth programs."

Admittedly, she was a little shocked. "That's respectable. Does it pay well?"

"I didn't think it was about the money." He spun her, then pulled her close to him.

"Curious, that's all," she said, a little light-headed.

"Fair enough." His smile evaporated. "The money won't make me rich, but it pays the bills."

And for whatever reason, Nora got the sense that money didn't matter to him, at least not in the traditional sense. Before she could ask another question, he put a hand at her back and dipped her.

"I think you were hustling me, John Patree," she said as their eyes met.

He gave her a sly smile and pulled her upright, his strong grip steadying her balance.

"You're a much better dancer than you let on."

His smile widened. "It's easy when you have the right partner."

Her heart raced. Despite his good looks and sneaky charm, there was something trustworthy about John that Nora couldn't ignore. Yes, it seemed John Patree was a rare breed indeed.

When the song ended, they returned to the bar and continued their conversation. Just after midnight, Whitney came over and said that she and Annette were ready to call it a night, so Nora thanked John for the conversation and the drink.

"Maybe I could I call you sometime?" he asked awkwardly as she gathered her things to leave.

Perhaps it was his disarming nature or the fact that he was light on his feet, but Nora didn't think twice about giving him her number.

Chapter Five

The next morning, Nora awoke to the roar of her neighbor's lawnmower and was greeted with a dull thumping in her head. Blinking her eyes open, she glanced at the clock—9:07. After a jog to the park and back, she called Nikki to see about returning her car. She had stayed the night at Rick's apartment, so Nora drove over and picked her up, then Nikki brought her back home, where they sat on the porch and talked for a while.

"Did you have fun last night?" Nikki shielded her eyes from the sun.

Thoughts of dancing with John filled Nora's head. "Yes, but probably not as much fun as you."

Nikki's cheeks blushed a shade of pink and she flashed a mischievous smile. "Rick is the first baseman for the Nashville Sounds."

Nora knew very little about sports other than the few times she'd watched football with her dad. "That's nice. Is it serious?"

"The baseball?"

"You and Rick."

"Oh." Nikki shrugged before responding nonchalantly.

"We're not exclusive, if that's what you mean. He and I just sort of hook up when he's in town."

Her candidness surprised Nora. Perhaps she wasn't as firmly in the Bible belt as she thought. "How long have you two had this... arrangement?"

"About a year." She ran her fingertips across her jeans absentmindedly. "He was seeing Whitney before me. Did she tell you?"

Nora shook her head, wondering if Nikki had done to Whitney what Erin had done to her.

Nikki leaned back in her chair and crossed one leg over the other. "Now that it's just the two of us, are you going to tell me why you changed your mind last night?"

"Like I told you before, it's a long story."

"Well"—Nikki glanced in her direction—"fortunately for you, I've got nothing but time."

Nora chewed her lip. Was she ready to open up about her heartbreak? "What the hell," she finally said. "You'll probably find out sooner or later anyway." She took a deep breath and exhaled before going on. "The truth is I received a call last night from my now-ex-best friend."

Nikki perked up.

"She called to inform me that she's dating my ex."

"And that's a problem because...?"

Nora felt the anger return. "Because he cheated on me."

"With her?"

Nora shrugged her shoulders. "Honestly, I don't know, and I don't care. The point is she was supposed to be my best friend, and she went and did the one thing we swore we'd never do to each other. It's bad enough that my fiancé cheated on me, but to have my best friend go behind my back and—"

"Wait! You were engaged? You didn't tell me that."

"For almost a year."

Nikki shook her head in disbelief. "Then you have every right to be upset. Your friend crossed the line."

Nora gave her a sidelong glance. "Says the girl who's dating Whitney's ex."

"That's different. Rick and Whitney only went out a couple of times, and they were never serious. Otherwise, I would never have agreed to go out with him. I might be a lot of things, but a backstabber isn't one of them."

Nora felt a little better knowing Nikki had at least some scruples.

"So Annette said you spent a long time talking to John Patree last night," Nikki said, changing the subject.

Nora's face flushed, and she spun the glass of sweet tea on her knee. "We had a couple of drinks... and shared a dance or two." Before she knew it, a smile had made its way onto her face.

Nikki raised an eyebrow. "Good for you. From what I hear, John's a respectable guy."

"Yeah, I picked up on that." She took a sip of tea before continuing. "Honestly, it was just nice to have an adult conversation with someone who wasn't a complete jerk for once."

"So are you going to see him again?"

She gave a half shrug. "I gave him my number, so we'll see."

When Nikki left, Nora made a trip to the store. Now that she had the essentials, it was time to stock up on all the things she liked. For years, Jeremy had been focused on fitness, so their cabinets had been filled with protein powder, vitamins, and supplements. Being a runner, Nora tried her best to always eat healthy, but occasionally she enjoyed a bag of M&M's or gummy worms, so today she decided to splurge.

She got home around one and parked in the drive. Opening the trunk, she reached in, grabbed a few bags, and started toward the porch.

"Nora? Nora Dawson?"

She glanced over her shoulder and froze in surprise at the sight of John Patree crossing the street in her direction. He looked different in the daylight. Better. "John? What are you doing here?" Fear pulsed through her. *Oh God! What if he's one of the bad boys Annette warned me about?*

"I live here—just there." He pointed to the brick rancher across the street. "So you're the new neighbor everyone's been talking about?"

Everyone. She gave a nervous laugh. "Guilty as charged."

He offered to help with the groceries, so she let him.

"Just set them anywhere," she said, showing him inside. "I'm surprised we didn't see each other last week when I moved in. I could have used your help unloading that U-Haul."

"I was out of town." He put down some bags on the countertop. "Otherwise, I would have gladly offered my services."

While Nora thought of something clever to say, John wandered off into the living room.

"Did you do all the decorating yourself or did you hire someone?"

"I did it all myself," she replied proudly.

He gave a nod of approval. "You did an excellent job. The house looks amazing."

"Thank you." She put away the perishables, then joined him. "My mother always said I had an eye for decorating, though God knows where it comes from."

"So you're a designer?"

"Far from it. I'm a nurse."

"Ah, that makes sense. The girl who lived here before you—Leslie—she was a nurse too."

"Yes. Did you know her well?"

"Not really," he said. "So did you buy this place or are you renting?"

"Renting for now. My contract with the hospital is only for six months, so I couldn't commit to anything long-term. Though I suspect if things go well, they'll want me to stay."

John gave a crooked smile, then shuffled to the bookshelf and picked up a picture of Erin and Nora at Disney World when they were eight. "Is this you?"

"Many years ago." She cringed inwardly at the sight of herself with freckles.

"And who's this?" He pointed to Erin in the photo.

"My best friend... at the time."

"Cute." John put down the picture and moved toward the door. "Sorry for lingering." He glanced back at her. "I'm sure you have better things to do than entertain me all afternoon."

"Pasta!" Nora blurted without thinking. "I was going to make pasta later if you'd like to join me. It's the least I can do to thank you for helping me with the groceries." She hoped he couldn't hear her heart beating like a drum in her chest.

"Sure. What time do you want me?" he replied smoothly.

Nora's mind went straight into the gutter, but she cleared her throat and managed to say, "I'll start dinner around five-thirty, so how about six?"

"Okay," John said, stepping out onto the porch. "Let me bring the wine. Do you prefer red or white?"

"Surprise me."

"Okay. Six o'clock it is." He backed off the porch. "See ya then."

As he crossed the street, Nora stared after him in disbelief, thinking the odds of them being neighbors had to be astronomical. It was at that moment she remembered Leslie's letter—*It may not look like much, but this little home has magic in its walls, and if you take care of it—it will take care of you in return*—and she wondered.

With time to kill, Nora sat down on the couch and began reading through the file Gail had given her on Mr. Carlisle. It was as thick as *War and Peace*, complete with charts, a detailed family medical history, and documentation of his time at Belle Haven. Since reading it word for word would have taken weeks, she scanned the pages for anything of interest.

According to the notes, Frederick Allen Carlisle was born July 2, 1920, in the Nashville suburb of Mount Juliet. Prior to moving to Belle Haven, he'd held the same Murfreesboro address since 1950. He had a wife—Judy—who died the previous year, and two daughters, Gloria and Suzanne, both of whom lived out of state.

Nora read on.

A few pages in, she located a note referencing a medical diagnosis. As she discovered, Fred Carlisle had recently been diagnosed with glioblastoma, an aggressive brain cancer, but there was nothing regarding a prognosis or plans for surgery. *So this is what Gail wanted me to find.*

Before she knew it, two hours had passed. Having made it through more of the file than she expected, Nora took a break and went for a run. When she returned home, she showered and started dinner before checking if John was headed over.

At precisely six o'clock, she heard a knock on the door. John was nothing if not punctual. He stepped inside with a bottle of white wine and an infectious smile, and while Nora finished dinner, he prepped a salad in the kitchen. Once the pasta was ready, they sat down at the table.

"I was thinking," John said between bites of Caesar salad. "What are the odds you and I would meet at a bar one night, find out we're neighbors the next afternoon, then be having dinner together all within twenty-four hours?"

"Well, when you put it that way, probably one in a million."

"More like one in a billion. Maybe it's fate?" he offered with a twinkle in his eye.

Nora had never been a believer in fate, but even she was starting to wonder.

When they had finished eating, they took the wine and moved to the back patio where the sun was setting on the horizon and crickets were singing their evening song.

"So tell me about your job as a nurse." John leaned back in the chair and crossed one leg over the other. "Is that what brought you to Brentwood?"

"Yes. I can't explain it, but I've always had this burning desire to help people, to comfort them in their time of need. What better way to do that than by being a nurse?" She sipped her wine, then continued. "After I graduated college, I was fortunate enough to land a job at a hospital near Trafford. That's where I'm from. It's nothing compared to Belle Haven, but it gave me an opportunity to get my feet wet."

"Trafford?" John wrinkled his brow and ran a hand through his hair. "That's near Birmingham, isn't it?"

"You know Trafford?"

"I know of it. A detour took me through there a couple of years ago on my way back from the beach. It was a nice town if memory serves."

Nora could count on one hand the number of compliments she'd received regarding her hometown, so she smiled in response to his kind words.

"Where do you call home?" She had already decided he wasn't a local. The last name, the accent, all felt deep South to her.

"South Carolina," he answered. "Monck's Corner, to be more precise. It's near—"

"Charleston. Yeah, I've heard of it. So is that where you

were last week?" She finished her glass of wine and set it down on the table between them.

He nodded once. "You mentioned Belle Haven. A friend of mine—Kyle—makes the rounds there once a week. Do you know him?"

"I know *of* him." She recalled the conversation with Annette and Whitney from last night. "Small world, isn't it?"

His eyes sparkled in agreement. "And getting smaller every day. So does nursing run in your family or are you the only one?"

"No, I'm the only one. Mom is a secretary at a law firm, and Dad is—was—in sales. He's recently retired. All he does now is play golf and drive my mom crazy." The corners of her lips twitched up slightly into an amused smile. "What about you—do you come from a long line of those seeking to help the underprivileged?"

"Hardly. My family is in politics. You've undoubtedly heard of them."

"Sorry, I don't follow politics. Wait a minute." Suddenly she recalled seeing a *Dateline* special a couple of years back about a Senator from South Carolina who had been suspected of misappropriating funds. "You're not related to Senator Robert Patree, are you?"

A hint of surprise and something else—was it shame?—flashed across his face. "Bob Patree is my father."

No wonder money didn't matter to him. His family was one of the most powerful and influential in the state.

"But don't hold that against me," he added with a rueful smile.

They watched as the sun cast its final orange glow over the backyard, the shadows drawing long and dark around them.

"How come you didn't follow in his footsteps—your father's, I mean?"

His brow furrowed. “I did for a while, but it wasn’t my cup of tea. More wine?”

Nora handed him the glass, and he disappeared into the house. But his sudden shift in mood and redirection of the conversation left her thinking there was more to the story.

John hung around until the wine was gone, then left, but not before promising Nora next time he’d treat her to dinner at his place. A man who helped the underprivileged, had wealth, knew his wine, and cooked. Nora wondered how he was still single—and how she’d gotten so lucky.

Chapter Six

WITH ANOTHER DINNER ALL BUT DECIDED, THINGS with John were moving faster than Nora had planned. She'd only been in Brentwood a week, and the last thing she wanted was to dive headfirst into another relationship

When Nora arrived at work Monday morning, Gail was waiting for her by the door. "How was your weekend?"

"Busy." They crossed the lobby and pushed through the double doors. "That file you gave me on Mr. Carlisle wasn't exactly a light read."

Gail laughed. "But you finished it, didn't you?"

"Yes, ma'am." They moved ahead a few steps. "How come you didn't tell me Mr. Carlisle was sick?"

"I wanted you to see the medical charts and read the doctors' notes rather than hear it from me. I think it makes us better nurses when we discover on our own versus being told."

They rounded the corner, Gail taking long strides that left Nora struggling to keep up.

"So what does Mr. Carlisle think about the cancer? I assume he knows."

Gail sighed heavily before she responded. "As you might

expect, he doesn't like to talk about it. We send him to Vanderbilt once a month for a PET scan," she went on as they made their way toward the nurses' lounge. "Just to make sure the tumor hasn't grown."

When Nora had put away her things, she asked Gail the question that had been burning in her mind for two days. "How long does he have—to live, I mean?"

"Two months. Two years. No one knows for sure." She took a deep breath before continuing. "Dr. Kenner tells me because of where it's located, once the tumor starts growing again, it'll be swift." Her lips pressed together in a thin line before releasing in a whisper of resignation. "But so far, so good."

"Can't they operate?"

"Yes, but the surgery is extremely risky, and any number of things could go wrong. But Dr. Kenner has made Mr. Carlisle aware of the risks, so it's in his hands now."

After clocking in, Nora hurried to the cafeteria. Once breakfast had been served, she set off on her rounds. Aside from Mr. Carlisle, Nora also provided care for a handful of additional residents, all of whom she had gotten to know quite well. But Fred Carlisle remained the thorn in her side.

By ten o'clock, the first wave of duties was done, so she grabbed a bag of M&M's and bottled water from the vending machine before easing her way down the hallway to Mr. Carlisle's room.

"Good morning, Mr. Carlisle," she said. "It's nice to see you again. How are you feeling? Listen, I've been thinking about your exercise regimen. Rather than go to the pool, how would you like to go for a walk instead? Maybe down by the creek or perhaps even the stables?" She'd read in his file that he loved horses.

Like all the times before, Mr. Carlisle said nothing. Deflated but not defeated, Nora reached into her pocket and pulled out a bag of M&M's. She placed it on the table beside him and whispered, "In case you get hungry." Then she turned and eased toward the door.

"Miss Dawson?"

Nora turned at the sound of his gravelly voice. "Yes?"

"Thank you."

"Well, I'll be damned—you can talk."

Mr. Carlisle shifted in his chair and looked up at her. "Of course I can talk. I'm old, not mute."

Nora shook her head in amusement. "In that case, I think proper introductions are in order." She smiled and extended her hand. "Nora Dawson. Pleased to meet you."

He accepted her handshake, his strong grip surprising for a man of his age. "Fred Carlisle," he said with a toothy grin. "And the pleasure is all mine."

To Nora's surprise, Fred Carlisle seemed affable, not grumpy or condescending in the least. She could only surmise that the nurses before her had not realized that the way to a man's heart was through his stomach. Lucky her. At some point in the conversation, she noticed Gail standing in the doorway watching them intently.

"Well, well, well, what have we here?" She glided into the room and planted her hands on her hips. "Does this mean you've decided to give Miss Dawson a chance?"

"I'm considering it." He looked at Nora and gave a sly wink.

"I'll take that as a yes," Gail said. Then, turning to Nora, she said, "A word." She gestured toward the hall When they were alone, Gail asked Nora what she'd said to charm Mr. Carlisle.

"Nothing, really. I just did what you said. I read the file, assessed the situation, chose a path I thought might work, and voilà."

Gail beamed. "See, what did I tell you? A little faith goes a long way." She patted Nora affectionately on the shoulder. "Nice work."

Only nine days into Nora's new life and things were going swimmingly.

As it turned out, Mr. Carlisle was a pushover. Contrary to what Nora had been told, Fred wasn't the monster everyone had made him out to be. He was temperamental at times, but who could blame him? To hear him tell it, he'd been ripped away from his home—a place where he'd gotten married, raised his family, and spent fifty years with his wife—and dropped off at Belle Haven with nothing more than a suitcase and the clothes on his back.

Nora spent the rest of the week getting to know Mr. Carlisle. If she was going to care for him properly, she needed more than notes in a file. They talked about everything under the sun—family, friends, jobs, hobbies. Nothing was off-limits.

"What did Gail tell you about me?" he asked one morning as they strolled along the path between the garden and the pond.

"I won't lie; she said you could be... difficult. She also said you were responsible for running off two of her best nurses. Is that true?"

He quirked a smile and laughed amusedly. "It's not my fault they had no backbone."

They walked on a little way, then he asked how old Nora was.

"Twenty-seven," she said. "But I'll be twenty-eight in September."

"You're but a child. What do you know about taking care of someone my age?"

"Well, for starters, I have a nursing degree," she said matter-of-factly. "And I've been taking care of patients your age for almost five years. I might not have the experience of Gail, but I'm more than capable of holding my own."

He seemed to consider that. "But what happens if I fall?" He looked her over. "You're no bigger than a minute. How could you possibly lift me?"

Nora didn't know whether to be offended or flattered, but she gave him the benefit of the doubt. "I'm stronger than I look. Plus, from what I've heard, you hardly ever leave your room, so a fall should be the least of your worries."

He cracked a smile and shifted the conversation in a new and more personal direction. "I don't see a ring on your finger. How come such a beautiful and engaging woman like you isn't married? Back in my day, you'd have been considered an old maid."

She glanced reflexively at her hand, where once the engagement ring had been.

"Forgive me." He said quickly. "That was insensitive of me."

"No, it's fine. I'm just... Well..." Nora composed herself, unwilling to give him the satisfaction of knowing he'd hit a nerve. "I'm taking some time to focus on my career, that's all."

"I see." He nodded knowingly. "So you're one of *those* women."

"I beg your pardon?"

"Oh, I didn't mean anything by it. Only that you're a new age, career-driven woman who doesn't have time for things like relationships or family."

She was beginning to understand why the others had left.

"I never said I didn't want those things. I'm simply taking some time for me, that's all. What's wrong with that?"

"Nothing, I suppose." They resumed their stroll. "I was only kidding, by the way. Truth be told, I admire modern women. Back in my day, most of them cooked, cleaned, and took care of the household. Not that there's anything wrong with that, but I always felt bad for them, like they weren't able to live up to their potential. That's what I loved about my Judy. She was a woman with a mind of her own. Oh, she could clean and made magic in the kitchen, but that was just the tip of the iceberg. Did you know she was a college professor?"

There was no mention of that in the file. "No, I didn't. Where did she teach?"

"Just up the road at Vanderbilt. She was the head of the mathematics department. God, she was smart as hell. Way smarter than me." He shook his head as a smile played about his lips. "To this day, I still wonder what she saw in me."

When they reached the stables, they paused for a moment to watch the horses, then turned and headed back toward the hospital.

"I've been thinking," he said as they topped the hill.

"About what?"

"About painting again."

His comment caught her by surprise. "I think that's an excellent idea! And I'm sure the others would be delighted to have you join them. Should I tell Olivia to be expecting you?"

"Let me think on it a bit more. I wouldn't want to get her hopes up."

"Fair enough." She didn't want to press her luck. "Until then, it'll be our little secret."

Chapter Seven

After an uneventful weekend, Nora arrived at work Monday morning to find everyone—nurses, administrative staff, residents—huddled in the corner of the common room. Her first inclination was that someone had taken a fall. After what she and Mr. Carlisle had discussed the week before, she prayed it wasn't him.

"What's going on? Is someone hurt?"

"Nora, there you are." Gail sounded relieved. "I've been looking all over for you. You seem to be batting a thousand with Mr. Carlisle."

"What do you mean?"

Just then, the crowd parted, and that's when she saw it. Staring back at Nora was a freshly painted portrait of a young woman whose eyes stared a hole through her.

"You mean Mr. Carlisle painted *this*?" Her mouth fell open in shock.

"I had the same reaction when I first saw it." Gail glanced at the painting and shook her head. "Marvelous, isn't it?"

Upon closer examination, a question formed inside Nora's head. "You don't think it's me, do you?"

"Now that you mention it..." Gail took another look. "It does bare a slight resemblance."

Slight? It was like looking in a mirror. The lips, nose, eyes—they were a perfect match. But no one else seemed to notice.

"Perhaps you're his muse," Gail said, then laughed it off. "And if not, maybe you just remind him of someone. Either way, his skill is remarkable." She shook her head in disbelief. "And to think this whole time we've had a Michelangelo in our midst."

After putting away her things, Nora went to see Mr. Carlisle.

"Miss Dawson." He glanced at his watch. "You're early."

"I know, but I couldn't wait to tell you how impressed I am with the portrait. When you said you were an artist, I thought you were joking."

He chuckled. "It's a little rough, I'll admit, but not bad for someone who hasn't held a brush in over fifty years."

She crossed the room and parted the drapes. Outside, a slate sky hinted at rain. "You're joking, right?" she said turning back to him.

He shook his head slowly, and his blue eyes filled with an emotion Nora couldn't quite place. "September 16, 1946—that's the last time I held a paintbrush before today."

"Why?"

He let loose a long and deep sigh. "Lots of reasons, I suppose..."

"Who else knows you can paint like that?"

"No one."

"No one! Not even your daughters?"

He shook his head in response.

"But Judy must have known, right?"

"No," he replied sadly. "I never told her."

Nora tipped her head to one side, thinking that there was something terribly tragic about the whole thing. "I don't understand. How can you be that great at something and not want everyone to know? I mean, if I had your talent, I'd show it off every chance I got."

As if by reflex, a humorless laugh escaped his lips. "When you're good at something, Miss Dawson, even great, and it comes effortlessly, you don't think about it. It's like walking or breathing." His demeanor shifted from cheerful to serious in an instant. "I made a conscious decision years ago to stop painting, and I never looked back."

When he turned away toward the window, she noticed the sadness in his eyes. Something tragic *had* happened.

The pitter-patter of raindrops on the window ledge caught Nora's attention. "It looks like we'll have to postpone our walk."

"I was afraid of that." He frowned. "I saw the weather report this morning, and it doesn't look good all week."

"No matter," she said, undeterred. "This building has miles of hallways. I think Nurse Pritchard has a swim class that starts in a few minutes. We could drop by and see if that cute redhead from down the hall is there."

"Thanks, but I think I'll pass."

"Suit yourself." She eased toward the door. "If you change your mind, just holler."

That afternoon, Annette joined Nikki and Nora for lunch. As usual, she was full of questions.

"So what's new in your world?" she asked Nora. "I feel like I haven't seen you in ages.

"I know." Where had the time gone? "Between work and settling into my new place, I haven't had time for much else. What have you been up to?"

"This and that." She unwrapped a ham sandwich and took a bite from the corner. "So word on the street is you and John Patree are neighbors."

Nora glanced at Nikki, who looked away before she could make eye contact.

"That's right. He lives in the house across the street from me," she replied carefully.

"Interesting." The corners of her mouth curved into a sly smile.

"Why is that interesting?"

Nikki stifled a giggle as Annette continued with a knowing smirk.

"Oh, nothing. I was just thinking how convenient it is to have someone like John so close. Has he asked you out yet?"

Nora's eyebrows shot up in surprise as she quickly shook her head in response to Annette's question. Dinner at his place didn't qualify... did it? "No."

Nikki's laughter broke through the awkward tension, and suddenly Nora felt as if she were on the outside of an inside joke.

With another glance at Nikki, Annette finished her thought. "But you have had dinner with him, haven't you?"

"It was my way of thanking him... for helping me carry in the groceries."

A hint of amusement danced in Annette's eyes. "Uh-huh."

Suddenly uncomfortable, Nora cleared her throat before Nikki stepped in to change the subject. "All right, enough about John. Let's talk about Mr. Carlisle." She shifted her gaze to Nora. "How the hell did you get him to come out of his shell?

And are you really the one responsible for getting him to paint again?"

Annette looked up from her sandwich and cocked an eyebrow. "What's this?"

"Mr. Carlisle—he's my patient," Nora explained. "You know him, don't you?"

She nodded. "Nice guy. Not much of a talker though."

"Until now," said Nikki. "Ever since Nora arrived, we can't get him to shut up. And apparently, he's a great artist. He painted a portrait today of a woman that will take your breath away."

"Well," said Annette, "that just goes to show you how little we know people, doesn't it?"

Before Nora's shift ended, she stopped by to check on Mr. Carlisle.

"I thought you'd already left for the day," he said, looking surprised to see her.

"Not yet. I was on my way out." She gathered her thoughts, straightening one of the photographs hanging on the wall. "There's something I want to ask you... about the painting."

He flashed a crooked little smile. "You want to know if it's you, don't you?"

Nora nodded sheepishly, her cheeks ablaze. "How did you know?"

He chuckled softly before replying. "Lucky guess. It isn't, by the way."

"Really? But she could be my twin."

He nodded slowly and said, "I can see why you would think that, but I assure you, Miss Dawson, it isn't you."

"Then who is she?"

He drew a ragged breath and his expression turned gloomy. "Someone from another life ago."

"Well, whoever she is—she must have been special for you to want to paint her." Nora went about the room, collecting Mr. Carlisle's dinner tray and cup.

"Yes." He looked solemn. "She was special."

"Forgive me for prying," she said on her way out, "but what happened to her?"

He offered a sad smile. "That, my dear, is a story for another day."

Chapter Eight

THE RAIN BEAT AGAINST THE WINDSHIELD, AND thunder echoed in the distance. As soon as Nora got home, she stripped out of her damp scrubs and into her faded, comfortable sweatpants and an old T-shirt before settling onto the couch with dinner. After eating a bowl of homemade chicken soup, she took a deep breath and dialed her mom's number, updating her on all that had happened since their last conversation.

"And you believe it's you in the painting?" Kathleen asked.

Nora's mind settled on the image of the young woman. "He says it isn't, but—"

"You don't believe him?"

"I want to, it's just..."

"Maybe you remind him of someone."

"Maybe." Nora pushed the thought out of her head. "How's Dad adjusting to retirement?"

"Like a duck to water. He's at the golf course this afternoon with Mike and Tim. I see him less now than I did when he was working."

"What about Gran? Have you talked to her lately? How is she doing?"

"As a matter of fact, we had lunch yesterday," Kathleen said. "And she's fair, considering."

Since Pap died, Gran had been on Nora's mind constantly.

"Do you think she's going to be okay? I mean, she's going to make it through this, right?"

"I suspect she will in time. After all, your grandmother is a resilient woman."

Nora had long been told that time is a great healer. Though her current situation was nothing like what Gran was going through, the agony she'd felt at the start of this journey had dissipated after seven months, leaving only intermittent flashes of hurt.

"I wish I wasn't so far away," Nora lamented. "Otherwise, I'd go see her."

"Well, her birthday is coming up next month. Maybe you could visit then."

Not that Nora was in a hurry to get back to Trafford, but she realized that at some point she'd have to go back to see her family.

"Thanks for reminding me. I'd almost forgotten. I can't make any promises, but I'll see what I can do."

By Friday evening, the rain was but a memory. Out of groceries but too exhausted to fight the crowd at the supermarket, Nora picked up a salad on her way home and ate in the living room alone. Afterward, she changed into her pajamas and lay down on the couch. No sooner had she gotten comfortable when she heard a knock at the door.

Peering through the peephole, she glimpsed John standing there in a blue suit, holding a bouquet of yellow daisies.

Nora looked down in dismay at her disheveled pajamas. "One minute," she called out. She rushed to her bedroom and changed into something more presentable before hurrying back to the door, running a hand through her hair as she opened it.

"John." She swung the door wide. "What brings you by?"

"I was in the neighborhood," he said with a smirk.

Nora smiled reflexively at his joke.

"These are for you." He handed her the flowers. "I picked them up on my way home. I hope you like them."

Overwhelmed by John's thoughtfulness, all Nora could do was smile and thank him as she took the bouquet in hand. "I'll get a vase." She turned toward the kitchen. "I was just getting ready to watch an episode of *ER*. You're more than welcome to join me."

"I wish I could," he replied sadly. "But unfortunately, I have a business dinner downtown."

"Oh?" She found a lilac vase, filled it with water, and carefully arranged the flowers.

"My associates and I are meeting with a group of investors who are interested in partnering to build a new youth sports complex. It's something we've been working on for a while."

"That sounds exciting." Nora set the vase on the coffee table. "Perfect."

He adjusted his tie and cleared his throat. "Listen, there's something I wanted to ask you. Since I know how much you like Italian food, I was hoping you'd join me for dinner tomorrow night. There's this great little spot downtown I think you'll love."

Flowers? Dinner? Nora didn't want to burst his bubble, but perhaps now was a good time to lay some ground rules. "Listen,

John," she said, speaking softly. "I'm flattered, but you should know I recently got out of a messy relationship, and—"

He held up a hand before she could finish her thought. "Say no more. I've been there myself a time or two." He took a step back. "Let's just pretend I didn't say anything."

"Thank you... for understanding and for the flowers. They really are beautiful."

"You're welcome." He rubbed the back of his neck. "Well"—he backed off the porch—"I should go. Good night, Nora."

"Night, John."

Closing the door, a pang of guilt rippled through her. Though she felt bad for having turned John down, Nora's gut told her that now was not the time to lead him on.

Saturday marked the first time Nora had seen sunlight in a week, so after breakfast, she put on her running gear, took one last sip of coffee, and headed outdoors. Rather than jog through the neighborhood as usual, she decided to mix things up and set off in the opposite direction toward Crockett Park. Twenty minutes into the run, she felt like her old self. Step by step she put behind her both the pavement and the past, concentrating solely on the road before her and what lay ahead.

As she neared the entrance to the park, a familiar figure came into view. He wore a black tank top that stretched across broad shoulders, and athletic shorts clinging to his toned legs that pounded against the pavement as he jogged closer. John. His jaw was set firm, brows furrowed in concentration, and even from far away, she could feel the intensity of his gaze upon her. Suddenly uncomfortable, she wanted to turn back, but it was too late.

"Hey," she said, regarding him with a wave.

"Hi there." John slowed his pace as Nora stopped to catch her breath.

"I didn't know you were a runner."

"Is that what it looked like I was doing?" He gave a quiet laugh. "I'm a jogger at best, but I'll take the compliment."

Nora wiped the sweat from her brow. "Are you on your way home?"

"I am, but I'll probably stop at Shiloh's first and grab a beer."

"That sounds tempting. Do you mind if I join you?" After turning down John's dinner invitation the night before, Nora wasn't sure he'd say yes.

"Not at all."

They jogged to Shiloh's and found a table on the outdoor patio overlooking a small creek. John pulled out a seat for her, then took a chair himself.

"Do you run for exercise or just to have an excuse to drink?" Nora asked when they were seated.

John laughed and leaned back in his chair, running a hand through his dark hair. "A little of both, I guess." He tilted his head to the side and scrutinized her face. "What about you? You seem in your element out there."

"I've been running my entire life. My dad introduced me to the sport when I was in elementary school, and I quickly became obsessed with it. From there, I ran cross-country and track in high school and college."

His brows shot up. "Impressive. Then you were taking it easy on me that last mile."

The waitress appeared and took their order. When she left, Nora turned to John and said, "Listen, I'm sorry about last night. It's just that—"

"Don't worry about it," he said matter-of-factly. "I wasn't aware of your situation. Besides, I get the feeling I'm probably the hundredth guy who's asked you out since you've moved here."

"Well," she said with a teasing smile, "maybe not the hundredth."

When the waitress returned with their drinks, Nora dropped a lime wedge into her Corona and took a draw before looking John in the eyes again. "I was wondering... is the invitation for dinner this evening still open?"

John gave a tiny twitch of his lips and nodded slightly. "It is. Why, do you know someone who'd like to go with me?"

"Yes, as a matter of fact I do." She hoped he couldn't hear the tremor in her voice. "I'd like to go, if you'll have me."

John placed his beer bottle on the table and smiled at her reassuringly. "Of course I'll have you."

"Then it's a date." She tapped her beer bottle against his.

They pulled up to the entrance of Valentino's, a dimly lit redbrick building that had once been a prominent residence, at six o'clock sharp. A smile curved John's lips as he watched the people gathered outside, waiting to be seated. He put the car in park and opened Nora's door, gently taking her hand in his as they made their way into the restaurant.

The maître d' greeted them warmly, then led them through clusters of tables to a private room in the rear of the building where they were seated near a mahogany wine rack filled with bottles of every color.

"Okay"—she dropped her voice to a whisper—"how did you pull that off? Do you know the owner or something?"

John pulled out the chair for her. "Or something," he said with a sly smile.

Nora chose the chicken marsala while John ordered veal and a bottle of pinot grigio.

"That shade of green brings out your eyes." He glanced at her dress.

"Thank you. Green has always been my favorite color."

"So..." John's eyes drifted away from her. "What do you think of this place?"

Nora took in the exposed brick walls, coffered ceiling, and hardwood floors. "It has charm. It reminds me of one of those speakeasies from the twenties."

A smile parted his lips. "You were right when you said you had a keen eye. A Prohibition-era setting is precisely the look we were going for."

"We?"

"My friend and I own this place. Well, he runs it. I'm more of a silent partner. It would have been demolished if we hadn't bought it. Restoring old buildings to their former glory is one of my many passions."

"You're just full of surprises, aren't you?"

Their wine arrived then, and he poured her a glass, his eyes twinkling in the candlelight.

John proposed a toast. "To what I hope is the first of many meals together." As they clinked glasses, Nora got the feeling something special was beginning.

When their food came out, they took turns eating and making small talk. Smiles graced John's lips as he listened intently to every word she spoke.

With the main course behind them, Nora found herself agreeing to dessert.

"What made you change your mind... about dinner?" John asked while scooping a spoonful of chocolate cake into his mouth.

Nora wiped the corners of her mouth and laid the napkin

across her lap before answering. "I had something of an epiphany last night after you left. I came to the realization that if my ex can move on and be happy, why can't I?"

"That's logical. And you're right—you should be happy. For what it's worth," he added, his tone quiet, serious, "I know how difficult getting over someone can be." The sadness in his voice gave the impression he too had recently gone through a breakup. "But I'm glad you changed your mind about dinner. I've had a wonderful time tonight."

"Me too. And you were right to assume I would love this place. The food, the atmosphere... Amazing. Thank you." Her smile fell away. "I'd forgotten what it was like to go to dinner with a man and not have to worry about him yelling at the waiter or complaining about the service."

John chuckled with amusement at her statement. "No offense, but your ex sounds like a real—"

"Asshole?"

His laughter echoed off the walls. "I was going to say jerk, but asshole works too."

"It's just... He was so full of himself, so arrogant. I don't know why it took me so long to see it. Honestly, I should have known from the beginning."

"Don't be so hard on yourself. People wear many masks. Some are just better at hiding behind them than others."

After leaving the restaurant, John drove them down a winding road until they arrived at the base of the Parthenon. There were scaffolds and cranes everywhere, but from where Nora stood somehow it still looked beautiful in the moonlight.

"Did you know that Nashville is called the Athens of the

South?" he asked as they walked along the path that circumvented the building.

"I didn't know that."

"The city has a long tradition of dedication to education and the arts. That's one of the things that drew me to the area. That and the weather."

As they continued walking, John's hand brushed against Nora's. It was a small gesture but enough to send shivers down her spine. Despite not wanting to jump into a relationship, there was something about John that drew her to him.

"I'm really glad I decided to move here. I almost didn't, you know. At the last minute, I had second thoughts."

"Why?"

Nora's gaze turned skyward, taking in the moon and stars. "Having grown up in a small town, I was insulated from the outside world. My parents both grew up in Trafford, so aside from the occasional family vacation, we rarely left home. In some respects, small-town living is second to none. Everyone knows everyone, and help is never far away. But it also has its disadvantages—mainly that the rest of the world seems scary in comparison. But I can see now how foolish I was to believe that. Since I arrived here, everyone has bent over backward to make me feel at home, and I haven't seen the first thing that is evenly remotely scary."

"I'm glad you feel that way. Hopefully, I'm one of the people who has made you feel at home."

"Yes." She set her gaze upon him. "You absolutely have."

When they returned to the car, John helped her inside.

"This was fun." As they drove south, Nora was glad she'd changed her mind about going to dinner with John.

"I agree." He flashed a gleaming smile. "Hopefully this was just the first of many dates."

"Yes." She grinned broadly. "I hope so too."

The drive back to Nora's place didn't take long, and she found herself wishing the night would never end. When he walked her to the door, Nora kissed John on the cheek and told him she would be open to going out again.

So much for not rushing into things.

From her window, Nora watched John cross the street to his house. As soon as he was inside, she slipped out of her dress and into bed. For some reason, this night had been different from all the other first dates she'd had. There was something special about John, and part of her wanted to take things further—but at the same time, with her heart on the mend, she knew she had to be careful.

Lying in the dark, listening to the hum of the fan above her, Nora realized something else: It had been almost eight months since she'd had sex—a new record—and for whatever reason, the crushing reality hit her right between the legs.

Chapter Nine

JUNE 1998

As the weeks passed, Nora and John grew closer. After their dinner at Valentino's, they went out several more times, and despite Nikki urging her to move faster, Nora felt comfortable with how their relationship was progressing. Slow and steady.

Despite Nora's optimism, there were those who didn't approve of John. Annette and Whitney had both warned her about his aloof attitude, but she chose to ignore them in favor of focusing on his attractive qualities: dark brown hair, chestnut eyes, and a soothing voice that made her heart flutter every time he spoke. Though she had promised herself to take time before committing to another serious relationship, she hadn't expected to meet someone like John.

Tuesday morning after serving breakfast, Nora found Mr. Carlisle already up and anxiously awaiting their walk.

"You look spry this morning." She helped him out of his chair.

"Thank you." He grabbed his blue cap and placed it on his head. "I've been ready since five."

"What time did you get up?"

"Four thirty, same as always."

"And I thought I was an early riser. Don't you get tired?"

"When you get to be my age, sleep becomes more of a luxury than a necessity," he explained as they left the room. "Besides, if I get tired later, I'll catch a nap after *The Price is Right*."

Outside, the sun beat down on them from a cloudless sky.

"It's gonna be a hot one," he said as they navigated the winding garden path. "The man on Channel 5 said ninety-two."

"I think you're right." Nora already felt the heat. In the distance, she spotted a pair of mallards coming in for a landing. She watched in silence as they glided gracefully across the surface of the water. "So Gail was telling me the other day that you fought in the war. Is that true?"

"Yes, ma'am," he answered proudly. "I was a captain in the United States Army."

"Really? I would never have guessed."

"No?" He stopped and stood at attention. "I don't strike you as the military type?" He gave a sharp salute.

"Not exactly." She gave a quiet laugh.

"I'll have you know that in my day I was a lean, mean fighting machine, feared by both friend and foe. At least that's what my buddy Albert used to tell me."

They walked on, passing beneath the canopy of a weeping willow tree as the sun filtered through the leaves and danced across the still surface of the pond.

"How was it—being in the military?" Nora asked.

His gaze fixed on something in the distance. "Tough," he said finally. "But equally rewarding. Some of my fondest memories are of my time in the service."

"I'll bet you have a story or two, don't you?"

He nodded as a ghost of a smile played around his lips. "Would you like to hear one?"

"Sure, but only if you promise to tell me more about the woman from the painting."

They found an empty bench at the far side of the pond beneath an old oak tree and settled down together. Fred removed his cap and ran a hand through what remained of his thinning silver hair. "Where would you like me to start?"

"It's your story, so start wherever you like."

He set his gaze on the horizon and drew a deep breath. "The year was 1920," he began. "I was born on a farm east of Nashville in the little town of Mount Juliet. First and foremost I was raised as a Southern boy, which meant I knew how to do four things—hunt, fish, cuss, and pray. Being from the South also meant that while the rest of the country was up to date on current affairs, we were at least ten steps behind. But that didn't seem to bother folks much. You've heard the saying *ignorance is bliss*? Well, that was us—ignorant as the day is long and blissfully unaware."

"So you've lived here your entire life?"

"More or less."

"What about your parents? What were they like?"

"Strict. God-fearing. But decent people." He gave a wistful smile. "Mother kept the house and took care of me and my sisters while Daddy was out working. But in the evenings, Daddy and I would sneak off to the pond and catch catfish and bass. That man loved the water almost as much as he loved Mama."

His words triggered something in Nora, and suddenly she

was five years old again, playing at the lake's edge while her parents hammered away at their new house.

A breeze ruffled the surface of the water, stealing her attention. "What about school? Did you go to college?"

"Sure did. When high school ended, I was fortunate enough to get accepted to David Lipscomb University. We didn't have much money, so I worked two jobs to put myself through school. There I earned a degree in business with a minor in religious studies. For a while, I tossed around the idea of being a preacher, but fate had other plans for me."

"The war?"

He gave a quiet nod.

Nora did the math in her head. "This would have been the Second World War, right?"

"Affirmative. After graduation, I debated taking a job with an accountant in town, but realizing that war was inevitable, I enlisted in the army instead. Later that year, the Japs attacked Pearl Harbor, ending any chance I had at a normal life. Fortunately, having already graduated college meant I was one of the first selected for Officer Candidate School, so by the time I completed my training, I had earned the rank of second lieutenant, which beat the hell out of going in as a grunt."

Admittedly, Nora wasn't educated on the military or its hierarchy, but even she knew that being an officer had its advantages.

"So does that mean you saw combat?"

"Yes, ma'am, and lots of it."

Suddenly, Nora had a whole new respect for Mr. Carlisle. "But what does that have to do with the girl in the painting?"

"I'm getting there," he said with a twinkle in his eye. After a few seconds, he continued. "Her name was Rose. She was someone I met during the war." He turned his gaze upon Nora and held it there. "You remind me a great deal of her."

Nora's stomach churned with emotion. "Is that why you started painting again, because I brought back her memory?"

"Yes. Don't take this the wrong way, but when I passed you in the hall that day, I thought I had seen a ghost. I guess seeing your face stirred something inside me I hadn't felt in over fifty years."

Nora didn't know whether to be disturbed or flattered, though she settled on the latter.

"My grandfather on my dad's side fought in the war," she said, attempting to find common ground. "He was in the air force, I think. Or was it the navy? Anyway, he died when I was young, so I didn't really know him all that well. And my other grandfather—Pap—was in the navy, but it was at the tail end of the war, so he didn't see any action."

"Were the two of you close?" Mr. Carlisle asked.

"Not as close as I would have liked."

"That's too bad. I assume he's..."

"He died about a year ago." She sighed. "Now Gran is the only grandparent I have left."

"Was she involved in the war effort, by chance?"

Nora gave him a funny look. "I didn't think women fought in those days."

"They didn't see combat," he said. "But they served in other ways. Many were nurses, just like yourself."

Nora shook her head, unable to imagine her grandmother anywhere near a battlefield. "To my knowledge, she worked at a knitting mill most of her life before she became a secretary for the telephone company." Glancing at her watch, Nora realized the time had gotten away from her. "Oh shoot! I'm sorry to cut our conversation short, but I have a staff meeting to attend. Can I walk you back to your room?"

"Thank you, dear." He leaned back against the park bench.

"But I think I'll stay a little longer and maybe think of Rose for a while."

"Suit yourself, but don't stay out here too long." She stood and fanned her face. "It's getting hotter by the minute."

They returned to the same spot the following day, and the story continued.

"The truth is," said Mr. Carlisle, "after Judy died, I was lost without her. I didn't realize how much I depended on her for things until she wasn't there anymore. Looking back, I know I wouldn't have been able to stay in that house by myself, at least not for very long. I just wish the girls had sat me down and told me what they were thinking rather than springing it on me at the last minute. My body might be worn out, but my mind is still sharp." He tapped a bony finger against his temple.

"Why don't you tell me more about the war," Nora suggested, hoping to move the conversation in a less sensitive direction.

"Good idea. Now where were we? Ah, yes. Casablanca..."

NOVEMBER 1942

I felt the roll of the waves beneath my feet as I leaped from the boat, sinking chest-deep into the salty surf. With a hundred pounds of gear strapped to my back, I could barely keep my head above water as I followed the men in front of me, wondering if this would be the day I would die.

To my surprise, there was little resistance, and by evening we had taken control of the port. I settled onto a fragment of wall that had survived the shelling while my men scattered around me, some taking naps in the shade.

The brief respite allowed me to take out my sketchbook and search for something to draw. As I scanned the street, my gaze settled on a young woman—a nurse with bloodstained hands—seated beside a medical tent and staring at the ground. The way the sunlight hit her, she looked almost angelic. Unable to pass up such an opportunity, I first sketched her silhouette, then roughed in her features before adding detail.

After ensuring it was accurate, I got up and eased in her direction. "Tough day?" I asked, hovering between her and the setting sun.

She peered up at me. "You could say that. Is there something I can do for you"—she looked at my uniform—"Lieutenant?"

"No, ma'am," I replied. "I just wanted to give you this." I handed her the sketch, and she inspected it closely.

"You drew this?"

"Yes, ma'am. Just now. I hope you don't mind."

She shook her head and scooted over, making room for me. "You've got talent, Lieutenant."

"Thank you, ma'am."

She shook her head in amusement. "An artist who fights. That's something you don't see every day."

"I was born an artist. I only fight because Uncle Sam says I must."

"At least you're honest about it. Most of these guys strut around here bragging about how tough they are." She looked down at her hands and frowned. "You should see the way they go on."

"You should see them out there." I nodded toward the beach. "It's all bravado until the bullets start flying. I can't help noticing you've been crying. Is this your first experience with combat?"

"Yes, but that's not why I was crying." She hesitated a

moment before continuing. "I recently lost someone close to me, so I'm still learning to live without them."

I could tell from the pain in her eyes that whoever she had lost was more than just an acquaintance. "I'm sorry to hear that. You have my condolences." After a moment of silence, I got to my feet. "Well, I'll leave you to your thoughts. I just wanted to stop by and give you that drawing and tell you that I hope things get better for you."

"Lieutenant?" she asked as I moved away.

"Yes?"

"Thank you." A flicker of a smile passed her lips.

"My pleasure. Oh, in case we ever meet again, you can call me Fred." I extended my hand toward her.

"Pleasure to meet you, Fred," she said as her grip tightened around mine. "Everyone around here calls me Rose. You can too if you like."

"So Rose was a nurse?"

Mr. Carlisle's expression softened at the thought. "Yes, she was. And a damn good one too."

"You said she lost someone close to her. Who was it?"

Mr. Carlisle took a breath before answering. "Her fiancé. He had been killed at the Battle of Santa Cruz just the month before."

Nora let out a gasp, unable to fathom the loss of a loved one at such a young age.

"She was devastated by it, and she carried that grief with her throughout the rest of the war."

"I can't imagine," Nora said. "That must have been difficult for her to continue treating wounded soldiers while dealing with her own heartbreak."

Mr. Carlisle nodded in agreement. "But she was strong. Stronger than most people I know." He leaned back and gazed into the heavens, studying the clouds as if they held the key to his memories. "I wish you could have seen her. She had a way of brightening up a room with just her smile."

Nora pictured Rose in her mind's eye. "She sounds like a remarkable woman."

"She certainly was," Mr. Carlisle said with a wistful sigh. "Which is why I'll never forget her."

They sat in silence for a few moments, lost in thought about the past. Finally Nora spoke up. "Do you think you'll ever see her again?"

Mr. Carlisle looked at her, his expression full of longing. "I don't know, but I hope so. There are very few things I want to do before I die but seeing her again is one of them. That way, I could die a happy man."

Chapter Ten

Nora arrived home that evening to find a note from John taped to her front door.

Brimming with excitement, she took a quick shower and donned her beloved blue jeans and an off-the-shoulder blouse. Then she did her makeup as fast as possible and fixed her hair.

On her way out, she checked her messages and saw that there was one from her mom. She said it wasn't urgent but wanted Nora to call her when she got a chance. It would have to wait. She had more important matters to attend to.

"You're not yourself tonight," John said after a lovely dinner.

Nora glanced away, that day's conversation with Mr. Carlisle still on her mind. "Sorry. I was just thinking."

He sat down beside her on the porch swing and draped an arm over her shoulder. "About what?"

"One of my patients—Mr. Carlisle," she said. "He's been telling me about his time in the war. I never thought I'd be interested in that kind of thing, but I find myself captivated."

"Sounds fascinating."

"It is. A few weeks ago, he painted this picture, and..." She put a hand to her heart. "It's the most beautiful thing I've ever seen."

John listened intently while she went on.

"But that isn't the most incredible part. He told me he hasn't painted in fifty years. I can't even begin to comprehend that."

"That *is* incredible. He must have had some formal training, right? Art school? Or perhaps he studied abroad?"

She shrugged, then turned to John. "At the risk of ruining what has been another lovely evening, there's something I need to ask you."

He set his beer on the ground and gave her his full attention. "I'm all ears."

Taking a deep breath, she continued. "This... thing we have between us—where do you see it going?"

He smiled. "That depends on you."

"Me?"

"Look, Nora." He took her hand in his. "I don't know about you, but these last few weeks have been some of the best of my life. It might sound clichéd, but you're a breath of fresh air. It's true I wasn't looking to meet someone, but sometimes these things just happen. And I know you said you just got out of a messy relationship and don't want to jump into anything serious, and I respect that, but the truth is I can't stop thinking about you."

His words left her breathless.

"I've been thinking about you a lot as well." She took a moment and cleared her throat. "Perhaps now is a good a time to tell you the whole story of why I moved here."

She turned and stared into the darkness, gathering her thoughts. "Growing up, I was of the belief that you met someone in school, fell in love, got married, and lived happily ever after." She held a brief smile then let it fade. "There was this guy named Jeremy. We met in high school, dated through college, and then a couple of years ago, he proposed to me."

She played with the hem of her shirt, the scene embedded in her memory. "I'd gone out with a couple of guys before him, but he was my first real love. After we were engaged, things were great for a while. I took a job at the hospital, and Jeremy went to work at a law firm in Birmingham. But about six months into our engagement, something changed. I didn't notice it at first. He started working odd hours, staying at his firm's apartment in the city on weekends... I thought it was all just part of the job. Little did I know he was cheating on me."

The onrush of tears took her by surprise. *Don't cry. Don't you dare cry.*

"When I found out, I was devastated. We had been together for so long that I'd forgotten what life was like without him. After I broke off the engagement, everything spiraled out of control. Word of our breakup spread like wildfire, and everywhere I went, whispers followed me. So I moved in with my grandmother for a while just to get away from everything."

John squeezed her hand. "I'm sorry you had to go through that. What made you finally decide to leave home and strike out on your own? That couldn't have been easy."

She shook her head. "No. It wasn't. Believe it or not, it was something my grandmother said to me while I was staying with her. She said that although I couldn't see it, my breakup with Jeremy was the best thing that could have happened to me. Gran was never a fan of his. But she also said that if I wanted to move on and start over, I'd need to look beyond the limits of Trafford. A few days later, I came across an opening for a job at Belle Haven, and I thought *what the hell*, so I applied, and the rest is history."

"That's quite a story." John turned his gaze toward two fireflies lighting up the night sky. "You've mentioned your grandmother before. I take it the two of you are close?"

She nodded. "Gran and I have this... unspoken connection. I don't know why, but she took a strong liking to me when I was very young. My mom says it's because I'm the only granddaughter, but I feel there's something else between us, that perhaps we're kindred spirits." Then Nora thought of Pap and dropped her eyes. "But she's not the same woman I once knew, not since Pap died."

"How long were they married?"

"Forty-eight years. Growing up I thought Gran was invincible. Even when life seemed to get everyone else down, she always had a smile on her face and a word of encouragement for whoever needed it. But now... It's like she's broken, and the worst part is there's nothing I can do to fix it."

John stayed quiet until Nora finished speaking, then said, "I learned many years ago that things are always darkest before the dawn. Maybe in the case of your grandmother, her dawn is just over the horizon."

His words lifted her spirits. "Thank you. You always seem to know exactly what to say to make me feel better."

"You're welcome. And thank you for sharing your story with me. I know that wasn't easy. And just so you know"—his dark, piercing gaze connected with hers—"no one, especially someone as kind and wonderful as you, deserves to be treated that way."

Nora's heart gave a flutter of anticipation, and for a moment she thought he was about to kiss her—but something seemed to stop him from doing so. Maybe he was keeping a secret of his own. Regardless, the moment passed, and though part of her was let down, something inside Nora had shifted, and for the first time since the breakup, she felt as if she was ready to love again.

Chapter Eleven

WHILE NORA CONTEMPLATED HER NEXT MOVE WITH John, she wanted desperately to learn more about Mr. Carlisle's artistic background. The fact that he could produce a portrait like the one of Rose without having touched a brush in decades astounded her, which led her to believe he must have had at least some professional instruction along the way.

Standing in Mr. Carlisle's room, her gaze fixed on the portrait of Rose, Nora asked him where he'd learned to paint.

"When I was in high school, I was fortunate enough to have an art teacher that recognized my potential," he said. "Mrs. Hall was her name. She took me under her wing and gave me a few pointers that helped refine my skills."

"So no formal training?"

He shook his head, and Nora opened the windows to allow a gentle breeze into the room, then adjusted the flowers in the vase.

"Did you ever try to pursue a career in art? You've certainly got the talent for it."

"Briefly, but it never amounted to anything." He sighed

deeply as his eyes took on a faraway look. "I always dreamed of having my work in one of those fancy New York galleries alongside the likes of Sargent or Cassatt, but it wasn't to be."

"There's still time."

"I appreciate your optimism, Miss. Dawson, but I'm afraid my time has come and gone."

Later that afternoon, Nora and Mr. Carlisle stopped at the pond to feed the ducks, then grabbed an ice cream from the cafeteria and sat in the shade beneath the awning. The last time they'd spoken, Nora got the impression his story of Rose was just beginning, and she could only speculate where it would go next.

"So what happened after that first meeting with Rose?" Nora asked. "Did you see her again?"

"Sure I did." Mr. Carlisle wiped the corners of his mouth before going on. "As our lines advanced east into Tunisia, casualties mounted. The farther we pushed the Germans, the fiercer the fighting. When I wasn't on the front line, which was seldom, I caught glimpses of Rose, mostly in passing. Unfortunately"—he turned to Nora—"when you're at war, there isn't much time for social calls. But we still said hello to one another and were friendly when we talked."

Nora felt a twinge of disappointment. "And here I was thinking you and Rose had some grand love affair." She took a bite of ice cream and kicked herself for letting her imagination get the better of her.

Mr. Carlisle glanced at her as his lips curled into a rascally smile. "Who says we didn't?"

. . .

DECEMBER 1942

"What happened to you?"

The voice was familiar, and as my eyes adjusted to the bright light in the room, I found myself staring into a familiar face—Rose.

"Mortar," I muttered, struggling to remain conscious.

"Don't worry, Lieutenant," she said with a sense of urgency. "You're safe now. We're going to take good care of you."

When I woke again, night had fallen, and an unfamiliar sense of peace blanketed the room. I noticed the thick bandage wrapped around my shoulder, and it brought back what had happened. Once I cleared the fog from my head, I sat up and searched for something to drink.

"Excuse me, miss." I stopped a passing nurse. "Could I trouble you for some water?"

She smiled warmly and poured me a glass before asking if there was anything else she could do for me.

"Yes. Is Rose still here? I'd like to thank her for taking such good care of me."

"Her shift ended a little while ago, Lieutenant, but let me see if I can find her."

A few minutes later, Rose appeared. She was still in uniform, but her auburn hair was down, cascading over her shoulder. "I'm glad to see you're awake, Lieutenant. You've been out for hours. How's the shoulder?"

"Hurts like hell," I said. "But I'll survive."

She checked the bandages. "It'll be painful for a few days. Might even mean you have to give up sketching for a while. But the good news is we were able to remove the shrapnel, so you should be good as new in no time."

I breathed a sigh of relief.

"You're lucky though." She added a blanket. "Some of the

other companies in your regiment really took a beating. I've been in surgery since ten this morning. What happened out there?"

Scenes of the ambush played inside my head. "We walked into a trap." I recounted the horrors of the day. "Honestly, I don't know how I made it out alive."

"Well, you're okay now." A smile creased her face. "Dorene will be working the night shift. She'll get you anything you need." She checked the time. "My shift starts at six, so I'm going to eat and get some shuteye, but I'll be back to check on you first thing in the morning. Until then, try not to cause too much trouble." She gave me a wink.

At dawn, Rose returned just like she promised.

"Did you get any sleep?" she asked.

"Very little. You?"

"Not much, but that's nothing new. I haven't had a good night's sleep since this whole thing began." She forced a smile, but it was short-lived.

"Don't worry," I told her. "It'll all be over soon."

"I hope you're right," she said as she changed out my bandages.

"Listen, I wanted to thank you for taking such good care of me yesterday. I'm ashamed to admit I was frightened by the whole experience, but your voice, the way you handled yourself, really set me at ease."

"My pleasure. And there's nothing to be ashamed of. You suffered a serious wound that left untreated could have been fatal. Being frightened at the prospects of your own mortality doesn't make you any less of a man—at least not in my eyes."

"You're right," I said, relieved. "I hope you don't take this the wrong way, but if I had to be wounded, there's no one else I'd rather have taking care of me than you."

She blushed and looked away. "That must be the morphine talking." She checked the line.

"No." I took her arm. "Ever since that day in the square when I first saw you, I haven't stopped thinking about you. You probably hear this all the time, but I think you're the most gorgeous woman I've ever seen."

She cast a wary glance in my direction. "I appreciate the compliment, Lieutenant, but—"

"Look, I know you're hurting and that we're at war, but that doesn't change the way I feel. And I was wondering"—I took a deep breath—"if maybe I could take you out sometime... for coffee or dinner?"

She hesitated for a moment, and I wondered if I'd overstepped my bounds. But then a sweet smile appeared on her lips. "That's very sweet of you, Lieutenant. But to be honest, I don't know if I'm ready for something like that."

"I understand." I felt a slight twinge of disappointment.

"Tell you what—for now let's just focus on getting you better. If and when I decide the time is right for me to starting dating again, you'll be the first to know."

As Nora waited for the next installment of the story, she had an idea she wanted to run past John.

"Remember the woman from the painting?" she said one evening as they walked to the park after dinner. "The one I was telling you about?

"Yeah," he said, nodding along. "What about her?"

"I want to find her. She was someone Mr. Carlisle met during the war, and I have a feeling they were in love."

"Is that what he told you?"

"Not in so many words, but I just know. And if they were in love," she went on, connecting the dots inside her head, "that means something tragic happened that has caused them to be apart for the past fifty years."

John plodded ahead. "I hate to play devil's advocate, but how do you know Rose is even still alive? I mean, what if she died in the war? And even if she didn't, she must be in her eighties by now."

Nora considered the odds. Knowing that the life expectancy for a woman was seventy-seven years, if Rose *was* still alive, she was living on borrowed time. Still, she had a feeling that Rose was out there, and that she was destined to find her.

"I know it's a long shot," Nora conceded, "but this is something I'm passionate about."

John ambled along, kicking pebbles, watching them tumble end over end into the street. "Assuming she is alive, how do you propose to find her? Do you have a mailing address, or at least a photograph?"

"No."

"Hmm. What about an internet search—have you tried that?"

"Yes," she replied despondently, "but without a last name or an address, there wasn't much I could find."

John scratched his head. "I might have another idea, but it's a bit of a stretch. Some friends of mine own an art gallery not far from here. They cater mostly to high-end clientele—local celebrities, politicians, country music stars. I could see if they have any ideas."

"Do you think they'd be willing to help?"

"Yes," said John. "We go way back. Plus they owe me one."

"That would be amazing. Thank you." Nora marveled at how John always seemed to have the right answers. "Wait. What if Rose isn't local? What if she's in Seattle or New York—or worse, Australia?"

"That's precisely why I think they could help. Stephanie and Owen have a huge online following. I'm talking worldwide. They probably have access to tens of thousands of people if not more. Even in Australia."

Chapter Twelve

ON SATURDAY, JOHN AND NORA DROVE TO Ravenswood to meet with Owen and Stephanie Langley. As they arrived at the antebellum-style mansion, Nora gasped at the sight before her. Even from the parking lot, she saw grand columns, a wide porch, and two soaring chimneys. Giant oak trees hundreds of years old provided shade around the house, contrasting with lush fields of Indian grass that stretched for miles in every direction.

They stepped out of the car to admire the view before heading up a brick sidewalk connecting the parking lot to the front porch. As they approached, an attractive woman with dark hair opened the door and welcomed them inside.

"You must be Nora," she said with a friendly smile. Stephanie's sapphire earrings sparkled in the light of the chandelier. "John has told me so much about you."

"It's nice to meet you, Stephanie." Nora admired the spacious foyer filled with expensive oil paintings. "This place is amazing."

"I see we have company." A tall, thin man with dark hair descended the staircase and introduced himself as Owen.

"Nice to meet you, Owen," said Nora. "I was just telling your wife what a lovely place you have. It's like something from a magazine."

"Thank you," he said kindly. "I still pinch myself every morning to make sure I'm not dreaming." He gave a lighthearted laugh. "I'm not sure if Stephanie mentioned it, but the gallery also doubles as a reception hall. We host intimate parties, rehearsal dinners, weddings..." He turned and winked at John.

"Okay, why don't we let these ladies talk." John put an arm around Owen's shoulders and led him away, leaving Nora with Stephanie.

"Men." Stephanie rolled her eyes, then showed Nora to her office.

The walls were lined with bookcases stacked full of leather-bound novels, and lush potted plants sat in every corner. Stephanie poured two glasses of tea from an ornate carafe, handed one to Nora, and they settled into their seats. "Tell me more about this woman, the one from the painting. John mentioned she's a friend of one of your patients?"

"Yes. Her name is Rose," Nora replied. "My patient, Fred Carlisle, met her during the war. Fred has been a patient at Belle Haven for seven months, and until recently, he's been something of a recluse. Then a few weeks ago, he shocked everyone by painting a beautiful portrait of Rose, and I don't know—something about it has captivated me."

Stephanie leaned forward in her chair, her eyes lit up with intrigue.

"I'm still learning about what happened to them," Nora went on. "I take Mr. Carlisle for walks, and he tells me about his time in the service. Anyway, to make a long story short, Mr. Carlisle is sick, and no one knows how much time he has left. Perhaps it's that or the fact that I feel connected to Rose in some way, but I feel compelled to find her, to reunite the two of them before it's too late."

Stephanie set down the glass and straightened in her chair. "I can certainly understand your desire to do so," she said warmly, "and the sense of urgency. If you don't mind me asking, what does Mr. Carlisle think of your plan?"

Nora stared into her glass while she considered her question. "He and I haven't really discussed it yet. I was hoping to surprise him."

A smile tugged at the corner of Stephanie's mouth. She stood and pointed at her copy of *The Notebook* on the shelf behind her. "I'm a sucker for a good love story. Besides"—she returned to her seat—"love and art go hand in hand. Assuming this is something Mr. Carlisle wants, I think Owen and I would like to be a part of it. How can we help?"

Her generosity threw Nora for a loop. "That's wonderful. Thank you. John says you have a large online presence. Since we don't know where she lives or if she's even alive, we thought perhaps we could take some pictures of the painting and distribute them to your followers. Maybe we'll get lucky, and someone will recognize her."

Stephanie smiled as though she had just gained access to a secret treasure chest. "Tell you what. I have a better idea." She leaned back in her chair, lacing her hands in front of her. "It just so happens that Owen and I have been tossing around the idea of hosting a summer event highlighting local artists. Based on what you've told me, it sounds as if Mr. Carlisle's work might fit in nicely with what we were thinking. I don't know if John told you, but Owen's a history buff, so this is right up his alley. But we'll need more than just the one painting." Her eyes widened with curiosity. "I assume there are others?"

Nora's heart sank. "I don't know, but I can find out."

Stephanie flipped open her planner. "We were thinking

sometime in August for the exhibit. Why don't I give you a few days to see what you can come up with, and then we can regroup and talk about next steps?"

"Perfect." Nora figured that should give her plenty of time. "And thank you. This really means a lot."

"My pleasure. Anything for a friend of John."

When they'd finished their tea, Stephanie gave Nora a tour of the grounds.

"I don't mean to pry," Stephanie said as they made their way along a dirt path at the edge of the woods, "but what's the story with you and John?"

Nora reached up and tucked a lock of hair behind her ear. "Story?"

"It's just that when he called, he mentioned you were friends. Forgive me if I've misread the situation, but I get the impression there's more to it than that."

A wave of heat made its way up Nora's neck. "What gave it away?"

An amused expression quirked Stephanie's mouth. "Call it woman's intuition."

"I didn't realize it was that obvious."

"It isn't. But in all the years I've known John, I've never heard him talk much about women, much less bring any around." She stopped beneath the shade of an oak. "He's not like most men, if you haven't already noticed. John appreciates privacy and is careful about who he lets get close to him."

"Is that why no one seems to know much about him?"

Stephanie's eyes flicked toward the ground before she laughed nervously. "Probably. I think most of it stems from him being a Patree." She locked eyes with Nora. "Between you and me, I think he's afraid that people will expect things from him if they find out who he really is."

Aware that Stephanie was sizing her up, Nora chose a diplomatic approach. "Oh, I can understand that, which is why I'm thankful that I'm an independent woman. Financially speaking, I never want to have to depend on a man."

A crooked smile quirked up one side of Stephanie's mouth. "I know what you mean."

As they resumed their walk, Stephanie's eyes were drawn back to the house. "Do you have plans to stay—in Brentwood, I mean? John said you were only here until November."

"That all depends on whether the hospital extends my contract."

Stephanie nodded thoughtfully before flashing Nora a warm smile as they reached the porch. "Well, in any event, welcome to the area, and if you ever need anything, don't hesitate to ask."

After thanking Stephanie for the tour and for agreeing to help get the word out about Rose, Nora was asked if she could do Stephanie a favor.

"Of course," she replied, wondering how she could possibly say no.

"Please take care of John. Not only is he one of my best friends, but he's such a wonderful man." She smiled sympathetically. "After everything he's been through, Owen and I just want to see him happy."

"Of course," said Nora. But in the back of her mind, she was starting to think she wasn't the only one with baggage after all.

Chapter Thirteen

After Monday morning rounds were over, Nora jammed two quarters into the vending machine slot and pressed the button. When the pack of peanut M&M's clattered down into the tray, she scooped them up, then tucked them into her pocket before anyone else could see.

As soon as the coast was clear, she snuck into Mr. Carlisle's room.

"What are you up to?" He cast a look of suspicion in her direction.

With a sly smile, she sank into the chair beside him and pulled out the M&M's from her pocket. "Here. These are for you."

He eyed her uncertainly. "Why do I get the feeling you're trying to butter me up?"

"Because I am. Mr. Carlisle, what if I told you I could make one dream of yours come true and possibly a second?"

He threw back a handful of M&M's. "I'm listening," he said as he chewed.

"John and I were talking this weekend, and we have an idea. Some friends of his own an art gallery not far from here. It's a lovely place. In fact, we met with them Saturday, and they're thinking of hosting a summer exhibit featuring local artists. I told them about your painting of Rose, and they're interested in showcasing your work."

Up went his eyebrows. "Go on."

"And while it isn't exactly New York or Chicago, it's a start."

Mr. Carlisle appeared to be thinking. "My work in a gallery?"

"Yes. Isn't that what you've always wanted?"

"It is, but... You mentioned two dreams."

"Right." She paused, taking a breath before going on. "If everything goes according to plan, having your work on display will help get the word out about Rose. I want to find her for you, Mr. Carlisle... If you'll allow me."

"Do you think you can?"

"I don't know, but I want to try."

To Nora's astonishment, Mr. Carlisle's eyes became moist with tears. "I don't know what to say."

"Just say yes, and I will take care of everything."

He nodded, then brushed the sides of his knuckles under his eyes. "But what if Rose doesn't want to see me? I mean, it's been a long time."

"Sure she does. Who wouldn't want to see an old friend?"

At last, he agreed. "All right. Let's do it. Let's find Rose."

Elated, Nora hugged his neck and thanked him for the opportunity. Now there was nothing stopping her from finding Rose... except finding Rose.

"Oh," she said as she stood. "There's one more thing. I'm going to need a few more paintings—and quick. Do you think you're up for it?"

He looked up at her and his eyes sparkled with a devilish glint. "Would a dozen more be enough?"

"Sure, but I don't think there's time."

Suddenly his expression changed; his smile turned sly.

"There's something you're not telling me, isn't there?"

"The paintings I have from the war are hidden in my attic... There are fourteen in all if memory serves. Some are of Rose, some of the men, some of the places I visited..."

Nora was speechless. Was it true? Had they been there all this time without anyone knowing? "Are you serious? You mean, they've been in your attic this whole time?" Her mind reeled. "Do you think Suzanne and Gloria would loan them to me... just until the exhibit is over?"

"You don't need their permission," he said. "But just in case, I'd better call and tell them what's going on."

When Nora got home that evening, she let down her hair and checked her messages. There was one from her mom and another from Gloria Delaney—Fred's daughter—asking Nora to call at her convenience.

She dialed the number right away.

"Mrs. Delaney, this is Nora Dawson returning your call."

"Nora, thank you for getting back to me so quickly. I've been anxious to speak with you. I received a call from my father this afternoon with the most incredible story." The excitement in her voice echoed through the phone.

"Then I assume he told you about Rose."

"Yes, as a matter of fact, he did. Needless to say, I was shocked. Neither Suzanne nor I have ever heard him mention her name." She paused briefly, then added, "But I'm not surprised. Dad never really talked much about the war. He kept that part of his life a secret from us... All of us. I always assumed it was because of what he saw when he was over there, but now I wonder."

"By any chance, did he mention the artwork?"

"Yes, he did. But I've never seen it. Suzanne and I cleaned out most of the attic a few weeks after Dad went to live at Belle Haven. We were afraid if anyone discovered the house was vacant, they'd rob the place. Between his Coheleach prints and Mom's antique collection, there must have been a couple hundred thousand dollars sitting in that attic."

Nora could relate. Her uncle's baseball-card collection, which turned out to be worth a small fortune, had sat in a closet for almost five years after he passed away.

"And you're sure there were no paintings, maybe in a trunk or—"

"Like I said, Suzanne and I were all over that attic, but maybe we missed them."

Suddenly Nora was struck by an idea. "What if I came by and helped look for them? I'm off on Wednesdays and Saturdays, and Murfreesboro is just a short drive from my place."

"Well... Suzanne and I were planning to visit Dad for his birthday next week. Yes, I think that would be fine."

"Wonderful," said Nora as a rush of excitement overtook her. "When should I come by?"

"We get into town Tuesday afternoon, so Wednesday would work. Say ten o'clock?"

"Yes, that's perfect. See you then."

With Nora spending Saturday afternoon shopping with her friends, John met Stephanie for lunch at their usual spot.

"So what did you think of Nora?" he asked as he reached for the basket of tortilla chips.

"I found her to be very charming. Smart too." Stephanie took a sip of tea. "It's been a long time since you brought a woman around. That must mean this one is special."

John nodded. "And the funny thing is I knew it right away."

"Love at first sight, huh?" She cracked a grin. "How did you two meet anyway?"

"It's the funniest thing... She was out with her friends at Tootsie's one Friday night. I was at the bar, minding my own business, when she walked right up and introduced herself. We talked, danced, and laughed like we were old friends. It wasn't until the next afternoon that I discovered she was my neighbor."

Her eyebrows shot to her hairline. "That's a hell of a coincidence."

"You're telling me. It's almost as if it was—"

"Fate?"

"I was going to say *meant to be*, but yes, fate."

Their food arrived, and the conversation continued. "I haven't felt this way about someone in a long time, so I don't want to do anything to screw it up."

Stephanie nodded. "If I didn't know any better, it sounds to me as if you love her." When John didn't respond she asked, "Do you love her?"

Despite all John had going for him—good looks, wealth, and pedigree—he had only ever been in love once in his life. Women had certainly come and gone, but none of them had captured his heart the way Nora had.

"I do," he answered without reservation.

Once the shock wore off, Stephanie asked, "Does she feel the same way?"

That proved to be a more difficult question for him to answer.

"I don't know. There's chemistry, and we've grown closer of

late, but Nora's last relationship ended with her heart being broken, so I'm not sure she's ready to love again."

"Well, just be patient, and don't force it. No one knows better than us what it's like to have a broken heart, and how long it can take to heal." Stephanie finished her meal then and pushed her plate to the middle of the table. "But the good news is Nora seems to be a wonderful person. I mean, anyone who would go to the lengths she's going to find someone for a patient she hardly knows must have a tremendous heart, and you're blessed to have found her."

On her day off, Nora made the short drive to Murfreesboro and parked on the street in front of Mr. Carlisle's home. The white Victorian house seemed to stretch up to the sky and boasted turrets, a wraparound porch, intricate woodworking, and a side yard filled with an array of colorful flowers and neatly manicured shrubs.

Walking up the drive, Nora could almost picture Fred and Judy spending countless hours together on the porch rockers, hands entwined as they laughed, talked, and stargazed.

As she approached the front door, Nora was greeted by a middle-aged woman who introduced herself as Gloria. Her sister, who had her mother's eyes, stood just behind her.

"It's so nice to meet you both," said Nora, stepping into the foyer. "I apologize for barging into your lives like this. It must be strange to learn that after all these years your father was hiding such a talent."

"Yes, but equally intriguing," said Suzanne. "Gloria and I both think so. I'm afraid our father was—is—a very private man. He never really talked much about his younger life with us. That's not to say he wasn't a good father. He was wonderful. But—"

"What my sister is trying to say is that if there's a chapter to Dad's life that we're unaware of, we want to be a part of uncovering it," Gloria said. "I think it would make us both feel a little closer to him."

They ushered Nora into the kitchen, where Gloria filled three glasses of tea. Then they made their way to the back of the house, passing through a paneled hallway to a cozy nook they affectionately called the Blue Room.

They settled onto a plush sofa, and Gloria began to talk about their father's move to Belle Haven.

"It broke our hearts when we told him we were moving him to a nursing home." A pained expression marred Gloria's face. "How do you tell the man who's taken care of you your entire life—a man that is strong and independent—that he can no longer live in the house he built with his own two hands? I'm just glad Suzie was here." She reached for her sister's hand and gave it a squeeze. "There's no way I could have done that on my own."

"I'm sure that wasn't easy." Nora sympathized with them. "But you'll be happy to know he's thriving at Belle Haven. Now that he's painting again, it's given him a new lease on life."

That brought smiles to the faces of Gloria and Suzanne.

"Tell me something, Miss Dawson," said Gloria, "is Dad angry with us for sending him to Belle Haven?"

Nora recalled the conversation with Mr. Carlisle in which he voiced his concerns over the way his daughters had handled his move. "I don't think he's angry," she answered carefully. "I imagine he was confused at first, but I think he understands that you all did it with the best of intentions."

A relieved look washed over Gloria's face.

When they had finished their tea, they showed Nora to the

attic. Gloria pulled the string, and down came a door with a ladder that unfolded to the floor like a gentleman's handshake.

"It can get a little warm up there this time of year," she warned as a wave of heat rushed down to meet them. "So we can't stay long."

"Yes, ma'am," Nora said, then climbed to the top. "We'll be brief." Once she reached the top, she pulled the chain for the light and surveyed the surroundings. The space was much larger than she expected. Gloria and Suzanne joined her, and they agreed to split up and search opposite ends of the room.

After a few minutes of searching, sweat dripped from Nora's forehead, mingling with dust and grime on the wooden floorboards.

"Any luck?" Gloria yelled across the room.

"Nothing yet. You?"

"Nada," Suzanne responded.

Nora was about to give up when she remembered something Mr. Carlisle mentioned: the place on the wall with a notch in the board. It clicked into place all at once—the paintings weren't hiding inside a trunk or dresser. They were hidden behind the wall, in a secret compartment. It was the only logical spot. After frantically searching for an opening, she finally discovered a small crack between two boards.

A shiver ran down her spine as she knocked on the board and heard an echo return to her.

"I think I might have found something," she called out, and Suzanne and Gloria hurried over. "Do you have something I could use to pry the boards?"

Gloria disappeared and returned a moment later carrying a tire iron. "Will this work?"

With excitement in their eyes, they watched Nora wedge the pointed end between two boards that had been nailed to the wall. After a few moments of prying and tugging, one flew off and clattered to the floor as a gust of stale air rushed in.

Nora shined the flashlight into the darkness.

Staring back at her were the fourteen paintings and sketches, just as Mr. Carlisle had predicted. They carefully removed them one by one and laid them out on the living room carpet.

Gloria's hand covered her mouth in shock while Suzanne's eyes brimmed with tears.

"You were right," said Suzanne. "They're beautiful. I still can't believe they were up here all this time."

"Why did he keep this a secret from us?" Gloria asked.

"I don't know," said Suzanne, "but this Rose, whoever she was, must have meant a great deal to Dad."

Chapter Fourteen

With the artwork in her possession, Nora phoned Stephanie to tell her the good news.

"That was quick," she said. "When can I see them?"

"I'm on my way there now." Nora could hardly contain her excitement. "See you in twenty."

When she arrived, Owen carried the artwork inside and placed each painting carefully on one table and laid out the sketches on another.

"These are wonderful." He ran his hands over the canvases while his eyes lit up with admiration. "I don't know if Steph told you, but history is my passion. I've been collecting pieces from the Second World War for years, and these will tie in perfectly with my vision for this exhibit."

"Will this be enough?" Nora asked.

"More than enough," said Stephanie.

They ordered lunch and talked about Mr. Carlisle's work as they ate. When Stephanie walked up to a painting of Rose sitting by an open window, she gasped in awe. "This one's my favorite. I can only imagine what must have been going through Mr. Carlisle's head when he painted this."

"Or hers," Nora offered.

"You can tell they were in love," Stephanie said softly, tracing her fingertips over the brushstrokes. "Just look at the attention to detail; you don't get that kind of effort from an impartial third party. This was painted by someone who loved his subject very much." She stepped away from the table and looked at Nora with wide eyes. "So how is the story coming along?"

"Agonizingly slow," she lamented.

"That's the difference between the older generation and ours. To them, patience is a virtue. To us, it's an annoyance. We want things now." She snapped her fingers. "Isn't that right, Owen?"

"Yes, dear," he answered and rolled his eyes.

"But I have a feeling he's building to a crescendo," said Nora, hoping her instincts about Rose were correct. She finished her salad and chased it with a gulp of water. "Oh, I talked to Mr. Carlisle about the exhibit, and he's on board. He said whatever you wanted to do was fine with him."

"Fantastic!" Stephanie beamed a smile. "Do you think he'd be interested in sitting down and talking with me and Owen? We'd like to get his thoughts on a few things. I'm not sure if Owen told you, but we've decided to make his work the centerpiece of the exhibit."

"Really? He'll be delighted. But I'll need to check with Gail and with his daughters. I promised I'd keep them in the loop."

"Take your time. Owen and I will be out of town for the weekend, so why don't we reconnect early next week?" She reached for her calendar and opened it.

While Stephanie searched for an open slot, Nora glimpsed a picture on the bookshelf behind her. It appeared to be of Stephanie, Owen, and John, taken when they were teenagers.

And there was someone else—a girl with long dark hair and green eyes.

"Is that you?" Nora gestured to the picture.

Stephanie looked over her shoulder. "Yes," she said with a wistful smile. "A hundred years ago. And that's Owen, John, and... Charlotte. Can you believe how long John's hair was back then?" She shook her head. "That picture was taken just before the start of our senior year. God, that seems like a lifetime ago."

"Charlotte? I've never heard John mention her before."

Stephanie turned back to Nora. "She's my sister," she said, then changed the subject. "So we were thinking August 15 as the date for the exhibit. And I would really like it if Mr. Carlisle could be here in person to talk to the patrons. Undoubtedly, there will be dozens of folks interested in speaking with him."

"I'll see if he's up for it. In the meantime, I'll go ahead and request that day off. I wouldn't want to miss Mr. Carlisle's moment in the sun."

The afternoon sun was low in the sky as Nora and John jogged along a winding path. Exhilarated by the unexpected cool breeze, she recounted her experience in Mr. Carlisle's attic and how Stephanie and Owen were determined to give the artwork its deserved attention.

John smiled. "I knew they wouldn't let us down. Those two have been working together for years and know what they're doing. The exhibit will be incredible!"

"I still can't believe you all grew up together... and that you're still close after all these years. How did the three of you wind up in Nashville together anyway?"

"Well... It sorta just happened... by accident. But I'm glad it did, because when I got here, I knew no one, so having Owen and Steph around made the transition a lot easier."

"That's nice. I'm glad you have them in your life. From what little I know of them, they seem like good people."

"Yes, they are. Well, I'll see you later."

They parted ways at the end of the drive, and as Nora walked up to the front door, she heard the phone ringing inside.

"Mom... how are you?"

"Fine. Is everything okay?"

"Everything's... great." Nora paused to catch her breath. "Sorry, I just got in from a run."

"Oh. That sounds... exhausting. Did you go alone?"

"Um... no. John went with me."

"Your neighbor?"

"Uh-huh."

"The same neighbor who took you to dinner a couple of weeks ago?"

"One and the same." Nora instantly regretting having mentioned his name.

"Does *John* have a last name?"

Nora hesitated, heart racing, wondering if her mom would make the connection. Kathleen wasn't into politics, but she watched *Dateline* regularly, so the odds were fifty-fifty. "Patree." She braced for the worst.

"Patree? Why does that sound familiar?"

Nora quickly changed the subject. "So how's Dad? It feels like ages since I've talked to him."

"You know your father. He's down at the dock piddling with the boat lift again. I keep telling him it's time to get a new one, but he insists it can be fixed."

A nervous laugh escaped Nora's lips. She imagined her dad cussing under his breath as he tried to disassemble the rusted contraption. "Yeah, that sounds like him, all right."

"Listen, the reason I called was to see if you were going to be able to make it to Gran's eightieth birthday party. We're finalizing the guest list. I know we talked about it before, but I wanted to make sure you hadn't changed your mind. Everyone is dying to see you."

Nora knew that was her mom's not-so-subtle way of telling her she'd been away from home too long. "I've already asked for that weekend off so, yeah, I'm planning on it."

"Wonderful. Hey, here's an idea... Why don't you bring John with you?"

Me and my big mouth. "Why on earth would I do that?"

"I just thought that since the two of you have been spending so much time together, it might be nice to have him meet the family. Besides, it'd give you someone your own age to talk to."

Over the years, Nora had wondered if her mom hadn't missed her calling. She had a passive-aggressive way about her that would have been well suited for a career in sales.

"I mentioned we're only friends, didn't I?"

"Yes, yes. Don't read too much into it. It was only an idea."

"I'll think about it," Nora said, ending the inquiry.

"Oh, I also wanted to tell you I ran into Erin the other day. She says hello. How come you never mentioned she and Jeremy were seeing one another?"

The back of Nora's neck burned red-hot. "Must have slipped my mind."

"Are the two of you still friends?"

"Why would you ask that?"

"I dunno. After talking to her, I got the sense that you might have had a falling out."

Nora let out a heavy sigh. "I'd rather not talk about it."

"Well, not to add fuel to the fire, but the rumor is she and Jeremy are engaged."

The shock left Nora speechless. She and Jeremy had been together for ten years before he popped the question—and now he was marrying Erin after only a few short months. Her heart sank in her chest. "Engaged? But they hardly know each other."

"That's what I said, but you know how these things go..."

"Apparently not." It felt like a direct attack.

"I hear it's going to be a fall wedding, which means invitations will be going out soon."

"But that's in just a few months. Why the rush?" Then it dawned on her that perhaps Erin was pregnant. *That's it!* That would explain why everything seemed to be coming together so quickly. *Serves her right.* The thought brought an involuntary grin to her face.

"I don't know, but I'd keep an eye on your mail."

"Ha. You don't really think I'll get an invite, do you?"

"Erin's still your best friend, isn't she?"

"Was," Nora muttered.

"Nora Jean! You don't mean that."

"Yes, I do."

"But you and Erin have been friends since... well, since as long as I can remember."

But the truth was Nora now hated Erin in much the same way she hated Jeremy. They'd both betrayed her trust, stabbed her in the back, and as far as she was concerned, she wanted nothing to do with either of them.

"Things change, Mom. People change. Isn't that what you always say?"

"Yes, but I say a lot of things," said Kathleen. "Look, the bottom line is if she's happy, then shouldn't you be happy for her? I know what Jeremy did to you was inexcusable, but you can't let yourself be burdened with that forever. Besides, you've moved on, haven't you?"

The next evening during their walk, Nora asked John if he would be her plus-one at Gran's party. Her mom was right, Nora needed someone her age to keep her company—and to keep Gran and her friends from feeling sorry for her now that she was on her own. "I realize it's a big step," she said, sensing some hesitancy, "so if you're not comfortable or not ready, I understand."

"It's not that. I'd love to come with you," he said, then frowned. "But I'm going to be in South Carolina that weekend."

"Oh." They walked on. "You know, for someone who's trying to distance himself from his family, you sure do make a lot of trips to see them."

"Yeah, well..." He lowered his eyes. "Sometimes we're forced to do things we otherwise wouldn't." He flashed an enigmatic smile that sent a chill down Nora's spine—something deep inside her sensing a hidden truth behind those words.

Nora had suspected for some time that John was hiding something from her. And while she wasn't ready to call him a liar just yet, he certainly was skilled at revealing only the parts he wanted her to see. Perhaps, she thought, he was a better politician than he let on.

Chapter Fifteen

Between spending time with John, her job, and helping with the art exhibit, Nora had neglected her new friends. So after work on Friday, the four of them met at Shiloh's to catch up over dinner and drinks.

"Where have you been hiding?" Annette asked. "I was just telling Whitney I thought you might have gotten homesick and moved back to Trafford."

"Are you kidding? I love it here. I've just been busy, that's all. I don't know if you heard, but Mr. Carlisle is going to be featured in an art exhibit later this summer. I've been working with the gallery directors to make sure everything stays on schedule."

Whitney chimed in then. "This is the one at the old Ravenswood Mansion, right?"

"Yes. How'd you know?"

"I'm on Stephanie's mailing list."

"Oh. I didn't realize you were an art connoisseur."

"I'm not, but my parents are. I bought a painting for them last year for their anniversary, so I get a notification anytime there's a new exhibit. By the way, what did you think of the place? Isn't it gorgeous? My dream is to get married there someday."

"That would require you to find a man first," Annette teased.

"I'm just glad to see that Stephanie is getting the word out," Nora said, cutting the tension. "John is the one who introduced me to her."

"Speaking of John"—Annette raised an eyebrow in her direction—"how are things with you two?"

"Good, actually."

"You sound surprised," said Whitney.

"I don't mean to come across as pessimistic," said Nora. "Perhaps cautiously optimistic is a better way to describe it. The truth is John seems to be a great guy. It's just... after the way things ended with Jeremy, I'm trying to temper my expectations, so I don't get my heart broken again."

"That's understandable." Nikki rifled through a bowl of bar mix. "Take it from me. I'm an expert in the field. I've had my heart broken more times than I can count. And trust me, it never gets easier."

Over dinner, Nora told them all about the exhibit and asked if they would come and support Mr. Carlisle.

"For sure," said Nikki. "I wouldn't miss it."

Whitney echoed the sentiment with a nod of her head and an assurance that her parents would be in attendance as well. Annette added that if the rest of his artwork was anything like the portrait of Rose, she couldn't wait to see it.

"Oh, it is," Nora said. "The paintings are incredible, and so are the sketches. I just can't believe they were hidden away in his attic all those years without anyone knowing about them."

"Don't you find that a little suspicious?" Whitney asked between bites of steak. "I mean, I feel sorry for his late wife. I'd hate to think the man I was married to would keep something like that from me."

Nora shrugged and suggested maybe it wasn't that he was hiding it from them but rather from himself.

"Well, whatever the reason, I think it's incredibly romantic." Nikki drew the napkin across her mouth "I mean, imagine a man so in love with you that he still feels that way after fifty years." She swooned. "That's what every girl dreams of."

"But that's just the thing... I don't know that he is in love with her," said Nora. "Or that he ever was. The only thing I know for sure is that they met at the start of the war, and other than a handful of encounters, most of them brief, I don't know if it ever went any deeper than that."

Whitney hailed the waitress. "Come on. There must be more to the story. I mean, who goes to all the trouble of painting these unbelievably beautiful pictures of someone they only met once or twice?"

"I'm sure you're right," said Nora. "But if he was in love her, what happened that kept them apart all these years?"

After Friday night out with the girls, Nora spent the rest of the weekend laboring in the yard. Now that the inside of the house was to her liking, she wanted the outside to match.

After a quick trip to the local nursery, she and John planted several rose bushes, a smattering of petunias and daffodils, then added a hanging basket to the porch. Stepping back to admire their work, Nora was satisfied with the way things looked.

"I wish Gran were here to see this." She took off her gloves. "By no means is it the sprawling garden she maintains, but it's a start." She filled two glasses with lemonade and handed one to

John. "Thanks for your help, by the way. You've got quite the green thumb."

John took a sip of lemonade then said, "I'm happy to do it. I don't know if I told you, but when I was in college, I spent several summers working for a landscaping company."

"You?" She had a hard time imagining him getting his hands dirty.

"Don't act so surprised." He moved to the porch and sat down on the steps. "Ever since I was a kid, I've enjoyed taking untouched pieces of land and transforming them into something both beautiful and functional. I was never any good at art or music, so I guess this is a way for me to express my creativity."

"Maybe you could use some of that creativity to help me come up with a plan for the backyard," she said. "That's next on my to-do list."

John chuckled. "I'll see what I can do."

When Nora returned to work Monday morning, Gail pulled her aside and said she'd heard through the grapevine that Mr. Carlisle's paintings were going to be featured in an upcoming exhibit.

"Yes, that's right," Nora said. "I'm so excited for him. Since we're talking about it, I'd like to request the fifteenth off if it's not too much trouble. That's opening day for the exhibit. According to Stephanie, there should be a large turnout, and I wouldn't want to miss it. I also hope you and Cecil can make it."

"Yes, that should be fine, and we wouldn't miss it."

"There's one other thing. The gallery owners would like to meet Mr. Carlisle to discuss the format. They'll also want him there on opening day. Stephanie thinks there will be a lot of patrons who will want to meet him and ask questions about his work. I told her I didn't think it would be an issue, but I'd have to check with you first."

"It's not standard policy." Gail rubbed her chin. "But given the circumstances, I think we can make an exception. So long as Mr. Carlisle is okay with it."

"Actually, I'm on my way to speak with him now, so I'll let you know."

"So did you find the paintings?" Mr. Carlisle asked as they rode the elevator to the first floor.

"Yes. We found them all—Gloria, Suzanne, and I. And the sketches too."

The doors opened, and they stepped into the hall.

"The girls didn't give you any trouble, did they?"

"No. They were very accommodating, especially considering I was rummaging through your attic like a cat burglar." She moved ahead and pushed open the double doors. "Honestly, I think they enjoyed the adventure more than me."

"What did your friends at the gallery think?"

"They loved your work. In fact, Owen wanted me to tell you he's going to make you the featured artist, which means all your pieces will be set up in the main gallery."

"You're joking."

"No. Owen says your work is as good as anything he's seen in New York or Chicago."

Mr. Carlisle shook his head in disbelief. "I never thought I'd live to see the day my work would be featured in a gallery. I've dreamed it many times, but never thought it would be a reality, especially at my age."

"Well, believe it, Mr. Carlisle. The exhibit is on the calendar for the fifteenth, and Stephanie will be sending out invitations soon." They found the bench beneath the shade of the willow tree and sat. "That reminds me... Do you think you'll be up for visiting the gallery next week? Stephanie and Owen want to meet you and share with you their vision for the exhibit."

"Will Gail allow it?"

"I cleared it with her this morning." Nora tore a few pieces of bread with the ends of her fingers and tossed them onto the water for the ducks. "I also asked her about you being there opening day of the exhibit, and she's okay with that too as long as you're up for it."

He got a little teary-eyed then. "I don't really know what to say. Before you came along, I was resigned to thinking my life was over. But now..." He bit back the tears. "What you've given me is a second chance, and I'm very thankful."

"You're welcome." Nora had to hold back tears of her own.

"How will I ever repay you?"

"Tell you what: if you'll finish telling me the story of you and Rose, I'll consider us even."

A smile broke across his face. "Deal. Now where were we? Oh yes." He put a finger in the air. "Once we wrapped up operations in North Africa, we sailed north and invaded the island of Sicily. After that, our attention turned to the big invasion everyone knew was coming. We arrived in England in November of that year, and as fate would have it, my company linked back up with Rose's medical unit."

NOVEMBER 1943

"Lieutenant!"

I turned to the sound of a familiar voice. "Rose!" I was overjoyed to see her.

Her face lit up when our eyes met, and she strode confidently toward me. We hugged, then she pulled away and scanned me with an appraising eye. "What are you doing here?"

"Same as everyone else—getting ready for the invasion. You look good," I said, admiring her golden tan.

She smiled gratefully at the compliment. "Thanks. You don't look so bad yourself. I see the shoulder healed up nicely."

"Good as new, thanks to you."

Without skipping a beat, she asked if I'd eaten lunch.

"Not yet. We just rolled into town."

"Come on." She took my hand and led me to a nearby mess tent, where she introduced me to some of her friends before getting us two plates of food. "So how have you been?"

"Well." I felt so thankful to be in her presence once again. "I can't get over your tan. Surely you didn't get that here in England."

"No." She shook her head. "We spent several weeks in Gibraltar before coming here. The weather there was amazing."

I watched her closely, noting that she was in better spirits than the last time I saw her.

"Some days are better than others, but overall, I'm doing okay. So..." She cleared her expression. "Are you here for a while or just passing through?"

"I think we're here for the duration," I told her.

A faint smile appeared. "Well, in that case, it will be nice to catch up." She raised her eyes, and in them I thought I detected something, a genuine interest on her part.

After lunch, we took a walk down by the creek that meandered along the edge of town, pausing beneath a tall elm tree as we watched birds flitting through emerald-green leaves.

"It's peaceful here, isn't it?"

I took in the gorgeous scenery and the hypnotic sound of the babbling brook. "Yes, it is. Do you come here often?"

"Almost every day," she said, then fixed her gaze on the southern horizon. "It's hard to believe a war is raging over there."

After a moment, she turned to me, fiddling nervously with her fingers. "Listen, I'm glad you're here. There's something I want to ask you." She went on to explain that there was going to be a dance at the rec hall on Friday night and asked if I wanted to take her as my date. "You dance, don't you, Lieutenant?"

"Not very well," I confessed.

The corners of her lips turned up in a light smile. "That makes two of us. My mother says I was born without any rhythm. Still..." She rested her gaze upon me. "It might be fun."

Her proposal took me aback, but I wasn't going to let the opportunity go out with Rose slip by. "I'm game if you are."

"Wonderful." A relieved smiled spread across her face. "It starts at seven. Why don't I meet you there?"

"Sounds like a plan." I could hardly believe my luck. "I'm looking forward to it."

On the way back, Rose shared stories from her adventures since leaving North Africa while I talked about our mission in Sicily. We compared battle scars and laughed at near misses we'd both experienced during combat—little anecdotes that made us appreciate these precious peaceful moments even more.

After escorting Rose to the medical tent, I eased over to the barracks and settled into my quarters. Only now there was a lightness about me, something missing since this terrible war had begun. It wasn't until I sat there on the edge of my bed, thinking about my date with Rose, that it dawned on me what it was: for the first time since this nightmare had begun, I felt human again.

When I entered the rec hall, my attention was immediately drawn to Rose, a vision of beauty in emerald. She was sitting at a table with some of the other girls from her unit. Her newly-done hair was carefully pinned and decorated with a red ribbon, and the white polka dots on her dress were like stars in the night sky.

For a moment, I stood there in silence, admiring her beauty, wondering what I had done to deserve the company of someone like her. Taking a deep breath, I walked up to her, clutching the canary-yellow rose I'd plucked from a garden on the way over.

"For me?"

"I hope yellow is okay."

She nodded, smiling. "Will you pin it on?"

My hands trembled as I fumbled with the pin but managed to get it on safely. "Wanna dance?"

We waltzed around the wooden floor for what felt like an eternity, talking and laughing as we moved together in perfect harmony. When there was a break in the music, we moved outside for some fresh air.

"I never knew dancing could be so tiring," I said.

"Neither did I." She took a breath of the cool evening air and leaned against the wall. "The girls seem to be enjoying themselves tonight."

"The fellas too." I peered through the window at them. "I'm glad. This is the first real break they've had since we landed in Sicily."

Rose's smile slipped. "How was it?" she asked softly.

I took a moment, feeling the weight of her question. Closing my eyes, I recalled images of blood-soaked earth, of limbs torn from young men like rag dolls, of the sound of shells screaming toward us. "Difficult," I said finally, opening my eyes.

"I know what you mean." The moonlight cast shadows across her face, creating pockets of darkness beneath her eyes that hinted at sleepless nights. “When I was in nursing school, I’d seen injured men before, but nothing like this. When I close my eyes at night, all I see is their faces. All I hear are their screams. They say it fades over time, but...” Her voice trailed off, heavy with emotion.

I hadn’t really thought about it until that moment, but in some ways what Rose experienced in the hospital was worse than what I saw on the battlefield. My hand instinctively went to the scar on my jawline where a bullet had grazed me during the last battle, and I wondered which was worse—the dead or the dying.

“It’s funny,” I mused. “You spend months mentally preparing yourself for what you think you might see, but no matter how hard you try, it pales in comparison to reality.”

Her lips pursed as she nodded thoughtfully, and I knew we were both reliving horrors in our minds. “How long do you think we’ll be here?” she asked after a long pause.

“In England, or in Europe?”

“England, silly.”

“A few months, maybe longer.”

“And after that?”

After that? I tried hard to focus only on the now, to avoid getting caught up in the prospects of tomorrow. I knew our odds of survival were low, but I kept hope in my heart that one day, God willing, these struggles would be behind us.

“It depends on who you ask,” I said, recalling all the stories I’d heard about when we might be going home. “Some say we’ll be home by next Christmas. Others think this could drag out for two or three more years.”

A deep frown creased her brow. “What do you think?”

I shrugged. “The sooner the better. I miss my old life.”

“Tell me about it—your life. What did you do before entering the war?”

I recalled the days leading up to enlisting. "I was planning to take a job as an accountant while I built up a portfolio of artwork. What about you? Were you a nurse before the war began?"

She nodded her head solemnly, her eyes shining with remembrance. "I graduated from nursing school two days before the attack on Pearl. Much to my family's dismay, I joined right away."

"That was brave of you."

"I don't feel brave," she said. "Most days I feel helpless."

I reached out to touch her arm, my fingers brushing against her skin as I tried to convey my understanding. "You're anything but helpless, Rose. You're doing everything you can, and you're making a difference."

A small smile tugged at the corners of her lips. "Thank you. You don't know how much I needed to hear that."

For a long moment, we sat there in silence, looking up at the stars as the music from the rec hall played in the background. Suddenly, I felt a sense of peace, a lull in the chaos of war. I looked over at Rose and wondered if she'd made the same silent wish as me—that one day this would all be over, and we'd be free to move on with our lives. Before I could finish my thought, she turned to me and smiled. And it was in that moment that I felt something indescribable—the realization that our lives were suddenly filled with fragile possibilities.

When the dance ended, we left the rec hall and strolled toward the center of town.

"I had a wonderful time tonight," she said as we passed beneath the glow of the streetlight. "You're a better dancer that you let on. I hope I didn't disappoint you."

"Never." We moved ahead, feeling the crunch of gravel beneath our feet. "Your mother was wrong, by the way," I told her. "You have plenty of rhythm."

She flashed a bashful smile. "I'll have to tell her you said so." We walked on a few steps before she asked, "Do you believe in fate, Lieutenant?"

"I don't know, but if it brought me to you, then maybe I do."

She smiled, and it was as if the sun had come out from behind a cloud. "Well, I do. And I think it was fate that brought us together that day in the square. For what reason, I don't know, but I think it was. Well, this is me." She came to a stop outside a small white cottage. "I'd invite you in for coffee, but I'm staying with a family."

I fought disappointment, wanting nothing more than to steal another hour with her. "I understand." I took a step closer, and in the moonlight, our eyes met. My heart pounded in my chest as I reached up to brush a strand of hair from her face. The moment seemed timeless; an electric longing coursed through me, a feeling that had been building all night. It was as if we were suspended in time in a moment that would be etched into my memory forever.

Rose didn't pull back, her eyes locked on mine, and it was all the invitation I needed. Leaning forward, I pressed my lips to hers in a gentle kiss, and it felt like the world disappeared beneath our feet. It wasn't passionate or heated; it was soft and meaningful, an acknowledgment of the connection we shared.

When I pulled away, her eyes were closed, and her lips were parted. I wanted to pull her close again and fall into a whirlwind of desire. Given our situation—living in a time where every moment could be our last—I didn't know if we'd ever get another chance like this. But a light came on inside, snapping me back to reality.

"I should go," I said softly, my hand still resting on her cheek.

She opened her eyes, and there was something in them that made my heart ache. "I wish you could stay."

"So do I." I had to summon every ounce of strength in me not to give in to her plea. "Can I see you tomorrow?"

"You'd better."

As we said our goodbyes and she disappeared into the cottage, I knew that this war had brought both horror and unexpected joy into my life. One day it would be over. But for now I would hold on to every moment with Rose, hoping it would be enough to see me through.

Chapter Sixteen

"Is something on your mind, Miss Dawson?" Fred asked one afternoon.

"As a matter of fact, there is," she answered as she plodded along the hallway between the pool and the library.

"This wouldn't have anything to do with that ex of yours, would it?"

"Sort of. Remember how I told you he and my former best friend were dating? Well, now they're engaged." Her shoulder dropped with a sigh. "I was talking with my mom the other day, and she thinks it's time for me to forgive Erin. What do you think?"

Mr. Carlisle pondered for a moment before giving his response. "That depends. Do you want her in your life?"

Nora considered his question, thinking that despite the anger, she missed having Erin to talk to. "I don't know. Maybe Mom is right. I mean, I can't stay mad at her forever, can I?"

"You could, but it wouldn't do you any good," said Mr. Carlisle. "Take it from me... Not being able to let go of something—even something as painful as betrayal—will only end in misery. Besides, I suspect your anger lies with Jeremy and not Erin."

Nora quietly contemplated his theory while they rode the elevator to the second floor. When the doors opened, they turned left and started down the hall.

"I'm going home this weekend," she said. "It's Gran's birthday, and I want to be there to surprise her."

A grin creased his face. "How old will she be?"

"Eighty. Mom and Dad are throwing a party for her at the lake house, and since I haven't been home since this move, it only seems right that I should be there."

"You're very thoughtful," said Mr. Carlisle as they entered the common room. "Your grandmother is lucky to have you in her life."

"I'm the lucky one," she said. "Besides, it's the least I can do for the woman who practically raised me."

They found a couple of empty chairs and sat near the window, observing a thunderstorm building in the western sky.

"So what happened after that first kiss?" Nora asked. "Did you and Rose become a couple?"

He nodded, his expression turning serious. "Yes, for a while... until the day she received a letter in the mail."

DECEMBER 1943

A couple of weeks before Christmas, I was on my way back from headquarters when I spotted Rose sitting on a bench near the creek. Her face was pale and drawn, her eyes puffy and red rimmed. She held a crumpled letter in her hands.

I approached her slowly, trying to make as little noise as possible. "Rose, what's wrong?"

She handed me the letter without looking up. The words were blurred from tears, but I made out enough to understand that she was being reassigned to a new unit in Cornwall. I returned the letter and sat down beside her. "When do you leave?"

"Tomorrow morning. Fred, what am I to do?" She laid her head on my shoulder. "I don't want to leave the girls—or you."

"Neither do I want you to leave." My heart was breaking. "Not that it counts for much, but I'm going to miss you, Rose. I feel like we were just getting started."

"So do I." She gave me a wistful smile. "I take back what I said about fate. Surely fate wouldn't be cruel enough to bring us together only to rip us apart."

I considered that. "Fate is a two-way street. Sometimes it giveth and sometimes it taketh away. But I don't think this is the end of us," I said, clinging to a shred of hope. "We were separated before and look at us now. We'll find each other again. I just know it."

My words brought a smile to her face, and although I had my doubts, I held on to the belief that someday, somewhere down the line, she and I would be *us* again.

We talked for a while longer, holding hands and watching the sun go down. When it was time for her to leave, I walked her back to her barracks, not wanting to let her go. As we stood outside, she turned to face me, her eyes shining with unshed tears.

"I don't want to say goodbye." Her voice broke.

"Then don't." I cupped her face in my hands. "Let's just say see you later instead."

She nodded, and I leaned in to kiss her. We stayed like that for what felt like hours, lost in each other, until we finally pulled away.

"I have to go," she said, her voice hoarse. "I have to pack."

"I know." I took her hand and kissed it. "Take care of yourself, Rose. And remember, thought time and space may separate us, we're never more than a heartbeat away."

"The next day, she left. And just like that, our romance was over before it ever got started."

Nora's cheeks were wet with tears, her heart heavy in her chest. "Just... like that? Tell me that isn't the end," she choked out.

Mr. Carlisle handed her a napkin to dry her eyes.

"For the next few months, we wrote letters to one another religiously," he said softly, "until D-Day. After that, I didn't hear from her again for a very long time."

Later that evening, Nora had dinner at John's place, and then they curled up on the couch and watched a movie. Afterward, they went to the backyard and lay in the hammock, looking up at the night sky filled with a sea of stars.

"Do you ever wonder how many people have gazed at these stars?" he asked thoughtfully.

Nora raised her eyes to the heavens, taking in the twinkling lights. "I can't say that the thought has ever crossed my mind. But I suppose every person, at one time or another, has looked at them."

"Fascinating, isn't it—how, even over millennia, we're connected to those who've come before us, and those who will follow in our footsteps."

The truth was she didn't exactly find it fascinating, not at first. But the longer she thought about it, the more the idea grew on her. Nora rolled her head to the side and looked at

John. And in his eyes she saw for the first time a man she could spend the rest of her life with.

"What is it?" He caught her staring at him.

"I was just thinking." She curled into his chest.

"About what?"

"You. Me. Us."

He put her arms around her and held her close to him. "What about us?"

"I was just imagining what we'd look like when we were older."

He smiled warmly and spoke gently. "I'd still have my devilishly handsome good looks," he said. "And you'd be just as gorgeous as ever."

His words melted her heart, and she kissed him tenderly. "I wish you didn't have to go to South Carolina this weekend. I think you'd enjoy meeting my family." She thought of her mom, dad, and Gran. No doubt they'd be impressed with John.

"I'm sure I would," he said, looking glum. "I'm sorry too. If there was any other way..."

"Can't you just go next weekend?" She was clinging to a shred of hope that he would change his mind.

"I'm afraid it isn't that simple."

Nora's heart was telling her there was more to the story, but instead of grilling him further, she decided to stop. After all, they were at that point in their relationship where they needed trust, not suspicion. And although they hadn't verbally expressed it yet, she knew he loved her. And she loved him too.

"Tell me more about your grandmother." He looked up to the heavens. "What was she like when you were growing up?"

"Gran was a firecracker." Nora chuckled, thinking of all the fun they had. "When I was nine, Dad took a job in sales, which meant he spent a lot of time on the road. Mom worked long hours at the law firm, so she relied on Gran and Pap to pick me up from school and take care of me until she got off work."

"That must have been hard," said John. "Being away from your parents for long stretches of time."

"At times, but I loved spending time with my grandparents. Gran had this garden, you see, and for a long time it was my favorite place in the whole world. I'd spend hours out there talking to the flowers and the butterflies, imagining they were my friends. And when I grew tired of that, Gran would serve tea in beautiful cups, and we'd play board games for hours. Oh, the fun we used to have."

"It sounds as if you have many wonderful memories there."

She nodded, recalling fondly days gone by. "I wouldn't trade those memories for anything in the world."

"Well, you're lucky. I hardly saw my family growing up, even my extended family. They were always on the campaign trail. My childhood consisted of butlers and housekeepers. For the longest time I thought Mrs. Devereaux—the nanny who took care of me—was my mother."

"That's sad."

He shrugged it off. "It wasn't all bad. I got to travel a lot, eat at the finest restaurants, see the most amazing sights. But enough about the past. I want to concentrate on the present." He rolled onto his side, and his eyes bore into hers until she felt like she was going to melt. "I've been thinking." His voice was low and sultry, and he entwined his fingers with hers. "About you. In fact, I can't stop thinking about you. Nora, would you be offended if I said I loved you?"

Her stomach fluttered and her heart raced. A wave of emotions washed over her—fear, excitement, relief—but more than anything, a feeling of reassurance that this man lying beside her could make everything okay.

She shook her head as a smile made its way onto her lips.
"Then I do. I love you."
"And I love you," she replied, feeling light as a feather.

Chapter Seventeen

After work the next evening, Nora gassed up the car and drove to Trafford. As she pulled into her parents' driveway and shut off the engine, a wave of nostalgia hit her. *Home sweet home.* Her mom stood out on the porch wearing a yellow sundress, her arms spread wide with excitement as if Nora had just come back from a long journey.

Nora grabbed her bag from the trunk and hurried to greet her. Kathleen drew her into an embrace so tight it felt like she was afraid Nora might disappear again.

"Hey there, darling. How are you?"

"I'm fine, Mom. It's good to see you."

Kathleen let go and beamed at her. She ran her hands down Nora's arms as she looked her over. "Gosh, just look at you. Have you gotten taller? You seem taller. And what have you done with your hair? It looks almost blond." She twirled a strand of Nora's sun-bleached locks between her fingers and laughed.

Nora smiled through the embarrassment and glanced past her into the foyer, where her dad stood watching them with a proud grin stretched across his face. He opened his arms as she walked in and hugged her close before planting a kiss on top of her head.

"Hi, Daddy," she said as they parted. "How are you?"

"I'm fine, doodlebug," he said. "It sure is nice to see your smiling face again. How was the drive?"

"Longer than I remember," she said with a sigh.

"Well, you look good," Mom said with a warm smile as she shut the door. "You must be running a lot. Are you hungry? I made your favorite—fried chicken with homemade mac and cheese. And there's banana pudding for dessert."

"Great." Nora felt a little spoiled. "I'm starving. Just give me a few minutes to get settled and I'll be right down."

She climbed the creaky stairs to her old room and dropped the bag on the bed. It had been almost five years since she'd lived in that house, but it felt more like twenty. A strange feeling filled her chest as she took in familiar sights and smells.

Once she'd freshened up, Nora headed back down to join her parents in the kitchen for supper.

"I see you decided to come alone." Kathleen spooned out a helping of mac and cheese onto each plate. "I was sort of hoping John would come with you."

"He was going to, but he's in South Carolina this weekend."

"What's in South Carolina?"

Nora ate a bite of mac and cheese, then used the napkin to dab at the corners of her mouth. "Some big family event." It was easier to lie than tell the truth. "But he sends his regards and promises to be here next time."

"So how's everything else going?" Bill asked from across the table. "Is your car still running good?"

Nora nodded. "Runs like a dream. I just had the oil changed and the tires rotated last week."

Bill gave a satisfied smile. "What about work? Have they offered you a full-time position yet?"

"Bill." Kathleen nudged him with her elbow.

"It's all right." Nora had grown accustomed to her dad's battery of questions. "To answer your question, no. I haven't received a full-time offer yet. But given my success with Mr. Carlisle and the fact that I've exceeded Gail's expectations, I think it's only a matter of time."

"Speaking of Mr. Carlisle," said Kathleen, "when is the exhibit you were telling me about?"

"In a few weeks. He's really excited, and so am I. Actually, we all are—me, John, Stephanie, and Owen. We've put in a lot of work getting everything organized."

"Well, your dad and I are proud of you." Kathleen beamed. "I think a project like this is exactly what you needed to get your mind off things. And in the process, it sounds like you've made a few friends."

That night as Nora lay in her old bed, staring up at the ceiling, her thoughts drifted to John and what he must be doing in South Carolina. To hear him tell it, he wanted to distance himself from his family, to be his own man, yet once a month it seemed he was there. Something didn't add up. As she tossed around the possibilities in her head, those old feelings of suspicion, the same ones she'd had about Jeremy leading up to his infidelity, crept in.

The next morning, Nora woke early to help her parents prepare for Gran's party. While Kathleen and Bill hung streamers in the yard and filled balloons with helium, Nora offered to pick Gran up from her house. On the drive over, she remembered all the afternoons spent in the garden and evenings in the sunroom eating snacks and playing board games. And as she pulled into the driveway, a sentimental smile spread across her face.

Nora gave a few brisk knocks on the door, and when Gran opened it, she could see tears welling up in her eyes.

"Hi, Gran." She gave her a hug. "Happy birthday."

"Well, I'll be... I wasn't expecting to see you." She welcomed Nora inside and offered her a seat on the couch in the living room.

"I wouldn't miss your birthday," Nora said. "After all, how often does a girl turn eighty?"

Gran giggled, her wrinkled cheeks creasing up like paper fans. "You didn't have to make a special trip just to see me, but I'm glad you did. So tell me, what news do you have from Tennessee?"

Nora glanced at her watch. "Tell you what—why don't I fill you in on the drive? Mom will have my head me if we're late."

They finally headed out the door and got into Nora's car. Being a few minutes ahead of schedule, Nora took her time as she navigated through winding country roads. As Gran meticulously applied her lipstick and blush, Nora thought of how beautiful she still was at eighty years old.

"I see things around here haven't changed much," Nora remarked as they drove through the center of town.

"You've not been gone that long."

"I wish you could see where I live now; it's such a nice neighborhood, and I've done so much work to the house."

Gran suddenly brightened up. "Your mother mentioned making a trip to see you this fall. I'm thinking of coming with her! It's been ages since I was last in Nashville."

"Yes, you should!"

"So tell me about work." She changed the topic slightly. "How are things at the hospital?"

"Honestly, I couldn't be happier," she told her as she negotiated a hairpin turn. "The hours are long but the work is rewarding. And the patients keep me on my toes, especially this one fellow; he's quite the handful but very sweet. Believe it or not, he has got me hooked on his stories from the war."

"Oh?"

"He hasn't made it to the end yet, but basically he met this woman while he was overseas and fell in love with her, and now that his wife is gone he's trying to find her again after all these years."

Gran put a hand to her heart. "He sounds like a very sweet man."

"Oh, he is, Gran. He really is. If you come to visit, I'll introduce you to him."

After crossing the railroad tracks, Gran asked if Nora had heard from Erin.

Nora's jaw clenched. "No," she uttered through gritted teeth, "and I can't imagine I will. I suppose Mom told you about her engagement to Jeremy."

"She sure did. The nerve of that girl," she growled. "She's supposed to be your best friend, and where I come from best friends don't do those kinds of things to each other, no matter how handsome or how rich the man is. Besides, she gave you her word that she'd stick by your side, and a woman's word is everything." She put away the lipstick in her purse. "Not that it's any of my business, but it seems to me like she could have found someone else."

"I agree, which is why we haven't spoken. Mom says I should reach out, but I don't know... Besides, I've got this group of girls at work, and we've all become good friends, so..."

"Well, whatever you decide, I stand behind you. You've got a good head on your shoulders, Nora, and I know you'll make the right decision."

Nora kept her distance during the party, watching from the fringe while Gran talked with old friends, ate cake, and opened gifts. When the sun had set, the party ended and one by one, the guests departed.

When everyone was gone, Nora said goodbye to Gran, then Kathleen drove her home. Alone now, Nora walked to the end of the dock where she used to come to be alone as a child. She stepped out of her shoes and let her toes skitter across the warm wood until she reached the edge. Peeling off her socks, she dipped her feet into the cool lake water and watched as dusk settled over the land.

Strangely, it felt both familiar and completely foreign at the same time—and for the first time in her life, Nora understood what people meant when they talked about not being able to go back home again.

"You look like you could use some company."

The sound of Bill's voice brought Nora back to her senses. "You know me too well." She offered a crooked smile while he pulled up a chair.

He motioned toward the water. "We had some good times out there while you were growing up, didn't we?"

She nodded, remembering fondly summer days spent boating and fishing.

"What I wouldn't give to have just one of those days back." He heaved a sigh as if wishing didn't make it so.

"Me too. Life was so much simpler back then."

"Give it time. Things will calm down eventually. Your mother tells me you're getting on well in Brentwood. Are you enjoying yourself up there?"

"I couldn't be happier." Nora thought of work—and of John. "It's just..." She dropped her eyes. "I guess after what happened with Jeremy, I'm suspicious of everything and everyone."

"There's nothing wrong with a healthy dose of skepticism. Is there something or someone that you're suspicious of?"

She picked at a splinter with her fingernail "I didn't want to say anything in front of Mom, and it's probably nothing, but I feel like John is hiding something from me. I don't think it's anything like what happened with Jeremy, but... The only thing I've been able to come up with is that he might be thinking of following in his father's footsteps and returning to politics."

"I see." Bill leaned back in the chair and laced his fingers behind his head. "Is that the real reason he couldn't make it this weekend?"

Nora shrugged a shoulder.

"Have you talked to him about it?"

She shook her head. "But I plan to when I get home. One way or the other, I need to know before this goes any further."

In the silence that followed, Nora wondered if her heart could withstand another setback. After the damage Jeremy had done, something similar might be her undoing.

"Look, sweetheart, I know this last year has been... tough. You've had your heart broken, gone through a messy breakup, moved away from home, and started a new job. That's a lot for anyone to have to deal with, especially someone your age. But you've handled yourself with dignity and grace, and there's something to be said for that."

"But?"

"Do you remember when you were a little girl, whenever you were upset by something—truly upset—you'd shut down, internalize everything?"

His question stirred a memory from the summer she turned seven. The boy from across the street—Stephen—had called Nora ugly. She remembered holding in her tears until she reached the safety of her room. It took three days and the promise of a hot fudge sundae to get her to come out.

"I realize that's your coping mechanism," Bill went on. "The only problem is internalizing all your feelings will eat away at you, consume you from the inside out. Not that you've solicited my advice, but if you did, I would tell you to keep an open mind. Life rarely turns out the way we want it to. There are always little surprises around every corner. These fairy tales that people talk about, seldom do they exist here in the real world. Unfortunately, reality is a bit more complicated. What I'm trying to say is talk to John. Tell him how you feel. And who knows—maybe he'll surprise you."

"Yeah, that's what I'm afraid of."

After breakfast the next morning, Nora packed her things and said goodbye to her parents.

"Don't be a stranger," Kathleen said, walking Nora to her car.

"I won't." She started the car and backed out of the drive.

But instead of getting on the interstate, Nora made a left at the light and went to see Erin.

"Nora!" Erin ran a hand through her tousled dark hair. "What a surprise. You're the last person I expected to find knocking at my door today."

"That makes two of us," she said, wondering if this was a mistake. "Can I come in?"

Erin showed Nora into the living room and offered her something to drink.

"No, thanks. This won't take long."

They settled uneasily into the chairs as the words to an Alanis Morissette song played in the background.

"Listen." Nora spoke up first. "I've come to apologize... for what I said on the phone that day. I was angry and upset and—"

"You don't need to apologize. You had every right to be angry with me. If I were in your shoes, I'd have been pissed off too."

"But it was more than that," said Nora. "You hurt me."

Erin dropped her eyes and stared at the floor. "If I had it to do over again, I would have driven to Brentwood so I could have told you in person."

Nora considered that. "I'm not sure that would have made it any better. Actually," she said, recalling how angry she was, "it could have been worse. Regardless, I've given this a lot of thought, and I finally decided that if I want you in my life, I have to learn to let go of the anger and resentment I've been carrying around. Besides, I realized it wasn't you I was truly mad at; it was Jeremy. You just got caught in the crossfire."

"And I'm sorry too," said Erin. "I never meant to hurt you."

That was a tough pill for Nora to swallow considering what Erin had done.

"Then why'd you do it? You're smart, beautiful... You could have had your pick of anyone, and you chose *him*."

Erin took a breath before responding. "The truth is Jeremy called me a few weeks after you ended things and asked if I thought there was any chance you'd take him back. I told him no, of course, and that he should move on. Honestly, I never thought I'd hear from him again. Then a few weeks later, he called again and spilled his guts to me about how sorry and heartbroken he was, and... I don't know... I guess I felt sorry for him. I know that sounds crazy, but I've always had a weakness for guys who need fixing. Anyway, we talked a few more times, and then one day, out of the blue, he asked me out. I didn't want to go at first, but eventually he wore me down." She sighed regretfully. "In hindsight, I should have told you right away."

Or not gone at all. Nora took a moment to process what Erin had told her. "So this is not just some fling? You really love him?"

Erin nodded. "I do. And he loves me too. I know this might be hard for you to believe, but Jeremy's a changed man."

Nora gritted her teeth. "And what if you're wrong? What if he does the same thing to you that he did to me? I'm not saying I don't believe you think he's changed, but try as it may, a leopard never changes its spots."

"And while I appreciate your concern," Erin replied delicately, "I'm aware of the risk. Jeremy and I have talked about this. And if I'm wrong, then I'm wrong, and you can be the first one to say I told you so."

Nora sighed, realizing there was nothing she could say to make Erin see the truth about Jeremy. "All right. As long as you're aware, I guess there's no reason to belabor the point."

"So does this mean we're... cool?" Erin asked.

"Yeah, we're cool."

Erin's face lit up in a smile as she breathed a sigh of relief. "You have no idea how happy I am to hear you say that. For a while there, I thought"—she dropped the smile—"that we were done."

Nora nodded along. "So did I, but we've been friends for a long time, Erin, and I suspect it'll take more than a guy, even one as devious as Jeremy, to split us up."

Erin rushed over and gave her a hug, then asked if she could expect Nora at the wedding.

"Don't push it."

When Nora got home that evening, she collapsed onto the couch and drifted off to sleep. Around seven, the doorbell jolted her awake. She opened the door to find John standing outside. He embraced her tightly and asked about her trip.

"It was good." She stifled a yawn and welcomed him inside. "Yours?"

"Not bad."

"Was your family glad to see you?"

He gave a one-shoulder shrug. "They were happy I was there, of course, but as usual the conversation turned to politics... and me taking over my father's senate seat."

Ah-hah!

"But I stood my ground."

"So you really have no interest in returning to politics?"

John shook his head. "Like I told you, it wasn't my cup of tea."

His comment left Nora more confused than ever. "Well, I'm glad you're back. I missed you."

"I missed you too," he said, then gave her a kiss that lingered longer than either of them expected. When they parted, John went to the kitchen to get something to drink. "Did you tell your family I was sorry for not attending?"

"Yes, but they're more curious than ever... especially Mom. They're already planning a trip to come see me... us. I doubt you'll be able to avoid that one."

"Actually"—he returned to the living room with a glass of water—"I was giving it some thought on the drive home, and I'm looking forward to meeting them."

"You are?"

"Why not? I figure the people who made you must be special. So yeah."

Nora was shocked. Jeremy never liked family get-togethers. In fact, he never liked much of anything unless he was the center of attention. Which only added to the list of reasons she loved John.

"But something else happened while I was there." Nora told John about going to see Erin.

His brows shot up in surprise.

"She also asked if I would be coming to the wedding."

John's expression shifted to one of concern as he processed the news. "What did you tell her?"

"That I'd think about it." Nora lowered herself onto the sofa. "Since we're friends again, I want to be there to support her, but to be in the same space with Jeremy... I just don't know if I'm ready for that."

"That's understandable." John reached out and gave her a comforting embrace. "But I'm fine with whatever you decide. And just so you know, you won't have to go it alone, because I'll be by your side the entire time."

Chapter Eighteen

With Nora back in Brentwood, the weeks leading up to the exhibition seemed to fly by. Now that she and John had settled into a comfortable routine, they spent every waking moment together, and any suspicions she'd had of him hiding something from her melted away with the summer heat.

On the eve of the exhibit, Nora and John met Owen and Stephanie for dinner at the mansion, dining on the back porch while they discussed the next day's events.

"I think that's everything." Owen struck the last of the items from his list. "All we can do now is cross our fingers and hope for the best."

Nora swallowed anxiously. "Do you think we'll have a decent turnout?"

Owen nodded. "Stephanie has a knack for drawing in a crowd. Don't you, dear? Given the response she's already received, I have little doubt the show will be an enormous success. And who knows? Maybe we'll get lucky, and Rose will be in attendance."

"Speaking of Rose." Stephanie downed the last of her wine. "I received an email just before you arrived." She went to her office and retrieved the printout. "It's from one of my patrons in Portland, Oregon—Cynthia Walden. She claims to be Rose's great niece."

Nora's heart jumped into her throat as she scanned the printout. "It says here that her great aunt, Rose Cunningham, worked for the army as a nurse during World War II. That sounds promising. But it also says she passed away last year." She had to force herself to breathe. "Oh, I hope this isn't her. Mr. Carlisle will be heartbroken if it is."

"There's a phone number for Cynthia in the email." Stephanie directed Nora's attention to the bottom of the page.

"I'll call her when I get home." Nora had suddenly lost her appetite. "If it isn't her, I won't bring it up."

"And if it is?" John asked.

Nora hesitated, thinking of Mr. Carlisle and the look on his face if she had to break this news to him. "Then I'll wait until after the exhibition. I wouldn't want anything to ruin his big day."

The next morning, Nora laced up her running shoes and hit the pavement early. She watched the sun rise above the horizon and heard birds singing in the trees. It was a glorious morning, which she took as a good omen. After a quick jog to the park and back, she grabbed a shower, put on a floral sundress and royal blue heels, and met John in the driveway.

"Today's the big day!" He smiled as she climbed in. "Nervous?"

She nodded and took a deep breath. "I just want today to be a success... for Mr. Carlisle."

He smiled reassuringly before putting the car into drive.

"Have faith. You've put so much work into this project, and I know things will turn out how they're supposed to."

She gave a small nod and looked out the window at the passing scenery. "Whatever happens, I wanted to say thank you for all your help. Honestly, I couldn't have done it without you."

"It was my pleasure," he said warmly. As they sped down the street, John asked her if she had been able to connect with the woman from the email.

"No, but I sent an email and left a message, so hopefully she'll get back with me soon."

"Well, let's focus on today," he said gently. "And let everything else fall into place."

They pulled up to Ravenswood and took in the sight of an enormous white tent bedecked with strings of twinkling lights. Beneath the roof of the tent, round tables were set with linen cloths and delicate floral arrangements while soft music played in the background. Even the outdoor stone patio had been transformed into an exquisite banquet hall, with high ceilings draped in sheer fabric and glittering chandeliers reflecting off every surface. With all that had been done, the mansion looked like something from a fairy tale.

Stephanie welcomed them inside amid laughter and clinking glasses as waiters bustled about in crisp uniforms.

When John had stepped away, Stephanie looked at Nora. "You should see how we do wedding receptions." She winked conspiratorially.

Nora smiled and said, "One thing at a time!" then asked what needed to be done next.

An hour before the start of the show, Mr. Carlisle arrived with his daughters in tow. Nora introduced Gloria and Suzanne first to John, then to Stephanie and Owen.

As she adjusted the knot in Mr. Carlisle's tie, Nora saw the tension visible on his face—a far cry from its usual jovial expression. "I'm nervous," he said shakily. "My hands haven't shaken this bad since the war."

"There's nothing to be nervous about, Mr. Carlisle," she reassured him. "This is the moment you've been dreaming of. Enjoy it!"

Nora led him inside to the main gallery where his artwork was on display. The room was lavishly lit to give each piece its due reverence, and they shone brilliantly under the newfound spotlight.

"Mr. Carlisle, it's good to see you again, sir," said Stephanie, coming over to greet him.

"Yes." Owen shook his hand firmly. "We're delighted to have you here. So what do you think now that everything is set up?"

Mr. Carlisle glanced around the room in amazement. "Everything looks beautiful," he said with a hint of pride. "It's beyond my wildest dreams."

"That's exactly the reaction I was hoping for," said Owen, grinning. "Now let's see what the public thinks, shall we?"

From the moment the doors opened, a sea of people flooded the gallery. Nora watched as Mr. Carlisle offered his warmest smile to each guest, regaling them with stories from the war and of Rose. Those who lingered long enough to learn the true purpose of the exhibit left with a resolve to help find Rose, each one eager to be part of such an important cause.

When the last of the guests had gone, Stephanie let out a sigh of relief and clapped her hands together. "The show was a success!" she declared. "We had over four hundred people attend, and I've sent emails to over twenty thousand more. Between this and other efforts, I feel like we might actually have a chance at finding Rose."

"I can't thank you enough," said Mr. Carlisle. "This has truly been a dream come true."

"It was our pleasure," said Owen. "After Rose has been found, I hope you'll consider bringing her by the gallery so Stephanie and I can meet her."

"Yes of course. It'd be my pleasure."

But in the back of Nora's mind, she wondered if Rose had already been found.

Later that evening after eating dinner at Shiloh's, Nora and John sat on her back porch where a fading twilight painted the sky with pink and purple hues.

"Well, how do you think it went today?" She eased into the rocking chair.

"I'd call it a success. If Rose is out there, word will reach her. You have to trust Stephanie and Owen."

"I do." Nora wanted to believe this would end happily for Mr. Carlisle—and for Rose—but the memory of what her father warned her about happy endings resurfaced in the back of her mind.

A few moments later, Nora's phone rang. It was Cynthia Walden returning her call. With cautious optimism, Nora asked for more information about Rose, including the color of her hair and eyes, height, and physical features like scars or birthmarks.

Cynthia paused before providing her with everything she was looking for.

As she rattled off the details—dark hair, brown eyes, a small scar on her chin—Nora realized this wasn't who she was looking for but requested a photograph just to be sure. The next morning, an email from Cynthia containing a picture confirmed that Rose Cunningham was not the same woman from the paintings.

Which meant the real Rose was still out there, waiting to be found.

Chapter Nineteen

WITH THE EXHIBIT BEHIND HER, NORA TURNED HER attention to her relationship with John. They were past the "I love you" phase, but there still was another hurdle to clear—and it was a biggie.

To celebrate their three-month anniversary, John surprised her with tickets to the Grand Ole Opry, so after work one Friday evening, Nora slipped into a green chiffon dress that highlighted her eyes, paired it with her cowgirl boots, and added some gold hoop earrings for an extra touch.

The doorbell rang at exactly six o'clock. John's eyes widened as he looked her up and down. "Wow! You look incredible."

She gave him a smile and welcomed him in before heading back to the bedroom to spritz on her favorite perfume. Then she grabbed her clutch, and they headed out the door.

"I didn't know you owned boots," she said, her lips curling into a smile.

"Why, yes, ma'am," he answered in a slow drawl. "Every good Southern man has a pair of boots." John held the car door for her and helped her inside. "So have you ever been to the Opry?"

She shook her head.

A smile pulled at the corners of his mouth. "Then you're in for a treat."

By the time they made it to the Ryman Auditorium, the crowd had already started to gather on the steps out front. But rather than get in line, they entered through a side entrance reserved for musicians and people of importance.

"You don't own this place too, do you?" Nora whispered as they slipped past security.

John chuckled. "No, but I know a guy." He flashed a smile.

Carefully, they weaved through the lobby and descended the stairs to their seats. The first row was packed with couples dressed to the nines, but John paid them little attention as he guided Nora to her seat. Even when they'd settled in, she could feel his excitement as he studied the program.

"I never asked if you liked country music," he whispered.

"As a general rule, I don't," she admitted. "But it depends on the artist. Who's playing tonight?"

He pointed to a name listed in the program. "Martina McBride. Have you heard of her?"

An involuntary smile made its way to Nora's lips as memories flooded back—the CDs of hers she'd collected over the years, the way she sang with such emotion and power behind each note—and she nodded her head. "Yes. I love her."

Relief spread across his face as he exhaled deeply. "I hope you know how proud I am of you for all the work you did on the exhibit. As I'm learning, you're quite a remarkable woman."

Nora felt her cheeks heat up at his kind words and looked away for a moment before responding sheepishly, "Thank you... Honestly, I'm a little surprised at how much fun I had. I don't normally get involved with these sorts of things, but this was different. I can't shake the feeling that I'm destined to find Rose."

John smiled tenderly and placed his hand atop hers. "Maybe you are. Life has a funny way of putting us in the right place at the right time."

As the lights dimmed and the show began, Nora wondered if tonight was the night. She and John had been dating for three months, and while she didn't have a rule about a specific number of dates before sex, if she went another night without it, she'd go insane. She looked over at John, trying to read his thoughts, wondering if he felt the same.

After the show, Nora escorted John back to her place, feeling a bit nervous and excited. Once inside, she asked him if he'd like a night cap and offered him a choice of drinks. He settled on wine and moved to the couch while she fetched two glasses. They clinked them together in a toast and began chatting about the evening's events. With each sip of wine, she grew more relaxed in his presence. His eyes never left her as he told her how beautiful she looked. Nora paused for a moment, unsure if it was just the alcohol talking, but accepted the compliment.

Then, out of nowhere, John set down his glass and leaned forward, capturing her lips with his own. The kiss started off slow and sweet, each exploring the other's mouth until they finally felt ready to take it further. His hands found their way around her waist and traveled up her spine as their lips danced together. Nora's breath quickened as he kissed down her jawline, pausing briefly near her ear before trailing kisses across her neck. She felt lost in him, her head spinning from the sensual onslaught of pleasure.

John seemed to sense that she wanted something more, his gaze meeting hers and asking for permission without having to speak a single word. She wrapped her arms around his neck in response, a silent agreement reached between them. He scooped her up into his arms and carried her down the hall to the bedroom. In haste, they discarded clothing piece by piece across the room until there was nothing left between them but air and anticipation. He caressed her as though he'd been waiting for this moment, wanting to explore every inch of her without restraint or apology.

Nora gasped as John's lips traveled down her neck, across her breasts, and curved around her stomach. He paused for a moment, looking up at her with a smile before diving between her legs. She cried out as his tongue sent shivers through her body. He was skilled and relentless, hitting all the right spots until she came undone underneath him.

"Now it's my turn," she said with a smile as John lay back onto the bed, eyes smoldering with anticipation. Nora crawled on top of him and ground her hips into his, teasing but indulging them both.

Desperate to feel all of her around him, John lifted her up into position. Her body arched as she slid down onto him, their bodies fitting together like two long-separated puzzle pieces.

Reaching the edge of ecstasy, John cried out with a scream that echoed through the room. And as the waves of pleasure subsided, Nora kissed him deeply one last time before collapsing on the bed beside him.

Nora awoke in the warmth of John's embrace with a sense of comfort and security she hadn't felt in a long time. The pale predawn light streaming through the bedroom window cast a soft glow across the room, illuminating their discarded clothes from the night before. She stifled a giggle as memories of their passionate night replayed in her mind.

John stirred beside her, lifting his head to plant a gentle kiss on her shoulder, softly whispering, "That was amazing," into her ear.

"Which part? Which time?" She grinned, turning to face him.

He laughed, wrapping an arm around her waist before pressing his lips against hers. "All parts... both times."

With one last kiss, Nora threw off the covers and reached for her robe. "Are you hungry?"

"I could eat," he responded with a smirk, slowly pushing himself up from the bed and slipping on his clothes.

Excitement rushed through Nora as they ventured into the kitchen together and opened the window to let in some fresh morning air. Images of their late-night romp danced in her head, making it difficult to focus on breakfast. As John stood next to her chopping vegetables for omelets though, she finally felt like all the pieces of her life were locking back into place.

Chapter Twenty

In the weeks that followed, Nora scoured hundreds of letters and emails, desperate to find a trace of Rose. But as summer faded, the hope that she'd ever discover her whereabouts gave way to doubt and resignation.

One afternoon while Nora and Mr. Carlisle watched horses grazing in the field, he asked if she'd had any new leads.

"Unfortunately, no." It was hard not to feel defeated. "Are you sure there's nothing else you can tell me about her—where she grew up or what she liked to do? Even the smallest detail could make a huge difference."

He stroked his chin in contemplation. "She didn't talk about her home situation much—I think because it was too painful—but I know she had a younger sister. She also mentioned having relatives in Muncie, Indiana."

"That's useful." Nora filed those details away. "Oh, that reminds me... I won't be here tomorrow. I'm going home to stay the weekend with Gran. But Nikki has agreed to check in on you while I'm away."

He looked at her with worry. "I hope nothing's the matter."

"No. I'm sure she's fine. It's just... since Pap died, she's not been herself, so I'm going to see if I can cheer her up."

"That's sweet of you." He was quiet for a moment before going on. "Losing a spouse brings a pain like no other. When you're with someone long enough, they become a part of you. So when they're gone, you feel lost." He reached down and plucked a few wildflowers from the lush grass, then took a piece of ribbon from his pocket and tied it around them. "I know it isn't much but give these to your grandmother." He pressed them into her hand. "Flowers always worked on Judy. Maybe they'll brighten her day as well."

"That's sweet, Mr. Carlisle. I'll make sure she gets them."

"Nora, my goodness." Gran smiled warmly. "To what do I owe the pleasure?"

"Hi, Gran. I was in the neighborhood and was hoping I could maybe stay the weekend... if that's all right?"

"Of course it is! Stay as long as you like." She opened the door and Nora stepped aside. "I hope nothing's the matter."

"No. Not at all. I just haven't had a chance to spend any meaningful time with you in a while, and since I had the weekend off, I thought I'd take advantage of the opportunity."

"Well, bless your heart." Gran poured some sweet tea in the kitchen while Nora got settled, then joined her in the living room. "Here we are." Gran set a glass on a coaster next to Nora's favorite chair. "Have a seat."

Nora eased into the green velvet as memories of her childhood played around her.

"This is such a nice surprise." Gran leaned in her rocker. "I'm so glad you came to see me. It feels like ages since you last stayed here."

"It has been." Nora sipped her tea. "Sorry about that. With everything that's been going on, I—"

Gran held up a hand. "You don't have to apologize to me, sweetheart. I remember how crazy life was at your age. So what's on your mind? You seem troubled."

Nora jerked a shoulder. "Just thinking about Pap." She took in the den and the empty recliner, which brought tears to her eyes. "I still can't believe he's gone."

Gran sighed heavily. "Neither can I. He was one of a kind, your Pap. And he loved you very much."

"I loved him too." Nora took a moment to compose herself. "How do you do it?"

"Do what?"

"Move on."

Gran sighed again, setting her glass of tea on the table beside her. "You do the best you can." She was silent a moment before going on. "I never told you this, but I was married once before."

Nora's mouth dropped open. "What?" The air between them seemed to grow thicker, and a million questions filled her mind.

"It was a long time ago. And I was young."

"How come you never said anything?"

"Because I didn't want to confuse you. The truth is my first husband died in an automobile accident about a year after we were married."

Nora shook her head, overwhelmed by the thought of Gran going through such grief. "That must have been so hard," she whispered softly.

Gran nodded before continuing her story. "For a while, I didn't know if I'd be able to go on. Then one day, Mother came to me and said I had two choices: either lay down and die or pick myself up and get on with my life. At the time it felt like the harshest thing anyone had ever said to me, but it was also just what I needed to hear... Mother might not have been the touchy-feely type, but she was right. Eventually I stopped feeling sorry for myself and got going again. Not long after that is when I met your Pap."

Nora glanced at her in admiration. "Your story sounds an awful lot like my patient at the hospital. He lost his wife last year, and he's only now starting to come out of the fog. Speaking of him..." Nora reached into her bag and pulled out the flowers he'd picked. "He wanted me to give these to you."

Gran pressed a hand to her chest as she let out a gentle sigh. "How thoughtful. He sounds like a very nice man." She slowly rose from the couch and went into the kitchen to place the flowers in water.

"Oh, he is." Nora finished her tea. "He's the one I was telling you about—the one who's looking for his long-lost love."

"Yes, I remember you saying something during your last visit. This ribbon..." She turned to Nora. "Wherever did you find it?"

"I didn't. It belonged to my patient."

Gran let out a heavy breath and turned away, staring into the distance.

"Everything all right?" Nora asked, finding her deep in thought.

"Yes... Everything's fine," she answered through a smile that failed to reach her eyes. "More tea?"

After an interesting weekend away, Nora returned home Sunday afternoon to find a note taped to her front door.

Inside, she took hesitant steps to the living room window and slowly parted the drapes. It took a few seconds for what lay in front of her to sink in. There was an array of various plants and trees, terraces with limestone walls and intricate brick pathways leading to the center of the yard where she saw a gazebo that held a wooden table with two chairs, beside which stood a tall stone fireplace. Everything was immaculately placed and unbelievably beautiful—it looked like a completely different world compared to the messy lawn she remembered seeing when she left.

Sensing John had something to do with this, she ran across the street and knocked on his door. When he answered, she hugged him tightly, unable to stop herself from planting a kiss on his lips.

"Thank you," she whispered, then pulled back to stare into his eyes.

"You're welcome," he said as she felt his hands grip her waist. "Does this mean you like it?"

She beamed at him. "I love it! No one has ever done anything like this for me before. How did you find the time? I was only gone two days."

John breathed an easy laugh. "I called in a favor."

They lay together that evening in the warmth of John's bed, entwined in each other's arms.

"Did you enjoy your weekend away?" he asked.

She nodded, still thinking of Gran's surprising revelation. "But I found out something about Gran that she'd kept hidden from me all these years." She told John everything.

When she finished, he looked thoughtful for a moment before speaking. "Does this change your opinion of her?"

"How can it not? But, if anything, it makes me realize she's far more interesting than I'd thought before. In some ways she reminds me of Mr. Carlisle." A twinge of regret shot through her—Gran was the last person she would have suspected of having secrets. "But now I'm curious as to what else I don't know about her." She rolled onto her side, crooking her arm, and propping her head on her palm. "You don't think I'm naive, do you?"

"Because you didn't suspect your grandmother of harboring secrets?" He shook his head adamantly. "No way! Besides, it's not like she meant to deceive or hurt you in any way. In fact, from what you told me, it sounds like she was trying to protect you."

"Still, I wonder..." Nora's gaze drifted to the window where a pair of robins played in the tree outside.

"I wouldn't read too much into it." John took her hand and absently played with her fingers, as if he were about to say something more. But then he just shrugged. "I mean, everyone has their secrets, don't they?"

Chapter Twenty-One

To christen her new backyard, Nora invited the girls over on Saturday for a barbecue. When Nikki and Whitney arrived, Nora led them out back and they marveled at John's handiwork.

"Oh my God." Nikki's eyes grew wide as she took in the scene. "Look at this place. John did all this?"

Nora nodded, proud of how much work he had done for her.

"And what did you do for him?" Whitney grinned and raised an eyebrow, sending a wave of heat surging to Nora's face. "But seriously, this is amazing."

"He must really love you," Nikki chimed in.

Nora smiled. "Yes, he does."

Annette was last to arrive, and she brought with her a bottle of tequila, which she quickly began to pour into shot glasses. Music blared from an old stereo system, and the four of them spun around to it, laughing as they clumsily danced in the twilight.

"So have you given any more thought to making Brentwood

your permanent home?" Annette asked as she filled her plate with the steak kabobs Nora had prepared.

"I'm considering it. As you know, my contract is up at the end of next month, so I'll need to start making plans soon. I keep waiting for Gail to bring it up, but she hasn't yet."

"She will," said Annette. "You're an excellent nurse. Everyone thinks so. Besides, you're the one who brought Mr. Carlisle out of his shell. I'd say your offer is only a formality at this point."

"I second that," said Whitney. "You're a shoo-in."

"I hope you're right." If not, Nora would be out of a job and out of a home, and she didn't have a plan B.

"I imagine part of your decision will depend on what happens with you and John, right?" Nikki asked.

A wave of anxiety washed over her.

Annette chimed in. "Do you think he'll ask you to marry him?"

Nora's brows furrowed as she pondered the question. "It's a little too soon to be talking about marriage, don't you think?"

"Is it?"

Nora shrugged her shoulders. "I don't know. Honestly, I still feel like he's hiding something from me." That got their attention. "He goes on these trips to South Carolina once a month, which isn't all that unusual except that he tells me he's trying to distance himself from his family."

Annette offered a logical explanation. "Maybe he's planning to take over for his father when he retires."

"I thought so too, but he swears he isn't. Besides, it feels like something more serious than that. Like—"

"Don't say it," Nikki interjected. "Don't even think it. John's a good guy, and he wouldn't cheat on you."

"I agree," said Annette. "I had my reservations about him in the beginning, but I've seen you together, and he's clearly smitten with you."

"You should talk to him," said Whitney. "Especially if you think he's husband material."

Whitney was right, and Nora's mind raced with doubts about John. Did he really love her? Yes. But did he trust her enough to tell her all his secrets?

When Annette and Whitney left, Nikki stayed behind to help clean up. "You didn't have to stay," Nora said as she carefully stacked the glasses in the sink. "But thank you."

Nikki nodded and smiled. "You're welcome, and I'm sorry if we ruined your evening. I'm sure everything with John is on the up and up."

Nora turned off the faucet and gestured toward the kitchen table. "You didn't ruin my evening. I've had my doubts for a while now, and I've just been avoiding having a conversation with him."

"Why?"

"Part of me is afraid he'll tell me something I don't want to hear."

"Like what?"

"That there's someone else." She took a deep breath, calming her nerves. "After what happened with Jeremy, I doubted my ability to love again, especially so soon. But along came John and swept me off my feet. Honestly, these last few months have been something of a fairy tale." A smile made its way onto her lips but didn't last. "Anyway, sooner or later, I will need the truth, and I just hope that whatever it is, it doesn't torpedo our relationship."

Nikki put an arm around Nora's shoulder. "Just remember —no matter what happens, we'll always be here for you."

"Thanks. That mean a lot."

Nora awoke the next morning with a pounding head and the bitter taste of tequila lingering on her tongue. The conversation from the night before came back to her, tainting her memories of the weekend and fanning the flames of suspicion she had been feeling toward John. Steeling herself against the throbbing in her skull, she drove off to Ravenswood to pick up Mr. Carlisle's artwork. Stephanie had called the day before to let Nora know it was ready.

Owen met her at the door, smiling warmly as he invited her inside. "Stephanie had to step out for a bit, but you're more than welcome to wait for her if you like."

"Not necessary," she told him as he led her to the gallery. "I'm kind of in a hurry anyway." She paused by a small table where a painting of Mr. Carlisle's company rested and asked why it wasn't with the others.

"I have exciting news." Owen flashed a wide smile. "A friend of mine who owns a gallery in Chicago heard about Mr. Carlisle's work and wants a piece for his private collection."

"Just like he always wanted. That's wonderful! He'll be thrilled."

Owen helped Nora carry the paintings to her car and load them into the back seat. "I can't wait to tell Mr. Carlisle the good news," she said, brushing off her hands. "And thank you for your help. You and Stephanie have exceeded my expectations. I only wish I was having more luck finding Rose."

"I was going to ask how the search was going."

Nora leaned against the car, letting out a deflated sigh. "Slow. I've received dozens of emails, but nothing bringing me any closer to finding her. Sometimes I wonder if this is a fool's errand."

"Well"—he patted her on the shoulder—"don't give up hope. In my experience, we find what we're looking for when we least expect it."

"You sound like John," she said, feeling her cheeks rise in a smile.

"Speaking of John, how is he these days?" His tone was light, but his eyes held concern.

Nora hesitated for a moment before answering. "Fine. Why do you ask?"

"I don't know," he said. "I just haven't heard from him in a few weeks, which normally means he's got something on his mind."

Perhaps her suspicions about John were well founded after all. "He's been busy, that's all," she said, hoping her answer would appease him.

Owen smiled politely. "You're probably right. Well, I should let you go." He turned and headed toward the house.

"Hey, Owen, can I ask you something?"

"Of course." He turned around when he reached the porch.

"You know John pretty well, right?"

"Better than most," he said with a grin. "Why do you ask?"

"It's just..." She joined him on the porch. "Is he always so... secretive?"

Owen gave a short, mirthless laugh. "Yes, but that's just his style. There's nothing to worry about."

"I see." She tried to keep the disappointment out of her voice. "Well, can you at least tell me why he makes so many trips home?"

"Business, I assume," Owen answered without skipping a beat. "Believe it or not, John's work takes him all over the country."

She mulled that over for a moment. "Do you think there's something more to it than that?"

Owen gave her a sympathetic look. "Look, John just isn't used to sharing his life with someone. He's been on his own for so long, I think he's forgotten what it's like to have someone in his life who has a genuine interest in his affairs—someone like you." He paused for a moment, then added, "But you might ask Stephanie. She and John have been friends longer than he and I have, and he tells her everything."

That surprised Nora. "I thought you all grew up together?"

"We did," Owen said. "But I didn't join their group until high school. John and Stephanie have known each other since they were kids."

Before Nora could respond, the phone rang inside the house, stealing Owen's attention.

"I should get that." He turned for the door. "Drive safe—and if you want my advice, go to the source and talk to John."

That evening, Nora and John ate at Shiloh's, then strolled arm in arm back to her house and settled around the fireplace in her backyard. A cool breeze blew through her hair as she stared into the crackling flames, lost in thought as she replayed the conversation with Owen in her head.

"Nora?" John's voice startled her out of her reverie. "Did you hear anything I just said?"

She shook her head apologetically. "Sorry."

He laughed, wrapping his arm around her. "My parents have a beach house on Kiawah Island that they never use. Now that the exhibit is over and things have calmed down, I was thinking that it might be fun to get away for a few days, just the two of us."

Images of sandy beaches and rolling waves filled Nora's

mind, pushing aside all thoughts of suspicion. She nodded eagerly. "Yes, that sounds nice."

John smiled. "If you're up for it, I was thinking we could go this weekend. We could leave Friday morning and be back in time for work on Tuesday. Does that sound okay?"

Nora grinned right back at him. "Sounds perfect!"

The next afternoon while John sat in his office, the phone rang.

"Hey, it's me," said Stephanie. "Listen, I know you're busy, so I'll keep it brief. Nora stopped by yesterday to pick up the artwork, and she started asking Owen questions."

John got up and shut his door. "What kinds of questions?"

"She knows that you're keeping something from her."

John was quiet for a moment, then asked if Owen had said anything to her.

"No. He told her she should talk to you about it. Look, John, it's obvious you care a great deal for Nora, and I think she's a wonderful woman. But unless you want to risk losing her, you need to tell her about Charlotte."

Charlotte. The mere mention of the name sent shivers down John's back. "I know," he replied quietly. "I just... Do you think Nora's the kind of woman that will understand? After what she went through with Jeremy, do you think I've waited too long?"

"In my opinion, I think she'll understand as long as you tell her everything," said Stephanie. "From what I can tell, she's levelheaded and doesn't overreact. But the longer this goes on, the greater the chance she'll feel betrayed when you tell her. And given how her last relationship ended, well—"

"You're right. I've put this off for far too long. Just so you know, I asked her to come with me this weekend to South Carolina. I'm going to tell her then."

"Good idea."

"Thanks, Steph," said John. "I don't know what I'd do without you and Owen."

"You're welcome. Besides, after what you did for us, we can never truly repay you."

Chapter Twenty-Two

JOHN AND NORA STARTED OUT BRIGHT AND EARLY, the sun just cresting over the horizon as they headed east on Interstate 40. The drive seemed to take forever; the endless blur of cars and road signs was punctuated by bathroom breaks and traffic jams that stalled their progress. Finally, after ten hours, they reached the outskirts of Charleston.

"How much longer?" Nora asked as they crossed the Ashley River.

"Not long." John exited the interstate and merged onto Highway 17.

"Remind me again why we're not going into the city."

"Mom is staying at her country home while my father is in D.C."

Talk of country homes had Nora feeling out of her element.

"Tell me about your mother again," she said, trying to keep the swell of anxiety at bay.

John glanced at her and smiled. "You're not nervous, are you?"

"A little."

"Because of my family?"

"That, and I want to make a good first impression."

"Relax," he said. "My mother is the most down-to-earth woman you'll ever meet. Besides, she's going to love you."

For her sake, Nora hoped he was right.

John steered them away from the city and down a winding rural highway. Nora noticed small farms and ramshackle houses dotting the landscape, with open fields full of swaying coastal grasses reaching out to either side.

"Are you sure you know where you're going?" She eyed him skeptically.

John chuckled. "Relax, I know this road like the back of my hand."

The sun had sunk low in the sky when John finally turned off onto a private drive that wound deep into a forest of ancient oaks. Soon the trees began to thin, and through an opening emerged a grand plantation home. Its whitewashed walls rose two stories high, crowned with two chimneys that jutted up against the orange skyline. Greek Revival columns lined its wraparound porch, and surrounding it were stately oaks and gnarled cypress trees draped in curtains of Spanish moss.

"This is your parent's home?" Nora leaned forward, her eyes widening as she took in the estate.

"One of them," he replied casually. "Their primary residence is downtown, in the South of Broad district. But this is where they come when they want to get away from things."

Including the beach house, that made at least three homes—each, Nora suspected, worth more than she would make in a lifetime. *What have I got myself into?*

John parked the car, and Nora stepped out onto the cobblestone driveway. The breeze blew through her hair as they walked up the flagstone path to the front porch. A well-put-together middle-aged woman with auburn hair was there to greet them with open arms. "John." She enveloped him a hug.

"It's good to see you." She turned her attention to Nora. "And you must be Nora. You're even prettier than John described."

Heat flooded Nora's face as an unexpected wave of joy coursed through her at the compliment. After a warm embrace, she said, "It's a pleasure to meet you, Mrs. Patree. John's told me so many nice things about you."

"I'm flattered. Please call me Marian." She led them into the kitchen, where a dinner of shrimp and grits was waiting on the table. "So Nora, John tells me you're a nurse. What's that like?"

"Very rewarding," she said between bites of food. "Nursing has always been a passion of mine."

John chimed in. "She works at Belle Haven."

"Oh yes. I remember you showing it to me once. It seemed like such a lovely place." She turned to Nora. "Is it difficult working with the elderly?"

"Not at all. Our residents are very polite and easy to get along with."

"And very talented too," John added. "Nora's got this one gentleman, Fred Carlisle, who is an amazing artist."

"Is he the one you were telling me about?"

John nodded.

"Did he ever find the woman he was looking for? What's her name...?"

"Rose," said Nora.

"Yes, that's it. Rose. John told me the whole story and about how you're trying to track her down. What you're doing is commendable."

"Thank you. John has been a big help," she said, not wanting to take all the credit. "I just hope we can find her before it's too late. I don't know if John told you, but Mr. Carlisle is sick, and time is of the essence."

"I'm sorry to hear that," Marian said with genuine concern. She raised a glass in a toast. "To hoping you find Rose."

After dinner, John and Nora spent the rest of the evening driving around John's old stomping grounds. He navigated winding roads with ease, pointing out schools he had attended and local landmarks like Cypress Gardens and the Biggin Church ruins, providing details that only someone who had grown up in the area could possibly know. On their way back, he took Nora by the country club where his family had held a membership since the seventies.

"I can see why you like it here so much," she said, admiring the beautiful surroundings. "This place reminds me of home."

"I'm glad you like it," he said with a smile. "I have many fond memories here."

And when he said it, Nora watched as the smile faded from his face. Fond memories? No doubt he had many. But there was something else—something dreadful—she feared.

In the dead of night, Nora was startled awake by distant voices piercing through the stillness of her room. A quick peek at the clock confirmed it was two in the morning. Puzzled and concerned, she slipped out of bed and silently made her way down the hall. As she neared the kitchen, she could make out Marian's voice in a low tone interspersed with John's replies.

"Have you told her?" she asked.

"Not yet," he said. "But I'm going to... this weekend. I'm just afraid that once she knows the truth, she might not want to be with me anymore."

"Regardless, if—as you say—she's *the one*, she deserves to know the truth."

Nora's heart raced and she inched backward, away from the entrance, and quickly tiptoed back to her room. Lying in bed, she wondered what truth would be so shattering that it could change the course of their relationship.

After a quiet breakfast, John asked if Nora would accompany him for a walk. They strolled in silence along an old dirt path that wound its way through the property, a slight chill in the air. As the sun rose, its warmth began to thaw the morning dew that had collected on the fields. Stopping at the edge of a small cemetery, John motioned for her to sit with him beneath a cypress tree.

"There's something I need to tell you." John brushed his hands across his jeans as he nervously looked out over the headstones. "And it won't be easy to hear."

Considering the conversation she'd overheard the night before, Nora's stomach twisted into a knot. "Let me guess: there's someone else, isn't there?"

John gave her a curious look.

"I overhead you and your mother talking last night. I was hoping this was all just my imagination, but after what I heard..." She took a breath and settled her nerves. "Just be a man give it to me straight. I know you think I'm fragile, and while that might have been true in the past, it isn't anymore. So if it's my feelings you're trying to spare, don't worry. I'll be fine."

"No," John said adamantly. "There isn't anyone else. I would never cheat on you."

"Then what is it?"

John drew a breath. "I know you're wondering why I've made so many trips home lately. Especially since I told you I was trying to distance myself from my family."

Nora nodded along.

"The truth is I love my family. Sure, we have our disagreements, and I get tired of them trying to drag me back into the political arena, but I never wanted to leave this place."

"Then why did you?"

"I had no other choice."

"I don't understand." Nora's mind was spinning. "Is this your father's doing?"

John shook his head. "The State of South Carolina." Confusion swept over Nora as John slowly explained that this was the result of a crime he had been convicted of years earlier.

"The truth is," he began, his eyes fixed on the horizon, "I haven't been honest with you, at least not entirely. But from now on I will be. You have my word." He took a breath before going on. "Just know that when I'm finished telling you what I need to tell you, there's a real chance you may never want to speak to me again."

Nora's heart raced with anticipation. It was hard for her to imagine anything that would be so terrible that she would never want to speak to him again, but the fear was still there.

John got up and led her into the cemetery by way of the open gate, stopping at a headstone that lay at the base of a sprawling oak tree. Staring at the headstone, Nora took a deep breath, bracing for what was to come.

NOVEMBER 1992

"Congratulations, Senator Patree!" Stephanie toasted, a glass held high in John's direction.

John paused for a moment, absorbing the enormity of it all. "Senator... I like the sound of that."

"I couldn't agree more," said Owen, giving his friend a congratulatory high-five.

John then turned to Charlotte whose emerald eyes were filled with delight. He pulled her close and planted a kiss on her lips. "We did it! I couldn't have done this without you, my soon-to-be bride." He glanced down at the engagement ring on her finger. "Let's celebrate!" He suggested they take out the boat for a moonlit cruise along the Cooper River.

Charlotte hesitated, noting how late it had gotten.

"Come on, sis," said Stephanie. "Don't be such a stick-in-the-mud."

Finally Charlotte relented.

By the time they left the dock, it was after midnight, the night sky illuminated by a brilliant full moon above them. Taking up captaincy of the boat, John steered them through a bend while Stephanie and Owen cracked open some beers. They offered one to Charlotte who politely declined in favor of admiring the scenery bathed in silvery light.

They cruised for an hour, enjoying the warm fall night. When they reached the Charleston city limits, John swung the boat in a wide arc and headed back home. But no sooner had the city lights faded when another vessel suddenly showed up in front of them. John jerked the wheel to avoid hitting the boat but in the process struck a fallen tree. The boat leaped out of the water, ran ashore, then flipped on its side and skidded back into the river.

When John came to, he was bleeding from a gash on his head. Dazed and disoriented, he stumbled onto the shore. He shouted for his friends, desperately searching the darkness for a response, but all he heard in return was an eerie silence. Then, just a few yards away, he spotted Owen floating face down in the water.

John quickly scrambled over to him and dragged him to shore. He then noticed Stephanie lying in the nearby grass, her body limp, and her breathing shallow. "Steph." He shook her awake. "Steph, are you all right?"

Stephanie groaned and slowly opened her eyes, squinting in the bright moonlight. She winced in pain as she tried to move her body, but John placed a hand on her shoulder, urging her to stay still.

"Stay here," he said softly, his voice shaking with fear and concern. "I'm going to look for Charlotte."

By then Owen was upright, and the two of them ran through the night, scouring the land and water for any sign of her. But despite their efforts, no trace of Charlotte could be found anywhere.

John felt a chill run through him as he realized something terrible had happened, something he could not bear to think about. He looked to Owen for comfort, but all he saw was despair. Charlotte was gone, and there was nothing either of them could do to bring her back.

When he finished talking, John glanced at Charlotte's headstone before dissolving into tears.

Nora's heart ached for him as his confession hit her like a ton of bricks. "John, I had no idea," she said softly. "Why didn't you tell me?"

He composed himself before answering her. "I was ashamed. And I knew if you found out the truth, there was a good chance you wouldn't want to be with me."

"That's not true." Her voice hovered barely above a whisper. "I mean, it was an accident, right?"

He averted his gaze before slowly nodding in agreement.

"But it doesn't make any sense," she said, thinking clearly.

"You did nothing wrong. How could they charge you with a crime?"

John looked at her helplessly. "I'm afraid you don't understand the way the law works around here. When the police searched the boat, they found open containers of alcohol. The fact that I hadn't been drinking didn't matter, not to them."

"What about Owen and Stephanie—weren't they able to corroborate your story?"

"Owen tried, but they accused him of covering for me. As for Steph, she had her own problems to deal with. Not only did she lose her sister that night but also the use of her legs. It took six months for the spinal fracture to heal and another six for her to learn to walk again."

The facts tumbled through Nora's mind like jagged stones. "And all this happened because of your last name?"

"Yes. Being a Patree means there is a target on my back wherever I go. There are a lot of people around here, including the cops, who would do anything, even lie, to see my family dragged through the mud. If it hadn't been for my father and his influence, I would have gone to prison for Charlotte's death. But he was able to strike a deal with the prosecutor whereby I gave up my seat in the senate and agreed to five years of probation in exchange for staying out of prison."

Nora did the math in her head. "Then that means your probation should be ending soon."

"Next month," he said quietly.

"Then you can be free of this, right?"

He stared at Charlotte's headstone a moment before shaking his head slowly. "As I've learned over these past six years, I will never be free of this. It's like a shadow, following me wherever I go."

Nora reached out to gently touch his hand, hoping to offer some comfort. John turned toward her, his eyes reflecting the pain he had kept hidden for so long. The truth had been revealed, but the burden of the past still weighed heavily on his shoulders.

"I'm so sorry," he said. "I should have told you sooner."

"No. I'm the one who's sorry," she whispered, her heart heavy with empathy. "I had no idea you were carrying something like this inside."

John took a deep breath before continuing his story.

"That night, which should have been one of the greatest nights of my life, I lost everything—my career, my innocence, and most importantly, Charlotte." He paused as if grappling with some inner turmoil. "And the worst part is I never even got to say goodbye."

The silence between them was heavy, but in that moment, Nora felt closer to John than ever before.

"John," she said softly. "I can't imagine how difficult this must be for you. But I want you to know that I'm here for you, and I'm not going anywhere."

John's face flickered with emotion before settling into a gentle smile.

"I don't deserve someone as understanding as you," he said, his voice filled with gratitude. "You're the only person I've ever met who was willing to overlook my scars."

She shrugged off his compliment and took hold of his hand.

"We all have scars," she said. "Some deeper than others. But that's not what defines us. It's our ability to move forward, despite our past, that makes us who we are."

Chapter Twenty-Three

The ride out to Kiawah Island that afternoon was quiet. While John listened to the radio, Nora tried to process everything that had happened. The news of the conviction that had put an end to his promising political career and the fact that he'd lost his fiancée left her torn.

"Listen," he said, breaking the silence, "I know today has been a lot to take in, so if you'd rather go home, I'll understand."

She shook her head, still struggling to come to terms with everything she'd heard. "No. I'm just processing, that's all," she replied as they crossed the Limehouse Bridge.

When they made it onto Kiawah Island, John pulled into the village square and parked in front of a small market. "Do you need anything?" he asked before stepping out into the sunshine.

She didn't, but rather than sit in the car alone while John shopped, Nora joined him inside and watched as he filled a shopping cart with various items. After loading the groceries into the trunk of the car, they crossed a walkway to a surf shop where she bought a pair of flip-flops, a foam boogie board, and a new pair of sunglasses.

By the time they reached the beach house on the east end of the island, it was after noon, so they ate lunch—grilled burgers and crispy fries—then changed into their swimsuits and stepped out onto the beach together.

An awe-inspiring view greeted them as far as the eye could see—sun-kissed sea and sand, glittering waves dancing on the shoreline—and Nora couldn't help but marvel at it all. "This place is gorgeous!" she remarked more to herself than John. "I still can't believe this is your life."

John sighed heavily and looked away from her. "Was my life," he said quietly.

She pondered that for a moment before asking him if he missed his old life.

"Sometimes. But I have a new life now." A smile replaced his frown. "A better life."

"I know I've asked you before, but now that your probation is coming to an end, do you ever think about reigniting your political aspirations?"

"I'd be lying if I said the thought hadn't crossed my mind, but I don't know if I want to put myself—or you—under the microscope of that world. And with the work I'm doing in Nashville, I feel like I'm making a real difference. Besides, maybe some things are best left in the past."

After dark, John made a fire on the beach, and they sat with their toes in the sand, drinking beer and listening to the waves crash on the shore.

"Tell me about Charlotte." Nora's mind raced with curiosity.

John shifted his gaze away and took a long draw from his beer before answering, "What do you want to know?"

"Start with how you met," she suggested.

John smiled slightly at the memory before replying. "We met in Monck's Corner when we were just kids," he began, turning wistful. "Our mothers were best friends growing up, so our families knew each other well. Charlotte and I were like two peas in a pod from the start. We used to ride bikes, play hide-and-seek, or go down to the creek and catch fish and crawdads. Then one summer she went off to camp, and when she returned she had transformed into a young woman. That's when our friendship evolved into something more. Even as teens, everyone used to joke that someday we'd be married. We just laughed it off, but I think even we knew it was our destiny." John paused, staring off into the darkness as if he was reliving some fond memory from his past. "But life had other plans," he murmured softly before returning to his beer.

Nora felt an unexpected wave of jealousy wash over her for this unknown girl who seemed to still have a piece of John's heart. Gathering her courage, she said, "It sounds like you loved her very much."

John's gaze met hers again, and he nodded slowly before replying, "As much as you can love someone."

She swallowed hard. "Do you love me like that?"

He reached out and gently cupped her chin with his hand. Turning to meet her gaze head-on, he said quietly, "Yes, I do. Which is how I know what we have is real. Because I've only ever felt that with one other person."

Nora felt her heart skip a beat at his words and leaned in to kiss him, feeling a sense of relief wash over her. She had been holding on to the fear that John would never be able to love her the way he had once loved Charlotte but hearing him say those words made her feel like she was truly special.

"I'm sorry again for not telling you everything sooner," he said. "It's just... after I lost Charlotte, I wasn't sure I could ever love with such passion again. So I promised her that I would never love anyone as much as I loved her. I know how irrational that sounds, but I felt like I owed it to her for not protecting her that night. And for almost five years, I held true to my word. Then you came along. Sweet, wonderful, amazing you." He gazed at her through the flicker of flames, his eyes burning with a vulnerability Nora hadn't seen before. "You made me realize it's possible to move on. You made me believe it's okay to love again."

She smiled, feeling her heart swelling with love for this man who had been through so much. "I'm glad I could help you see that. John," she said, scooting closer to him. "I want you to know that I love you, and I'm here for you, no matter what."

His face broke into a wide smile, and he leaned in for a kiss. As their lips met, Nora felt a deep sense of connection and love between them. It was as if all the pain and hardship that had brought them to this moment was worth it just for this one moment of happiness.

They spent the rest of the night wrapped up in each other's arms, talking about everything and nothing. Lying there, gazing up at the blanket of stars, Nora couldn't help but think about how far she and John had come from the tragedies that had once defined them. They had both been through so much, but they had emerged stronger, more resilient than ever before.

And as they drifted off to sleep, with the sound of waves lapping at their feet, Nora knew that they were exactly where they were meant to be—together.

The following morning, after a run on the beach, they returned to the veranda and dug into plates of scrambled eggs and bacon while taking in views of the ocean. That afternoon, they challenged each other to a game of tennis, then took a leisurely bike ride around the island until a storm drove them to seek shelter.

Inside, they made a little thunder of their own, then got

dressed and drove off to the golf course for dinner, watching as the sun dipped below the horizon and bathed the coast in its golden light.

"Must we really go home tomorrow?" Nora asked after their meal.

John sighed sharply. "I'm afraid so; we both have jobs, remember? Besides, aren't you anxious to get back to Mr. Carlisle?"

"You're right." She'd almost forgotten about him. "My top priority when I get home is to find Rose," she said with a newfound resolve.

"If—when—you find her, I can't imagine what that moment will be like for Mr. Carlisle. Or for you."

John was right; Nora had been so focused on finding Rose for Mr. Carlisle that she'd failed to acknowledge the emotional impact this search was having on her. All she could do now was hope and pray that nothing happened to Mr. Carlisle, or else all her efforts would have been for nothing.

Nora and John spent the remainder of their evening strolling along the beach, letting the wind blow through their hair and listening to waves before writing their names in the sand and bidding farewell to the ocean. Their time in South Carolina had been emotional yet satisfying, and they were returning home closer than ever.

Chapter Twenty-Four

THE SOUND OF NORA'S PHONE JOLTED HER AWAKE. When she answered, Nikki's panicked voice filled the line.

"Nora, it's me," she said. "There's been an accident."

Nora knew right away that it was Mr. Carlisle. "Is he all right?" she asked, struggling to get her bearings.

"He's stable, but he's going to have quite a headache when he wakes up."

Nora glanced at the digital clock—five a.m.—and quietly told John to get ready, that they were heading home early.

The drive back was silent as Nora's thoughts raced with worry for Mr. Carlisle. When they reached Brentwood, she drove straight to the hospital where Gail met her at the entrance.

"He's going to be okay," she said before cautiously adding, "but there's something you need to know." Gail paused, her forehead creased with worry. "The results came in this morning from his PET scan. It appears the tumor is growing again."

The air left Nora's lungs.

"Keep this between us for now." Gail put a hand on Nora's

shoulder. "Mr. Carlisle doesn't know, and I don't want to do anything to upset him while he's in this fragile state."

"Yes of course," she said, her thoughts drifting.

Nora went in and found Mr. Carlisle sleeping, so she pulled a chair up to the bed and sat down. "What have you done to yourself?" she whispered, looking him over.

"Rose?"

Nora swallowed the lump in her throat. "No, Mr. Carlisle. It's me—Nora."

His eyelids fluttered open, and he turned to her with a faint smile. "Miss Dawson—for a moment there, I thought you were someone else."

She gave his hand a gentle squeeze and asked how he was feeling.

"I'll survive," he said. "So how was South Carolina? Did you get to see the beach?"

"Yes, it was beautiful. And heartbreaking. But that's a story for another time. Right now the main thing is to get you back on your feet."

"How are you holding up?" Nikki asked Nora later that evening as they sat down to dinner.

"I've been better," was Nora's response.

Nikki placed two plates of pizza on the table and handed one to Nora. "Sorry about calling you so early this morning, but I figured you'd want to know."

"Don't apologize." Nora picked up a slice. "You did the right thing." She took a bite of pizza and shook her head.

"What is it?" Nikki asked.

"Nothing. I was just thinking about this weekend and everything that happened."

Nikki straightened in her chair. "Everything?"

"First with John and then with Mr. Carlisle. I guess it's true when they say *when it rains it pours.*"

"What happened with John?"

Nora took a deep breath, then told Nikki everything that had happened—about the accident, Charlotte's death, and John's probation.

"I can't believe it," Nikki said after Nora finished speaking. "Are you all right?"

"I think so," Nora replied wearily. "But let's keep this between us for now. The last thing I need is Whitney or Annette chiming in with their opinions."

After a sleepless night, Nora returned to the hospital the next morning, her heart heavy with sadness. To her surprise, Mr. Carlisle was awake and sitting up in bed. The swelling on his forehead had subsided, and he seemed to have regained some of his old vigor.

"Good morning." She placed a vase of yellow daisies in the window. "It's good to see you back among the living."

"It's good to be back," he said in a raspy tone. "For a minute there, I thought I might be down for the count."

She glanced over at the charts and checked his vitals. "How's your head?"

"It's been better."

"Your sarcasm is back—that's a good sign."

He shared with her that Dr. Kenner had come by earlier that morning and informed him that the tumor was growing again.

Nora's throat tightened as she asked about next steps.

He gave her a wistful smile. "I'm afraid there are only two options—surgery or let nature take its course."

"You're not seriously considering doing nothing, are you? That would mean certain death."

"Death is a certainty either way, Miss Dawson," he said matter-of-factly. "The only question is: How do I want to spend my final days?"

Tears welled up in her eyes, and she quickly turned away from him to gaze out the window. Dark clouds had blanketed the sky, and rain was starting to fall.

"Do your daughters know?" she finally managed to choke out.

Mr. Carlisle nodded solemnly. "I spoke with them this morning. They're upset, naturally, but we all knew this day was coming. I only wish we'd been able to find Rose. Now I fear it's too late."

Nora felt a pang of sadness at the mention of the name. She'd promised Mr. Carlisle she would find her, but so far, she had come up empty-handed.

Nora spent the next few days tirelessly searching for Rose, leaving no stone unturned. She checked every lead and followed up with anyone who might have seen or heard something concerning her whereabouts. But her efforts were in vain. If Rose was still out there somewhere, word of the search hadn't reached her. Or perhaps it had, and she didn't want to be found. It was an angle Nora hadn't considered. Then there was a third possibility—maybe Rose was dead. It was a morbid thought, but it would explain why they hadn't heard from her.

Out of options and time, Nora got up early Saturday

morning and went for a run. When she returned home, she saw someone had left a package on the porch while she was gone. Curious, she went inside and tore away the tape. Pulling open the flaps, she was shocked to find a letter addressed to her, along with a sketch of Rose.

Dear Ms. Dawson,

I hear you've been looking for me. I'm Rose—the Rose—though most now know me by another name. I would have reached out sooner, but the truth is I'm shocked to hear that Fred wants to see me considering I'm the one who broke his heart. But that was a lifetime ago, and perhaps what they say about time healing all wounds really is true. As proof of my identity, I've included a copy of a sketch Fred gave to me when we were in France, along with a note I want you to give him. If, after reading it, he still wants to see me, I will make arrangements to come to Brentwood. And if not, I understand. Either way, I'm glad to know he's still alive and kicking, as the world would be a much dinner place without him in it. If you need to contact me, I can be reached at arosebyanyother-name@aol.com.

Sincerely,

Rose

A wave of joy crashed through Nora's body, sending warm tears spilling down her face. She couldn't keep the news to herself a second longer and darted across the street to find John. He scanned the letter before looking up at her with wide eyes.

"Oh my God! You did it! You found her!"

"More like the other way around," she muttered. "But at least we know she's real and that she's alive."

John took another look. "What's this about her breaking his heart?"

"I have no idea, but it must have been awful considering it's kept them apart all this time."

"And the letter?" John asked. "Did you read it?"

"No. I would never. Whatever it contains is between Rose and Mr. Carlisle. I just hope after reading it he still wants to see her."

The next morning, Nora was back at Mr. Carlisle's bedside, feeling a mix of emotions. After telling him about the package she received, she handed him the sketch and the letter.

His eyes widened with surprise and disbelief as he examined the sketch. "It's really her!" he exclaimed, his voice thick with emotion.

"She's given me a way to contact her." Nora showed him the email address. "But she's insisting you read the letter first."

Without hesitation, Mr. Carlisle opened the letter and

began to read it. As he read, a look of sadness washed over his face.

"What does it say?" she asked, unable to contain her curiosity.

"It says... she's sorry for the pain she caused me all those years ago." With a shaky finger he wiped away a single tear. "And that she's willing to meet with me if I still want to see her. But she also says that if I choose not to, she'll understand."

Nora watched as Mr. Carlisle stared at the letter, lost in thought. It appeared he was contemplating what to do next.

"You want to see her, don't you, Mr. Carlisle?"

He nodded slowly. "Yes, I do. I need to see her and speak with her one last time."

It took several days, but eventually Mr. Carlisle healed. When the doctors gave the all-clear, he and Nora resumed their walks, and he continued to tell her about Rose.

"After D-Day, the tide had turned in our favor, and we had the Germans on the run. We chased them all the way across France and into the Ardennes, but by Christmas, everything ground to a halt."

DECEMBER 1944

One evening, my good friend Albert Pilkins and I were devouring our C rations in a small foxhole we had chiseled out of the frozen earth when he asked me if I thought we'd get out of this thing alive.

"I try not to think about it," I said, not wanting to jinx it. Despite my lack of superstition, war had changed me. "But no one is getting out of anything if this weather doesn't break."

Above us, as it had for weeks, the sky remained an unbroken sheet of gray.

Albert smiled and pulled a small black-and-white photograph from his coat pocket.

"Jenny?" I asked.

"Yes, sir," he said proudly. "Did I tell you we're getting hitched as soon as I get back home?"

I chuckled. "Only a thousand times."

"After we're married, I think I'll go to work for my dad and uncle at the plant so me and Jenny can afford our own place. She'll want to start a family soon, and I already told her I want six or seven kids, and a lab named Rosco."

His words took me back to a simpler time. "That sounds nice, Albert," I said with admiration.

He put away the photograph and turned to me. "You got a girl waiting for you, Fred?"

Instantly my thoughts went to Rose. "I did," I admitted reluctantly, "but I'm sure she's forgotten about me by now. I haven't seen her in a long time."

"That's too bad. Hey, maybe you can come to Detroit with me when this is over, and I'll introduce you to Jenny's sisters." He winked playfully at me. "Hey, we could be brothers if you play your cards right!"

I chuckled softly and shook my head at his optimism. "One step at a time, Albert," I said cautiously, not wanting to give myself false hope.

As the winter dragged on, our situation went from bad to worse. Our food supplies had run out, we were down to our last few rounds of ammunition, and the trenches were full of excrement. Everything we owned was either frozen solid or waterlogged, and morale among the men had plunged to an all-time low. To make matters even worse, we were under constant bombardment from German artillery. For weeks, they'd been shelling us, poking holes in our lines.

But it was nothing compared to that fateful night in January, a night I'll never forget.

As I went around checking if my men were properly settled for the night, the air lit up with mortars and tree bursts. I scrambled for cover beneath a fallen tree, praying to God that if he let me survive this attack, I would never ask for anything again.

The bombardment stopped soon after, but two of my men had been killed and many others were badly injured, including Albert Pilkins.

By the time we made it to the field hospital, Albert was barely alive, so I ran inside and shouted for a nurse. And wouldn't you know it, Rose appeared—only she was different; she had thinned out since the last time I saw her, and her once jovial expression had turned deathly serious.

Before either of us could say anything, they carried Albert inside, so Rose and another nurse immediately went to work on him. All I could do was stand by and watch as my friend succumbed to his injuries.

A little later, Rose found me sitting among a pile of rubble outside.

"I'm sorry for your loss," she said quietly. "Did you know him well?"

"Yes," I answered, fighting back tears. "Albert was probably the closest friend I had here."

"It's not fair, is it?" She sat down beside me. "This war does nothing but take from us."

"He was engaged," I said as I showed her a photo of his fiancée. "They were supposed to get married when this was over. Now Jenny won't be able to do that; she won't ever see him again."

Rose turned away and wept softly, letting out a few sobs.

"I'm sorry," I said, remembering her own lost fiancé. "I didn't mean to—"

"It's all right," she replied, but I could hear the pain in her voice.

I looked out at the ruins of the town. "What a waste," I muttered sadly. "Of everyone and everything..." My words trailed off as emotions overwhelmed me and I broke down into tears. Rose held me close and told me it would all be okay, but inside I knew that even if I survived this terrible war, nothing would ever be the same again.

When he finished speaking, Nora noticed the tears dripping onto Mr. Carlisle's cheeks. Even after all those years, all that hurt was still raw inside him.

"Whatever became of Albert's fiancée?" she asked carefully. "Did you ever speak with her?"

"I promised Albert on his deathbed that I'd go see her when the war ended," he said. "So after I got home, I made the drive to Detroit and presented her with Albert's dog tags and the photo that he kept close to his heart. It was by far the most difficult thing I've ever had to do."

She waited a few seconds before asking the question that had been on her mind since the day she received Rose's letter. "So how did Rose break your heart?"

A grim smile crossed his face. "I'm getting there."

FEBRUARY 1945

Finally the weather broke, and we continued our march east. In the weeks following Albert's death, I said very little, kept a strict schedule, and told the men to take every precaution. We all sensed the end of the war was near, and I hated the thought of losing someone when we were so close to going home.

Rose's unit was ordered to stay back and help with some of the wounded being transported from the front lines, so I lost contact with her again. But in March while on leave one weekend, she and I crossed paths once more.

"This must be fate," I said, finding her on the platform in Brussels. "You still believe in fate, don't you?"

The corners of her mouth curled into a smile. "I suppose so." She looked me up and down. "You look better than the last time I saw you... Captain. Congratulations on the promotion."

"Thanks. You don't look so bad yourself," I told her, admiring the way her blue dress brought out her eyes. "So are you coming or going?"

"Going," she said. "I'm waiting for the next train to Paris. I'm spending the weekend there."

I couldn't help but laugh at the coincidence. "Me too."

She raised an eyebrow.

"It seems the men believe I need a weekend away for some much-needed R&R."

Rose chuckled. "The girls said something similar to me."

We stood there for a moment, lost in each other's gaze, wondering if it *was* fate that had brought us there.

When our train arrived, we sat beside each other and got reacquainted. It was nice to be in her presence again, to have someone other than the men to talk to, and it almost made me forget about the horror I had just come from.

We arrived in Paris in the late evening as the sun was setting. As we walked out of the station, I couldn't help but feel a sense of relief. The city that had only months before been under German occupation was alive and bustling again, and it gave me hope that a return to normal was still possible.

We both agreed on staying at a cozy little hotel on the outskirts of the city, away from the main thoroughfare. It was perfect—dimly lit with an old-fashioned charm that immediately put us at ease.

The first night was spent exploring the streets, taking in the sights and sounds of Paris at night. We dined at a small bistro that Rose knew from her previous visit and enjoyed a bottle of wine with our meal. Afterward, we took our time as we passed beneath the Arc de Triomphe and stood in awe of the Eiffel Tower.

As we walked back to our hotel, I felt the same as I had that night at the dance. If possible, Rose was more beautiful than before, and being around her made me more aware of just how much in love with her I was.

Sitting in the lobby of the hotel, we talked for hours, reminiscing about the first time we met. We discussed our hopes for the future and shared stories from our time apart. We laughed and joked and for a moment felt carefree, as we had before the start of the war.

After midnight, I escorted her to her room.

"Well, here we are," I said, stopping outside her door.

She turned and looked up at me, her eyes soft and inviting. "Stay with me," she whispered. "Just for tonight."

How could I say no? I leaned down and pressed my lips to hers, tentatively at first but then with more passion as she sighed and opened her mouth to mine. Twisting the doorknob, I stepped into her room as we undressed each other, then crawled into bed.

The war had taken so much from us both—friends, family, and innocence—but it couldn't take away the love we had for each other. That night we made love with such tenderness and intensity that it felt as if we'd outrun the darkness that threatened to consume us.

In the pale morning light, I sat quietly, tracing the silhouette of Rose's body. Diligently, I worked until a familiar figure emerged from the page.

"Fred?"

I raised my eyes from the paper. "Here, my love," I whispered.

Rose rolled over and glanced at me. "What are you doing?"

"Sorry," I said softly. "I couldn't pass up an opportunity such as this."

Rose wrapped a sheet around her naked body and stepped closer, examining the drawing carefully. "I see you haven't lost your touch."

I smiled, knowing that despite all the war had taken from me, my ability to create something beautiful remained. "It's easy when the subject is so beautiful."

Rose picked up the sketchbook and placed it on the bedside table before sitting down on my lap. She locked into my eyes and said, "Kiss me." So I did.

As our lips met, a deep passion swelled within me. I wrapped my arms around her waist and pulled her close, feeling the warmth of her skin against mine. Soon we were lost in each other's embrace, our bodies intertwined. This was where we truly belonged, in each other's arms, lost in the ecstasy of our love. And as we collapsed onto the bed in a tangle of limbs and sheets, I knew that weekend in Paris would be one that I would never forget.

When our magical time came to an end, we boarded the train and held hands the entire way back. Now, after years of desolation, we had a little bit of hope. When the train came to a stop in Brussels, neither of us wanted to let go. I knew this was the woman I wanted to spend my life with, so I made a silent vow that if we survived the war, I'd find her and ask her to marry me.

Rose stepped off the car and onto the platform, her eyes misty with tears. I wiped them away lovingly before whispering in her ear, "This isn't goodbye—just until we meet again." I kissed her softly and watched as she slowly walked away from me, wondering if I'd ever see her face again.

Chapter Twenty-Five

Mr. Carlisle's tale was nearly finished, and after hearing about their weekend in Paris, Nora wondered what could have happened between them to make Rose want to shatter his heart.

While she pondered the possibilities, a soft knock sounded through the living room. Thinking it was John, she opened the door without looking. But instead of seeing his smiling face, she found Erin standing there, her eyes red, face streaked with tears.

"Erin." Nora embraced her in a hug. "What are you doing here? And why are you crying?" Immediately, her thoughts went to Jeremy.

"I'm sorry to barge in on you like this," she said, "but Jeremy and I just had a big fight, and I didn't know where else to go."

Nora ushered Erin in and offered her a seat on the sofa. After grabbing two sodas from the fridge, she handed one to Erin, then took the easy chair across from her and settled into place.

"All right, tell me what happened."

Erin's gaze dropped to the floor, and tears started flowing again. "I'm pregnant," she said quietly.

"Pregnant?" Nora's mind raced, and it took her a few moments to process. "How long have you known?"

"Not long."

When Nora had gathered her thoughts, she asked Erin if it was the pregnancy that had caused the fight with Jeremy.

She brought her hands up to cover her eyes and nodded slowly. "He said he isn't ready to be a father," she choked out between sobs. "And the worst thing is he suggested I get an abortion."

"Abortion! You're kidding?"

She pulled a wad of money from her pocket and showed it to Nora. "He even offered to pay for it. He says I should get it done right away and never breathe a word to anyone."

Appalled, Nora said, "That's not why you're here, is it?"

"Of course not. I could never think of killing a baby."

Nora breathed a sigh of relief. "Good for you." Then a fresh wave of anger coursed through her veins. "How dare he suggest such a thing?" She knew Jeremy was despicable, but this was low even for him. "You're not still thinking of marrying him after this, are you?"

Erin shrugged a shoulder and lowered her chin to her chest. "What choice do I have? Whether I like it or not, we're going to have a child together."

"You could always raise it on your own," Nora suggested. Anything had to be better than staying with Jeremy. "Or give the baby up for adoption. There are plenty of people out there who can't have a child of their own."

"But that's just it—I want this baby," she insisted. "I've always dreamed of being a mother. You know that." She smiled briefly. "I just wish the circumstances were different, that's all." She looked at Nora. "You're lucky you got away when you did

—from Jeremy, from Trafford. I knew I should have listened to you."

"Don't beat yourself up," said Nora. "There's nothing you can do about it now. Who else knows about this besides you and Jeremy?"

"Just you."

A sense of shock warred with a strange flicker of satisfaction inside her. When Erin's tears subsided, Nora suggested they order takeout from the Chinese restaurant down the street and insisted on her staying the night.

"I don't want to impose," Erin said. "I'm sure you have better things to do than sit and listen to me whine all night."

"I was going to have dinner with John," she told her. "But I'll reschedule."

"No, don't do that just because of me." She gathered her things.

"It's fine," Nora reassured her. "Besides, John's a big boy. He can manage one night without me."

A sad sort of smile graced Erin's lips before she bowed her head and thanked her softly. Nora squeezed her shoulder and said cheerily, "Best friends have to stick together, especially at a time like this."

By the time their food arrived, Erin's tears had subsided, and she was acting like her old self again.

"This food is amazing," she said as she picked up a piece of cashew chicken with her chopsticks. "How'd you find this place?"

Nora smiled and said, "John turned me on to it."

Erin fell quiet as she picked at some beef broccoli before speaking again. "I envy you, Nora... your job, your relationship with John... You've got the perfect life here." Then her smile faded into a frown. "I thought I had that with Jeremy, but..."

Nora wanted to tell her *I told you so* but didn't have the

heart. "So did I. But you can have that with someone, someday."

Erin looked away quickly but not before Nora saw a flicker of hopelessness in her pale blue eyes. "Maybe before... But once I have the baby, no decent man will want to be with a single mom..."

Nora scooted closer and put her arm over Erin's shoulder in a comforting embrace. "That's not true. Lucky for you, not every man is like Jeremy. There are good men out there—men who aren't scared away by less-than-ideal circumstances."

For the rest of the evening, Nora and Erin watched movies and vegged out on the couch, purposefully avoiding talking about Jeremy. It was just like old times, only now Nora knew that Erin's life would never be the same.

When Erin left the next morning, Nora sighed and told John everything. He sat down beside her on the porch swing, his brow furrowed in deep concentration as he asked, "Is she really going to raise the baby on her own?"

Nora took a sip of her coffee, steam rising from the cup. "She's not exactly alone. Her parents are well off, and they'll help her out. That is if they don't disown her."

John nodded thoughtfully. "And you don't think Jeremy will have a change of heart?"

She shrugged, trying to remain hopeful. "I wish I could say yes, but if I know him, he's already distancing himself from the situation, planning his escape." An uncomfortable silence fell between them until a thought came to mind. "What would you do if I told you I was pregnant?" she asked John. "Would you freak out like Jeremy, or would you be calm about it?"

John stared ahead at the horizon, eyes distant like he was already considering all the possibilities. After what felt like forever, he finally spoke. "I'd need to take time to process of course," he said softly. "But I wouldn't overreact, and I certainly wouldn't tell you to get an abortion. I value life too much for that. Honestly, I'd probably just start thinking about the future and how we'd get through it together."

His words were sincere and gentle yet strong enough for Nora to know he meant them—a perfect mix that melted her heart in an instant.

Nora spent the next few days adjusting to all the new developments in her life. John's confession, Mr. Carlisle's deteriorating health, and Erin's pregnancy had turned her once harmonious reality upside down, and it would take more than flowers or kind words to set things right again.

Fortunately, she didn't have to wait long for the first ray of sunshine when Gail met her after work one evening with an offer for a full-time job.

"I'm sorry it took so long. I wanted to do this weeks ago, but with all the hoops we're forced to jump through these days... The truth is you've been a breath of fresh air, Nora, and I would be delighted if you stayed on."

Although she'd been hopeful, Nora couldn't believe her ears. A full-time-job offer from Gail, the woman she had come to admire and respect as a boss and mentor. Her heart sang with joy.

"Yes," she said without hesitation. "I'd be delighted to continue working for you. This place is like a second home to me, and I can't think of anywhere I'd rather continue to grow my career."

After filling out the necessary paperwork, Nora left Gail's office, ready to conquer the world.

She couldn't wait to tell John the good news. When she got home, he was already there, cooking dinner for her.

"You won't believe what happened today," she said as she burst into the kitchen.

John looked up at her, his eyes twinkling with excitement. "What? Tell me!"

"Gail offered me a full-time position!"

John set down the knife and lifted her off her feet in a bear hug. "That's fantastic news!"

"I know! It's like everything is falling into place."

They spent the rest of the evening celebrating her new job and their future together over a bottle of Chardonnay and creamy chicken piccata.

As they lay in bed that night, Nora couldn't help but feel grateful for everything that had led her to that moment—the good, the bad, and the ugly.

"You know," John said as he stroked her hair, "I've been thinking a lot about what you said the other day."

"What did I say?" she asked sleepily.

"About if you were pregnant," he replied. "And I realized something—when the time is right to start a family, I want it to be with you."

Her heart swelled with love for him, but a flicker of doubt nagged at the back of her mind. "But what if everything gets too overwhelming?" She was thinking of recent events. "What if we can't handle it all?"

John brushed a kiss against her forehead. "We'll handle it together. Just like we always do." And with those words, he lulled her into a peaceful sleep.

The next morning, Nora woke up feeling hopeful and excited for the future. As John left for work, he pressed a quick kiss against her lips. "Love you," he said softly.

"Love you too," she replied.

Before she left, she checked her email and found a message

from Rose. After several days of correspondence, she had finally settled on a date to come to Brentwood: October 24.

When Nora mentioned it to Mr. Carlisle later that day, he let out a sigh of relief. "Thank goodness. I was beginning to think she'd had a change of heart."

"Me too." She opened the window for some fresh air. "So how are you feeling today?"

He held his stomach and shook his head slowly. "Still nauseated, but Dr. Kenner said that's normal."

"Any headaches, dizziness, or weakness?"

He hesitated before shaking his head again. "No, not really, just some light discomfort."

She nodded in response, relieved that he seemed to be doing better overall. "Keep me updated on how you're feeling, okay?"

"I will," he promised.

The weather took a turn, so they spent the afternoon in the theater, watching an old black-and-white film, and listening to jazz on the radio. It was a peaceful respite from all the chaos of recent weeks.

As the movie came to an end, Mr. Carlisle closed his eyes and leaned back in his seat. "You know," he said softly, "I've been thinking a lot lately about my life, about the people I've known, things I've done, places I've been. And I can't help but feel it might be time for me to move on."

Her breath caught in her throat. "What do you mean, *move on*?"

"I mean it might be time for me to say goodbye," he said with a small smile. "To accept that my time here on earth is coming to an end."

She looked at him, tears prickling at the corners of her eyes. "Don't say that, Mr. Carlisle," she whispered. "You'll get through this. All you need is the surgery to remove the tumor, and you'll be as good as new. You are still considering it, aren't you?"

He reached out and squeezed her hand. "Yes, but either way, everything's going to be okay." He was silent for a moment, then asked if she was ready to hear the rest of the story.

She took a deep breath and nodded.

APRIL 1945

A few weeks before the end of the war, I ran into Rose on the outskirts of Weimar. Just the sight of her took my breath.

"Hello, beautiful," I said, giving her a hug and kiss. "How I've missed you."

"Not as much as I've missed you," she said, then planted a kiss on my lips. "Do you think the war is over?"

I nodded, confident that we had finally reached the end. "Which means we can finally put all this behind us and get on with our lives."

"About that," she said, pulling back. "What will you do when you get home?"

We walked the streets hand in hand while I pondered. I'd kept thoughts of home out of my head for fear that I'd become distracted and catch a bullet. Now, with the end in sight, I allowed myself to dream again.

"Get a job, settle down, maybe get married." I glanced in her direction.

She smiled. "Does that mean you've got someone in mind that you'd like to ask?"

"There's one or two girls I can think of," I teased.

She nudged me with her elbow. "I'm ready to start a family," she said, which surprised me. "After everything I've seen and done here, I just want to forget this whole thing, to live my life, and be happy."

"And you think a family will do that for you?"

"I'm certain of it," she said. "I want a boy and a girl, maybe a year apart so they can play together and be friends. And we'll have a house on the hill with a white picket fence. That's the American dream, isn't it?"

"Sounds like a dream to me." I imagined it in my mind. "Do you see yourself working as a nurse when you get back?"

She shook her head as the smile evaporated. "After this, I can't stand the thought of seeing another wounded man. I don't quite know what kind of work I can find at home, but anything will be better than this."

"But you're so good at it."

"Be that as it may, the pain is too hard."

We walked to the edge of the occupied zone, then turned and headed back.

"Rose, when we get back to America, can I... call on you?"

She flashed a sly smile. "Don't you think we're past that stage, or have you forgotten about Paris?"

Heat touched my face. "How could I forget?" I said, recalling our passionate weekend. "I just mean that I want to see you... properly. I want to take you out and buy you whatever your heart desires. And I want to travel across the country with the top down and the wind in our hair, just the two of us. And I want to live and go on adventures with you by my side." I stopped and took her hand. "I never expected to fall in love while I was away, but at the same time, I never expected to meet someone like you." I gazed into her beautiful eyes, seeing in them the rest of my life. "What I'm trying to say is I think we have a future, you and I, and I want to do this right."

Her eyes became misty, and she nodded. "Yes, I'd like that very much."

The next morning, Rose and I ate breakfast together and talked about the future. But before we had finished our meal, a runner burst in and handed Rose a letter, telling her it was urgent. I watched her closely while she read and noticed the color drain from her face.

"Rose—what is it?" I asked, fearing something dreadful had happened.

I waited for her to respond, but she just sat there, looking as if she'd seen a ghost.

"He's a-alive," she breathed, and put a hand to her heart.

"Who's alive?" I asked. "Who, Rose?" She handed me the letter. When I finished reading, I couldn't believe it.

"There must be some mistake." She shook her head in disbelief.

I tried to control my emotions, to make sense of it all. "Let me make a call," I told her. I got up and found the nearest phone and called my superiors. They quickly confirmed that Corporal Harold Colson—Rose's fiancé—was in fact alive and well. "It appears the mix-up occurred when his plane went down in the Pacific," I explained to Rose after the call ended. "He was taken prisoner and held in a camp until it was liberated a few days ago."

Rose stared ahead, still trying to process the situation.

I could tell that she was struggling to hold back tears, but wanting to offer comfort, I put my hand on hers. She turned to face me, her eyes filled with a mix of emotions: shock, relief, and confusion.

"What will you do now?" I asked, fearing the worst.

"I-I don't know," she said. "I still can't believe this is real."

As she spoke, I watched her closely, trying to read her thoughts. And that's when it dawned on me—with Harold back in the picture, where did that leave me?

Nora held a hand to her mouth, not knowing what to say. "He was alive the whole time?"

Mr. Carlisle nodded slowly. "Unfortunately, there were many cases just like Harold's. In war, there are so many moving pieces that mistakes are inevitable."

"Mistake? But this wasn't just a mistake."

"You're right. It was life altering, for everyone involved."

In her head, Nora was putting the pieces together. The reemergence of Rose's fiancé, her breaking Mr. Carlisle's heart. It could only mean one thing.

"She chose him, didn't she?" She was hardly able to get the words out.

Mr. Carlisle turned away, his eyes reddening. "I tried to make my case, but I knew I was fighting an uphill battle. I could see the conflict in her expression—torn between two loves and a sense of responsibility. She had made a promise to Harold, and I wanted to respect that. But I also adored her and felt like the love she and I had for each other might be enough to tip the scales in my favor."

MAY 1945

When news of Germany's surrender echoed over the loudspeaker, I was filled with an overwhelming sense of joy and elation. Thinking back on the years of battle—the close calls and narrow escapes—I was astounded that I had managed to survive it all. Finally free from the fear of death, I longed for home—the place that had been absent from my life for three long years. The thought of returning made me anxious; everything must have changed so much, and so had I.

"It's all over!" I told Rose, who was in the process of folding blankets when I found her. "We're finally going home."

She looked up at me and smiled, her eyes filling with tears of relief. "Thank God," she said, embracing me tightly. "I couldn't have done this without you, Fred. You've been my rock, my... everything."

A wave of emotion swept over me, overwhelmed by the tenderness in her voice. Somehow, through all the chaos, she and I had found each other, and she had become the one constant in my ever-changing life.

"I couldn't have done it without you either," I whispered into her ear. "You're the one who has kept me going through it all. Which is why I don't want this to end."

Rose looked up at me, confusion etched on her face as she pulled away from our embrace. "Fred, I—"

"I know you said you needed time and that you weren't ready to make a decision, but...." I took her hand in mine and looked deep into her eyes. "We'll be going home soon, and I'm terrified of never seeing you again. As awful as this war has been, it's nothing compared to the thought of losing you."

Rose's eyes widened in surprise as she listened to my words. I could see the emotions taking over her, the tears streaming down her face. She opened and closed her mouth a few times before finding her voice.

"Fred, I... I don't know what to say. Like I told you before, I have a lot to think about, and I need time to process."

"What's there to think about? I love you, Rose, and want to spend the rest of my life with you. Isn't that enough?"

"I love you too, Fred." Her voice quivered with emotion. "But things are not that simple for me. I wish I could make you understand."

But the truth was I did understand, far greater than she realized. And despite the love she had for me, it stung knowing she had feelings for someone else.

"I do understand." I tried to keep my voice steady. "No matter what happens, somebody will have their heart shattered. All I can do is hope it won't be mine," I added, my voice cracking with the weight of my words. "But if more time is what you need, then I'll wait as long as it takes, because you're worth waiting for."

Rose nodded slowly, still holding onto my hand. "Thank you, Fred. Thank you for understanding."

In the months that followed, amid the chaos of the occupation, I lost contact with Rose at precisely the time I needed to be with her. But after our last conversation, I wasn't sure there was anything left to say.

JANUARY 1946

By the time my unit finally made it back to America, a new year had dawned. Many of the ceremonies and ticker-tape parades had already taken place, so when I arrived at the shipyard in Virginia, there was little excitement or fuss.

I caught a bus in Norfolk that got me as far as Knoxville, then boarded a train that took me the rest of the way home. Waiting at the platform were my parents and sisters, who welcomed me home with open arms.

Once I was settled, I took some of the money I had saved up from the war and bought a car. The first thing I did was go see Albert's fiancée in Detroit. After an emotional couple of hours with her, I dried my eyes and set off in search of Rose. Aside from the occasional letter, we hadn't talked much in recent months, which left me worried. It took me a couple of days to track her down, but eventually I found out that she had been staying with her sister in Cincinnati. So I bought a suit, a bouquet of yellow roses, and set out to win her heart.

After taking a deep breath, I stepped up onto the porch and knocked on the door.

A young woman who favored Rose answered after a minute and surveyed me from head to toe. "Can I help you?"

"I hope so. I'm looking for Rose," I replied nervously.

"You must be Fred," she said quietly.

"Yes, ma'am, I am. Is Rose around?"

"Just a minute." She stepped inside, then returned a moment later holding a letter. She handed it to me and said, "Rose said to give this to you if you stopped by."

I sat down on the stoop and opened the letter, reading it word for word.

Dearest Fred,

If you're reading this, then it means you've come looking for me. As much as it breaks my heart to have to tell you this, I've decided to marry Harold. You see, there was a promise made some time ago, and despite the love we shared, I couldn't go back on my word. Rest assured, this decision was not made lightly, and in the millions of tears I shed while making it, you were always at the forefront of my mind. I know this will be difficult for you to grasp, but I will never forget you or our weekend in Paris and the passion we felt for each other. You will have a special place in my heart forever, and I only hope one day you can accept why I've chosen this path. Though I realize I've broken your heart, I wish that at some point in your life, you might find someone who lights up your world like you once lit up mine. I'm sorry for the informal nature of this letter but delivering this message to you in person would have required a strength that I simply do not have.

Until we meet again,

Rose

"After that, my life was never the same. I was angry—not because Rose had married Harold, but because the woman I was in love with, the one I thought I would spend my life with, was gone forever. In the months that followed, Rose was all I could think about: Where she was, what she was doing. Her memory haunted me, yet nothing seemed to take the pain away. I even considered ending it all at one point. Then a ray of light appeared on the horizon. Judy." The corners of his mouth curled upward into a smile. "Suddenly I felt alive again. We were married within a year, and joy found its way back into my heart. As the years passed, my love for Judy only grew stronger. But even then, sometimes when no one was around and everything was still, a sudden thought of Rose would strike me, and it was as if she was right there with me again."

When he had finished speaking, Nora asked if he'd ever truly gotten over Rose.

He paused before answering, considering what he knew to be true. "I moved on," he finally said with a sad smile. "And lived an amazing life with a wonderful woman. But no," he said regretfully. "I never got over her. Sometimes, no matter how hard we try, there are just some people we can't get over."

Tears streaming down Nora's face, she made her way home, still unable to process what Rose had done. For the first time since hearing Rose's name, Nora wished she'd never gotten involved, and it made her question why Mr. Carlisle was so desperate to see her again.

To take her mind off things, she sat down in the living room after dinner and called Erin. They hadn't spoken since her visit, and Nora wanted to make sure she was doing okay.

"Mom and Dad know," Erin told her. "And surprisingly, they were rather laid-back about it."

"That's a relief," Nora replied. "My parents would have had a coronary!"

Erin laughed at the joke.

"What about Jeremy? Is he still pushing you for an abortion?"

Erin's heavy sigh spoke volumes. "Actually, I haven't heard from him since I came to see you. He left town for a few days... said he needed time to think things through."

Nora's blood boiled. "Do you want me to call him and give him a piece of my mind?"

"I'd love that," Erin responded dryly, "but I doubt it would make a difference." She sighed again, deeper this time. "I suppose I'll have to call everyone soon and let them know the wedding is off—that'll be embarrassing."

"Well, if you need any help, just say the word. And if you

need me to come down there, I can. Trafford isn't that far away."

"That's sweet of you, but I think I have the situation under control. But if it ever gets too overwhelming for me again, you're the first person I'll call."

Chapter Twenty-Six

"You look deep in thought."

The sound of Mr. Carlisle's voice startled Nora. She looked up and found him hovering between her and the sun, his face unreadable. "Mr. Carlisle, what are you doing out here? Shouldn't you be inside?"

"Probably. But I've never been any good at following directions. Do you mind if I sit?"

She reached for what was left of her lunch and cleared a place for him.

He eased onto the bench and propped the cane against the armrest. "Nice day, isn't it?" he said with a smile as he set his gaze upon the water.

Nora nodded mindlessly, her thoughts drifting.

"You couldn't have picked a finer place to eat your lunch. Of all the spots on this property, this is my favorite."

Nora removed herself from the daydream and looked around, taking in the trees ablaze with the colors of fall, the rolling pastures, and the blue-green water. He was right; it was beautiful.

"Sometimes I like to sit here and reflect."

"On what?"

"Life," he answered, squinting against the afternoon sun.

"Have you had a good life, Mr. Carlisle?"

He thought for a moment. "Yes, I believe I have," he said, nodding. "Is something troubling you, Miss Dawson?"

It was like he could read her mind. "How did you know?"

"I raised two daughters, remember?"

She sighed and looked down at her hands.

"Rose didn't change her mind about seeing me, did she?" he fretted.

"No." She shook her head. "It's my friend... Erin."

"The one who's marrying your ex?"

She nodded, thinking how ridiculous it sounded. "She came to see me a few days ago and told me that she's pregnant with his baby. And that's not all. To make matters worse, he wants nothing to do with it."

Mr. Carlisle let out a low whistle. "I can see why you're troubled."

Nora looked up at him, feeling tears prick at the corners of her eyes. "I just wish she had listened to me. I tried to warn her."

Mr. Carlisle leaned back against the bench, rubbing his chin thoughtfully. "Unfortunately, despite our best efforts, people have to learn things on their own even if it means making mistakes along the way."

"But this is a huge mistake," she said, her voice cracking. "They're supposed to be getting married in a few weeks, and now everything is ruined. And I can't even imagine what it's going to do to her if she has to raise the baby on her own."

Mr. Carlisle reached over and placed a comforting hand on hers. "It's not your responsibility to fix their mess, dear. All you can do is be there for your friend, support her, and help her through this difficult situation. And as far as that ex of yours…" His tone grew cold, and a spark of anger flashed in his eyes. "Someone needs to light a fire under his ass!"

"You're right." Nora composed herself. "What am I saying? You're always right."

His eyes lit up. "I don't know about that, but I have been around the block a few times."

Her thoughts then wandered from Erin to Rose, who had been on her mind constantly ever since Mr. Carlisle revealed that she'd broken his heart.

"Are you sure you want to see her again after what she did to you?" Nora asked him. "It's not too late to change your mind."

He paused before answering with a smile. "I appreciate your concern, but yes, I want to see Rose. Despite what she did to me, I loved her very much. A part of me still loves her."

"But I still don't understand how she could choose Harold over you. I mean, I get making a promise to someone, but for nearly three years she thought he was dead. Not to mention she'd fallen in love again."

"What can I say? She loved him before she loved me. Which means they shared a history that she and I didn't, and while that may seem unfair, it's the only explanation I've got. Besides, I know in my heart that if Harold hadn't come back, Rose and I would have gotten married and lived a happy life together. Knowing that is enough to give me peace."

Nora considered that. "I see your point… Still, I wish the two of you had ended up together."

He smiled. "You say that now, but in time I think you'll change your mind. Besides, if that had happened, our lives would have turned out different, and you and I would never have met."

"I don't know." Nora pondered the possibilities as a dark

cloud shuttled across the sky. "Perhaps we would have... in another place or time."

He smiled knowingly. "Ever the optimist," he said, then turned wistful. "I think that's what I'll miss most about you, Miss Dawson. You have an unbreakable spirit, the kind of spirit I've only seen in one other woman. In spite of all Rose endured, life never kept her down for long. It was one of the things I admired most about her."

"You're very sweet, Mr. Carlisle." What a shame it was that the nurses before had missed out on an opportunity to get to know him. "And wise too."

He chuckled. "After eighty years, I don't know much, but I know this one thing. Life has a funny way of working out the way it's supposed to. We may not always see the bigger picture, but things happen for a reason."

"So you don't have any regrets?"

He didn't answer right away, his expression shifting from cheerful to wistful. "Only one," he said solemnly.

"Rose again?" she guessed.

"No." He dropped his head and turned away.

"Well what is it?"

"I don't want to talk about it."

"Come on, Mr. Carlisle. You've told me everything else. Why not this?"

He was quiet for a moment, appearing to struggle with something. "Because I don't want you to think ill of me."

"I could never."

He seemed to come around. Eventually, he reached into his shirt pocket and pulled out a photograph of a young man in uniform and showed it to Nora.

"Who is he?" she asked, studying the picture. "Is this Albert?"

He shook his head. "His name was Julian Wentz. He was a German soldier."

Puzzled, she asked, "Why do you carry a picture of a German soldier with you?"

Mr. Carlisle took a deep breath and exhaled. "When Albert died, it nearly broke me. Any hope I'd had of emerging from the war unscathed died along with him. In the days that followed, the only thing I could think about was revenge, and it didn't matter where I got it. One afternoon, we assaulted a small town that had been occupied by a unit of SS troops during their retreat. The fighting was fierce, and in the confusion, I got cut off from my men. I hid in a ditch until dark, then crawled into the forest on the edge of town. Even under the cover of darkness, I had to be careful. The Germans were close enough that I could hear them talking, and I knew one wrong move could cost me my life. After most of the men had turned in for the night, I crept to the edge of the forest and began looking for a way out. Luckily, there was only one guard standing sentry that night. If I'd had my rifle, I could have easily dispatched him from my position, but all I had on me was my field knife. I waited quietly until he was within striking distance before jumping out of the trees. He never saw it coming."

"You mean you...?"

"I'd killed before," he said as tears flowed freely. "Many times, in fact, but not like that—not close up. To feel the weight of another man's life, to look him in the eyes and watch the light fade... That's something that not even years of war can prepare you for. The truth of the matter is I could have waited until he was out of sight, maybe snuck across the road, and disappeared into the wilderness, but all I could think about was Albert and the look on his face in those final moments." He hung his head in shame. "For a long time, I struggled with what I had done to that young man. Everywhere I went I saw his face staring up at me with terror in his eyes." When he had composed himself, he turned to Nora. "I bet you think I'm a monster, don't you?"

"No," she replied, struggling to comprehend the horrific nature of war. "I think you're a wonderful person that was put in a terrible position."

"Thank you," he said, and squeezed her hand, "for understanding." They sat in silence for a long time, letting the sound of nature fill their ears. Eventually, Mr. Carlisle spoke up. "So are you anxious about meeting Rose?"

"I was... I suppose I still am. There are so many questions I have for her. I just hope she shows."

"Oh, she'll show," he said with confidence.

When Nora's lunch was over, she stood and helped him to his feet. "In the meantime, I've got to get ready for visitors of my own. Mom and Gran will be here this weekend, and I still have so much to do."

"That's right. I'd nearly forgotten. Are you still planning on bringing them by?"

"Yes, if you're feeling up to it."

"I am. Actually, I'm looking forward to meeting them."

"Really?"

"Sure. After everything you've told me, I feel as if I know them already."

"They're looking forward to meeting you as well, especially Gran. She really appreciated the flowers you sent."

He smiled warmly as they eased toward the hospital. "Dr. Kenner came to see me this morning," he said, changing the subject.

"And?"

"The tumor's still growing, but my vitals are good and so is my white cell count. I'm not foolish enough to think this will go away on its own, but so far so good."

Nora smiled at his optimism. "Never say never, Mr. Carlisle. Medical miracles happen every day."

That evening, Nora did something she swore she'd never do again. Despite what Erin had told her, she was furious with Jeremy and felt like he needed someone to shake the sense into him, so she dialed his number and waited for him to pick up.

"Hello."

Just the sound of his voice made her skin crawl.

"Hey... It's me."

There was a moment of silence on the other end of the line before Jeremy replied. "Nora... H-How are you? It's been a long time."

"I'm fine," she said, trying to steady her voice. "Listen, I know about the pregnancy... and about you asking Erin to get an abortion, and—"

"And you're angry," Jeremy said. "I know, and I'm sorry. I overreacted."

"Overreacted?" She scoffed. "You did more than overreact. Most men are over the moon when the woman they love tells them they're going to be a father, but not you. All you cared about was getting rid of the problem. If you knew Erin at all, you'd know how much she wants to be a mother and how much it hurt her when you asked her to get an abortion. And you know the worst thing of all? I told her you'd do something to break her heart. When she told me you'd changed, I didn't believe her. And as it turns out, I was right."

"Look, Nora, I'm sorry for the way I acted. Truly, I am. And I told Erin the same thing last night, though I don't think she believed me. The truth is I just feel like I keep making mistakes—with her, with you..."

"Don't bring me into this." Nora shook her head. "What happened between us was a long time ago... another life ago, and I've moved on."

"I know," he said softly. "But I still regret how things ended between us. You were the one I should have spent the rest of my life with, and I threw it all away. Not that it matters, but I'm sorry."

Nora's heart pounded in her chest as she tried to process his words. Jeremy had always known how to manipulate her emotions, and she couldn't help but wonder if he was trying to do it again. "Look, I made my peace with what happened a long time ago, and I suggest you do the same. But as far as this situation with Erin," she said, redirecting the conversation, "if you care for her, even the slightest bit, then man up and do whatever it takes to make this right."

Nora slammed the receiver down, feeling a blend of anger and confusion. Whatever happened now would be up to Jeremy, but she had, for the first time in her life, stood up to him and could look anyone in the eye knowing he no longer had any control over her.

As Nora got ready for her mom and Gran, she couldn't help but wonder what they'd think of her house. She'd worked hard to turn her little cottage in Brentwood into a cozy home, and all she could do was hope that it made an impression.

The night before they arrived, Nora and John had dinner with Stephanie and Owen at the mansion. It had been weeks since they'd last talked, and Nora was anxious to fill them in on everything that had happened with Rose.

"I'm so relieved you were able to find her," said Stephanie.

"So am I. For a while there, I was starting to think she didn't exist."

"So how is Mr. Carlisle holding up?" Owen asked.

"He's determined but anxious. Thankfully his condition has stabilized."

They ate in silence until Stephanie posed a seemingly random question: "Do you think wedding bells are in your future?"

John blushed as he stammered an answer while Owen beamed with amusement. "I know that look," he snickered. "Whenever it does happen, you have to hold it here at the mansion!"

John nodded toward Nora and muttered, "That's up to Nora."

She quickly agreed. "Yes, I'd be honored, and I can't think of a more perfect place."

When dinner was over, Nora helped Stephanie carry the plates into the kitchen while the men sipped whiskey on the porch.

"I hope all that talk of marriage didn't make you uncomfortable," said Stephanie. She reached into the refrigerator and brought out a tray of chocolate cakes. "Sometimes Owen gets carried away."

"Not at all. In fact, John and I have been talking about it a lot lately."

Stephanie's eyes widened with excitement. "Really? That's so exciting! Have you thought about the kind of wedding you want—big, small...?"

Nora shrugged. "Not really. I just know that I want it to be special."

"Well, if you need any help planning, let me know. I've planned plenty of weddings in my time."

"I appreciate it." Nora smiled gratefully, but felt it slide into a frown. "I just hope Mr. Carlisle is still around when it happens. It's funny, but after what we've been through, I consider him part of the family now."

Stephanie nodded in understanding. "I know what you mean. Fred means a great deal to Owen and me as well. Tell you what," she said a moment later, looking as if an idea had just occurred to her. "Let me see what I can do about lighting a fire under John."

Chapter Twenty-Seven

The morning of her family's arrival, Nora woke early and straightened the house. Afterward, she made breakfast and sat in the garden until nine, enjoying the crisp fall air.

When Kathleen's car pulled into the drive, Nora went out to greet them, and led them into the house.

"Nora, dear, you've outdone yourself," said Gran. She eased around the house, taking in every detail.

Kathleen was just as complementary. "And where does John live?" she asked, gazing out the living room window.

"There." Nora pointed to his place.

"Will he be stopping by?"

"A little later," she said. "He had some business to attend to this morning, but he'll be joining us for dinner."

As soon as Kathleen and Gran settled in, Nora gave them a tour of the garden. They walked around for half an hour, admiring the flower beds, the pond with the lilies, and the gazebo where Nora liked to read in the afternoons. Gran took a seat on one of the benches.

"Oh, Nora, this is just lovely," she said.

"Thank you, Gran," Nora said, beaming. "I'm glad you like it."

When they'd rested a while, Nora took them for a drive around Brentwood, showing them the places where she spent her time—the stores and restaurants, the park where she ran, and the church she attended. They then drove to Belle Haven, where she introduced them to Gail and her coworkers.

After giving them a tour of the hospital, Nora led them into the common room to wait for Mr. Carlisle.

"Why don't I go see if he's ready for us," she said. She walked to his room but found it empty.

When she returned to the common room, Kathleen was sitting alone.

"Where's Gran?" she asked.

"She said she needed to go to the bathroom."

When Gran didn't return a few minutes later, Nora got worried and went to look for her, imagining she'd taken a wrong turn and was hopelessly lost in the labyrinth of hallways or had stumbled upon the bridge game going on in the card room. If so, it'd be hours before they'd see her again.

As she was walking down the hallway, something outside the window caught Nora's eye. She stopped and looked out to find Gran and Mr. Carlisle standing at the end of a path just short of the pond, gazing silently at each other as if stuck in time.

"Gran?" Nora asked out loud, not sure what to make of it.

Kathleen grabbed her arm and held her back from opening the door, mouthing *wait* as if she knew something that Nora had missed.

Suddenly, it all made sense—the nurse with the blue eyes, her grandmother's checkered past, why she and Rose seemed so much alike. It wasn't a coincidence that she found herself in this moment; it had been planned for her to be here. Her skin prickled at the realization that the woman she had known her entire life as Gran, the one who had been her best friend growing up, whom she thought she knew better than anyone on earth, had been holding on to the biggest secret of all. From now on, Nora would know Gran by another name—Rose.

And as Nora stood there, processing the scene before her, John's assertion that Rose was likely closer than she imagined played in her head. Like usual, he had been right; she *was* closer than Nora could have ever imagined, though without seeing it with her own eyes, she would never have believed it.

Nora found herself in a mix of emotion—of joy and sadness. After all these years, fifty of them, the nurse and the soldier who had so long ago fallen in love were finally reunited. What began as a ripple of emotion quickly swelled into a tidal wave that washed over her, ending in a flood of tears.

"She's her," Nora cried, breaking the silence. "She's his Rose."

"I know," Kathleen whispered. "Gran and I had a long talk on the way up this morning. I guess you never really know someone, do you?"

Nora shook her head, thinking that perhaps not knowing was what attracted us to certain people in the first place. It was that constant discovery that intrigued us, that kept us guessing, longing for more. And in that moment of reflection, she felt the rise in her cheeks as a smile broke across her face. Her father had been wrong. Happy endings did still exist, and not just in fairy tales. And although it had taken a lifetime to get to this point, it *was* happy—for both, it seemed.

As they continued to watch from afar, the scene between Nora's grandmother and Mr. Carlisle began to unfold. They slowly made their way closer to the pond, holding hands as if afraid to let go. Nora's heart swelled with emotion as she watched them find each other once again. A lifetime had come and gone since they'd last seen one another, and yet it appeared to vanish the instant their eyes met.

Nora could see the tears streaming down Gran's face as she looked up at him with a mix of joy and sadness. Mr. Carlisle gently wiped away her tears with his thumb, a small smile forming on his lips.

For a moment, they just stood there, lost in their own world. Nora knew that they were reliving all the memories they had shared together so many years ago. It was a beautiful and bittersweet moment all at once.

Eventually they made their way back toward the entrance, still holding hands. As they approached, Nora could see the happiness etched into their faces.

"Well?" Gran said, looking at her with a twinkle in her eye.

Nora ran to her and wrapped her arms around her tightly. "I'm so happy for you," she said softly into her ear.

"Thank you, dear," she replied, tears welling up in her eyes once again.

Mr. Carlisle stood beside her, smiling widely. "It's been a long time coming," he said, looking at Nora and Kathleen in turn.

They all hugged and smiled together, tears streaming down their faces. It was a moment that would stay with Nora forever—the moment when love had triumphed over distance, over time, over everything that had ever tried to keep them apart.

As they made their way back inside, Nora noticed that the whole facility had gone silent. Everyone seemed to be watching them, smiling and nodding as they walked past.

Word must have traveled fast, Nora thought, smiling to herself. But it didn't matter. In this moment, it was just the four of them, Rose, Mr. Carlisle, Kathleen, and Nora. They sat in a small sitting area near the entrance, sipping on tea and reminiscing about past memories.

Rose told them stories of her time with Mr. Carlisle, about their first date, their first kiss, and their adventures together. Mr. Carlisle chimed in from time to time with his own stories, making them all laugh.

When visiting hours were over, they went back to Nora's house for dinner, where Nora told the day's events to John. He listened attentively as she recounted the emotional reunion between Rose and Mr. Carlisle. His eyes widened with surprise when she revealed that Rose, her grandmother, had been keeping her true identity from her all these years.

"I can't believe it," he said, shaking his head.

"Neither can I," Nora said, still trying to process the fact that the woman she had known her whole life was actually someone else entirely. But despite the shock of this discovery, there was no denying the happiness that had come from this reunion. It was a reminder that love, no matter how long it takes, can conquer all.

After dinner, John entertained Kathleen while Nora searched for something to drink. She thought about wine, but after the day she'd had, she needed something stronger, so she opened the cabinet and grabbed what remained of the fifth of Jack Daniel's and drank straight from the bottle.

"You all right?" Gran asked as she joined her under the gazebo.

Nora had to think about that for a second.

"That was some day, wasn't it?"

Nora nodded, thinking it was likely the most shocked she'd ever been in her life.

Gran grabbed the bottle of whiskey and took a sip of her own. "That's better." She looked as though it had been a while since her last drink.

Nora should have been shocked, but after what she'd seen, nothing would surprise her.

They sat silently beneath the full moon, both reflecting on the day.

"There's something you want to ask me, isn't there?"

Nora nodded, gathering her thoughts. "How come I never knew your name was Rose?"

Gran smiled. "Because it isn't. Rose was a nickname the girls in my unit gave me because of my rosy cheeks. I tried to get them to call me by my real name, but they refused, so Rose stuck. It wasn't until after the war that I let that name go."

Nora then asked another question. "If Mr. Carlisle's unit hadn't been held in Europe for so long at the end of the war—if he'd been around—do you think you would have gone ahead and married Harold?" She was still trying to reconcile what, to her, seemed like an irrational decision.

Gran thought a moment, then said, "I don't know. Not seeing Fred during those months of indecision was difficult, and no doubt made it easier for me to be with Harold. If he'd been there, well..." She gave a rueful smile. "I guess we'll never know, will we?"

"No, I guess not. Did you ever tell Harold... about Fred?"

"Yes. In fact, I told him everything. Part of it was because of guilt; the other part because I felt I owed it to him. I know it hurt him to hear that I'd fallen in love with someone else, but in the end, I think he understood."

For a moment, they sat in silence while Nora digested her words.

"But you're satisfied with how things turned out, right?"

"Yes," she answered without hesitation. "Despite the many heartbreaks, I've lived a wonderful life, and have had the pleasure of being loved not only by one terrific man, but by three. Life is seldom simple, Nora, but we do the best we can with the hand we're dealt."

"I guess you're right," she said, thinking of her own situation. "I mean, if Jeremy hadn't cheated, I would never have left Trafford, never met John or Mr. Carlisle, and I may never have known your story. In the end, you were right—it was the best thing that ever happened to me." Then another thought jumped into her head. "When did you know?" she asked, realizing that it must have been before today. "About Mr. Carlisle."

"Not until the last time you came to see me."

Nora tipped her head to one side.

"That ribbon was a dead giveaway," said Gran.

Nora recalled how her mood had shifted when she saw it. "It belonged to you, didn't it?"

"Yes. I used it to tie my hair up when I was on duty. I had given it to Fred early in the war for good luck. I can't believe he kept it all these years."

"How come you didn't say anything?"

"I had to be sure. Besides, even if I'd said something, I'm not sure you would have believed me."

She was right about that. Nora turned and stared into the darkness. "I still can't believe it's you."

"You're not upset, are you—that I didn't tell you?"

Nora turned and stared at her. "Why would I be upset?"

"I just know how much you loved your Pap. The last thing I wanted was to do anything that could tarnish his memory for you."

"No, Gran. I'm not upset. I could never be upset with you. Besides, what happened between you and Fred was a long time ago, before you met Pap. But it does make me appreciate you more. All my life, I thought you could do no wrong. Now I know you're just like all the rest of us, and that makes me love you even more. It also lets me know that I'm going to be okay. Sure, there'll be bumps along the way, but every setback is only temporary, and there are great things waiting for me out there."

When Kathleen and Gran had gone to bed, Nora and John sat together beneath the stars.

"This has been quite a day," he said.

"You can say that again." Nora replayed the day's events in her head. "Never in a million years would I have guessed that Gran and Rose were one and the same." She took a breath, recalling the first day she moved to Brentwood. "Leslie was right... about this place having magic, and about me being in the right place. I guess some would call it fate."

"I've never been a big believer in fate," said John, gazing into the stars. "But I do believe things happen for a reason."

It wasn't until much later that they finally made their way back inside, tired but happy after a long day of revelations and surprises.

As she lay in bed that night, listening to the sounds of the old house settling around her, Nora knew that life would never be the same again.

Chapter Twenty-Eight

The next morning, Nora woke up early and sat on the porch sipping her coffee. Her brain was whirring with yesterday's revelations. Even though they had discovered Rose's identity, there were still so many unanswered questions.

Gran soon joined her on the porch with a look of determination, ready to start her day.

"Good morning," she said.

"Morning, Gran," Nora replied and motioned for her to take the empty rocking chair. "Sleep okay?"

"As a matter of fact, I did," she replied. "It's amazing what having the weight of the world off your shoulders can do for you."

Nora smiled. "Yeah, I know the feeling." She took a sip of her coffee and looked out at the serene landscape.

"What's on your mind?" Gran asked, breaking the silence.

"I was wondering if you ever saw Fred again... after the war?"

She drew a deep breath and exhaled slowly. "Yes, I saw him once," she said, then paused. "After Harold died, I started wondering if I'd made a mistake—if I should have chosen Fred instead. So I decided to find him and see if there was still any hope for us. But by the time I finally tracked him down, he had already married Judy. I never saw him again after that until yesterday."

"That must have been so hard," Nora said, imagining the pain she must have felt.

"Yes." She sighed. "Losing both Harold and Fred at virtually the same time was heartbreaking. It took me a while to get back on my feet, but eventually I realized that sometimes God puts people into our lives for a certain amount of time. They're not meant to stay forever; it's simply how it is. But that doesn't make them any less important. I like to think that Fred and I met each other at just the right moment, and we only survived the war because of one another."

Nora nodded, understanding the bittersweet sentiment. "Do you ever regret not pursuing him further?"

"I used to," Gran said with a wistful smile. "But then I met your Pap, and I knew that he was the one for me. Sometimes we think we know what we want, but life has a way of surprising us."

Nora furrowed her brow slightly, pondering her words. "Do you think I made the right choice to leave Trafford?"

"Absolutely," she said without hesitation. "I would never say this in front of your mother, but there was nothing left for you there. Here you have opportunities and, from what I can tell, a man that adores you."

Nora smiled, feeling reassured by Gran's words. It was true; she loved her life here—her friends, her colleagues, and of course John.

"I was thinking." Gran took a sip from her mug of coffee. "What if I were to take Fred home with me? To live? I know about his diagnosis," she continued. "But since your Pap died, I haven't had anyone to take care of, and it's lonely in that old house."

Kathleen stepped out onto the porch then. "Mom, have you thought this through? Do you really think that's a good idea?"

Gran nodded. "I've had plenty of time to consider it. He's dying, his wife is gone, and the nearest family he has is ten hours away. No offense," she said, looking at Nora, "but I don't want his last months on earth to be spent in a hospital. He should be at home, surrounded by those who love him. Besides, I have a house full of empty rooms just filled with furniture and memories. It'd be nice to have someone around; someone to take care of, to talk to, to make breakfast for. I know it's a lot to ask, but I really want to do this."

"Have you asked Mr. Carlisle yet?" Nora questioned.

"No," Gran answered. "I was hoping to speak with him this afternoon."

Kathleen glanced at her before speaking her mind. "If this is what you really want," she said slowly, "then I support you." She looked to Nora.

"You'll get no objection from me. But you'll need to clear it with Gail and his doctors. Oh, and someone will need to tell his daughters."

That afternoon, after getting Mr. Carlisle's approval, they took their proposal to Gail. She leaned back in her chair and rubbed her chin thoughtfully. "It's a big decision, Mrs. Thompson. You're taking on a lot of responsibility."

"I understand that," Gran said. "But I can't stand the thought of leaving him again."

There was a moment of silence as Gail considered her words. Finally she nodded. "I understand where you're coming from. I'll need to consult with Dr. Kenner and make sure it's safe for him to be discharged into your care, but if he gives the okay, I don't see any reason he can't go home with you."

The next few days were a whirlwind of activity as they prepared to bring Mr. Carlisle home. Gran had never been one to procrastinate, and she threw herself into the preparations with a fierce determination. She cleared out one of the guest rooms and set it up with a hospital bed, a bedside table, and all the medical equipment that Mr. Carlisle would need. She stocked the kitchen with healthy foods and snacks and sourced a caregiver who could come in to help with his care.

Nora watched her bustle around the house, her eyes shining with excitement. It was clear that she was relishing the challenge of taking care of Mr. Carlisle, and Nora couldn't help but feel proud of her.

When the day finally arrived for Mr. Carlisle to leave Belle Haven, everyone came out to see him off.

Nora stood alongside Gran at the front of the crowd as Gail and the doctors wheeled Mr. Carlisle out of his room and down to the entrance. He was pale, but there was a glimmer of hope in his eyes that Nora hadn't seen before. Gran rushed over to him and took his hand.

"We're taking you home," she said softly, smiling at him. "You're going to be okay."

He looked up at her with a mix of gratitude and fear. "Thank you," he said. "I don't know what I'd do without you."

As they loaded him into the car, Nora was struck by the notion that the man whom she so admired, the man that she had taken care of for almost seven months, was leaving her. But she knew that it was for the best.

The drive to Gran's house was quiet. When they arrived, they were greeted by the caregiver that Gran had hired, a kind woman named Margaret who had years of experience in caring for cancer patients.

They spent the day helping Fred settle into his new room and making sure he had everything he needed. They put up pictures of his family on the walls and arranged some of his things around the room until it started to feel like home.

After they were done, they all sat in Gran's living room, sipping on lemonade and talking about old times. Fred told some more stories about his time in the war that made Nora appreciate him even more. Despite all that he had gone through, he was still kindhearted and full of love for those around him.

Later that night, after dinner, Nora went to check on Fred in his room. She found him sitting up in bed, looking out the window at the stars.

"Beautiful sky tonight," she said as she walked over to him.

"Sure is," he said with a smile. "Makes me wonder what's out there beyond what we can see."

"Yeah," she said with a chuckle. "Maybe there's another world where things are just a little bit different. Where everything that's lost isn't gone forever."

Fred looked at her with a wistful expression. "I sure hope so," he said softly.

"You were right," she said after a few moments.

"About what?"

"About things turning out the way they were supposed to."

He smiled warmly.

"Did you know all along that Rose and I were related?"

He gave a sly smile. "I had an inkling. An artist forgets names from time to time, but never a face. That day when you passed me in the hall, I knew I'd seen those eyes before. I considered saying something to you then, but when you told me your grandmother hadn't been involved with the war, I thought that perhaps it was just my imagination."

"That's why you tied the ribbon to the flowers, isn't it? To see if you'd get a reaction out of her?"

He nodded knowingly.

"How come you didn't say anything?"

"And spoil the surprise?" He laughed an easy laugh. "Don't you think this way was better?"

Nora smiled. "Yes, much better."

"I want to thank you," said Mr. Carlisle after a moment, "for everything you've done for me. I can honestly say my life is now complete."

Her heart swelled with emotion, touched by his kind words. She had come to care for Mr. Carlisle deeply in the time she'd known him and knew that even if she lived to be as old as him, she would never forget the adventure they shared together.

"It was my pleasure," she replied sincerely. "I'm just glad I could help bring some happiness into your life."

He reached out and took her hand in his, giving it a gentle squeeze.

"You're a remarkable young woman, Miss Dawson," he said with a smile. "And I'll never forget you or what you've done for me."

She felt humbled by his praise. "I should go." She rose to her feet. "John will worry about me if I don't leave soon. But you take care of yourself, all right? And I promise I'll call and check on you every day."

"I look forward to it," he said, then told her goodbye.

Before Nora left, Gran pulled her aside and handed her a box of old letters she'd been saving for her.

"What's this?" Nora asked.

"Little pieces of me," said Gran. "I thought you might appreciate them."

Nora thumbed through the dozens of letters, noting the dates. "Are these...?"

"The letters Fred and I wrote to each other during the war," she said. "These should answer any lingering questions you have. Since you've heard Fred's side of the story, I thought you might appreciate mine as well, and then maybe you'll have a greater understanding of why I chose the path I did."

Nora was torn. On the one hand, she couldn't wait to devour the letters, to discover what treasures lay hidden in the lines of text. But another part of her was hesitant about infringing on her grandmother's privacy.

"Are you sure you want me to read these?" Nora asked. "It feels like these should be kept private, between you and Mr. Carlisle."

"Nonsense," said Gran, brushing away Nora's concern. "There's nothing explicit in there from what I remember, just some good old-fashioned love letters from a time long ago."

"Thank you," Nora said, giving her an extra-long hug. "I'll return these as soon as I've had a chance to read through them."

When Nora finally made it back to Brentwood, John was there to welcome her home.

"Did you get Mr. Carlisle settled?" he asked.

She nodded, letting out a sigh. "Yes, he's all settled in." She plopped down on the couch and kicked up her feet.

John sat down beside her, his hand reaching out to brush the hair off her face. "Are you okay?" he asked softly.

She leaned into his touch, feeling comforted by his presence. "Yeah, I'm fine. It's just been a long day."

He wrapped his arm around her, pulling her closer. "I don't know how you do it, Nora. Taking care of people like you do every day."

"I guess it runs in the family," she said, knowing now where she got her instincts as a nurse.

"Speaking of taking care of people, why don't I take care of you for a change?"

She smiled, feeling her heart flutter. "What did you have in mind?"

John cooked a late dinner and brought it to her in bed.

They ate in comfortable silence, enjoying the simple pleasure of each other's company. When they finished eating, John leaned over and kissed her softly on the forehead and told her he loved her.

"I love you too," she said in reply.

As John got up to clear the dishes, she couldn't help but feel grateful for him and everything he did for her. He was always there, whether it was to listen to her vent about a difficult day at work or just to hold her when she needed comfort.

"Thank you for this," she said as he came back into the bedroom.

"Anything for you." His eyes sparkled with love.

Nora scooted over, making room for him on the bed. He climbed in beside her, wrapping his arms around her. They cuddled together under the blankets, feeling the exhaustion of the day catch up to them, and as she drifted off to sleep, Nora couldn't help but wonder what tomorrow would bring.

Chapter Twenty-Nine

A FEW DAYS LATER, NORA WAS TAKING IN THE VIVID colors of fall while seated in the garden when her phone suddenly rang. Nervousness coursed through her. Assuming Mr. Carlisle's health had suddenly worsened, she slowly entered the house and answered the call with apprehension.

"It's Erin," came her voice over the line.

"Oh, Erin," she said, relieved. "I was wondering when I might hear from you."

"I just called to thank you... for talking some sense into Jeremy. I don't know what you said to him, but he's like a completely different person now."

"Well, I'm glad I could help," Nora said, smiling in satisfaction.

"You'll be happy to know he's coming with me tomorrow for my first doctor visit. And he says he's all in when it comes to the baby."

"That's great, Erin! I'm glad to hear it. Does this mean the wedding is on again?"

"About that... Jeremy and I talked, and we decided that it might be best if we waited until after the baby is born before getting married. I know we'll catch hell over it, especially from our parents, and everyone down at the church, but Jeremy doesn't want to put me or the baby under any more stress."

For the first time in a long time, Nora agreed with Jeremy on something. "I think that's a wise decision. Well, whenever you have it, I can't wait to be there. And Erin, if there's anything I can do for you, don't hesitate to ask. No matter what happens or where life takes us, I hope you know that I'm never more than a phone call away."

After that, Erin vanished from her life for a while. Nora and John spent Thanksgiving with his family in South Carolina, followed by Christmas with hers in Alabama. They celebrated New Year's Eve with their closest friends, and as a new year dawned, things slowly returned to normal.

Despite Mr. Carlisle's decision to forgo the surgery, his condition improved. Dr. Kenner called it a medical miracle. To celebrate his recovery, he and Rose spent every waking moment together, making up for lost time.

As the chill of winter set in, Nora took advantage of the downtime and read the letters Gran gave her word for word, and with each passing one came a greater understanding of Gran's life.

"I know why she did it," Nora said to John one night as he finished up washing dishes.

"Why who did what?" he asked.

"Why she picked Harold over Fred."

John dried his hands and came closer, giving her his full attention.

"I don't know why I didn't think about it sooner," she said. "Gran used to tell me that our word was our most valuable attribute; that if we made a promise, we should keep it no matter what. After reading all these letters, I see how madly in love she was with Fred, but ultimately she stayed true to her word to Harold. If he had really been dead, I'm sure things would have turned out differently."

John contemplated this before moving even closer. "No offense, but I'm glad things worked out the way they did. If not, you wouldn't have been born, which means I never would have known you or had the chance of having you in my life. And what a tragedy that would've been."

He put his arm around her and kissed her gently on the forehead.

"I guess in the end, things turn out the way they're supposed to, don't they?" she mused.

As winter gave way to the warmth of spring, Nora found herself celebrating one year living in Brentwood. One afternoon while she and John were walking hand in hand in the park, he suddenly stopped in front of her. His eyes were filled with a mix of determination and nervousness.

"I know we've talked about this a lot lately," he said, taking both her hands in his, "but I want to make it official."

She looked at him, eyes wide. "What do you mean?"

"I mean I want to ask you to marry me." He pulled a small box from his pocket.

Nora gasped as John got down on one knee. People around them stopped to watch as he opened the box, revealing a stunning diamond ring. "Nora Jean Dawson, will you do me the honor of being mine forever?" he asked, gazing up at her with love in his eyes.

Tears filled her eyes as she nodded. "Yes!" He slid the ring onto her finger, and they embraced, kissing passionately while the world faded away around them.

SEPTEMBER 1999

After months of planning every last detail, John and Nora exchanged vows on a lovely Saturday afternoon in September. They said their *I do's* in front of the people who mattered most to them at the majestic Ravenswood Mansion. And in the front row, seated beside Nora's parents, were her grandmother and Mr. Carlisle, their hands, like their love for each other, intertwined during the entire ceremony.

And for a while, life was perfect. But, as they say, nothing lasts forever.

On a cold December morning, Margaret phoned to tell John and Nora that Mr. Carlisle had passed away peacefully in his sleep, with Rose at his side. Nora was beside herself with grief, imagining her grandmother sitting in her rocking chair, tears streaming down her cheeks.

John and Nora drove down right away and did their best to console her, but it made little difference. She had experienced the loss of the man she loved twice in her life, and it was too much for her to bear.

The funeral was held at the Baptist church in Murfreesboro where Mr. Carlisle had been a member for the better part of five decades. People from all over attended, lining up to pay their respects to a man they all admired and loved. Gran sat in the front row, wearing black and clutching a handkerchief in her hand. John and Nora were there too, along with Stephanie, Owen, and everyone from Belle Haven.

As the reverend spoke, his words rekindled memories of Mr. Carlisle. Nora reminisced about those awkward days in the beginning when he gave her the cold shoulder and how, once she'd broken the ice, he became one of the kindest people she had ever met.

Losing him was like losing a member of the family, and she kept thinking how unfair life was, that after all this time, he and Rose had been united only for them to be separated again, this time for eternity. And her mind could not comprehend the cruel nature of life.

That night was one of the most difficult nights of Nora's life, but John stayed by her side and comforted her while she cried herself to sleep. She slept longer that night than she had in her entire life, and when she woke the next morning, it was as if the slate had been wiped clean.

A few weeks later, John and Nora were enjoying lunch one afternoon when a knock echoed through the door. John got up to answer it and returned with a large package in his hands. "It has your name on it," he said, handing it to her.

Nora opened it cautiously and tears began to run down her cheeks. On his own, when no one was watching, Mr. Carlisle had painted one final picture. It was of her on the park bench by the pond, where she used to spend her afternoons having lunch. "He must have done it from memory," she said, showing it to John.

The painting was so lifelike it was as if Nora could see herself sitting on that bench all over again. The way Mr. Carlisle had captured the light in her hair and the curve of her smile was simply remarkable.

"I can't believe he did this."

John pulled her into his arms. "He wanted you to have something to remember him by."

She nodded, tears still streaming down her face. "I know," she said softly.

He smiled and kissed her forehead. "It's absolutely beautiful, just like you."

Nora looked up at him and smiled, feeling a sense of warmth in her heart. John always knew how to lift her spirits. He was her rock, her support, her everything.

John suggested they hang the painting on the wall of their living room where it could be seen by everyone who came over and act as a beautiful reminder of the kindhearted man who had touched her life in such a profound way.

"I think that's a wonderful idea," Nora said as she dried her tears. "I think Mr. Carlisle would have liked that."

While John went to get his tools, she examined the painting more closely and discovered a note taped to the back with her name on it.

To the woman who authored the last chapter of my life. You will forever be in my heart. May your days be filled with health, happiness, and love. And remember, it isn't the mistakes of our past that define us, but the hope for what's ahead and the hearts we leave behind.

Epilogue

"That's the last of them," John said, appearing in the living room. He drew a hand across his brow and snapped the sweat. "I still can't believe you did this by yourself."

Nora smiled, reflecting on the first day she arrived in Brentwood. That felt like a lifetime ago. All the ups and downs—at work, with her peers, John, and of course Mr. Carlisle—flashed through her mind as she glanced around the empty house. The walls stared back at her as if to memorialize all the laughter and tears that they'd shared there.

"If we're going to make it before dark, we'd better get a move on," John said, breaking her trance.

The girls gasped and crowded around her, embracing Nora in a group hug. Nikki noticed a tear rolling down her cheek and spoke up. "Don't cry! It's not like you're moving across the country."

Whitney stepped forward and gave Nora an encouraging look. "Yeah. It's only thirty minutes away, and you'll actually be closer to me now."

Annette wiped her own eyes and added her support: "Me too... But don't worry; we promise to help you make new memories in your new place!" She waggled her eyebrows mischievously.

Nora glanced down at her baby bump and smiled reassuringly. "We can't wait."

"Give us a call when you get settled," Nikki said.

"Will do," she replied gratefully, then walked them out. As they said their final goodbyes, Nora went inside and took one last sad glance around the house before scrawling down a personal note in the kitchen.

A little piece of goodbye...

Do you believe in fate? I didn't. Not before I came here. My name is Nora Dawson, and for the past two years I've been fortunate enough to call this place home. When I arrived in Brentwood, I was brokenhearted and full of doubt about the future. However, I soon discovered that the rest of my life was waiting here for me. I don't know what has brought you to this little corner of the world, but rest assured, you are in the right place. It may not look like much, but this little home has magic in its walls, and if you'll take care of it, I promise it will take care of you.

All the best,

Nora

END

Keep Reading for a Sneak Peek of The Keeper of Stars

Prologue

You don't find love. It finds you. It's got a little bit to do with destiny, fate, and what's written in the stars.
—Anais Nin

May 2020
Sims Chapel, TN

THEY SAY OUR LIVES ARE WRITTEN IN THE STARS, that our fate is predetermined. But after the life I've lived, I believe that we are the authors of our own destiny, endowed by the Almighty with the power to choose our own paths, and, when necessary, to rewrite the stars.

Tonight, I sit alone under a chilly Tennessee sky. My only company, aside from a crackling fire and a glass of Jack Daniels, is a chorus of crickets and bullfrogs. It is a tune I know well. From the comfort of my rocking chair, I lean back and gaze deep into the heavens. Above me, the stars stretch to infinity like lighthouses on a thousand distant shores, waiting to guide my thoughts across the velvet sea.

But before they set sail, the sound of the telephone ringing brings me back to earth, so I push myself out of the rocker and shuffle into the house.

"Hello."

"Hey, it's me. It's done."

"Everything? Are you sure?"

"The moving truck is on its way to the storage facility, the door is locked, and the alarm is set. Sherrie will be by in the morning to stick the sign in the yard, so there's nothing left to do now but wait."

Between the alcohol, and the notion that the house that had known sixty years of love and laughter now sits empty, it takes me a moment to process.

"I can't thank you enough, sweetheart. I don't know what I would do without you."

"You're welcome, Daddy. I only wish I could do more. Speaking of that, I know you said you didn't want any company tomorrow, but I wish you'd reconsider. I could leave first thing in the morning and be at your place by noon. That way we could go together."

"Who would run the store?"

"Annalise can manage. She practically runs the place on her own as it is."

"I appreciate the offer, Caroline, but you've more than held up your end of the bargain. The last mile is my cross to bear."

"Well," she says, sighing heavily into the phone, "if you change your mind, you know how to reach me. I don't mind dropping everything and leaving at a moment's notice."

"I know, and thank you. Oh, before I forget, did you find your mother's memory box?"

"No, I'm afraid not, and I searched every inch of the house.

Twice in fact. The only thing I can figure is she must have moved it without telling you."

"You're probably right," I say, fearing it is lost forever. "I'll check again in the morning before I head out."

"Just promise me you'll be careful. I don't know what I'd do if I lost you too."

"I will. But try not to worry. I've been making this trip since before you were a twinkle in your mother's eye."

"Yes, but not like this—this will be different."

I consider that, thinking that tomorrow will be one of the toughest days of my life.

"Well, I should go," she says a moment later. "I've been at it all day, and I'm exhausted."

"All right, darlin'. Tell Don I said hello, will you? Annalise too."

"Sure thing, Daddy. I love you."

"I love you too, sweetheart."

I mosey outside, add a log to the fire, and settle in for the long night ahead. "Now where was I?" At the bottom of my glass, it all comes back to me. Leaning back in the rocker, I catch the glimmer of the North Star as the tail of a comet's light streaks across the sky.

Chapter 7

GULLY WASHER

May 1950

"JACK, IF YOU GET US KILLED, SO HELP ME GOD..."

The storm that had been building in the western sky rolled east, and a column of low, swirling clouds swept up the valley, blotting out the sun. By the looks of things, this was going to be a gully washer, which meant Jack Bennett had one shot at getting the motor to turn over. Otherwise he and his passenger would have to ride out the storm on Rock Island.

With the last bolt tightened, Jack turned and shouted into the wind. "All right, George, here goes nothing." Bracing himself, Jack pressed one hand firmly against the engine, grabbed the pull cord with the other, and yanked with all his might.

The engine spat and sputtered until finally, to Jack's delight, the steel beast gurgled to life as, from the bow, George Duncan put his palms together and raised his eyes to the heavens.

Jack grinned. But with a mile of open water between them and the dock, they weren't out of the woods yet.

A little while later, Jack and George huddled in the weathered shack at the end of the dock as rain fell in wind-driven sheets around them. Thunder echoed over the vast expanse, and like starlight pulsing through the graphite sky, lightning twisted and forked, bridging the gap between the heavens and the earth. It was as awesome a display of Mother Nature's power as either of them had ever witnessed.

As the dilapidated shack swayed and creaked around them, Jack took in a couple of deep breaths, smelled rain, gasoline, and the sweet aroma of chewing tobacco, then turned and stared out the window. "God must be angry today."

"I don't know nothin' about that." George lumbered to the icebox, plucked two beers from the top shelf, and tossed one to Jack. "But if we'd waited five more minutes, we could have asked him ourselves."

Jack smiled amusedly and opened his beer. "I ain't gonna let nothing happen to you, George. Besides, you keep forgetting I'm the best damn mechanic around. No one knows boats like me—or how to fix them."

"Speakin' of that, you should think about making a livin' out of it."

"What, boats?"

George shook his head as he took a long pull from his beer. "Bein' a mechanic. I mean, you can fix just about anything, and since there's no shortage of things breakin', you'd never run out of work."

Jack entertained the idea while he took a sip of beer. "Maybe you're right," he finally said. "I may look into that. Thanks, George."

"Don't mention it." George gulped his beer and drew a hand across his mouth. "I'm sure glad to get outta that hot sun... and away from the storm. Now look at us." A smile worked across his weathered face. "We got a roof over our heads and somethin' cold to drink. A man don't need much more'n that." When he'd finished, he nodded toward the icebox. "There's more beer in the chest if you get a hankerin'."

"Thank you kindly," said Jack. "But you know I only drink one. I wouldn't want to get you into any kind of trouble, not on account of me."

George leaned back and let out a laugh that filled the small room. "The way I see it, if you're old enough to fight, you're old enough to have a beer. It's one of them rites of passage I heard the preacher talk about when I was younger. B'sides, there ain't nothin' wrong with it so long as you don't go burnin' up the roads. The water, on the other hand." He nodded toward the lake. "Why, you could go off course for pert' near an hour and not run into anything."

While George fetched another beer from the chest, Jack pulled out his wallet and counted the bills. *Thirty-five plus the four sixty-five I have at home makes...* He did the math in his head. *Five hundred big ones. Not bad.*

"Whatcha gonna do with all that cash?"

"I reckon I'll save it."

"For what?"

"Same thing as the last time you asked me."

"You mean that house on the hill?" Before Jack could respond, George shook his head in disgust. "Don't be a damn fool, boy. Like I told you before, only rich folks live on the hill. Folks like you and me—real folks—we ain't got no chance at a life like that. It ain't in the stars. We're lucky to scrape by down here at the water's edge. Which, if you wanna know the truth, ain't a bad deal."

George leaned in his chair and belched. Then Jack watched as a smile spread across his face.

"That's what you keep telling me. But even rich folks gotta start somewhere." Jack put away his money and stared out at the dark water, disinclined to accept the fate George had predicted for him.

"Think what you want, but someday you'll see what old George is talkin' about." George finished his second beer. After crushing the can and tossing it in the corner, he said, "Hey, listen. I appreciate you decidin' to stay on with me this summer. Honestly, I don't think I could run things without you. Not anymore."

Jack wondered if it was George or the alcohol doing the talking. Probably a little of both, he concluded as the man started on his third beer. "Aww, come on, George. That ain't no way to talk. You still got a few years left in you." He watched as George stared sullenly at the rain. "But in any case, I'm glad to do it and thankful for the work. Besides, it beats the hell out of working at the mill. I was talking to Ray Tucker the other day, and he said with all the windows they have in that place, it's like an oven in the summer. And in the winter you nearly freeze to death. That's no life I want. No, sir." He shook his head and glanced outside as the rain tapered off. "At least here I get to be on the water, and like you said, that ain't bad."

"Amen!" George slapped the table with an open palm. "I'll drink to that."

By the time Jack's house came into view, the storm had pushed east into the mountains, but evidence of its passage remained. The hike from the dock to his house, which was over a mile, took Jack along the lakeshore, through a dense stretch of woods, over a creek, and across a field of heather so thick he had to cut a path with his machete.

When Jack finally reached the porch, it was nearly suppertime, so he slipped out of his clothes, set them on the rail to dry, then pushed open the front door.

"That you, JB?"

"It's me, Mama," Jack answered wearily. He shuffled into the bathroom, washed his hands and face, and changed clothes before coming to supper.

"How was work today? You didn't get caught out in that squall, did ya? Donna Rae said Deep Springs Road is a mess."

"The woods too," said Jack. "On the bright side, there's a couple of trees down at the edge of the yard I can cut up and use for firewood. And to answer your question, me and George made it back just in time."

She looked at him dubiously. "You didn't pull that engine-trouble trick on old George again, did you?"

The fact that she remembered shocked him. "What if I did? You gonna to tell old George on me? I was only having a little fun." He rocked back in the chair, balancing on two legs. "Besides, I got us back with five whole minutes to spare."

Helen Bennett narrowed her eyes at him. "Jack Edward Bennett. I thought I taught you better'n that. And put that chair on all fours. If God had intended it to have two legs, he'd have made it that way." She shook her head in disgust. "You got too much of your daddy in you. That's your problem. If you ain't careful, one of these days you're gonna fool around and give old George a heart attack. How would you feel then?"

"I'm sorry." He set the chair right. "It won't happen again. Promise."

"Well, good. After all, George ain't as young as he used to be. I reckon none of us are." She checked the biscuits. "You hungry?"

"Starving."

When the biscuits were golden brown on top, Helen took

them out of the oven, covered them with a towel, and set them on the table to cool. Next, she brought over the jar of honey and a plate of fried bologna, put it beside the biscuits, and finally collapsed into her chair. "You wanna say grace or should I?"

"You go ahead. You're so much better at it than I am."

"Very well. Bow your head."

When the prayer had been said, Helen filled a plate and began eating while Jack poked and prodded at the fatty meat. Usually, he didn't mind bologna and biscuits, but this made the third day in a row. Even he had his limits.

"Mama, I wish you'd let me help with the groceries. I was counting my money this afternoon, and—"

Helen raised a hand, cutting him short. "Listen, I know you want to help, and God knows you'd give me your last dime if I asked you, but that's your money. You've worked hard for it, and hopefully someday it will help you get that house on the hill you're always goin' on about. So don't go wastin' it on me. B'sides, this may not be steak and potatoes, but it's nourishment to our bodies, and we got the good Lord to thank for that. Which is more than I can say for some folks."

Feeling a tinge of guilt, Jack dropped his eyes. "Yes, ma'am."

"But it's mighty kind of you to offer, JB. You're turnin' into a fine young man."

"Thanks, Mama." He took another bite of biscuit and chased it with a sip of tea. "Well, if I can't buy groceries, can I at least paint the kitchen? George has a couple of gallons of chiffon sitting in the shack that came from a man in White Pine. He said it's mine if I want it."

"Well, now." She chewed her lip for a moment. "I suppose there's nothin' wrong with that so long as it don't cost you nothin'."

"Not a cent," he said. "Cross my heart."

"All right, it's a deal—under one condition. You promise not to make a mess of my floors."

"Yes, ma'am."

After supper, Jack cleared the table and took the scraps outside to feed to the foxes and raccoons before drawing a bath. When he'd finished scrubbing the dirt from his body, he put on his pajama pants and opened the window to let in the cool breeze. The little house he and his mama called home was no mansion, and it didn't have any modern conveniences like a telephone or air-conditioning, but it had gobs of windows. Most nights they left them open to let in fresh air and be sung to sleep by the crickets and bullfrogs.

He spent a few minutes talking to God then wrote in the journal Fleta Pickle had given him for his birthday.

Dear Lewis,

You should have seen the big storm we had this afternoon. The way the wind was howlin', you'd a thought the Rapture was coming. In all my days, I've never seen whitecaps like that. Luckily, I got me and George back in time without as much as a single raindrop hitting us. According to Mama, I nearly gave George a heart attack with that old engine-trouble stunt. Maybe she's right, and I should take it easy on him from now on. After all, I don't know what

I'd do if anything ever happened to George. Anyway, when the storm passed, I dropped a line and caught a couple of crappies from the dock on some minnows I snagged with the net this morning. Neither of them any size but a promising sign. Maybe tomorrow I'll head up Flat Creek and see if I can't catch me a catfish for supper. I haven't had a good mess of fish in a while, and it'd sure beat having bologna again. Well, I gotta get some shuteye. Talk later.

Jack

To continue reading THE KEEPER OF STARS, go to:
Amazon

Or, listen on Audiobook:
Audible

Acknowledgments

As always, I would like to thank the individuals who played key roles in shaping this story into what it is today.

To my beta readers, Jane, Carol, and Chloeey, for their time in scrutinizing this manuscript and helping make it the best it can be.

I must also thank my wife, Josette, for her patience and understanding as I delved into the world of Nora, Fred, John, and Rose. None of this would be possible without your love and support.

And last but not least, to my readers your unwavering support is what keeps me writing. You're the best!

About the Author

Buck Turner is the bestselling author of nine novels, including *The Keeper of Stars, A Thousand Distant Shores, Promises Promises, and The Long Road Back to You.* A former IT professional turned writer, he lives with his family in Northern Kentucky, where he spends his free time golfing, drawing, and exercising.

Discover Your Next Read

BUCK'S TITLES:

The Keeper of Stars
A Thousand Distant Shores
Promises Promises
The Long Road Back to You
Between Your Heart and Mine
Evergreen
Losing Adam

Printed in Dunstable, United Kingdom

70095311R00154

Back from the Dead and Back in the Game

My Survival and Recovery from Cardiac Arrest

Paul Feeney

Published by Close Shave Publications 2021

ISBN: 978-1-9168799-0-4

Dedicated to those who formed
the links in my chain of survival.
Without whom, none of this would
have been be possible.

Contents

Just Another Day....11
Aaaaaand I'm Back....29
Out Of The Frying Pan, And Into... Another Frying Pan....37
The Results Are In, And It's Not Good....41
The Zipper Club....47
Doctor's Rounds....57
Enter Stage Left. A Hero....63
'O' Day....73
Post Op. Panic....77
The Worst Kind Of Nurse....81
Catheter Removal (How Not To)....85
Back to '11', Where's Everyone Gone?....89
In The Pink (Literally)....93
A Fluttering Heart Causes Concern....97
Finally, Some Good News....101
More Heart Checks (And More Wires). 103
Panic At Midnight....105
Noooooooo!....109
An Unexpected Surprise....111
Tested To Go Home....115
Home Sweet Home....123
'Schooled' by the 'Pink Blur'....129
I'm No Male 'Gym Bunny', But....133
Back to 'Beechcroft'....137
Return To The Scene....143
Fixed....157
Back In The Game....161
The Birmingham County Regional Trials....171
A Successful Year....177
The WFA Regional Final....179
Last Game Shootout, Who's The Best In The League? ..183
Rock Bottom, The WFA National Finals.. 187
Birmingham WF 'Peaky's On Tour....191
The Year In Short....199
Facing Cardiac Events....201

The Importance Of AED's..205
Acknowledgements...209

"And once the storm is over, you
won't remember how you made it through,
how you managed to survive.
You won't even be sure, whether the
storm is really over. But one thing is certain.
When you come out of the storm , you
won't be the same person who walked in.
That's what this storm is all about."

- Haruki Murakami

Your story could be the key to unlock someone
else's prison. Don't be afraid to share it.

Foreword

There's a popular misconception that cardiac arrest and heart attack are one and the same. They're not.

Although, both relating to the heart. Heart attacks are caused by circulatory problems (i.e. coronary arteries that become blocked, which prevent blood flow from reaching the heart,) whereas cardiac arrest is triggered by electrical problems within the heart.

A heart attack may lead to cardiac arrest if an irregular heartbeat (arrhythmia) occurs, as with the heart's pumping action disrupted, it is no longer able to supply blood to the brain, lungs or other organs.

Sudden cardiac arrest (SCA) can happen to anyone, anywhere and at any time. There is usually no prior warning, with gender, age or ethnicity not being factors. SCA's happen so quickly, that within seconds a victim will lose consciousness and have no pulse. Death will occur within minutes if no treatment is received. Literally, one minute you are alive, the next you are dead.

The survival rate for victims of sudden cardiac arrest is 8%, whereas for heart attack sufferers it is 70 to 80%.

Every victim of sudden cardiac arrest or heart attack has a different story to tell. This is mine.

Just Another Day

It was late afternoon on Friday the 21st of September 2018, and after kissing my wife goodbye, I reversed the car from the drive and set off on the 20 minute trip to 'The Oval', the home of Bedworth United football club.

I was on my way to meet my teammates from Birmingham Walking Football Club and to take part in a charity football game in aid of Prostate Cancer (something that I'd recently been checked for and thankfully been cleared of).

At 6:15pm, I waited for a gap in the oncoming traffic before turning my car off the Coventry Road and into the entrance to the ground.

Then...

[The Referee
"I saw a player go down, so I immediately stopped the game, ran over to where he lay and put him into the recovery position."]

[Mark Gibbons: BWFC over 50's player
"I was playing in a game on another pitch when I looked over and saw a group of people gathered on the next pitch. Something had happened and they looked to be in some distress, so I rushed over.
When I arrived, I could see that a player was lifeless on the ground. I turned him onto his back and proceeded to administer CPR."]

[Mark Welch: BDWF over 50's player
"I heard a commotion coming from the adjoining pitch and I quickly realised that something serious had happened, so I ran to the scene to offer my help. I could see that there was a player on the ground being given CPR, and I helped by performing mouth to mouth resuscitation."]

[Dave Whatmore: BWFC Player
"I had my back to the oppositions goal. Paul was playing in midfield and I noticed him rubbing his thigh. I thought that he had picked up a muscle strain or something. Then he collapsed like a ton of bricks. Everybody swarmed around him. We knew exactly what had happened but felt useless as we didn't know what to do. Looking to the sideline, I could see that my friend was making a call on his

mobile. I just hoped that it was to the emergency services. My friend was an ex-professional footballer (and a manager) who I later discovered was trained in CPR and had seen this type of event before. Then, two people appeared and started administering CPR and mouth to mouth. I thought, thank God that someone knows what to do. They were quickly joined by two women, and with the increase in the number of people involved, there was a general feeling of relief that Paul was now in capable hands. But as we stood there and the minutes passed, it seemed that the CPR wasn't having any effect on Paul. It wasn't looking good. Oh my god is he going to die?

I remember being shocked as the CPR was being performed on Paul and how his body looked like a piece of meat being pounded."]

[Roy Williams: BWFC Player

"We'd been playing for about twenty minutes and the game was going well. Our striker Dave Whatmore had put us three goals ahead and I'd just won the ball in midfield, when I became aware that the referee had stopped the game. Looking around for the reason, I noticed that a blue shirted player (one of ours) was lying face down on the ground, and as I quickly checked around for my teammates, I realised that it was Paul who was down. I knew that by the way he just lying there motionless, that it was serious. I could see that there were no signs of life.

As I approached Paul, he was turned over, and CPR had now started to be performed on him by a woman (who I later discovered was a nurse.) He was clearly struggling to breathe, and I could hear him making a deep snoring sound which then stopped (agonal breathing, or agonal respiration. A medical term for the gasping that people do when they're struggling to breathe because of a cardiac arrest.)

Within a few minutes a man arrived on the scene carrying an AED (automated external defibrillator.) Paul was still receiving CPR as the man prepared the AED by removing the sticky pads from their protective packaging, and then attaching them to Paul's body.

Finally everything was ready, and everyone stood clear as Paul was shocked by the machine. But although Paul's body jumped with the shock, nothing happened. There was no response. It had not worked.

Following this shock, the AED advised that further CPR be administered, as it monitored Paul for any signs of life. We just stood there looking on in dread as they worked and struggled to try and save him. Someone said, "It's OK, he's in good hands, he (pointing to the man who had brought the AED and was now performing CPR). He is ex-military and has done this before over in Afghanistan."]

[Russell Watkin: BDWF Manager
It was clear to us all that the AED shock had done nothing and as we stood on helpless many of the players who were gathered around just turned away with their heads in their hands.
"We all thought, he's dead, there's going to be no

hope of reviving him."

There were other games being played at the time, but they had been stopped, the pitches cleared, and the matches abandoned. What had once been a busy stadium with noisy football games taking place, had now become a hushed shell of a place with vacant pitches. All except one, where a small group of players gathered around a fellow player who lay at their feet motionless, between life and death.]

[Dave Whatmore: BWFC Player

"The quiet was suddenly broken by the sound of a nearby siren.

It was an ambulance and it was close, but then, the sound of the tone suddenly changed as it sped straight past the entrance to the ground. Why is it so damn difficult to see that entrance?

I remember thinking, 'this isn't looking good. Everything's taking far too long! That's it, he's dead.'

Then the siren sound changed again and became louder as it came into view at the far end of the ground. Yes, come on, hurry up!

I heard someone say 'it's been over eight minutes since he collapsed. Does that mean that he could have brain damage?

The AED pads were attached to Paul's body and the machine determined: 'NO LIFE SIGNS PRESENT' Surely, we must now be close to running out of time?

Everybody stood well clear as the AED produced a loud click and a thump and Paul's body jerked in response. But nothing seemed to happen. The machine went through the checks again, searching for signs of a heartbeat. As it did so, it instructed that CPR be resumed.

A short while later, another shock was given to Paul, but looking on, we didn't hold out much hope as there were still no obvious signs of life. But we just when we thought that we had lost him, the 'defib' indicated that a low heartbeat had been detected. NO FURTHER SHOCKS REQUIRED. It said. 'Thank God, does this mean that Paul is going to be OK? Where is the ambulance crew? They seemed to be taking so much time to get from the far end of the pitch to where Paul was laying. "Come on, bloody hell run. Why are you walking? Why is everything taking so bloody long?"

After what seemed like an eternity the crew finally got to where we were all standing and loaded Paul onto a stretcher, which they slowly wheeled to the waiting ambulance. The ambulance remained in the ground for what seemed to be an eternity, perhaps twenty or thirty minutes. Was this a good sign or a bad sign? We just didn't know".]

[Roy Williams: BWFC Player

"We were surprised that the ambulance didn't leave straight away and just sat there for a further twenty minutes. Maybe Paul was still having problems and the medics were having to provide further CPR to keep him alive in the ambulance.

On a personal note, I have never witnessed this type of event before and found it extremely emotional, especially as it involved someone that I'd come to know well. And whilst I would not describe myself as being religious in any way, that day I actually said a prayer for Paul to be saved. Thankfully that prayer was answered".]

[Dave Whatmore: BWFC Player
"With nothing else that we could do and Paul hopefully now in good hands, we all retired to the changing rooms, where we showered and dressed in silence before meeting up in the club bar.

Nobody knew what to say or what to think. Was Paul already lying dead in the back of the ambulance or was he safe and alive in the hands of the paramedics? That night, we received an email from our manager, "Paul is in the Intensive Care Unit. He's currently on a ventilator and his heartbeat is still irregular but it's now under control. Further updates when we know more. 'Thank God that Stuart and Mark from Bedworth were there. The team are so thankful to them. I didn't think that I would ever see Paul again.

Of all the players in the team Paul has the most passion for the game. So I suppose that if you were going to die, then what better way to go than when playing the game that you love.
No. On second thoughts, that's a shit way to go. Only in your early 60's and without the chance to say goodbye to your wife or family".]

[BWFC Manager
"I accompanied Paul in the ambulance to the hospital and was sat in the front seat. All I could hear coming from the back was "come on Paul breathe, breathe for us Paul, stay with us."]

[Roy Williams: BWFC Player
"All the time that Paul was being worked on, we were trying to get in touch with his wife Dawn, but the only contact name we had was for a person called Jenni, (we later found out that Jenni was one of Paul's daughters.) I had briefly met Paul's wife before and I knew that her name was not Jenni, but Dawn, so I volunteered to take the responsibility of calling her. However, I wondered how I would go about breaking such terrible news without panicking and frightening her and I knew that this would be impossible, so I just forged ahead. The conversation went like this:

"Hi Jenny (because of the confusion over the name)"

"Sorry you have the wrong number"

"Is that Dawn?"

"Yes"

"Dawn, its Roy from Birmingham Walking Football. Paul has collapsed when playing football, but don't worry he's alright and an ambulance is going to take him to the hospital.
You need to get to UHCW hospital) as soon as possible".]

[Stuart Roe: Bedworth United Stadium Manager

"I was working in the bar when Karen (a female Bedworth 50's player) ran in, shouting, 'Someone's collapsed on the pitch, we need the defibrillator.' So, rushing to the wall where it hung, we detached it and ran outside and onto the nearby pitches. Thankfully, the incident had taken place on the closest pitch to the bar, so it didn't take long for us to get to the crowd of people who were gathered there. As I arrived, I could see that CPR was already being performed upon the prone figure, so I opened up the AED case, switched the machine on and prepared it for use by attaching the sticky pads to the chest of the patient (who I later knew as Paul.) As the AED started up and ran through a series of checks, I took over the giving of CPR as I awaited the results.

The machine indicated that 'no life signs could be detected' and that the patient was deceased, therefore it would be possible for the AED to deliver a shock (AEDs are deliberately designed not to be able to administer a shock if any life signs are detected in a patient.) I pressed the button and Paul was shocked.

The AED then monitored the results of the shock and checked again for any signs of life. There were none! I therefore resumed the CPR. At one point I heard a loud crack, and thought that I'd possibly broken one (or more) of Paul's ribs, but distressing as that may be, I knew that fracturing a bone whilst giving CPR is secondary to delivering effective CPR that would possibly help to save a patient's life. But

Paul had now been without any signs of life for over eight minutes, and time was beginning to run out.

I heard someone from the crowd say, 'He's gone, we've lost him, shall we stop?' I replied 'No, we don't stop' and I continued to push on, performing CPR, whilst Mark resumed with mouth-to-mouth resuscitation: 'Analysing, shock advised, clear patient. 'And with another push of the button a further shock was delivered into Paul.

Awaiting results...No further shock advised...

YES, thankfully, this time the shock had proved successful, and collectively, we all breathed a sigh of relief as a very low heartbeat had now been detected by the AED. Paul's body had reacted. The emergency services now arrived at the scene, which I was thankful for, as I was dripping with sweat and absolutely shattered with all the effort of helping Paul. The ambulance crew re-confirmed that Paul did now show life signs, but asked me to continue to attend to him while they prepared the equipment in the ambulance that they would need to provide advanced life support."]

There were two ambulances that attended the incident, both coming from the local hospital (George Elliot Hospital in Nuneaton.) Both had been at the end of their shifts and were just about to go off duty when they received the emergency call, and from the time of that call to their arrival at the scene took them only six minutes. Upon their arrival and having made an initial assessment of the incident, the ambulance crews then decided that, rather than take Paul to the local Nuneaton hospital, it would be in his best interests to take him directly to the University Hospital Coventry and Warwickshire (UHCW.) This decision was made on the grounds that UHCW is renowned for having not only a world class heart unit, but also a first rate team of heart surgeons.

This was a major factor in helping to save Paul's life.

Upon arrival at UHCW, Paul was rushed from the ambulance straight into the intensive care unit, where he was put into a medically induced coma.

> *[Medical Note: Patients who have been subjected to and have survived a major trauma such as a cardiac arrest, are often administered a paralytic drug to put them into a medically induced coma. This is done for a number of reasons: The patient's body (being in a paralysed state), is helped to recover by not having to expend any energy or effort on physical movement. This not only reduces any physical discomfort, but also aids in repair to the heart and recovery of the brain (unfortunately, many patients have survived cardiac arrest only to then have permanent brain damage, including some who then have to live in a vegetative state.) So, without any physical movement, the heart is now in a situation whereby the cardiac workload has been greatly reduced, and the heart only has to do the bare minimum, to continue to pump and circulate the blood.*
>
> *During a heart attack a part of the heart will*

essentially die due to lack of oxygen, and surrounding that dead area, there will be an area that is dying, which if not stressed further, will have a better chance for recovery (as the heart requiring less energy to contract is able to use more energy to repair itself.)]

[Dawn Feeney
Today had been another lovely day. We'd just returned from a beautiful holiday in Thailand, and earlier that morning we had been to the local village hall to make a booking for our planned family Christmas party in December. Tomorrow we would be meeting up with our children to discuss the plans for the exciting times ahead.

Everything in life looked to be perfect, but little did I know that it wasn't going to last. Within the next four hours my idyllic world was going to be turned completely upside down. Paul had left home around 6pm to go and play football. He was pretty excited about meeting up with his teammates and getting back on to the pitch again after our holiday break. So having some time to myself, I had arranged to meet-up with a good friend and have some 'me time.' To pamper myself with a face mask and to have a nice glass of wine.

At around 8pm my phone rang.

"Hello is that ???? (unclear)", the caller asked.
Thinking that someone had dialled the wrong number, I was about to end the call when I heard.

"Is that Dawn?"

"Yes, I replied"

"Dawn, It's Roy from Paul's walking football team. Paul has collapsed and has been taken to hospital in an ambulance."

What? I couldn't believe what I'd just heard. I tried to calm myself. I'm sure that it couldn't be anything too serious, he must have just feinted or something.'

But then Roy's words replayed in my head. Collapsed on the pitch? Taken to hospital in an ambulance? Why would they do that? Maybe it's just as a precaution, I thought. I'll go and collect him and bring him home.

"OK, thanks Roy, I'll go and get him."

The eight mile drive from home to hospital seemed to take an eternity, with every set of lights seeming to conspire against me and turn red as I approached. And with every delay at every set of lights, the panic started to set in, bit by bit. Trying to keep myself calm, I told myself, 'He's probably just overdone it a bit, or he's concussed or feinted with dehydration or something, anything!

Arriving at hospital, I was relieved to see that the car park was mostly empty, so pulling into the nearest space, I abandoned the car and ran to the A&E department.

"I'm sorry Mrs Feeney, the ambulance carrying Paul hasn't arrived yet. If you would like to go to the other reception area and wait, it's closer to where the ambulance will pull in."

At the second reception, I explained, "I'm Mrs

Feeney ...," to which I was bombarded with questions, "Are you Paul's next of kin?" "What's his date of birth?" "What's his medical history?" etc. etc. "Thank you Mrs Feeney, you can wait in the family room. Someone will come and speak to you once Paul has arrived."

It seemed like I had waited for an eternity, when the silence was broken by Paul's team manager and his teammates arriving.

"I've just travelled with Paul in the ambulance from the football ground" said the manager. "The doctors have taken him to get him settled."

Settled? What does that mean?

He then said, "Paul was complaining before the game that he'd got pain in his calf muscles, so he massaged some heat cream into them."

Why was he telling me this? It wasn't unusual for Paul to do this before playing. I had the feeling that I wasn't being told the full story. As time dragged on, I was starting to become more and more anxious. They had promised that someone will come and speak to me, so why haven't they? Why was everything taking so damn long. They need to tell me what's happening. I need to be able to see Paul. Eventually a doctor arrived and as he approached, he said, "Please sit down."

I now knew that this was serious. I didn't want to hear, I just wanted to run away. Why won't they just take me to Paul?

The doctor said, "Paul has been made comfortable. But due to him becoming quite agitated, it has been necessary for us to put him into an induced coma to keep him calm. We will monitor Paul closely and carry out further tests to ensure that he hasn't suffered a stroke, and that there aren't any signs of brain damage present. But we won't know for sure until he is awake. Please be prepared for him to possibly not be the same."

My head swam as Paul's manager turned to the doctor, saying, "she doesn't know anything."

The doctor looked at me, "oh I'm sorry, I thought you knew."

"JUST STOP!" I said. "Are you telling me that my husband has had a heart attack?"

The doctor replied, "Yes, and a cardiac arrest."

The room spun. This couldn't be happening. Whatever the doctor said next was just noise that passed over me, everything was just a blur.

"I need to be with Paul, NOW," I demanded.

As we approached the room that Paul was in, a nurse turned to me, "be prepared that Paul has got some tubes and drips attached to him, and although things don't look very good, we are doing all we can to help him." Her warning didn't prepare me for what I saw next.

As I entered, I could see that Paul had been propped up in bed. He was surrounded by, and had been connected to, a mass of electrical equipment, whose purpose was obviously to keep him alive. From these various machines, snaked wires and tubes that had been inserted into him. The sound of Paul's heartbeat beeped from an overhead monitor, and an eerie sucking and clicking sound came from a ventilator that was breathing for Paul, via tubes that disappeared down into his throat. How the hell could this be happening? Paul is so fit and healthy. Activity around the bed was frantic, with doctors and nurses hurriedly rushing back and forth.

Paul's football shirt had been cut from his body, and although he still had one shin guard on, both of his socks were rolled down around his ankles and his football boots lay strewn across the floor. The person that was laid out before me didn't look like 'my Paul'. His eyes were open, but they were cloudy and unseeing. His body was just a shell, unaware detached, helpless and vulnerable, and now fully reliant on others for continuation of his life.

The sight of him lying there like that will haunt me forever. I'd barely had time to catch my breath, when a monitor attached to Paul sounded a shrill alarm, causing the nurse to rush me from the room.

"Is there anybody that you can telephone to be with you?" She said. But my only thought was that I didn't need anyone. I just wanted to be with my husband. On the nurse's insistence, I phoned my daughter Niki's mobile, which was answered by her husband Simon.

Quickly sensing that something was wrong, Simon asked, "Are you OK?"

"No" I replied, "Paul is in hospital. He's had a heart attack."

"We'll come right away" he said.

The nurse spoke again, "Have you got any other

children? They will need to come to the hospital."

Her 'straight to the point' question shook me to the core.

"What, do you mean that Paul might not make it?" I asked.

"Yes. He may not make it through the night."

My worst nightmare was now unfolding before me. Suddenly, my mobile rang and my son Matthew's name appeared on the screen.

I pressed the button to answer but found myself unable to speak. I could hear him talking, trying to reassure me that everything would be alright. "Paul is the fittest and strongest person we know, he will be OK mum." But no words could come out of my mouth in response. Finally my senses kicked back in. Of course, he will be OK, this is Paul, he won't leave me.

"Matt, can you please contact Paul's two daughter's Joanne and Jenni, to let them know?" I was glad of the help, my priority was to concentrate on Paul and not have to think about anybody else.

Before long, I was allowed to return to Paul's room, where thankfully the alarm was now silent.

Happy as I was at being let back in, I was still unable to get close to Paul as his bed was still surrounded by half a dozen people, all frantically working to provide him with assistance. But as I strained to see between the gaps in the crowd, I could at least tell that Paul was still alive. This was backed-up by a reassuring beep that came from the overhead monitor.

Thirty minutes later and I was joined by our

children, who although clearly upset by the sight of Paul, managed to hold it together and show strength and support for one another. I was proud of them, Paul needed us to be strong. It wouldn't help if any of us were to break down now. As time ticked slowly by, activity around Paul lessened, and in the early hours of the morning, he was finally moved out of emergency and into the intensive care unit, where once settled, I asked the children to leave. I wanted Paul to be able to rest, I wanted him to myself.

Everyone kept telling me to go home, to rest and get some sleep, but there was no way I was going anywhere. What if Paul needed me? What if he died? No, I needed to be here in case anything happened. If I'm here with him, Paul will know it and he won't leave me. Eventually, the hospital staff realised that I wouldn't leave, so they arranged for a bed in a nearby private room, promising me that they would awaken me if there was any change in Paul.

Later that morning I was back at Paul's bedside, when a doctor came to see me.

"If Paul remains in a stable condition, we will start to reduce his medication and bring him out of his coma. But due to him being without oxygen for so long, we don't know if he has suffered any damage to his brain. So, once he wakes, there is a chance that he may not be as he was."

I was shocked. Completely numb, and I was more scared than I had ever been in my life. I hadn't even considered this possibility.

I just held onto Paul's hand and I prayed.]

Aaaaaand I'm Back...

It was late afternoon on Saturday 22nd of September, when the drip that was providing me with sleep inducing anaesthetic was slowly reduced, causing me to gradually awaken from my coma.

Looking around (and only being half-conscious), I tried to focus upon my surroundings. The lights seemed to be so bright that they were hurting my eyes. I was laying propped up in bed with electrical wires stuck all over me. Tubes that came from bags, hanging from stands, arced down to disappear under plasters and into my arm. There were doctors in white coats, nurses in blue and other people who were just like me, laying there immobile on their beds.

Rolling my head onto the side, I could see my wife and family. It was then that I realised. I was in a hospital. Focusing on my wife, I asked, "what's happened, why am I here?"

Her (choked) reply came like a hammer blow, "you've had a cardiac arrest while you were playing football."

"What do you mean, I've had a cardiac arrest? No... there must be some mistake."

What she'd said wasn't right. It couldn't be.

Casting my mind back, I searched for a scrap of memory to confirm what I'd just heard. There was nothing. So, without that confirmation, there could only be one other explanation.

"This isn't happening is it. Am I dreaming this?"

My wife replied, "No darling, I wish it was a dream."

Scanning the faces of the other people around me, I hoped to make some sense of it all, but all that came back were pitiful expressions and uneasy smiles. Clearly, something had happened, and it must have been something serious or they wouldn't all be here, but what it was, I hadn't got a clue.

Hearing a rhythmic beep coming from somewhere above, I lifted my head to see a monitor that was flashing orange numbers and a wavy line.

Aargh! A sharp pain lanced into my neck, bringing any further movement to a sudden halt. Bloody hell, what the .... there was something sharp pulling at my throat.

Reaching up, my fingers made contact with half a dozen lengths of plastic tube, that seemed to come together at the base of a thick needle that had been inserted into the side of my neck.

[I was to find out later, that this is called a central venous catheter. An intravenous line that is used when medication is administered directly into a patient's jugular vein.]

All the dangling tubes were hurting like hell, and their

combined weight made them hang down like a plastic chandelier, that swung to and fro and caught on everything possible, constantly pulling at the needle and causing it to move inside the vein. Shit, that hurts!

The sudden pain forced me to lay back down, now only daring to move my eyes in case the jolt came back again. Apart from my now stinging neck, I was feeling absolutely fine. Yes, I was a little groggy from whatever had been pumped into me, but I'm sure that once it had worn off and everyone could see that I was Okay, then they'd probably realise there had been some kind of clerical error, and they will turf me out of bed and pack me off home.

Needless to say, this didn't happen. What did happen though, was a regular procession of nurses back and forth to my bedside. They were taking notes, monitoring dials, sampling fluids, checking numbers and adjusting settings. With no mention whatsoever of when I would be able to leave.

As I lay there, trying to make some sense of what was happening around me, there was an almighty rumble that came from somewhere beneath the sheets. The sound was so loud that it seemed to catch the attention of everyone within earshot causing heads to slowly turn in my direction.

"It's just my stomach" I announced, feeling mightily relieved at the culprit. Then it dawned on me that it had been over thirty hours since I'd last eaten. Little wonder my stomach was grumbling.

That was it. Once this fact was in my head, I

became consumed by hunger and could think of nothing else.

Before I knew it, my mouth opened and, "can I have Kebab and Chips?" spilled out.

Where that had come from, I had no idea, as I very rarely eat Kebab's.

My impromptu food order brought a laugh from my wife. "Sorry, there are no Kebabs. But there is an M&S, a Starbucks and a Subway in the hospital."

"OK, anything from Subway" I said, "you choose, I'll have anything." I was desperate for food.

Fifteen minutes later (and after a painful do-or-die struggle with the swinging Christmas Tree Decoration in my neck), I was sitting up in bed, tucking into the best Chicken Tikka Salad Baguette that I had ever had in my life (well, this new life anyway.)

Later that evening I was starting to concede to the argument that something serious had happened to me. Everyone that I'd spoken to were all saying the same thing. "You had a cardiac arrest and heart attack whilst you were playing football." This was finally reaffirmed, when the nurses who had worked the previous day's, night shift (and had attended to me upon my admittance) started to return to the ward. Upon seeing me, they were overwhelmed that I was sitting up in bed and chatting merrily away.

Several of them approached my bedside and greeted me with big smiles, and chorus's of compliments, congratulations and well wishes.

"Look at you, it's amazing how fast you've recovered" and "how incredible you look compared to when you were brought in last night" they said. Several even confided, "honestly, we didn't think that you were going to make it. We are so pleased for you."

I was taken aback by all the sudden and unexpected attention, plus I was slightly embarrassed that all these people standing before me, and who were showing me such affection, were completely unknown to me. It was clear that they obviously knew me pretty well, but bizarrely, I didn't recognise any of them.

This had me a bit confused. That is, until I was reminded that I was put into a coma as soon as I arrived last night, and had been unconscious for over ten hours. So, by the time I had emerged from my sleep, these nurses before me had all finished their shifts, gone home and had been replaced by the nurses on the day shift. Now it all made sense. It was no wonder that I didn't recognise them. Then a thought came to me. All throughout my enforced slumber, these very nurses had spent countless hours at my bedside, monitoring and caring for me to make sure that I had the best chance of surviving through the night and making it into this morning. It was as a result of their dedication that I was still here, still in the land of the living. So, being the recipient of their accolades made me feel like a bit of a fraud. I hadn't done anything had I? If anything, any praise or acclaim that was due should really be going to them, as well as the surgeons, doctors, paramedics and ambulance crews that had also fought to keep me alive.

[It's a sad fact that the fantastic service provided by the NHS, only seems to get recognised when people find themselves at the sharp end, and are in need of serious healthcare.
When feeling well, we all take it for granted that the NHS will be there to help should we need it, and we don't give much thought for the dedicated but underpaid and undervalued staff who regularly work well over their allotted hours to save lives on a daily basis.
Ironically, at the time of writing this, the UK has entered a state of 'lock down' due to the Coronavirus (Covid19) pandemic, with the NHS now receiving nationwide acclaim, as they put their own lives (and the lives of their families) at risk to help save the lives of the public.
Last night (26/03/2020) at 8pm, across the UK, millions of people stood in the street outside their homes to show their appreciation by applauding the NHS front line staff for their bravery and dedication.
Hopefully this appreciation and recognition of our NHS services, will continue once this pandemic has been beaten.
All I can say is, God bless them for the incredible job that they do! I don't know where we would be without them].

The rest of the evening passed by in a bit of a blur, and despite a valiant effort by my visitors to comfort me, by holding my hand, gazing into my eyes and smiling at me relentlessly (which was all a bit creepy), the drugs finally won the day and I gradually became less aware of my surroundings and slowly drifted off, back to sleep.

It had been a busy day.

Out Of The Frying Pan, And Into... Another Frying Pan

Sunday 23 September 2018

Suddenly, I was awakened by a burst of activity around my bed.

Two or three nurses had sprung into action and were busy collecting everything that lived on top of my bedside locker, putting it all safely inside. This included my water jug and glass, get well cards, tissues, magazines and even my chocolate collection. All the stuff that had become important to me since my arrival.

"What's happening?"

"Getting you ready" said the nurse, "we are moving you out of Intensive Care and upstairs into the Coronary Care Ward."

"That's fantastic" I said, "let's go."

Health wise, I was feeling pretty good, and any advance from the critical care stage of my admission was great news. Life was suddenly looking a lot more promising. Rather naively, I still held onto the hope that after a few days of care, I would be sent home with a few tablets and 'a note for my mum'. Little did I know what was in store for me!

As the hospital porters secured my bed for travel, I looked around for someone to say my farewell's to, but I was surrounded by blank faces. Everyone around me was so medicated and deep within their own personal traumas, that they just lay on their beds like empty husks of people, unaware of their surroundings and with minds that were far removed from the present. The only movement visible were the amber lines that slowly traced across their monitors, accompanied by a metronomic beep that signalled that a life was still being lived.

I hadn't thought about it before, but looking at the scene around me, it struck me that some of these people may not make it back into the world. The Intensive Care ward is like a waiting room between life and death, where drugs, medical expertise, a patient's strength and determination and a large slice of luck all have a hand to determine who makes it out of here and who doesn't. I felt sorry for those I was leaving behind, but there was nothing I could do for them. I could only hope that, like me, they got another chance. But, I had enough worries of my own, I needed to concentrate all my energy on getting better myself, so I just lay back and watched as the white spotty ceiling tiles sped past on the journey to my new home.

Upon arrival in Coronary Care, I was wheeled into a vacant dark corner space and the curtains quickly pulled around, as everything from inside my locker came back out again. Once everything was back as before... Swoosh, the curtains were pulled back like the reveal of a magic trick.

"What the..." This was just the same as where I'd come from. Another dark and depressing windowless room, with everyone laying quiet and motionless on their beds. My heart sank! I'd hoped that: As I was no longer considered to be in danger. And was in a stable condition. And was able to sit up and hold a conversation (plus make short work of a Chicken Tikka baguette), that I would be considered well again and any change in accommodation was going to be an upgrade. But here I was, without a paddle and still up shit creek. Why am I here anyway?

IF I'd had a cardiac arrest, and

IF I'd had a heart attack, and

IF I'd been clinically dead for ten minutes (like they were saying), then why was I feeling Okay? Why was I just the same person that I'd been before?

IF all these terrible things HAD happened, then surely I should be more like these poor sods around me, who spend their days motionless, drugged and asleep in their beds. Whereas I (on the other hand), would pass the time, fully alert, sitting up in bed and looking around like a Meerkat?

But, like it or not, I was outnumbered, and whatever I thought or however I felt, I was now confined to this bleak and demoralising room. Another place where life was so fragile and the distance between life and death wasn't too far. The reality of this was demonstrated only a few days later, when in the early hours of the morning I was awakened by the sound of someone crying at the next bedside.

The curtains had been drawn around, but it was clear

that a number of people were distressed and were having quite a difficult time. I wondered if they had been given some bad news or something, or maybe the man in the bed has woken up and is in pain. But, there wasn't much I could do in any event, I couldn't even leave my bed, so, I blocked out the noise, closed my eyes and focused on getting back to sleep again, making a mental note to talk to him later and try to cheer him up.

The next morning when I opened my eyes, I looked across to the next bed where the noise in the night had come from. It was empty. It didn't even have any sheets or pillows on it.

"Where's the bloke in the next bed gone" I asked,

"has he been moved out?"

"Err, no. Mr ... died during the night" said the nurse.

I was speechless. I hadn't really known this person, but our paths had crossed and we had been brought together in similar circumstances. But now he'd died, only feet away while I'd slept.

Things suddenly became very real for me, and with his death, a realisation of my circumstances hit me like a ton of bricks. I thought: If I was considered sick enough to be put into a ward with patients who were 'just like me' and who have 'similar medical conditions.' And those patients could suddenly die, just like that, then maybe I DO have something seriously wrong with me. It had taken me a few days, but I'd finally accepted the grave situation that I now found myself in.

The Results Are In, And It's Not Good

The next day (Monday the 24th September), and a nurse came to my bedside.

"Morning Paul, we are going to take you down to theatre for an angiogram today."

"Fantastic, I'll look forward to that" said I (with more than a hint of sarcasm), "what's an angiogram anyway?"

"It's where we inject a dye into you, so that we can see how your heart is performing" came the reply.

This was actually the first good news that I'd had (well, obviously apart from when they said, "you died and then came back to life again.) and I was happy that something was going to be done that would explain what had happened to my heart (which incidentally was now on it's best behaviour and ticking away quite nicely.) Within thirty minutes a doctor had appeared.

"Hello, I'm your cardiologist. Have they told you what your procedure will entail today?" he said.

"Nope, not really."

"Well, the correct name for it is, cardio catheterization with coronary angioplasty."

'That would be a great score in scrabble' I thought.

He added, "we will also carry out stenting if necessary."

I had no idea what any of that meant.

"Sorry, you'll have to simplify that for me" I said.

"Well, what we are going to do is: We will insert a tube into a vein in your wrist and inject a dye into it. The dye will then travel up into your heart and will allow us to see what's happening on a monitor."

"What's the stenting bit then?" I asked.

"Well, if an artery of your heart is restricted, we can insert a tiny mesh tube called a stent to keep it open."

"Fine" I said, "But, will I have to be put to sleep?"

"No, you'll be awake throughout. But don't worry, you won't feel a thing. This is bread and butter for me, I do them all the time."

"Is there anything else you'd like to ask?" he said.

"No, I can't think of anything"

"Good, we will see you later then".

And with nothing more to add and with no further questions from me, he was gone.

No sooner had he passed through the doors, than a nurse swooped in and hung a 'nil by mouth' sign above my bed.

"Hang on a minute" I said, "does that mean I won't be getting any breakfast this morning?"

"I'm afraid so. You are not allowed any food or drink for several hours before your procedure" she replied. Bloody hell... What a start to the day.

[Medical note: An angiogram is an X-ray test that uses a special dye and camera (fluoroscopy) to take pictures of the blood flow within an artery

(such as the aorta) or a vein (such as the vena cava.) This procedure is normally performed by inserting a plastic tube (catheter) into the radial artery of the wrist, or the femoral artery in the groin.
The tube is then slid all the way up inside the artery until it arrives at the heart, at which point a contrast dye (which shows up under X-ray) is injected into the tube and a special X-ray camera is moved around the heart area to create a 3D image. The image shows up any arterial narrowing and how bad it may be.]

After what seemed like an eternity of waiting (with a rumbling stomach), two hospital porters finally appeared.

"Paul Feeney?" One of them asked, as he checked out the chart at the bottom of my bed.

"Yep, that's me"

"We are here to take you down to theatre" said the other (as he checked the hospital band on my wrist.)

"OK, I'm ready" said I (snapping the bed's safety belt closed, just in case I flew off on a corner), "let's go." Being certain that I was who I'd claimed to be (and not a nutter who would insanely swap their chart and band with someone else's), the porters positioned themselves front and rear and 'clunk clunk', the brakes were off, and we sped out of the ward, along the corridor, down the elevator and through a set of doors that were signed 'Catheterisation Laboratory.'

[Cath. lab, where 'minor' procedures are performed]

"Hello, I'm your anaesthetist today" came the cheery welcome as my bed came to a halt.

"Let's just make sure that we've got the right person for the procedure" checking my band), and then I'll give you a little something that will help you to relax".

Let's hope it's a rum and coke or a bacon sandwich I thought. But no surprise, it wasn't, and a syringe full of 'happy juice' found it's way into my bloodstream. More doctors then appeared from out of nowhere, and after several minutes of studying my forearm, a discussion took place in which there was much shaking of heads.

"Mr Feeney, we are unable to find a suitable vein in your arm for the procedure, so we will be performing the catheterisation via your groin."

No sooner had they said that, (and before I had a chance to process what it meant), my hospital gown was unceremoniously whipped up and my naked undercarriage was exposed to the world.

Good God, whatever next?

"A little something to help you to relax" he'd said!

Well, I wasn't feeling very bloody relaxed, as I watched the needle fast approaching my prized possession. Thereafter, I just lay there in a daze, unconcerned, not feeling anything and not really knowing or caring what was happening to me. Before I knew it, it was all over and I was once again watching the ceiling tiles rush past overhead, as I was wheeled back upstairs and onto the ward.

Arriving back at my parking space, I could see that my wife was there waiting for me. In fact, she had been there all the time, even when they had taken me down. But with the anaesthetic still active in my system, my brain was completely muddled. I tried to sit up to drink some water, but as I pulled myself up in the bed, there was a sharp pain down in my groin that stopped me dead in my tracks. Gingerly I lifted the sheet and looked down to see two large strips of adhesive plaster, which ran from my lower stomach, into my groin and down onto the top of my thigh.

"What the bloody hell's that?' I said (mentally checking that everything down there was still intact.)

"That must be where they..." began my wife.

But just then, the cardiologist arrived.

"What are the plasters doing in my groin?" I asked.

"Ah" said the doc, "don't you remember? We had to catheterise into your femoral artery"

No, I didn't remember. It felt like I'd been kicked by a mule.

"Well Mr Feeney, the results of your angiogram have shown that you have a severe narrowing in a number of arteries that go to your heart."

"We would normally insert stents into these arteries, but we don't believe that stenting would be a sufficient solution to the problem, therefore a bypass procedure may possibly be required."

What...? I was absolutely staggered. Struck dumb by

what I'd just heard. Last time I'd seen him, he'd said, "we will also carry out stenting if necessary." I specifically heard him say that.

Before I'd been taken down, I'd thought: If there's a problem, they will probably just insert a stent (or two), which will open things up a bit. Now he's saying that putting stents in may not be enough.

Now I was completely shitting myself!

"One of my colleagues will be along to see you soon, to give you a little more information."

And with that he left, leaving me open mouthed and feeling utterly sick.

The rest of the day passed in a mixture of fear and uncertainty, with the words: 'A bypass procedure may possibly be required," playing on continual loop in my head. I was struggling to come to terms with it all.

"I'm not sure I would have surgery to open the arteries," I told my wife.

"I'll ask them again if putting some stents in will make any difference."

"I don't want to have an operation just for the sake of it."

I was looking for any way to avoid this surgery. Grasping at anything that would get me out of this nightmare.

Visitors came and went throughout the evening, but I wasn't good company and contributed little to any conversation. My mind was elsewhere. I was empty and worn out. It had been a day that I wouldn't forget and I was glad when it was over.

The Zipper Club

Sunday 23 September 2018.

The next morning I was on the move again. The porters (who I was getting to know quite well by now) had arrived early, so my bed and I were being whisked to a new ward called 'Step Down'.

Yep, I was sure that I'd heard it right. 'Step Down'. The name sounded awesome, and I was delighted at the thought of being moved further and further out of the danger zone. Away from all the suffering of Intensive and Coronary Care. They were both awful places where lives hung in a state of limbo, as critical care was given to those on the very edge of existence, before waiting and seeing. Either they responded to the treatment (and re-joined the rest of the world) or (in the case of my unfortunate neighbour), they didn't, and they died. It was as clear cut and as simple as that.

But now (thankfully) I was on my way to Step Down. And as I was being wheeled-in through the doors, I was delighted to see that patients here, were either, out of beds and walking around, or relaxing in comfy bedside chairs, or chatting in small groups with others.

Everyday life in this ward was in complete contrast to where I'd just come from. I felt so much better. But as my bed came to rest in it's new space, the nurse set to work reconnecting all my electrics to the monitoring equipment again.

"Excuse me" I said, "Do I still need to have all these wires attached?"

"Yes, while we continue to monitor you."

"So, does that mean that I still can't leave my bed?"

"Yes."

Bloody hell, it's so frustrating! I had finally got what I had wished for and had been moved to more pleasant and relaxed surroundings, but my freedom was still dictated by the length of the bloody electrical wires and plastic tubes that kept me shackled within a two metre bed-space, along with the beeping monitors that checked and reported on me 24 hours a day (just in case I popped off again.) I felt like a prisoner that could see the world 'going on' just beyond arms reach, but wasn't allowed into it.

Once 'plug-in' was complete, I was greeted with a number of warm 'hello's' and friendly introductions.

"What are you in here for?" they asked.

"I don't know" I replied, sounding like an idiot, "I'm having tests, but the results are not certain yet."

"Oh, but you have got a heart problem, haven't you?"

"I'm not sure" I said (wishing the bed sheets would swallow me up).

Further conversation revealed that everyone here on 'Step Down' ward, was either awaiting various heart surgeries (pre-op) or had recently undergone their heart surgery (post-op.) The 'post-op boys' were easy to spot as they all sported livid six-inch long purple scars that ran down the middle of their bare chests. They also wore knee-high white surgical stockings to help prevent Thrombosis, which comically made them look a bit like geriatric schoolgirls. But, looking comical or not, they were the lucky ones. Their operations were now behind them and they had all made it safely out the other side. They had now become members of 'The Zipper Club' (so called, due to their raised scars resembling zippers, which had been the route into their chests.)

Zipper Club members wore their scars like badges of honour and could recognise and relate to 'fellow zippers', who they knew had travelled the same path. There was a kinship that now existed between them. And what was also noticeable, was that, despite the wide spread in ages, (from the early 30's to the mid 70's), there was a tremendous feeling of camaraderie within the group. It was widely acknowledged that despite the differences in age, creed, colour or background, that everyone here shared something in common. And that was, that each and every one of them was in the same life threatening situation, and had now been brought together to undergo life saving, or life changing heart surgery. And with that, came an appreciation for what each other was going through, as well as an understanding of the pain, anguish and fears that they were all facing.

I discovered that everybody on the ward was nearing the end of a standard process, which had started with them experiencing some sort of chest pain, which had then prompted them to make an appointment to see their local doctor. The doctor (not being a heart expert), would invariably have then referred them to see a specialist cardiologist (who is a heart expert.) The cardiologist would then have conducted checks and sent the patient for further tests, (which would unfortunately have confirmed that a heart condition had been detected).

The patient would then have been given the news that he'd been dreading: 'Mr ..., I'm sorry to have to inform you, but ...' A few weeks later, the postman would have made everything official, by pushing a letter of hospital admission through the patients' letterbox, which would then wind up as a hot date with the heart surgeon.

My arrival at the hospital hadn't been anything like theirs. I had arrived in very different circumstances. Those being: In a critical condition and in the back of an ambulance with blue flashing lights. I never told anyone this and I was never asked (I suppose it was taken for granted that everyone arrived in the same way), but it didn't take long for gossip on the 'hospital grapevine' to get around, and it was soon revealed that I was the only one on the ward who'd been admitted in an emergency situation.

The result of this, (through no wish of my own,) was that I seemed to become a bit of a minor celebrity, which resulted in patients appearing at my bedside to ask questions like, "Did you really die?" And, "What was it like when you were dead?" And 'Did you see anything?" Or, "Could you hear anything?" And, "Did you feel it when they shocked you?" And a multitude of other death and after-life related enquiries. It didn't bother me answering all of their questions or even having to constantly re-live my experience to them. Everyone was just curious, and to be honest, I would have asked the same questions had I been in their shoes (or in this case slippers).

Later that day, my 'celebrity status' was elevated further when my wife was overheard telling me that 'my event' was now being reported in the local newspapers, (the Coventry Telegraph, Bedworth Echo and Nuneaton Tribune) as well as appearing on their respective websites. I was unsure how I felt about this. I had mixed feelings.

On the one hand, I was pleased to know that the value of having portable defibrillators available in public places, had been demonstrated so effectively, and hopefully with the story having a successful outcome, this may then encourage 'decision makers' within these places to install AED's themselves, which would then help to save further lives. I was also happy that the staff and players at Bedworth on that day, were receiving the accolades that they truly and rightfully deserved. BUT, the unsolicited reporting of my 'event' had also left me feeling a little aggrieved. I felt that what had happened to me had been a very personal affair, the details of which were now being blurted out very publicly to a very wide audience. Furthermore, the journalist who had dug deep to report the darkest day of my life, had acted without my knowledge or consent, with no regard for my privacy and without the decency to ask me if I wanted the whole world to know what had happened to me.

And if I did want them all to know, then surely it was my privilege and my place to do it, not theirs.

Maybe my biggest problem with the newspaper article lay with me still having no recollection or knowledge of what had happened. But here it was in black and white, a blow-by-blow account, now being told to everyone by a complete stranger.

The public reporting of my incident left me feeling uncomfortable and very exposed.

25 September 2018 – Coventry Telegraph, Bedworth Echo and Nuneaton Tribune Newspapers and website report

Quick-thinking footballers praised for saving life of player who collapsed on the pitch

Quick-thinking footballers managed to save the life of a fellow player who collapsed on the pitch during a charity game at Bedworth United.

Two members of the Walking Football team at The Oval, as well the stadium manager, literally had to put their life-saving skills into practice when a player collapsed on the pitch.

It was a member of a Birmingham Walking Football team who collapsed during a fundraising match in aid of Prostate Cancer at the home of the Greenbacks on Friday.

Russ Watkin, a director at the club, explained: "A

gentleman collapsed on the pitch - the game was stopped by the ref and we quickly realised he had had a heart attack."

The stadium manager and two other members of the Walking Football team started administering CPR and then they shouted for the defibrillator.

"It happened about 40 yards away from where it (the defibrillator) is kept outside the club house," he explained.

"It seemed liked hours but it was actually only seconds that the whole thing happened.

"Normally it is just something we all just walk past but on Friday night, without it (the defibrillator), the man would not be here right now."

The trio continued to work on the man while calls were made to West Midlands Ambulance Service, which sent two ambulances in just six minutes.

"They (the three) managed to get his heart started again and found a pulse and then the paramedics arrived," Mr Watkin added.

"The ambulance services were brilliant, they sent two ambulances in about six minutes and soon took him off."

The player, who has not been identified, was taken to the University Hospital Coventry and Warwickshire, where he is still receiving treatment.

"His wife came to pick up his car, she was so thankful and there were a few tears. I am just so glad that we were able to help him, hopefully he will be OK," the director added.

"His teammates said he was the fittest one among them. He had just got back from holiday and was as strong as an Ox, that just goes to show that this can happen to anyone".

The Walking Football community across the Midlands has united in their response to the shock incident on Friday night.

"My phone did not stop pinging all weekend. The concern that has been shown I think is a compliment to the walking football league we have," he said.

"So many people wanted to see if he was OK and say well done to our players. You don't expect to have to use a defibrillator, but when it happens it shows just how important they are."

He paid tribute to the players who stepped in to help: "They were incredible. I am so glad that they did their training," said Mr Watkin, who is himself a member of the award-winning Walking Football team.

"I would recommend anyone undertake the CPR training and the British Heart Foundation training too. I know that defibrillators can be expensive, but this just goes to show how important they are."

A spokesman for West Midlands Ambulance Service said: "CPR was being carried out prior to our arrival, a defibrillator was in use, ambulance staff took over and performed advanced life support.

"Crews managed to successfully re-start the man's heart prior to arrival."

He went on to add: " West Midlands Ambulance Service would like to take the opportunity to praise the actions of the quick-thinking bystanders who started CPR prior to our arrival.

"Every second is vital when trying to save someone's

life and by starting to treat the man with the help of a defibrillator, they helped to give him the very best chance of survival.

"We would encourage anyone who can, to undertake first aid training, as one day it could be your turn to try and save a life."

On a psychological note: I've started to have this fear that I'll be judged as being weak to have suffered a heart attack, plus I have also started to relive the scene in my head, becoming upset (maybe embarrassed) that I'd lain helpless on the ground in front of a crowd of people whilst my life hung in the balance.

I know that these emotions are irrational and completely unjustified, but no matter how many times I'm told 'don't worry, it's quite normal to feel like that after what's happened to you', I still have these feelings all the same. Maybe it's the cocktail of drugs that are making me overly emotional, but It's hard to come to terms with the thought that I'd simply gone out to play a game of football with my mates, and one minute everyone was happy and having fun, and the next I was dead, and they were having to witness it. Enough. Come on Feeney, snap out of it. Stay positive.

Needing a distraction from the dark thoughts, I picked up my book and settled back to lose myself within its pages. But no sooner had I started reading, I was distracted by a noise, which happened to be a man in a white coat pushing a trolley towards my bed. As he drew near, he told me his name, but I wasn't paying much attention as I was too busy checking to see if he was the bearer of my long-awaited dinner. No such luck. The trolley contained only surgical supplies, rolls of plaster, bandages, scissors, tape etc.

"I'm here to remove the plasters from your procedure yesterday" he said.

"Ah, that's good, they've been pulling at the hair every time I move."

I pulled the bed sheet back to expose the two long plasters that covered the spot where the catheter had been inserted during the angiogram. They began on my stomach, passed through my groin and ended on my thigh.

"Well, you can have a free wax then" he smiled, as he gripped the top of the plasters. And before I knew it, he had quickly raised his arm into the air.

"aargh, bastard!" I said, looking down at the smooth landing strip along the side of my groin.

"You've given me half a bloody Brazilian."

"Look at that, I've got one bald testicle and one woolly one"

"What kind of an idiot would trap someone's nut sack under a sodding plaster?" Needless to say, I was less than impressed!

He gave me a sorry smile, and with a clear sense of accomplishment and his mission now complete, he reversed his trolley and made off before I could launch further expletives in his direction, leaving me to sadly inspect my now glowing plums.

Doctor's Rounds

26th September 2018

The next morning, I was rudely awakened at 6:30am (despite not having ordered an early wake up call.) It was something they called 'Doctor's Rounds,' and although I hadn't heard of this before, it's when a gang of specialist doctors, (and one not quite so specialist who just pushes the drugs trolley), visit each patient in turn, flip through their notes and discuss with them, their ailments and their individual medical programs.

> *[They told me that the collective noun for a group of doctors was 'a dose of doctor's, but I'm not having that.]*

So, without any apology for the noise, this crowd of white coated professionals bomb burst onto the ward like a detachment of SAS and pounced on the unsuspecting patient in bed one. Poor bloke, he'd only just woken up and hadn't even had time to do his hair.

"Morning Mr J...., how are you feeling today, shall we ..."? etc.

Next patient.

"Hello Mr B..., is your ... still giving you trouble?" etc. The scene continued as I watched them out of the corner of my eye as they made their way up the ward. Finally it was my turn and the head doctor approached my bed, where he picked up and examined the notes on my clipboard.

"Aaah, Mr Feeney"

"Firstly, I would like to congratulate you on being here."

"Oh, thanks" I said, nodding my head (I hadn't a clue what he meant. Maybe it was because I'd managed to snag a bed by the window.)

"We will continue to monitor you following the result of your angiogram."

"Err, OK" said I, "so no chance of going home then?"

"No Mr Feeney, not today."

As he replaced my clipboard, I'm sure I heard him chuckle as he turned away. Then he was gone.

A short while later, the nurse came to see me, bringing with her a bowl of water, a wash-cloth and a towel. My heart sank, oh God it was wash time. Out of all the discomforts I was facing, wash time was the worst. The procedure consisted of: Drawing the curtain around the two inner sides of my bed (as the other side was a window.)

Standing next to the bed, on a towel, starkers and 'tackle out', whilst wiping myself down with a flannel from a bowl of lukewarm water. All the time, the chandelier of tubes swung to and fro (making the hole in my neck even bigger,) whilst doing their best to tangle up with the six coloured electrical wires (oh, didn't I mention those?) that had recently been attached to my body with super sticky pads, and which connected to yet another monitoring box that hung on a tape around my neck.

Every morning I would stand there naked and thoroughly miserable as streams of cold water cascaded down my legs, whilst wires and tubes dangled, tangled and swung in the breeze, making me look like a busted robot. And all throughout my wash, the pigeons on the window ledge looked in, laughing. Bastards!

During today's wash, I was concerned to see that the whole of my groin and down most of my leg was now covered with a large and vivid purple and yellow bruise. The doctor had previously warned, 'It's common to expect the angiogram procedure to leave a little bruising.'

'Leave a little bruising?' It looked like I'd been hit by a car.

Morning wash accomplished, I got dressed, opened the curtains and sat back in my bedside chair.

“Are you finished Mr Feeney, shall I take your bowl?”

“Yes, all done thanks”. “Nurse? There's something confusing me.”

“What's that” she said.

“Well, earlier this morning, when the doctor came to see me, he said: 'Congratulations on being here.' What did he mean by that?”

The nurse smiled and replied, “when people are brought into the hospital through the emergency route and in the condition that you were in. They are only given a 1 to 3 percent chance of survival and they don't usually make it here onto the ward."

Wow, I was lost for words.

9:30am, breakfast is over, and the sun has broken out, streaming through my window and lighting up the ward.

And as I sit here, bathed in sunlight and in my comfy chair, my thoughts start to wander, as I gaze at the gently swaying trees and the green fields that stretch all the way into the distance, and to the banks of Coombe Abbey fishing lake, which is just a few miles down the road.

What am I going to do today, I'm pretty sure that I don't have any pressing engagements? Wouldn't it be nice to be out in the fresh air?

Between me and you, they've made a big mistake by putting me next to the window and letting me see the outside world. They think that it will be visually stimulating for me. But little do they know, that when I'm bored, I have a dark and mischievous side that is awakened.

My present thoughts are not, 'ooh, look at the lovely countryside or aah, look at all the various birds (meaning different coloured pigeon's.) No, I'm thinking more like: OK, I don't have anything on for today, so maybe, it would be a good time to arrange an escape! What if we get a few of the lads together, 'borrow' an Ambulance and all go fishing at 'Coombe?' We wouldn't have to be gone for that long and could even be back for lunch. Just enough time for us to catch a few fish and have a bit of a change of scenery. And anyway, the fresh air would do us all good.

Now we just needed a driver. I beckoned to a few of what I deemed were the 'most likely candidates', and put my splendid idea to them, but what I had thought to be a feasible plan seemed to fall on deaf ears, with them all thinking that I was quite mental.

In hindsight, maybe they were right. The image of us all standing in a line fishing, in our slippers and 'tie up the back' green hospital gowns (with our bums showing) is a vision that would have been quite disturbing, especially had it made tomorrow's newspaper. I can see the headlines now: 'Heart op gang do hospital runner to 'hang out' at popular fishing spot'.

Enter Stage Left. A Hero

Thursday 27th September 2018

Today a man came to my bedside, and after shaking my hand, he proceeded to introduce himself.

"Hello, My name is Mr Tom Barker. I'm a cardiothoracic surgeon (easy for him to say), and I will be the person who'll be looking after you".

[Note: A cardiothoracic surgeon is a specialist who operates on the heart, lungs and other thoracic (chest) organs. As well as performing surgery, they also diagnose and treat diseases of these organs.]

He looked just like an ordinary bloke, aged mid to late 30's and dressed in normal clothes of chequered shirt, casual trousers and Crocs. You know, the kind of stuff you'd wear everyday (well, not Crocs! Unless you live on the beach or have limited fashion sense.)

Mister? A Cardiothoracic Surgeon? To look after me? Now I don't want to seem pernickety, but if I were to be choosing a medical professional to 'look after me', then first off, I would obviously plump for a Doctor (not a Mister), that's a no-brainer right?

Furthermore, they would ideally be dressed in a long

white coat (without bloodstains), have a stethoscope around their neck and boast a full set of coloured pens sticking out from their top pocket. That would seem like the bare minimum to me. Anyway, what the hell's a Cardiothoracic Surgeon, and how come I need one to 'look after me'?

[Note: My ignorance was later corrected when I discovered the meaning behind the different salutations in the medical profession and the use of the title Mr. versus Dr.
Surgeons who have passed examinations and are Fellows of one of the Royal Colleges of Surgeons are called Mr. and are Surgical Doctors rather than Medical Doctors (who are called Dr.)
Medical doctors are mainly concerned with diagnosing and treating medical conditions i.e. diseases that can be treated with medicines, whereas Surgeons diagnose and treat conditions which need surgical intervention to cure them.
In the UK, it is common practice for a doctor working in a more surgical speciality to have the title 'Mr'.
With hindsight, I now realise that I had done Mr. Barker a great disservice and for that I truly apologise. It was an uneducated and improper assumption of someone who I consider as being one of the most important men to have touched my life].

"Well, Mr Feeney (whoa! Not a good way to begin a sentence, I thought.) As you are aware, the results of your recent angiogram have indicated that you have three coronary arteries that are showing signs of being dangerously narrowed. This narrowing would undoubtedly have reduced the flow of blood to your heart, and would most likely have been enough to have caused your recent cardiac arrest. Your arteries are not constricted through the accumulation of fatty deposits (which are normally associated with poor diet), but have merely been constricted in their width due to age."

Mr. Barker went on to say. "From your medical records I am aware that both your father and brother died from 'heart attacks' at the ages of 62 and 56 respectively. Therefore, it is always a possibility that a hereditary condition may exist within your family, and that one day this affliction could potentially effect you."

I have got to admit that I'd always been aware of this possibility, but I'd hoped that by living a life of regular exercise and with a good diet, that maybe I could have 'dodged the bullet' and the Feeney curse' would hopefully have passed me by.

But clearly this wasn't to be, so I now took consolation in the thought that, I had experienced and survived my cardiac arrest and now I was feeling Okay again. Just like I had been before. It was then that Mr Barker dropped the bomb.

"We will therefore be performing a triple heart bypass on you."

There it was, the news that I had always dreaded. I did have a heart condition just like my dad and brother before me. I felt sick. I just sat there open mouthed and feeling completely numb as I listened to him, quite matter of factly, and very calmly outline the procedure that I was very soon to undergo.

"The procedure will take place on Monday (1st October 2018, in four days time.) And following five to seven days of monitoring (to make sure that all is well,) you will then be able to go home. The surgery will take approximately five hours to perform, during which, we will remove veins and arteries (called grafts) from your leg [greater saphenous vein] and chest [internal mammary artery.]

Your chest will then be opened up and your breastbone cut through and spread open to expose your heart beneath. Your blood will then be re-routed though a heart-lung bypass machine, (which will continue to provide your body with blood and oxygen), whilst we stop your heart and attach the new grafts onto it. These grafts will then take over diverting the blood supply to your heart and bypass the blocked arteries. Your heart will then be re-started with controlled electric shocks. Your breastbone will be fixed together again using permanent stainless-steel wires, and finally the skin on your leg and chest will be sewn up again".

Mr Barker underlined it all with. "Obviously a heart bypass procedure is not without it's risks, but it is something that is performed every day and which has an excellent rate of success."

I was absolutely terrified by what I'd just heard.

"Do I have to go through with this operation?" I asked.

"Yes, if you don't, you are putting yourself seriously at risk of having another cardiac arrest, but next time you may not be so lucky as to survive it."

My head spun with a million different emotions. I was baffled how, in such a short space of time, my life could have changed so much. Only ten days ago I was enjoying a holiday in Thailand without a care in the world, then I returned home and six days later, I'd been playing in a charity football match when I'd collapsed and died following a cardiac arrest. Fortunately, I had been revived and rushed to hospital, where I was beginning to believe that I'd been nursed back to good health. But now, I'd just been told that I had to undergo a major surgical procedure if I didn't want to risk dying again. So much for my hope of them 'pushing a couple of stents in.' I was completely unprepared for this 'solution' to be so graphically laid out in front of me. But on the bright side, at least I was still here with a chance of a solution. I'm sure that it's difficult at any time to give consent to have heart surgery performed on you. But it's bloody hard to give it when you are feeling perfectly fit and healthy.

But, what choice was there given the alternative? Firstly, I owed it to my wife and family not to put them in a position whereby they would be living in constant fear that I could possibly collapse and die at any time.

Secondly, I also believed that I owed a debt of gratitude to all the people who'd shown the courage to 'step-up,' and help to save my life only a few days ago.

Looking up at Mr Barker, I nodded my head in resigned acceptance. “Okay”.

Once Mr. Barker had gone, I just lay there on my bed. I was overcome with emotion and shed a few tears as I tried to come to terms with what I'd just agreed to. A hollow, sickly feeling lay in the pit of my stomach and I knew that I wouldn't be able to face this alone. Hopefully, by sharing the burden, then maybe it would somehow ease the turmoil that was going on inside my head.

Retrieving my phone from the bedside table I messaged my wife to tell her about Mr. Barkers visit and the awful news that I'd just been given. I couldn't help myself and I let it all out, flooding her with a barrage of messages in which I poured out all my fears:

'I don't want to be put back to sleep', 'I don't want them to cut me open', I don't want my heart to be stopped', 'I don't want a f***ing operation' and so on. When my outburst had finally subsided (and I'd got all of the I don'ts out of my system), she calmly explained to me: “Having this operation is going to put things right. All of the things that have hung over our heads and that have worried us for all of these years. They will be gone. Look, nobody wants to lose you, and everyone wants you here with them for many years to come. So, if you want the best chance of giving them and yourself that, then you've got no other choice but to go ahead with the operation. Yes, I know it's a massively scary thing to have done to you, but Mr. Barker is the best there is, and he performs this surgery every single day. Everything is going to be okay and in the long run. It will all be for the best."

My wife's word's were like an epiphany and slowly everything started to become clear. I realised that it wasn't just about me and my fears, I'd also got other people's feelings to consider as well. She was absolutely right. There really was no other choice but to go ahead with the operation. Her explanation was like a switch had been thrown, and with it I became resigned for what was to come. Wiping my eyes, I looked around at my fellow patients. They all seemed perfectly happily getting on with hospital life and even seemed untroubled as to the reason why they were here. How can they carry on as normal when they know what lies in store for them? I thought. Why did my feelings seem so very different to theirs?

Later that evening I mentioned this in conversation, and the answer I got back was obvious.

"You've only just received the bad news about having to face heart surgery, whereas we've all known for months that we were coming into hospital. We've been expecting it for months and have had considerable time to mentally prepare for it. You on the other hand, coming in as an emergency and then being told (within 6 days) that you need a heart operation, hasn't given you that time to prepare."

What they said made complete sense. Months ago,

they had all faced the same fears and battled the same demons that now confronted me. It would seem that as time has passed, their initial fears had eased somewhat and the feeling of utter dread that would have once gripped their stomachs had subsided. Time had allowed them to accept their situation. Now I had to accept mine.

The next few days passed by in a whirlwind of checks, tests and monitoring in preparation for the big day. I started to gain strength by watching those around me, both the pre-ops, who like me were on countdown, and the post-ops who had been returning to the ward every day following their successful procedures. Seeing how everyone came together as a group to help each other, give support, provide encouragement and lift one another's spirits was inspiring. There were no individuals on the ward. We were all in it together, and nobody had to face this difficult time alone.

As 'O day' drew nearer, I could feel my worries starting to disappear and I was becoming much more relaxed. Dare I say it, I actually wanted 'my turn' to come around. Now that I had accepted that it was going to happen, I just wanted to get on with it.

On the eve of the operation a nurse came to my bedside brandishing a pair of electric hair clippers.

"We need to shave your body hair and the hair from your legs in preparation for your procedure tomorrow. Do you want me to do it, or would you prefer to shave yourself?" She asked.

"I'll do it myself" I quickly replied (as I was still

traumatised by the last body hair experience) and I reached out to take the shaver from her. She laughed, "I'll pull the curtains around, so you can have some privacy, let me know when you're finished."

I swung my legs out of bed and switched on, 'buzzz', and somewhat reluctantly I set about the task ahead, slowly taking my time with each stroke to make sure that I did a thorough job (I didn't want to end up all stripey did I?) And I didn't stop until my chest and legs were as smooth as a Dolphin's beak. Turning the shaver off, I looked down to check out my handy work and I slowly shook my head in despair. Throughout my life, I have been proud to have sported a well groomed, manly, hairy chest, but now standing here, I just looked like an overgrown baby. The last shreds of my dignity lay in a heap of hair on the floor. I had more hair on my one surviving woolly bollock than I had on the rest of my body.

It was a sad day.

'O' Day

It was Monday the 1st of October 2018, and I was awoken at 6:30am by the ward slowly coming back to life. As soon as my eyes were open the first thing that entered my head was: 'Today's the day. The day of my operation. It's finally here.'

Laying there, I was feeling pretty good and felt comforted with the thought of: By the end of the day, one way or another, it will all be over. There will be no more waiting and no more worrying, Mr. Barker was going to put things right, and all I've got to do is to be there for that to happen. Friends and family have been saying that I'm brave to face such an operation, but bravery really doesn't come into it. Realistically, when it's all laid out in front of you, it all comes down to two choices: Either you turn away and risk living a life in constant fear of what may happen, or you face the problem head on, put things right and hopefully live your life without further worry. For me, there was only one way to go.

I no longer felt any fear in having this operation (that had been overcome during the last few days,) but I admit to being acutely aware that I was having a five-hour surgical procedure in which my heart would literally be in someone else's hands.

Now that the day was here, I just wanted to get things underway, to get it all over and done with. But the day was passing slowly as I watched everyone tuck into their breakfast (I wasn't allowed any), followed by morning wash routine (which I hated), then Doctor's Rounds (which didn't include me), and finally the 11am Tea and Biscuit break (which I was also banned from.)

But eventually, the hands of the clock both met at midday and two hospital porters appeared by my bed to take me down to the operating theatre. My time had come. There was no turning back!

After following my usual route downstairs, I found myself being pushed through some doors and into a small room adjoining the operating theatre. Here I was met by the anaesthetist, who introduced herself and explained the steps that would be necessary to put me to sleep in preparation for my surgery. Her voice was extremely calming, putting me at immediate ease, and I guessed that her caring and understanding manner came from years of dealing with patients who had lain here feeling scared to death. Removing the bed sheet, she looked down at my smooth-shaven (large baby) body.

"You've done a magnificent job of shaving everywhere" she said.

"Oh, thank you" I said proudly, "I took my time to make sure that I didn't miss anywhere."

Then her lips creased into a slight smile.

"Mr Feeney, you did know that you only had to shave your chest, plus one leg, didn't you?"

Shit. They never told me that!!

When she had finished talking and had turned away, I raised my head to catch a glimpse through the open doors and into the operating theatre beyond. I was surprised to see how small it was. It was nothing like the huge expanses of shiny steel and overhead lights that you see in the movies or on TV. But although small in size, it was filled wall to ceiling with every conceivable piece of equipment needed to sustain life whilst a human body was being fixed. In the middle of it all and dominating the scene was a big stainless-steel table with lights overhead, which gazed down like giant eyes. I couldn't help but think, “I'll be on that table, under those lights soon.”

Theatre staff in different coloured gowns were buzzing everywhere. I was amazed by just how many people were going to be involved. They all had a role to play specific to them, and each had their own work area. They were each one piece of a puzzle, that when linked together with others, formed the complete jigsaw of skills that were needed to make up a modern operating theatre. And today, they were all there just for me, and I was greatly appreciative.

I heard the anaesthetist's voice, “Paul, I'm just going to give you an injection that will put you to sleep. I want you to slowly count down from Ten, okay?”

“Yep. Ten, nine, eight ...”

Post Op. Panic

(Choking) I can't breathe, I can't breathe. Panicking, I looked left and right, looking for someone to help me. My wife's voice rang out, "Paul, its okay, I'm here. You've had your operation, it's over."

I tried to talk back, but couldn't. Pointing to my throat I croaked, "I can't breathe, I can't get any air. There's something stuck in my throat."

Gasping, I frantically made the hand signal for writing, and a pen and paper was quickly produced. 'I CAN'T BREATHE' I wrote, still desperately trying to get some air into my lungs.

I wasn't aware at the time, (and hadn't been given any prior warning), that during my surgery I'd been put onto a ventilator to help breathe for me. This apparatus consists of a 'breathing machine' with a connected ET (endotracheal) tube which is placed through your mouth and into your trachea (windpipe).

Fighting for breath, I thought that I would choke to death and seriously considered ripping the whole thing out of my throat. Seeing the commotion, a nurse appeared at the bedside.

"He's saying that he can't breathe" said my wife. The nurse looked at me. I was on the edge of panic and pleaded with my eyes. Please take it out.

"Yes, he can breathe fine" said the nurse. "The ventilator is just to help him recover after his operation. The tube will have to stay in place for 30 minutes more, and it can then be removed when Paul can show that he is able to breathe on his own. But if he continues to panic, then we will have no choice but to put him back to sleep again."

Whoa! Now she had my full attention! Being put back to sleep again was something that I definitely didn't want (especially as I'd only just come back), so having no choice other than to force myself to relax, I lay back and tried to slow my breathing, trying to put all of the discomfort to the back of my mind. My wife helped calm me further, by reminding me of a special moment that we'd shared in the Maldives. And so, I concentrated on her words as I watched the clock tick slowly by.

Waking up to feel my throat blocked and being unable to breathe, was the most traumatic experience of my life. It was sheer panic.

But it wasn't my only discomfort. There's a line in a pop song by the artist called Pink, that says, 'all that morphine's making me itch.' Well, I can tell you from first-hand experience that those words are not an understatement. The constant itching was driving me crazy, turning me into a mad man as I tried to remove every piece of skin that flared-up in response to the drug. And by the end of the day, I considered myself lucky to have had any skin left on me at all.

As well as making you feel like there's a million bugs crawling all over you, morphine can also raise your temperature to astronomical levels and does a terrific job of making you feel violently ill, with projectile vomiting high on its list of specialities. I don't know what was worse, the pain from the surgery I'd just had, or the morphine to ease that pain.

On second thought, yes I do. I'll rather keep the pain thanks.

I also came out of surgery sporting a new and extremely large purple scar. It began at my ankle and progressed up my leg to my knee, and then continued a further six inches from my knee up my thigh. This was where the greater saphenous vein had been removed, so that it could be used as a 'graft' to replace the blocked arteries around my heart. Yes, I had been aware that they would be 'taking a piece of vein' from my leg, but I was bloody surprised that they needed three foot of it. You could do some skipping with that much!

With no vein, what's supplying the blood to my leg now then?

The Worst Kind Of Nurse

Following a night in which I had remained stable, my bed was relocated to a side ward of Intensive Care and I was placed under the 'care' of a senior nurse, who can only be described as an absolute cow.

She was a short, rotund and stern looking woman with a large ample chest (that would appear on the ward several seconds before she did), and when she was 'on shift', she would demonstrate her authority by being brash, rude and arrogant.

Being unable to divulge her name, but believing her to be the most impatient, inconsiderate, insensitive, uncaring, unfeeling, conceited and heartless nurse at the hospital (did I miss any?) I will therefore refer to her as Nurse Worst.

Now, as most people will be aware, a patient who is spending time in Intensive Care will, more often than not, be in a critical condition, and therefore, they will probably just lay motionless on their bed. But, unfortunately, this immobility brings with it the possibility of painful pressure sores forming (often called bed sores), where a patient's skin has been subjected to prolonged pressure.

To help prevent this condition, it is recommended that an immobile patient is physically moved, so that their body position is made to change on a regular basis. Well, here is where my trouble with Nurse Worst began. At this time (and to my misfortune) Nurse Worst had been tasked with 'showing the ropes' to a young foreign junior student. The student shadowed the teacher everywhere that she went, and Senior Nurse Worst relished in this opportunity to show her experience, share her knowledge and give the young girl the benefit of her vast and endless advice. BUT, there was a negative in this arrangement: With nurse Worst holding such a position of power and being considered as 'the Oracle of all knowledge' by her student, the ego of the Senior Nurse had inflated to astronomical proportions. And with her high self-image (and when in the company of her student), there was a tendency for Nurse Worst to perform everything she did, in an extreme, exaggerated and often unnecessary manner.

After breakfast, Nurse Worst' and her student approached my bed.

“Mr Feeney, are you able to turn your body from your side, onto your back, and back onto your side again?”

“I think so” I said, as I slowly started to do what she had asked.

“Hmm, you're struggling somewhat, aren't you?”

I felt like saying, 'well, that's probably because I've just had a f***ing heart operation.'

The teacher turned to her pupil “This is how we would perform a bed roll-over.” And with that, she took a folded sheet and pushed it under my body, gripped one side of it with both hands, and pulled sharply upwards, causing my body to quickly roll onto it's side.

Aargh! This sudden movement sent a sharp pain into my chest. Having the entire weight of my body pushed from one side to the other was agonizing. It not only stretched all my stitches to their limits, but also forced all of my weight to press down on a breastbone that had recently been cut up the middle. The whole process had been conducted as if the 'Senior' had been demonstrating 'her technique' on a rubber training dummy and not on a real person. It was performed without care or compassion.

I was speechless at what she had done. I'd had no warning or time to prepare for such a movement. It had been completely unnecessary. And had she given me just a little more time, I'm positive that I could have achieved the same manoeuvre myself without all the pain.

Yes, I'm sure that she has probably performed that same procedure a million times before, but just because it may have become routine to her, it doesn't make it acceptable to perform it roughly and without care on a vulnerable and weak patient as part of 'her demonstration.'

Job done, she walked away, leaving me on my side, facing the wall.

Later that day, a doctor prescribed me some tablets that would help my body to pass water, and flush any residual chemicals from the operation out of my system. This medication was brought to me by Nurse

Worst, who one hour later, gave me some more, and then more again throughout the day. Every few hours seemed to be either bladder flushing tablets, or a session of full contact Olympic speed bed rolling (or sometimes both). And it came as a great relief when the nursing shift ended and she left the ward, mounted her broomstick and flew home to a no doubt scared shitless and quivering husband.

The nurse who arrived to replace her came straight to my bed and introduced herself.

"Hello, I'll be here to look after you throughout the night. If there's anything that you need, just press the buzzer. I'm just around the corner and I will be with you straight away."

Well, this was a bit different. She was sensitive, gentle and compassionate. A total contrast to the pompous and overbearing cow that had just gone home. And with the change in shifts, a curtain of peace descended over the ward. My body still had to be 'turned' throughout the night, but I was awoken gently, with the nurse allowing me to perform this process slowly by myself, only assisting if needed. A proper nurse.

Catheter Removal (How Not To)

During a visit by the nurse the next morning, she was alarmed to find that my urine bag (I'd had a urinary catheter fitted during my surgery), had been completely filled to capacity, and that I had passed over 5 litres of urine since the previous evening. This was far from normal and was considerably more than what they had been expecting. Nobody told me directly why this had occurred, but I heard it suggested that I had been given far too many tablets (by Nurse Worst) the previous day.

The effect of passing so much urine in such a short space of time, meant that the potassium levels in my body had now plummeted to a dangerously low level, and in order to correct this, I had to be prescribed with yet another tablet.

I had just settled into the day when I heard a familiar set of hooves clicking on the tiled floor. Looking up, my heart sank as I spotted the bosom of my nemesis appearing around the doorway, 'bloody hell, she's back.'

The evil one appeared and proceeded to clip clop up the ward with only her eyes moving from side to side, scanning each patient in turn. No words were uttered, and no pleasantries exchanged as she passed from bed to bed. When she got to me, I quickly averted my eyes to avoid her death stare. Strangely, she didn't mention anything about over medicating me yesterday, and I decided it was probably for the best if I didn't mention it either, just in case she cast a spell and turned me into a frog or something.

Once the inspection of her domain was complete, she swept past and onto the adjoining ward, so that she could also spoil the mood of the patients there.

Breakfast came and went as did the dreaded wash time, and I received the good news that my urinary catheter would soon be removed. This was like music to my ears. I'd never been the 'lucky bearer' of one of these contraptions before and I'd always thought of this part of my anatomy as being 'strictly one way only', so I'd been quite horrified when I regained consciousness to find that I had a length of plastic pipe coming out of it.

It's an extremely uncomfortable feeling to have something attached to you down there, and it makes you think about every move you make, before you dare make it.

Of course, that's all well and good whilst you are awake, but once you've dozed off it's a different story altogether. When moving about in your sleep, it is all too easy to lay on the tube as you attempt to turn over, and should this scenario happen, it will cause your prized possession to be stretched to it's limit, until that is, the tube breaks free, and it flies back to it's normal 'resting place' with a resounding thwack.

I was catching a quick snooze in my bedside chair when Nurse Worst approached with her student.

"Mr Feeney, we've come to remove your urinary catheter," she said.

I gave this careful consideration. 'Not bloody likely' I thought, 'I'm not trusting you with the family jewels.'

And as I looked for a way out, the young student piped up (attempting to impress her teacher.) "Would it be okay if I was to remove it?"

I checked, "have you done it before?"

"Yes" she replied. So I agreed, and down she went.

What a sight we must have been as the young student fiddled about under my gown, whilst I nonchalantly tried to look detached by gazing everywhere except down between my legs where the action was going on. If the bloke in the next bed had woken up, he wouldn't have believed his eyes.

One moment later and "arghhhhhh" I cried, as my genitals shrunk back, searching for a place to hide.

"Sorry, sorry" she said, looking up at me sheepishly.

She had only tried to pull the catheter out from inside my penis without deflating it first.

Nurse Worst glared at me as if I had over-reacted and it was me that had done something wrong. I felt like saying 'What? She nearly pulled me inside out.' But I held my tongue just in case she insisted on finishing the job herself. It then took several minutes for me to compose myself again, (and several more to coax my startled todger back out into the open), but eventually we all relaxed and were ready to have another go at it.

Fortunately, this time everything went according to

plan and the tube was slowly removed, although I didn't see it happen as I had my eyes firmly clamped shut, but I could feel it being pulled out every inch of the way. An experience that I don't ever want to repeat. I reflected on my last forty eight hours in Intensive Care:

1. I'd had my chest crushed by being rolled back and forth like a piece of pastry.
2. I'd been over medicated (making me pass water like an out-of- control fireman's hose) and,
3. I'd had my manhood stretched to the maximum by having a space hopper pulled out of it.

That's enough now, it's the final straw. I've got to get out of here.

At this point, I feel the need to put the record straight. Throughout my time at University Hospital Coventry and Warwickshire (UHCW), I found all of the medical staff to be absolutely incredible. Unfortunately, there will always be exceptions to the rule and Nurse Worst was that exception. Maybe she was just having a bad couple of days, I don't know, or maybe she just didn't like me. But whatever it was, sadly she just didn't possess the temperament or the qualities that are required to care for patients in an Intensive Care Ward.

Back to '11', Where's Everyone Gone?

Wednesday 3rd October 2018.

Great news! I've just been told, that today I will be moving back upstairs to ward 11 'Step Down.' Back to my mates and far away from the wizened claws of the evil nurse Worst.

So, I've packed up all my belongings, and all that is left to do, is to wait for the hospital porters to turn up. Hopefully they won't take too long, or I may have to put one of my shaved legs out of the bed sheet and scoot the bed up to ward 11 myself.

Luckily for me (and due to the need for ICU space), the porters arrived just after breakfast, and once I'd been strapped in and disconnected from mains power, the brakes came off and I was back on the familiar trail between ICU and Ward 11, Step Down.

As I was pushed into the ward, I was met by one of the coronary nurses.

"Welcome back Paul"

My eyes quickly flicked around the seven beds and the unfamiliar faces that were staring back at me.

"Where is everyone? Where are all the lads that had been here with me only a few days ago?"

"Oh, they've mostly been discharged and gone

home" she said, "apart from Mike, Dave and Bob who have been moved into the other side wards."

These were my mates. The 'post-op' patients who were further into the process than me, and who were already on ward 11, recovering from their surgeries when I had arrived. I felt deflated as I had expected the 'old gang' to still be here. The lads that had helped and supported each other through such a difficult time. Yes, we hadn't known each other for that long, but we had shared the experience together and a bond had formed between us.

But now, the group had been broken up, with most being sent back out into the world, and able to carry on with their lives, thanks to the extraordinary skills of the UHCW heart surgeons. To be fair, this is what we had all hoped for in the beginning, so, I was happy for them. But, like it or not, I was going to be stuck here for a little while longer. My time to go home would come eventually, but until then, it was back to re-focusing on the positives again.

In the last eleven days: I'd had a cardiac arrest, a heart attack, been dead for 10 minutes, been resuscitated, had undergone heart surgery, been in intensive care (twice) and had survived nurse Worst. It had been a tough time, but I had come through it.

The end was now in sight, with the hardest part now behind me. I was on the recovery ward, where I was just about to be pushed into a vacant bed-space next to the window (Mwuaha, evil laugh, don't they know about my overwhelming urges to escape?)

Once all my electrics had been connected to the monitoring equipment again (yes, I'd still got all the bloody wires), people slowly started to approach my bed and introduce themselves.

They were mostly pre-op patients, who were in the same position that I'd been in myself, only a few days ago. Some were curious, some were scared and some just wanted reassurance, but they all came armed with a million questions. It was my turn to lead. To pass on my experience, afford some help, give them support and provide encouragement. I was now considered to be one of the lucky ones. I had been there, done it and come safely out the other side. I wore the white surgical support stockings, I had the long scar running down my leg and the six inch scar down the middle of my chest. I had become a 'zipper man.'

During the next few days I settled into life back on Step Down ward 11, but things were not as I had expected. Although my operation had been a success, I was frustrated that I still had to remain connected to the stack of monitoring equipment that had been my unwanted companion for the past 14 days. And that I would still unable to leave the bed. I had hoped that following the surgery, all the electrical equipment would no longer be needed and would therefore be disconnected, but as it was, I still couldn't go for a walk, visit the toilet or go for a shower like everyone else on the ward. I grumbled to the nurse, “How much longer will I need to be attached to all this equipment?”

"You are still being monitored because of the way in which you arrived at the hospital," she said. "And because of that, there are also additional concerns, meaning that you have to be monitored more closely. All the other patients have been expected on the ward. They have no immediate complications and their hearts are working sufficiently well enough at this time. But in your case, your heart has recently been 'arrested' and was stopped for a long period of time. Your monitoring will have to remain, until we can see that your heart is reacting in a stable way following surgery, and that you've recovered sufficiently and it is safe to send you home."

Her answer didn't come as any surprise, I should have known before I even asked.

In The Pink (Literally)

Still being attached to the monitoring equipment, meant that I was still having to use a bedpan and commode for my toilet needs, and that the dreaded 'wash routine' would have to continue. But, if I hated having to stand up and wash from a bowl before, it was now going to be taken to a whole new level, with my introduction to a product called Hibiscrub. As wash time approached, the nurse brought the bowl of water to my bedside as usual, setting it down upon the nearby table.

Producing a plastic bottle, she said,

"Paul, following your operation, we want you to add a little of this Hibiscrub into your washing water. It's an antiseptic and antibacterial liquid that will protect your wounds from any infection."

'Fair enough' I thought, 'I don't want any problems that may complicate my recovery.' And with that I added a good double glug of the liquid into the water. Once the curtains around my bed had been closed, (and the window ledge checked and cleared of voyeur pigeons), I stripped naked and proceeded with the job of washing myself down. I knew that I had to be extra careful with this wash, as along with the threat of dislodging one of the many wires, I also had the risk of snagging or pulling out any of the stitches from my wounds. So, with this hazard at the forefront of my mind, it's fair to say that I became quite absorbed and focused on the task.

In fact, I was so absorbed that I failed to notice, that with every wipe of the wash-cloth, I was painting on a broad line of pink liquid. Initially I didn't pay much attention to this discolouration, as I assumed that my skin was just reacting to the heat of the water. But the more I washed, the pinker I seemed to become. Even the bits that I'd previously washed and that had now become cold, were still pink.

It was only when I was about halfway through my wash, that I stopped to inspect further.

'Hang on a minute, this isn't right.'

Tracing a finger across my wet stomach I examined it. 'Hot Pink. I've turned bloody pink!'

I looked like a sun burnt ginger on the first day of his holiday.

Picking up the bottle of Hibiscrub, I tipped it up to see past the label. The liquid inside was bloody pink. For God's sake, somebody could have at least warned me! It took two days of rigorous scrubbing to dull down the initial glow. And after this, I decided to only add the Hibiscrub at the end of my wash, and then to wash my wounds only, not the whole of my body (top tip).

Another fun addition to my life, were the daily injections of an anti-coagulant that were administered into the area of my lower stomach. Given to me to help thin my blood and to avoid the possibility of clots forming, which could break free and travel to my heart. These injections, although uncomfortable, were bearable, but they left behind quite large bruises, which after a few days of injecting, joined up to form one long blue, black and purple line across my stomach. Which, when added to the yellowing bruises on my groin and the hot pink patches of Hibiscrub, made me more colourful than a chameleon on a disco light.

A Fluttering Heart Causes Concern

Thursday 4th October 2018

One day started to merge into the next as the monotony of hospital routine started to kick in. Being fresh out of surgery I was still under close 24 hour observation, with nurses constantly arriving at my bedside to either inject, test, adjust, monitor or medicate me. And it was during one such early morning visit, that my heart rate was recorded at 195bpm, (beats per minute).

This had happened quickly and without any warning. One minute I was lying in bed, gazing out of the window and ticking along nicely. The next, I had the RESTING heart rate of an Olympic Sprinter in full flow. My heart had also started to beat erratically, constantly 'fluttering' within my chest, as if there was a butterfly trapped inside. They told me, that the 'fluttering' sensation was called arrhythmia, which was something I'd never heard of before. Although, when thinking back, I had experienced this feeling a few times in the past, but I'd never paid it much attention as it was just a gentle vibration under the skin which would then quickly disappear.

[arrhythmia: A condition in which the heart beats with an irregular or abnormal rhythm]

But if I hadn't given this anomaly much attention before, it was certainly getting some attention now, as the area around my bed became awash in a sea of blue uniforms.

The look of concern on everyone's face told a story. That was, having a patient whose heart was beating so fast and so abnormally only two days after surgery, wasn't a good sign. It didn't take long before a doctor appeared and I was quickly connected to an intravenous drip and a bag of 'magic juice', that would help get my heart back to a more reasonable level.

I was also made the recipient of a Holter monitor (a small box that measures and records heart activity, such as rate and rhythm), which was ceremoniously hung around my neck like a winners medal, before it's wires were firmly attached to my body with super sticky pads. Just what I needed, more wires. I was now festooned with so many wires, that I was starting to look like a bloody Christmas Tree!

I could hear the doctor deliberating: 'We need to determine if Mr Feeney's heart problem is hereditary, or does he have an underlying heart electrical problem?'

Obviously, neither answer was going to be good news for me, but what was worse, was the realisation that due to this latest 'complication', I wouldn't be going home anytime soon.

With the days now spent largely motionless and being confined to the hospital bed, my mind had starting to wander. Asking questions that I didn't have any answers for:

Why had all this happened to me?
Why hadn't there been any signs beforehand?
Why can't I remember what happened?
What if they hadn't saved me?
How would my family have coped without me?
How will the heart surgery effect my life?

Not having any physical or mental stimulus to occupy me, was giving me too much time to think, and I was starting to become quite emotional. They said: 'Don't worry, it's quite natural for you to feel like this at your stage of recovery. With all the trauma taking place in such a short period of time, your brain hasn't had the opportunity until now, to process what has happened to you.

But now that you have survived your cardiac event and have safely emerged from heart surgery, the worst is all behind you. And without the need to focus on, or worry about these, it's perfectly normal for the emotional floodgates to open as you reflect on what has actually happened, and also to think about what could have happened (the what-ifs)'.

Finally, Some Good News

Friday 5th October 2018.

I'd now been restricted to the bed and connected to the equipment for 14 days, and the lack of physical activity was starting to take it's toll Sometimes, when I would get out of bed to have a wash (or to scare the pigeons from the ledge), I would become quite dizzy and unsteady. Just to be able to walk around the bed would have helped, but if I tried to take more than a half dozen steps in any direction, all of the monitor wires would become tight and stop me dead in my tracks. Being so immobile was starting to become a real worry, I had already noticed a change in definition of my leg muscles, caused by their lack of use.

My surgeon has just been to visit me.

"Mr Feeney, I'm not overly worried about the fluttering in your chest (which was still happening) as it is quite normal for the heart to take a little while to settle down again after such an operation. We will remove the monitoring box to review the data, but you will need to stay on the drip to reduce your heart rate further.

You will not be able to go home this weekend, but it may be possible from Tuesday, next week."

It came as no surprise that I wasn't allowed home just yet. My irregular heartbeat had put paid to that. But to hear him say that 'the fluttering' was 'quite normal' and not too much to be worried about was a relief. It had been something that I was becoming anxious of. The last thing I wanted was any more problems.

And "it may be possible (to go home) from Tuesday?" Well, that was just the icing on the cake that lifted my mood sky high. I would have leapt out of bed and danced a jig, if I could have got more than six steps away from it.

More Heart Checks (And More Wires)

6th October 2018.

Saturday morning was here. And following my morning wash (and yes, I was still pink), a nurse arrived at my bedside.

"Good morning Mr Feeney, I see that your intravenous drip has finished, so we can now have that removed. Also, today, you will be having an ECG (Electrocardiogram) so that we can have a better look at your heart's rhythm and electrical activity."

An ECG did mean having even more wires stuck onto me, but within 30 minutes all was complete, with the results showing that my heart was beating strongly and behaving 'mostly' normal.

Everyone seemed fairly pleased with the results, even though I was still told the usual, "yes, it's a little bit fluttery now and again, but it's nothing to worry about. We are not overly worried."

Little did they know what lay in store for them tomorrow.

As a result of my (sometimes) irregular heartbeat, the doctors decided that the best course of action would be to fit me with a temporary external 'heart pacer' (pacemaker), which would send electrical signals to my heart and stimulate it to beat regularly and at a more normal and regular pace.

Unfortunately, this new addition came with yet another wire, which was inserted through the skin half-way down my chest, before running up inside me and then connecting directly to my heart.

> *[Heart pacers operate by delivering an electrical impulse to the patient's heart muscles. These impulses stimulate the muscles to contract, thereby normalizing the heartbeat. The most common use of external pacemakers is as an emergency measure to restore and regulate abnormal heart rhythms.*
>
> *During use, an external pacemaker takes over the job from the body's own natural pacemaker of telling the heart when to beat. For some patients, the device can be removed after a short time and the heartbeat returns to a normal, healthy rhythm. But if the heartbeat reverts to an abnormal rhythm, the patient will need a pacemaker implanted into the body to control the heartbeat on a permanent basis.]*

Along with my new pacemaker, I also received a fresh bag of magic juice.

Panic At Midnight

The nurse has just told me that I can disconnect from the monitor and visit the toilet, providing I take the portable heart pacer (pacing brick) with me. So, I'm out of bed and into my racing slippers, ready to be unplugged before she changes her mind.

And upon her words "All done Mr Feeney, you can go now", I was off, pushing myself away from the bed and stepping out into the passageway.

Whoa! What's happening?

My feet were not responding (a legacy of being inactive for so long.) They were numb, like I had sat with them tucked beneath me and they'd gone to sleep. I tried again, but they still refused to budge. And the only way that I could manage to move forward was by sliding each foot slowly along, like I was skiing. But, walking like one of the 'undead' wasn't going to stop me, and with a look of defiance on my face and a refusal to be beaten, I made my way up the ward in a loping zombie shuffle, pacing brick in one hand, IV drip in the other, and a determination to reach the toilet door without falling over. And with gritted teeth I finally make it across the threshold. I was in!

Truth be told, I don't really need the toilet. So I'm just standing here, looking in the mirror and relishing in my new found sense of freedom.

But sadly, there is only so much adventure to be had in a toilet if you don't want to go, so after a mere handful of minutes, I head for the door and the long slide back. On my way, I can see through the doors and out into the corridor beyond, where groups of people are streaming in to visit their loved ones. How easy it would be to turn left instead of right, and then to make a break for it in a taxi. I don't suppose I would have gained too much attention, pushing an IV stand as I scooted through the parting crowds, with my hospital gown flapping behind me in the breeze, would it? On second thoughts, maybe it isn't one of my best ideas. And anyway, what taxi driver in his right mind would take a fare dressed in a long white robe, and carrying a box with a bunch of wires coming out of it?

That night, just before midnight I was fast asleep, when I awoke to a disturbance and the piercing sound of an alarm wailing.

I actually thought that I had been dreaming, that was until I opened my eyes to see that the curtains had been drawn around my bed, and I was surrounded by a crowd of doctors and nurses. There looked to be a real panic going on, with people rushing in and out through the curtain, people leaning over to examine me and people preparing various bits of medical equipment (including a rather large hypodermic needle. The contents of which, soon found itself inside my arm.)

Looking up, I noticed that my monitor was lit up like a Christmas Tree with all it's numbers flashing, and I realised, that the alarm making such a God awful din was mine.

What the hell's going on? What's with all these people? I was actually feeling fine (although pissed off at having been woken up) and I couldn't understand what all the fuss was about. But looking around me, and judging by the concerned look on all the faces, I couldn't say the same for them. It was being treated like a real emergency situation.

Only when the initial panic had subsided and things were under control, that was I told what had actually happened: Apparently, my heart rate had 'gone irregular' again, sounding the alarm as it rocketed from 55 bpm to 185 bpm, which put me at risk of having a possible stroke.

Did someone say earlier, 'we are not overly worried?

Noooooooo!

Monday 8th October 2018

It was during Doctors Rounds the next morning when they hit me with the bad news.

"Mr Feeney, due to your incident last night, we are going to have to monitor your heart rate closely (no shit Sherlock). Unfortunately, this means that you will not be discharged for at least another four days."

What!, hang on a minute (my mind sprang into action.)

Okay. So it's Monday today and four days would make it Friday. Then it will be the weekend (when no doctors are here to discharge anyone.) Then we will be back to Monday again. So that means that I will be stuck in here for at least another seven days, not four!

I was absolutely distraught. This was the worst news possible, and it sent me plummeting into the depths of despair.

For three days I had clung to the hope of possibly going home tomorrow (Tuesday), but with one single statement, the doctor had condemned me to another seven days of boredom (which would make my stay in here, nearly one month.) I was now at the end of my tether. Frustrated, that since my surgery one week ago, I had looked on every day as other patients around me were being discharged, and allowed to go home with their loved ones. Yet here I was, seven days after surgery and with at least seven more to go, still 'under observation' and still wired to all of these damn machines.

It seemed that every time I took a step forward, I then slipped two steps back.

Looking back, I can see that the decisions taken by the doctors had all been for the best. They had a duty to put my health first, and couldn't discharge me until I was in a stable condition and out of all immediate danger. But, at the time, I felt that I'd been through enough.

All I wanted to do was to go home.

An Unexpected Surprise

Tuesday 9th October 2018.

The morning peace was shattered as 'Doctors Rounds' exploded onto the ward again, making me loose count of the number of trees that surrounded the field outside. Today's the day that I should have been going home, but after yesterday's bad news, I'm not. So I'm laying here sulking, and not paying much attention to anything that the doctor's have to say. That is, until I hear a familiar voice.

Looking up, I was surprised to see that my surgeon Mr. Barker had joined the rounds (this was quite unusual as surgeons didn't normally attend.)

"Good morning Paul, how are you feeling this morning?"

"Yeah, I'm okay thanks Mr. Barker (I replied grumpily)"

"When was your 24 hour heart monitor box removed?"

"Four days ago" I said.

"And have we had the results back yet?"

"No, because the monitor box went back on Saturday and the Cardiologist (blood and heart specialist) wasn't on duty over the weekend."

"Right," he said, turning on his heel, "I will go and see him now."

And with that, he was gone.

Clearly, Mr. Barker was on a pointless journey. It was pretty obvious what the results were going to be, based upon the evidence.

<u>The case to keep me here</u>: 'Mr Feeney has been directly responsible for two bedside emergencies, during which he scared the crap out of the nurses by elevating his heart rate from a steady 55bpm to an alarming 185bpm, 195bpm. Also, during his time here, Mr Feeney has shown to possess a persistently irregular and erratic heartbeat. In fact, the only time that Mr Feeney's heartbeat hadn't been irregular, was when it was stopped.'

<u>The case to let me go home:</u> Errr ... (silence)

So, the verdict will obviously be: 'The patient continues to have irregular heart beat, recommend he remains on ward, further monitoring required.'

Thirty minutes later and Mr. Barker returned to the ward. "Good news" he said, "the Cardiologist isn't too concerned about your irregular heartbeat and rather than monitor you any further, we can control your heart rate with drugs. So you will be going home today."

Well, I'm sure that you could hear my jaw drop all the way from Cardio down to Maternity. I gawped at him open mouthed, and checked that my ears weren't playing tricks on me. "Did you just say that I can go home today?"

"Yes, we will have all of your wires removed and arrange for some medication that you can take home with you."

I was completely stunned. Since my surgery, I'd been on a downward spiral as I had watched everyone around me go home, everyone but me that is. I'd even joked with the nurses that I would still be around for the Christmas Party in two months time. But now, completely out of the blue, I had just heard the words that I was starting to believe would never come. And, what had made then even better, was that they had come from the 'main man' himself, Mr. Barker. So, I could be 100% certain (ish) that it was going to happen!

As soon as Mr Barker had left the ward, and at the risk of tempting fate, I began packing up all my worldly possessions (which was mostly chocolates), and put them into a 'bag for life' (which I thought was quite appropriate.) I was absolutely delighted and couldn't wait to share the good news with my wife. Mr. Barker, you're a star!

One of the nurses came to see me.

"I've just heard that you will be leaving us" she said.

"Yep, I'm off", said I (giving her my best Cheshire Cat smile.)

And just to discourage any thoughts that she may have had about keeping me, I added, "Mr. Barker has just told me himself, that I can go."

"Well, firstly, before we can discharge you, your external pacemaker and all of the monitoring wires will need to be removed. Plus, you will also have to demonstrate to us, that you are capable of looking after yourself, by completing a few simple tasks, including walking up and down a flight of stairs, and being able to shower yourself."

No worries, I thought, what can be hard about standing under a shower? And I've been going up and down stairs since I was two years old.
This will be a breeze (or so I thought).

Tested To Go Home

By watching when other patients had been discharged, I was aware that the process could sometimes take as long as ten hours to complete. With the major stumbling block being the time taken by the hospital pharmacy, to put together the goody bag of medicine that a patient would need to take home with them. So, with that in mind (and although it was only 10am), I hatched a plan to do everything possible to help speed the process along. I was determined that now I'd been told that I could go home, that nothing was going to stop me, so from that point on, every time I spotted a nurse, I would badger them about removing my monitoring wires. And by midday, my persistence had paid off, and for the first time in 18 days I became 'virtually' wire free. I say 'virtually', as my only remaining wire was the one that disappeared inside me. The pacemaker wire.

"This may be a little uncomfortable as we remove it", the nurse said (with an apologetic smile), "but one way or another, it will have to come out before you can go home."

So I clenched my teeth (and my buttocks) as she firmly took hold of the end of the wire, and slowly started to retrieve it.

Actually, the process wasn't too painful, more unpleasant than anything else, but with it being quite a stiff wire, I could feel every inch of it as it made its journey the six inches down from my heart. And it was quite a relief when I saw the end of it pop clear of my chest. Yes, at long last, I was completely unrestrained, and free from the bed and all of the equipment.

And with perfect timing Dawn arrived. She was so excited that I would be coming home, and couldn't wait to help me with the next stage of my preparations. That being, to get me out of bed and moving around again.

"What do we need to do" she asked.

"Well firstly, I have to show the nurses that I can walk unaided. Then I've got to be able to go up and down a flight of stairs."

It didn't seem like much, saying it like that. But judging by the way my last 'excursion' went, when I'd lurched down the ward like one of the undead, I knew that it wasn't going to be that straightforward.

So, with the first test simply being able to walk, I swung my legs from the bed to the floor and slowly got myself upright. And with the help of Dawn supporting my arm and with a face set in grim determination, I focused on putting one foot in front of the other, in an attempt to leave the sanctuary of the bed. Initially, nothing seemed to happen. It was like my feet were glued to the floor and they stubbornly refusing to budge, but after several minutes of dogged persistence (along with a fair amount of swearing), they finally surrendered and I slowly started to move forward. It wasn't pretty and it was far from graceful, but I didn't care. As long as it satisfied the 'mobility police', that was all I was bothered about. It was good enough for me. And with my new ability to venture further afield, there followed an hour spent shuffling around the wards, visiting those that had always visited me, and letting everybody know why I was up and about.

"See me?" I said. "I'm walking about I am, I'm going home today I am." I was on cloud nine.

Next up came the stairs test. To be able to negotiate a flight of stairs, both up and down, without anyone's help.

I expected this to be a bit of a challenging one, given the difficulty I'd had lifting my feet from the floor when walking, and it could go a number of ways. Either I would bound up the stairs like a young mountain goat (highly unlikely), or I would miss a step on the way up and face-plant into the steps above, or I would miss a step on the way down and 'go airborne' straight to the bottom (either of these last two were very possible). And it was now time to find out, which one it was going to be.

Making my final approach, I arrived at step one, where I looked back to see my wife and the nurse willing me on. Okay then, brain send a message to my foot to do it's thing.

Whoa! I didn't expect that! My foot lifted straight up off the floor. In fact, it came up much higher than I had needed it to, about two feet in all. It was as if gravity had been 'switched off' under it, or it had been pulled up by an invisible string or something. So, without further ado (and before gravity could be 'switched back on'), I took full advantage and planted it down firmly onto step two. Lifting my other foot, I repeated 'the stomp', and became another step nearer to my goal. You could have described my movement as being clumsy, awkward and ungraceful, or even like I was climbing stairs in lead diving boots. But it was working. It was getting me up there. And by recreating this stomping motion, I slowly and methodically ground my way, step-by-step, all the way up, until finally I reached the safety of the top landing, where I stood triumphant and majestic like Sir Edmund Hillary.

[Sir Edmund Percival Hillary, mountaineer, explorer, and philanthropist, who on 29 May 1953, along with Sherpa mountaineer Tenzing Norgay became the first climbers confirmed to have reached the summit of Mount Everest.]

'Well, that was half the job done, wasn't so bad was it?'

And full of confidence, I turned around and set off on the return journey. But what had worked for me on the way up, was now working against me on the way down. With my feet feeling so light, that all they wanted to do, was dangle about in the air in front of me, rather than doing what they were supposed to. But I quickly worked out, that if I held onto the stair rail and pulled myself forward (until my balance shifted), this 'toppling over' motion would persuade my foot down onto the step below, where it would be ready and (hopefully) able to take my weight.

Eventually, with this technique I was able to lumber my way back down to the bottom, where it was mission accomplished and another step (pardon the pun), nearer to me going home.

[The strange lightness (pins and needles type feeling) that I experienced in my feet during this test only lasted for around thirty minutes or so, after which I could accomplish the task with full control over my movements. I can only guess that it may have been caused by the return of full blood flow to my legs, after having not walked for so long.]

My final challenge was simply to 'be able to shower myself', and after washing from a bowl for the past seventeen days, this one I was looking forward to. Moving around had started to become a little easier now, and following an hour of 'upright activity', I had stopped 'skiing along' and had progressed to a kind of fast shuffle (a bit like a toddler heading for the TV remote), so the journey from bed to bathroom was accomplished in record time.

Stepping through the door and shutting out the world behind me, I had an overwhelming sense of being alone. There was nobody here to watch over me, or to assist me should anything unforeseen happen. And after being so closely monitored for the past three weeks, it felt strange to be alone.

Turning on the shower, I slipped out of my gown as the water heated up, pleased to note that I was slightly less 'Hibiscrub pink' than I used to be. And as I stepped under the steaming hot jets, I was overcome by a feeling of complete bliss, which caused me to just stand there mesmerised as the flood of water crashed against my head and cascaded down over my shoulders. After having to wash from a bowl for so long, the shower felt amazing, and I could have remained under it for hours! But, tempting as that would have been, I knew that being away for too long would cause a real panic, which would cause the nurses to crash through the door like a Police SWAT team, to make sure that I was okay.

So reluctantly, I set about the task of washing myself down, and scraping off the stubble that was making me look like I belonged on a wanted poster.

Apart from a brief bout of dizziness when I closed my eyes to avoid the shampoo from going into them, the shower test was sheer heaven, and all to briefly I was towelling myself dry and was returning to the ward, buffed-up and shining like a new pin.

Being able to wash and shave properly was a joy, and to feel independent again and able to function unaided was a definite corner turned in my recovery. A sense of normality was now returning, and with it, I started to feel like I was getting back to being myself again.

It was now 1pm and with all the tasks successfully passed, no more wires to remove, and with everything packed up and ready to go, I just sat on the edge of my bed, dangling my feet and watching a clock that didn't seem to be moving. Nurses flashed past here and there, going about their daily routines. And with each one, I willed them to turn in my direction and to say the words that I longed to hear.

"Okay Mr. Feeney, we can discharge you now."

"You are free to go home."

Surely it wasn't going to be that much longer? It wasn't the nurses fault that it was taking so long. 'My release' was in the hands of the hospital pharmacy, and depended on them having the time to put together my take-away medication. But on the stroke of 2pm, an angel did appear, and she did come my way.

"Okay Paul, I've got your discharge form here, and once you have signed it, you can go."

There was no need to tell me twice, and after a quickly scribbled signature and with my 'party bag' tucked under my arm, I said my farewell's and left Coronary Care behind to join the crowds in the hallway, where I 'sped off' towards the exit. Actually 'sped off' is a slight exaggeration, but it was certainly a good and nippy shuffle. I was going home, and I was a man on a mission.

I left University Hospital Cov & Warks. with a new found respect, and a great appreciation for all the surgeons, specialists, doctors and nurses who had shown such skill, devotion, compassion and tenderness in their care of me (except nurse Worst), and I will be forever grateful. Thank you one and all.

Home Sweet Home

The feeling of being back in my own home was incredible.

I could do whatever I wanted, when I wanted. I could sit on the sofa, watch TV, eat my own food, drink proper coffee, use my own toilet and sleep in my own bed. All of these little things were priceless. And if I'd ever been guilty of taking any of them for granted in the past, I vowed to never do so again. And by far, the biggest pleasure of all, was that I was back home again with my loving wife. I know it's a cliché, but she is so much a part of me and I'm not complete without her. We are best friends and soulmates and I had missed her so much. But, if I thought that being at home was going to be just like it was before, I was wrong.

Courtesy of the six-inch scar that I now had running down the middle of my chest, tasks that I had accomplished before without even thinking, now presented me with a whole new set of challenges.

Before I'd left hospital the surgeon had warned me:

"Although your wound may look to be healing well on the outside, the bone and tissue on the inside will take considerably longer to knit itself back together again. Therefore, you should avoid putting any strain on it, by not lifting anything heavy for a period of six weeks. This includes pots, pans, kettles of water and even full plates of food. And if you do need to lift or carry anything, you should do it by keeping it tucked in and close to your chest."

Other things I had to avoid doing were: Reaching up, stretching down, twisting or straining. And God forbid if I was to cough or to sneeze (or any other spontaneous bodily emission), I would be rendered helpless, doubled up in pain and clutching at my chest. Oh, and one more thing. Driving a car for the next six weeks wasn't allowed either. There was a positive though, I was now ruled out of doing any ironing!

When you get home from hospital, there is a great temptation to just sit around and do nothing. All the time feeling sorry for yourself, and telling everyone how much it hurts and how difficult everything is. But as easy as that path is to take, being 'sick and helpless' and living your life in an armchair, isn't really going to help you to recover, either physically or mentally. It is also hugely unfair on those around you, who would have been consumed by worry, and would also have been through a tough time. And now that they have you back at home, all they want is for you to recover, and to be back to how you were before.

So it's important to help them to help you, by being positive towards your recovery. What the heck, you've just been given a second chance at life, grab it with both hands and appreciate just how lucky you are to still be alive.

One of my biggest concerns, was just how much my fitness had been effected by the surgery and my stay in hospital. Only seventeen days ago, I could easily have played football for one hour, sprinting short distances and running for miles without very much effort.

But now everything had changed, and even performing the simplest of physical activities would leave me gasping and struggling to get enough air to fill my heaving lungs. Even climbing the stairs to go to the bathroom was a challenge, and although we only have thirteen steps to negotiate, I would find myself having to stop half-way up in order to catch my breath. And when I eventually did reach the bathroom, I'd be so light-headed, that I would need to steady myself against a wall until the feeling had passed. Becoming so breathless so easily was quite frightening, and although I'd been 'out of breath' many times before (whilst playing sport), those times were nothing compared to this. It was like having a tight band wrapped around my chest, which hampered all efforts to get the air that I so desperately needed.

Trying to get to sleep at night was also a challenge, as it's next to impossible to lay on your front or your side without putting pressure on the sensitive chest wound. So, the only option is to lay on your back and stare at the ceiling until sleep finally overcomes you, that is, until you move again and are jolted back to reality). Fortunately, this sensitivity in your chest only lasts for about three weeks, after which the area around the wound starts to become numb, which allows you to tentatively change position without wincing in pain.

After a few days at home, and with my wounds now healing nicely, my thoughts had turned to getting more active again, and regaining some of the fitness that I'd lost over the past month.

It was now time to make a plan. I would start small, with some easily achievable goals, a few daily targets that I could reach and surpass (with a little bit of effort). These would give me something to focus on and keep me motivated as I progressed throughout my training. Also, any goals set would have to be measurable and become progressively more difficult. That way, I would be able to recognise and gauge my progress along with any improvement.

But before I did anything, first up was the purchase of a sports activity tracking watch. Something that would not only allow me to set targets, track progress and record goals in my exercise routine, but also, it would display my 'live heart rate', something that was of great importance to me. And just by having my heart rate displayed in 'real time', it would greatly reduce the worry that I had of suffering another cardiac arrest or attack due to heart arrhythmia.

I hoped that by seeing instantly if my heart was behaving abnormally, then I may have the time to be able to react to it. Also, by being able to monitor my heart rate whilst performing exercise, I could learn how my heart would react as it progressed up through the various 'workout zones', before it levelled out, and slowly descended back down to a normal resting pace as the exercise ceased. Being able to see and know that my heart was now working as it should was a great comfort, and would allow me to exercise without fear of a repeat performance of my incident. The activity tracking watch was a great investment, and I would highly recommend the use of one to anybody who may be concerned about arrhythmia, or the performance of their heart whilst exercising.

'Schooled' by the 'Pink Blur'

The first step on my road back to physical fitness was going to be a visit to the local park, where I could amble sedately around the perimeter at my own pace, (attack dogs, kids on bikes and pushchair mums permitting). So, I slipped into my shorts and trainers and I headed for the door.

"Where do you think you're going?" said the wife.

"I'm just going for a quick run around the park" I said, screeching to a halt and thinking 'bugger, now I'm in trouble.'

Slowly turning around, I was greeted by two pairs of raised eyebrows, and the two slowly shaking heads of my wife and my daughter Joanne, looking back at me.

"You're bloody well not" said the wife, "you're not going out on your own. We will come with you."

This wasn't a request, it was more a statement of intent. So, being outgunned and outmanoeuvred, I smiled and grudgingly agreed. I didn't mind the company really, and thinking about it, they were both obviously concerned that I may go 'belly up' half-way around. I had to remember that they had been through a lot as well.

So, off we went, with a goal of 1000 steps (½ mile) set on the watch.

I thought that 1000 steps was about right, and a pretty realistic and achievable target for a first session. And all was going well until I reached the first incline, where I slowed dramatically and started to struggle for breath. It was here (as I stood hands on hips and puffing like an old steam train), that a grey haired old lady flashed past me in a blur of pink Lycra and spangly trainers.

"Bloody hell" I thought, "I've just been done by a racing granny"

So, calling upon all my reserves of energy (which were roughly zero), I sucked in a monster breath and set off in an attempt to catch her up.

Unfortunately, my pursuit of 'the blur' was very short lived, and after another twenty steps I was forced to concede defeat as she disappeared over the horizon, where no doubt, she would go on to embarrass another poor soul. To be fair, my respect goes out to 'the blur'. She is an example to us all, that age, or illness, or injury are not reasons for us to stop trying to live a life.

My first foray into the outside world was more difficult than I had expected, and it came as a real shock when I'd had to rest half way up that first hill. But it had clarified the situation and had taught me a valuable lesson.

As things stood, I was no longer able to do what I used to, so I would have to start again from the bottom. But I wasn't in a race and I wasn't in competition with anyone, so my return to fitness could be at my pace and in my own time. And although I went on to reach the 1000 step goal, the old adage of starting small, building gradually and not expecting too much too soon, was the answer, and the safest and most effective way back to playing football again.

Someone once said 'A journey of a thousand miles begins with a single step.' Well, this was my first step.

Over the next two weeks, further sessions at the park saw my fitness slowly start to improve. And with each visit, I was able to gradually increase my target steps, until I could manage a 2000 step goal (approximately 1 mile) without too much difficulty, (and without too many rest stops).

Back at home, tackling the stairs had also become less of a mission, and I could now scale the full set of thirteen, without 'face-planting' or sucking in air like an old hoover. Toilet visits were also enhanced, with the ability to now 'do the business standing upright, and without having to lean against the wall and wee at a 45 degree angle.

It had now been ten days since I'd been discharged from hospital, and with the small increase in fitness, my mind had started to become dominated with thoughts of football again. It wasn't solely the need to play again that was now haunting me, (as I wasn't foolish enough to think I was ready to kick a ball, just yet). I was also starting to miss the social side of being part of the team.

To be able to meet up with my mates, share some tales, tell a few jokes and grumble about our latest aches and pains, as well as reminiscing about 'the game' back in 'the good old days'. Then repeating most of it again (that happens at our age) over some 'post training' tea and biscuits, or a slice of home-made cake if we were lucky. Priceless!

The importance of being involved as part of a team or club cannot be underestimated. It is equally important to keep your mind active as well as your body.

Unfortunately, during further visits to the park, I never saw my nemesis 'the pink blur' again. But if I had, I would have given her a high five (probably as she sped past me again).

I'm No Male 'Gym Bunny', But...

After being at home for a couple of weeks I had started to become more and more confident. Thanks to the daily walks in the park, my chest was now starting to feel less constricted, and I'd lost that initial fear of my 'new heart' failing, when it was being put under pressure.

I wasn't a runner and never had been, (unless I had a ball at my feet), so I knew that the park was just going to be the opening step for me, a toe in the water so to speak, that would give me the confidence to 'push on' in my quest to regain a reasonable level of fitness. And fourteen days in, I now felt comfortable that I could do that.

The step-up in my exercise took the form of attending a local gym, where I was booked onto a thirteen week program, arranged by the hospital's cardiac team in conjunction with a company called Atrium Health. The program consists of a personal tailored exercise plan, which is specifically aimed at helping people to rehabilitate and to regain their health, following cardiac (heart) or pulmonary (lung) problems.

Now I've always disliked the idea of going to the gym, but this one turned out to be quite different.

As soon as I walked through the doors, the first thing that struck me, was that all those inside were in their 'golden years.' There were no pouting gym bunnies, no buffed-up and flexing muscle men and no one working on a summer six pack or a pair of bulging biceps. Everyone was there for one reason and one reason only, that being, to improve their health by increasing their fitness, (was that two reasons?)

To achieve this, first time visitors will have a personalised training plan created for them, which has been specifically designed to help them raise their level of fitness, in order to achieve their own personal goals.

All gym training takes place under strict supervision, and with the full support of the ever present staff, who are not only trained fitness instructors, but are also trained to provide emergency medical assistance should it be required, (a major consideration when dealing with this type of group, where it is quite possible for someone to collapse, require CPR or even defibrillation.) And should such a medical emergency occur, the victim would certainly be in the right place, with the right people to give them full and proper medical support.

When asked, I told them that my goal at the gym was real simple: 'To get fit enough to return and play football again.'

So, after signing on the dotted line and coming up with a 12 week plan, I trudged along to the gym each week, where I pushed my legs on the exercise bikes, pumped my arms on the rowing machines, and did a strange kind of arm flailing, uncoordinated wild man dance on the cross trainer.

Then, after I had attended for around eight weeks, my fitness just seemed to turn a corner, and I felt that it was time for me to make a decision. Either I could stay at the gym and continue to fall off the cross trainer for a few more weeks, or I could ease myself back into football training. Starting with a social visit.
It was a tough decision indeed, but in less than one nanosecond I had my answer, 'football here I come.'
I suppose I could have spent a little longer at the gym, but I knew that once I started playing football again, my fitness would increase so much faster.
So I gave thanks for all the help and support I'd been given, bid them all a fond farewell, and broke the news to my wife (and part-time chauffeur), that it was time to go back to Beechcroft Multi Sports Club in Birmingham, so that I could catch up with all my footballing mates.

Back to 'Beechcroft'

Friday 19th October 2018. (19 days post-surgery).

It was 10am and I was on my way to Beechcroft for the 11am over 60's training session.

Obviously, I wasn't able to take part (just yet), but I would be able to catch up with everyone and rejoin the social side of being part of a club again. But, I was nervous and apprehensive, I was still feeling self-conscious about what had happened to me. How would they all react? What would they say? What would they think? These were the questions I was asking myself.

And to be totally honest. Before it happened to me, I used to think that people who had suffered a cardiac arrest or heart attack, must somehow have contributed to it themselves by possibly having some kind of underlying condition. Whether it was by having a bad diet, or through lack of exercise, or maybe they'd been carrying excess weight or something, or some other 'lifestyle choice' that had been the reason why their 'arrest or attack' had happened. But now, after experiencing it myself, I can see how naïve I had been.

The truth is: Anyone can suffer from a cardiac arrest

or have a heart attack at any time, at any age and for any number of reasons.

But unfortunately, long held beliefs (even totally wrong ones) can be hard to shake off sometimes, and for whatever reason I still had this feeling of embarrassment that it had happened to me.

Due to not knowing how I would be received, I planned to limit my exposure to only a few people at a time, so we had left home early. The last thing I wanted was to turn up to a crowd and be the centre of attention, although I knew that just by being there, I would arouse some curiosity, and would probably be the subject of a million questions. I suppose it's to be expected. It's not every day that you are told your friend has died, only to have them turn up for training three weeks later.

As we pulled into the car park, I was relieved to see that we were the first to arrive, so we 'parked-up' and waited as the other's started to appear one by one, until in no time at all, a group of around eight players had gathered. Feeling that this was as many people as I could handle in one go, I couldn't put things off any longer, so rather self-consciously I left the car and made my way towards where they were all standing. Needless to say, the expressions of surprise came first,

"hey it's Paul" and "look who's back" and "Paul's here."

Followed by the customary compliments of,

"you're looking well" and "how are you feeling, and you're looking good."

And after a suitable amount of time, the direct and

unreserved statements,

"we all thought you were dead" and "we didn't think we'd see you again" and "nice to see you upright," that sort of thing.

Everything had gone as I had hoped, with all feelings of discomfort soon forgotten, as I was greeted with a genuine show of affection.

Handshakes, back-slaps, man-hugs and some woman hugs came in quick succession, as everyone came forward to tell me how pleased they were to see me, and how relieved they were that I had survived my ordeal.

I don't care if it sounds 'un-manly' or even a little 'soppy', but within the walking football community there is a genuine feeling of care and consideration for one another, and although we may come from different backgrounds, from different cities and have different accents, we all have that one thing in common, (well two if you count that we are all old buggers). We all share a passion for the beautiful game of football. Yes, we know that we are no longer as fast, athletic or as skilful as we used to be, and yes, there are more than a few dicky backs, dodgy hips and wonky knees around, but what we now lack in speed and mobility, we more than make up for with a sense of fun, friendship and enthusiasm. It's just a blessing that we are still here and still able to take part.

My apologies, I went off on one then. Back to the story.

Once everyone had finished declaring how happy they were that 'I'd made it', there followed the inevitable questions that everybody wanted to know.

'What actually happened?'

'Did you feel any pain?'

'What did it feel like when you died?'

'Did you know you were dead?'

'Were there any lights?'

'Out of body experience?'

'Did you see anything at all?' etc. etc.

But sadly, the answers I gave, were not going to be much help to them.

No, I didn't have any memory of the day. No, I didn't have any pain, one minute I was here, the next I was gone. No, I didn't know that I was dead, and I wasn't aware of anything happening (a good job really, as there had been two big hairy and be-whiskered blokes giving me mouth to mouth). And no, I didn't see anything either (although I must admit to sometimes having a little fun with the last one.)

"Yes, I did see something actually, (crowd go silent and gather around.) I was in a long dark tunnel that looked to have a glowing light at the end. And ever so faintly I could hear a soft voice, it was telling me that everything was going to be okay, if I would just go to the light. And when I reached the light, there was a man, who seemed to be floating on air as he moved towards me. And once he got close, he leaned forward and said something to me. And do you know what he said? (beckoning the crowd closer and pausing for dramatic effect.) He said, ...

"I'm sorry son, you're not allowed in here wearing trainers!" (Cue groans from the crowd).
[NB: Sports shoes for our overseas readers].

I hadn't really given it much thought before, but once you reach a 'certain age', it really makes you think when one of your number experiences a life-threatening event. And it doesn't take long before the inevitable pops into your head, 'bloody hell, that could so easily have been me' (a 'there but for the grace of God...' scenario.) And judging by the look of it, that is exactly what had happened at the club. So many people had come forward to say that it came as such a shock to them when they heard that I'd had a cardiac arrest and heart attack whilst on the pitch, especially as they considered me one of the fittest in our group of over 60's players. They said: That what happened to me had made them think about the need to enjoy life and to live it day by day, as you really don't know what fate has in store for you, or what lies just around the corner. So true!

Standing on the sideline, watching everyone else play was so frustrating. Every time the ball came close, I had to fight back the urge to stick out my foot and make contact with it. But at half-time, when play had stopped and everyone was walking from the pitch, I spotted a stray, lonely and unloved ball, just sitting on the half way line, longing to be kicked. So, after a quick look around (to check that the wife wasn't looking,) I nonchalantly strolled over to it, flicked it up and volleyed it into the empty net. Goaaaaal!

I had hoped that nobody was going to notice, but unfortunately the ball rattled in off the crossbar with a bit of a clang, and as I winced at the sound, I could sense my wife's head slowly turning in my direction (a bit like the possessed girl from the Exorcist movie) to give me 'the look.' Oops, spotted!' I slid back to the sideline 'tail between my legs', where I remained on best behaviour for the rest of the game.

Going back to Beechcroft had been just what I needed. Yes, it was frustrating to watch and not be involved, but it was great to see everyone and to feel part of the club again. It raised my spirits and strengthened my resolve to work hard, and to get back to full fitness as soon as possible, so that I could take my place back on the pitch again, back out there with my mates.

Whilst I was there, I heard that in two days time, my over 60's teammates would be playing in a competitive league game at 'The Oval' (Bedworth United's ground). The place where all this had started only 30 days ago, so I pencilled it into my diary. I needed to know what had happened to me on that day.

Return To The Scene

Sunday 21st October 2018. (21 days post surgery).

It had been a long two days of waiting, but Sunday was finally here. Today I was going back to 'The Oval' in Bedworth, but as with my recent visit to Beechcroft, any excitement of 'going to football again, was mixed with a good dose of the jitters. Yes, I was looking forward to seeing my teammates again, and yes, I was eager to find out what had happened to me, but I was nervous about meeting the other people who'd been at 'The Oval' on the day that I had my 'incident.'

They were people that I didn't know, but they were the people responsible for saving my life. I mean, what do you say to someone that you've never met before, and who's actions have determined whether you lived or died? And just to say thank you to them is not enough. It doesn't even come close to being enough! But, being nervous to meet them or not, it was something that I had to do. It was important to see them and to express my gratitude for what they did.

Arriving at the ground around 3:30pm and after Dawn had parked the car, we made our way around the side of the pitches, to where I could see the blue shirts of the Birmingham lads, who's game was already underway. Now, normally I'd be quite happy to just stand and 'take in' a game of football, especially when it's my mates that are playing. But today, I had something much more important to attend to. First and foremost, I had to go and meet Stuart Roe, the person who'd rushed to my aid with the defib, and the person who was largely responsible for saving my life.

So, after waving a quick greeting to the lads, I put the pitches behind me, and made my way to the players' lounge, where I knew that I would find him.

As I entered, it was empty, that is, except for a young blonde girl who sat in the corner with two small children (little did I know that the girl was Stuart's partner.)

"Hello, I'm looking for Stuart," I said.

"Oh, he's out the back," she replied, "I'll go and get him for you."

A short while later a man appeared. Was this Stuart? I didn't know, so I tentatively walked towards him, hoping that I wasn't going to make an idiot of myself with a random stranger. But as we drew closer, he broke into a big smile and held out his hand, which I shook vigorously as I thanked him for everything that he'd done for me.

"Well, you look a lot healthier than the last time I saw you" he joked.

"Yeah" I said, laughing, "I'm better now that I've got some blood pumping around my body again."

And as we talked further, Stuart recounted his side of the story, of what happened.

"You were really lucky you know. On the day you collapsed, I wasn't even scheduled to be at work. And the defibrillator that we used to save you, had only just been fitted with new batteries, as the previous week it had been checked and the batteries had needed replacing."

He jokingly added, "You're so lucky, you should probably choose this weekend's lottery numbers for me."

We chatted for a while longer, and although we had so much to catch up on, Stuart had work duties to perform, so we shook hands again and arranged to catch up later, once the games outside had finished.

Vacating the players' lounge, Dawn and I returned pitch-side, where we took to the sideline and watched the remaining 20 minutes of the Birmingham game. As is usual when watching, I was mentally kicking every ball, longing to be on the other side of the line and able to take part. And hopefully, with my wounds continuing to heal well and with a noticeable increase in my fitness, it wouldn't be too much longer before I could do that.

The team were playing well and were winning without me, but I could sense a strange mood hanging over the game, with some of the lads seeming to be a little subdued and not performing at 100 percent. Something wasn't quite right, something that I was unable to put my finger on at the time. I was told later, that by sheer coincidence, this game was being played on the exact same quarter of pitch, where my incident had taken place during the previous game. Maybe this was the reason for them being so unsettled?

As the final whistle blew, the players came over to gather on the sideline, where amongst much hand shaking and back slapping, it was expressed how happy they were to see me, along with the relief that everything had worked out okay in the end. Nobody could believe that it happened only four weeks ago, and everyone agreed that on another day and under another set of circumstances, it could easily have all ended so differently.

They asked, "don't you feel uneasy, coming back and being in the place where it happened?" But no, I didn't feel anything at all. I still had no memory of the day, so coming here today was just like arriving for any other football game.

Before disappearing to the changing rooms, one of my teammates, Steve Evans surprised me by presenting me with a large framed photograph of myself (in B'ham colours), which he had taken at a tournament a few months earlier. And as Steve handed his gift to me, I could see that he was quite emotional about it. Putting this gift together had obviously meant a great deal to him. And as he gave it to me, I too became emotional. I was overwhelmed by such a thoughtful and moving gesture. The picture now hangs 'pride of place' on the wall in my lounge, and is the photo that has been used to grace the front cover of this book.

With the team now gone, I wandered around to the other side of the pitch, to where the Bedworth team were still playing their game. As I approached, I was puzzled to see that a number of spectators had turned in my direction and were smiling at me.

I had no idea who these people were, but judging by their collective behaviour, it was clear that they knew me. I was met by a beaming Russ Watkin (BDWF Manager), who was so pleased to see me, that he shook my hand as if he wanted to remove it from my wrist, before introducing me to some of the people present, who turned out to be mostly staff and players of Bedworth & District Walking Football Club (BDWF). Aah, the penny dropped. It all became clear.

No wonder they had recognised me. These were people who had been there on the day of my 'incident', and who (in one form or another) had attended to me.

And as I met each in turn and the details of their involvement became clear, I could only shake my head in disbelief, lost for words, as the full picture of what had happened began to emerge.

"You were laying on the floor",

"we were all gathered around you",

"you wasn't breathing",

"the CPR didn't seem to be working",

"we thought, he's dead",

"the defib didn't work",

"we shocked you again",

"faint signs of life",

"two Ambulances came",

"they put you on a stretcher",

"took you away."

All of their tales were sprinkled with their personal thoughts and feelings at the time. It painted a grim scene. And the one reoccurring thing that everyone said was, “None of us thought that you were going to make it. You were really, really lucky.”

But, by the grace of ... (insert God of choice here) I did make it, and with the help of these people, plus some amazing medical staff, here I was, surrounded by a crowd who showed great delight that I was back in the land of the living. I was truly moved by the number of people who approached me, (people that I didn't know or recognise), to shake my hand, and tell me how happy they were to see me, and how fantastic it was that I was still alive.

And with the game now finished, people started to disperse. I had met and spoken to so many today, and I had endlessly relived the event over and over, but now I was done. It was time to go home.

But before leaving, we made a point of calling into the Players' Lounge, to see Stuart again, and to say our goodbye's.

Meeting for the second time was much more relaxed for both of us. And with the initial 'what do I says' now behind us, we resumed with the inevitable, and returned to the topic that had brought us both together. We laughed as Stuart recalled:

“As you had obviously left the ground in an ambulance, I had been given your car keys (to move it to a more secure area), and when I inserted them into the ignition, your car stereo blasted out with Bon Jovi's 'shot down in a Blaze of Glory', followed by, 'Shot through the heart ...' (from Bon Jovi's, you give love a bad name.)" He laughed at how ironic it was, that these were the last song, and the next song on the Bon Jovi playlist, that I'd been listening to on my way to the ground.

And there was further irony to come, (in relation to Stuart's earlier comment of, "you're so lucky, that you should choose this weekend's lottery numbers for me.") Well, a short while later, Dawn picked out a random team (from 50) on the club's lottery card. And when the card was complete and the sticker removed to reveal the winner? Yep, you guessed it, Dawn.

Returning to 'The Oval' to meet everyone, and hearing all the personal accounts, told with such emotion had been incredibly moving. And although my previous visit had been 'a tad traumatic', I count myself very lucky to have been in the right place, at the right time, and with the right people around me. And now that everything is behind us, the negative experience that we all shared, has turned into a positive, with new friendships being formed and with a special bond now existing between us. And although I'm still part of the Birmingham WF family, I now have another family at Bedworth and District WF.

[To give an example of the relationship I now have *with the Bedworth WF team, I would like to share an amusing story that happened a few months later, when the Birmingham WF and Bedworth WF teams were playing at the same venue. Prior to the game, I had changed into my*

Birmingham kit and was heading out of the dressing room, (with my teammates), just as the Bedworth team were queueing to enter. As we walked out past the line of waiting players, there was a chorus of,
"hello Paul, you OK?"
"Hi Paul, how's it going,"
"hello mate, how are you" and,
"hey Paul, how you feeling?" etc. etc.
Walking past, I shook outstretched hands and answered each in turn, "Hi Russ, feeling great" "hey Brian, I'm fine thanks" "hello Phil, much better now" etc.
And upon arriving at the end of the line, Martin (one of my teammates) turned to me and said,
"bloody hell, it's like following a celebrity."
To which I replied (tongue in cheek) "yeah, but don't forget, I had to die to get that reception".]

I feel that I can't end this chapter without saying a few more words about Stuart. Whenever I've met Stuart, I've found him to be a very quiet and modest person, who shuns the spotlight and doesn't seek any praise or any recognition for what he did. He has always underplayed his involvement with an approach of, 'well, you just do what you need to do.'

One of the stories that Stuart shared with me, occurred whilst he was serving in the British Army (Stuart served for nearly twenty years, including out in Afghanistan.) When out on patrol one day, Stuart was unfortunately caught in an IED blast (Improvised Explosive Device), that was intended for somebody else. And when the device exploded, the impact caused an tremendous amount of damage to Stuart's legs. The first responders to the incident were a squad of American soldiers, who informed Stuart that his injuries were so severe, that one of his legs would have to be amputated at the scene. Stuart's response was, "there's no way that I'll give you consent to do that. You are not leaving any part of me in this god forsaken country."

Following the incident, Stuart was evacuated back to the UK, where he spent the next two years in a wheelchair, as he underwent numerous operations and physical rehabilitation, aimed at rebuilding and strengthening his damaged legs.

The process of learning to walk again was a long, slow and frustrating one, but with dogged determination and strength of character Stuart persevered, with the result that today, he is now able to walk again completely unaided.

[When I sat and thought about Stuart's story, I found it incredible how an event which had taken place decades ago and over 3500 miles away, and which had involved a person, who was unknown and unconnected to me, could now have had such an effect on my life.

To put it simply: If Stuart's incident in Afghanistan had ended differently for him, then my 'event' would probably have ended differently for me, with

the end result possibly being that neither of us would be alive today!
It's amazing to think how people's lives can be connected, and how something that happens within a stranger's life, can later have an impact and an effect on what happens within yours].

I know that Stuart would never consider himself to be a hero, in fact he would hate the thought of anyone calling him one, but if he ever reads this book, he will know that I will always hold him in the highest regard. The fact remains, that if it wasn't for Stuart and what he did for me, then I wouldn't be here today.

22 October 2018 – Coventry Telegraph, Bedworth Echo and Nuneaton Tribune Newspapers and website report

'Thank you for saving my life' says grateful Coventry grandad

A Coventry grandad says he will be forever indebted to Bedworth United Football Club for literally saving his life.
Had it not been for the quick actions of members of the club and its walking football team Paul Feeney says he would not be around to share his remarkable story.
The Eastern Green resident, who collapsed on the pitch at The Oval while playing a walking football game, simply said: "I cannot put into words how thankful I am, I am indebted to all of the people at Bedworth.
"Without the people at Bedworth I would not be

here, there aren't enough words to say how grateful I am.

"Having met them and spoke to them, they said they didn't really know what skills they had until they were put in the situation to use them, they said they all pulled together and that is incredible."

What happened?

The Birmingham Walking Football team player collapsed during a fund-raising match in aid of Prostate Cancer at the home of the 'Greenbacks on Friday, September 21.

Two members of the Bedworth walking football team as well the stadium manager put their life-saving skills into practice and used the club's defibrillator to literally bring Mr Feeney back to life.

"I don't really remember a lot, I remember turning into Bedworth United, I was really, really looking forward to taking part in the game for prostate cancer, but then I can't remember a thing, it was almost as if I had been switched off," the 61-year-old explained.

Unbeknown to him, the first aid and defibrillator trained 'Greenbacks members fought to save his life while West Midlands Ambulance Service paramedics were en-route.

The former manager at the Coventry Chamber of Commerce was then taken to the University Hospital Coventry and Warwickshire (UHCW), where he underwent a triple heart bypass.

Indebted to the 'Greenbacks

After spending more than ten days at UHCW, Mr

Feeney was able to return home to his grateful family, including his wife Dawn.

Keen to thank those who saved his life, Mr and Mrs Feeney returned to the Oval - the place where the drama happened and it proved to be an emotional day.

"I am really indebted to club, without the skills of some of the people there, I would not be where I am today," he said.

"It is not just the people who saved my life, it is whoever took the decision at the club to get a defibrillator, they also saved my life with that decision.

"It was strange to go there (Bedworth United) I don't know anyone there but they all knew me. I just wanted to say thank you to everyone who helped me."

"It was okay for me, I didn't know what was going on, it is my wife and kids who have had to deal with all of the trauma of it and the people who saved me.

"Until I spoke to them, I didn't realise how traumatic it was for them and how touch and go it was for me.

"It just goes to show how important defibrillators are and how much of a difference they can make, I know they are expensive, especially for small teams but you can't put a cost on a life."

It could happen to anyone

By his own admission, Mr Feeney was fit, having played Saturday and Sunday football league all of his life, twice a week and then been playing walking football for Birmingham for the past two years.

"It just goes to show that it can happen to anyone," he added.

" I have spoken to the lads on the Birmingham team

and told them to look after themselves because you never know when this is going to happen."

The famed family spirit among the walking football community has astounded the grandad: "I had well wishes from as far as Canada, New Zealand and Australia, I couldn't believe it.

"I am so surprised with how many people have been in touch, especially other walking football clubs, they have been brilliant.

He is now due to see a specialist on November 13 and then hopes to be able to go back to the gym to get fit again: "I would like to start playing football again in January," he said.

"I am going to take it steady, get my fitness back up there first."

Proud club

Russ Watkin, one of the directors at Bedworth United Football Club and a member of the walking football team, said they were delighted to welcome Mr and Mrs Feeney along to their first county FA game on Sunday.

"We had kept in touch with them, they kept us updated when he was coming out of hospital and so we gave Paul and his wife an open invite to come back whenever they could," he said.

"It was great to see them both, it was nice for our walking football team players and the ground manager, who saved his life, to see him again."

Mr Watkin said the football club has also been inundated with messages following the life-saving, on-pitch drama

"It was quite remarkable the response we got back from it, the amount of lower league clubs who explained how they had just got a defib and how the story showed how important they are," he said.

"Walking football is like a huge family, we have had so many messages and so many people saying how they too now have a defibrillator.

"I just think it is such a shame that they cost so much money and very little is given to grass roots football for things like this."

Russ' wife puts on a legendary buffet after games: "We always run a little 'black out' to pay for the buffet so that it doesn't have to come out of club funds and Dawn had a go and won it."

She said: "This must be my lucky club, first you save my husband's life and then I win the 'black out' card".

Fixed

Mid November, six weeks since the operation, and today I'm on my way back to the hospital for a six week check-up with my surgeon. I was looking forward to meeting Mr. Barker again, (or Tom, as I like to call him, now that we are bro's.) I wanted to thank him for taking such good care of me and, to reaffirm to him how the work he does, truly is life changing.

I suppose deep down he probably knows that, but it doesn't hurt to show appreciation to someone for their expertise, and for the many years of training that they've had to put in to get them there.

I'll admit to being a little in awe of Mr. Barker, but hey, who wouldn't be. This is a man who has the power to extend life at his fingertips. Now that's what I call a real superpower!

Health wise, everything was going well, with my wounds having now transformed from lumpy and livid purple gashes, to barely visible smooth and flat creases (kudos to the man or woman with the needle.) My heart had remained stable and was no longer beating like an old tractor engine, and my fitness had improved to the point where I could now bound up and down the stairs like a young mountain goat.

At the hospital, it wasn't long before I was whisked into the consulting room.

"Hello. Mr Barker."

"Hello Mr Feeney, how are you feeling now, any problems?" Damn it, he didn't call me Paul! Oh well, I suppose he's saved dozens of lives since he did me.

"I'm feeling great thanks, no problems at all"

"That's good to hear. We'll take a look at your wounds, have a quick check of your medication and let you be on your way, back out into the world."

It was as easy as that! No high fives, no exchange of phone numbers and no meet up for beers down the pub. Was I disappointed? Yeah, maybe a little, but at the end of the day, I suppose that I was just another patient saved, and tomorrow there will be more to save, and more the day after, and the day after that, ad infinitum.

The conveyor belt of patients, waiting to have their bodies repaired is relentless, and only makes the job that these specialists do, more remarkable. It's just another day at the office.

"So, what was the problem then?" I asked.

"You had extremely narrowed arteries around the heart, which I believe were the result of a hereditary problem within your family, as your mother, father and brother all died young from heart related conditions. Following your surgery, the problem that caused you to have your cardiac arrest no longer exists. You've been fixed. Your heart is as strong as it could possibly be, so it will probably be something else that pop's you off now."

"Am I able to drive again then?"

"Yes you can"

"Will I be able to fly?"

"Yes, no problem"

"Can I go back to playing football?"

"Yes, as long as you are careful"

"Will I still be able scuba dive?"

"Yes, after completing a stress test"

"So, is that it?"

"Yes, that's it, as long as you are healing well and have no pain, there's nothing more we need to do."

So, safe in the knowledge that I was now 'fixed', I thanked Mr. Barker again for everything that he had done, and I exited the hospital, jumped into the car and drove home, where I circled a date on the calendar for my expected return to the game.

Back In The Game

It was the 30th of November, a day that I had looked forward to for so long. Two months had passed since 'the op.' and my recovery had gone better than expected. Back then, at the hospital, I had set an ambitious (some said ridiculous) target of returning to football in just eight weeks. And now, after much determination (and the support of a good wife), that day had finally arrived. No longer would I have to be excluded, forced to play the game in my head from the side-line. Today, I was going to be 'out there', 'in amongst it' and taking part in a one-hour game.

I hadn't given much thought that something untoward could possibly happen, or that my 'new heart' may not be ready to be pushed to where it hadn't been in a while, I was just excited to be back doing something that I loved.

Anyway, if I did 'go floppy' and tombstone into the ground, I was comforted by the thought that all the Birmingham WF facilities have AED's on site (not that I wanted to be zapped again), along with staff trained in giving first aid and CPR, should it be required.

This had actually been a major consideration when I moved from Coventry WF to Birmingham WF in the first place. So if anything unfortunate were to happen, then I was comfortable that I would be in good hands.

Dawn and I arrived at Birmingham's Beechcroft Club early, and 'parked up' in an empty space. I knew that most of the lads wouldn't be here yet. But just like my previous visit, I didn't want to turn up and walk into a crowd of people, many of which would think I was crazy to be coming back to training so soon. But I had thought long and hard about this, and had discussed my feelings with a very protective and fully supporting wife, and between us, we had weighed the level of risk against the mental and physical benefits of playing again, and had both agreed, that as long as I took it easy, curbed my enthusiasm, and constantly monitored how my body was reacting, then returning to football was the best thing that I could possibly do.

Opening the boot of the car, I smiled as I removed my kit bag, enjoying the wave of familiarity that swept over me. And although I had performed this task a hundred times before, this time it seemed a little more poignant. I was struck by the thought of: how easy it would have been for things to have turned out differently. And if they had, then I wouldn't be here doing this today. But it would all still be happening anyway. Life goes on with or without you.

I struggled to contemplate the depth of what that all meant.

But I was here. One month earlier than anyone expected and I was itching to play.

Entering the club house I could see a number of 'early birds' already getting changed, and I dropped my bag in the corner as I headed to the kitchen area to make myself a pre-game drink. In the kitchen I bumped into Neil the club trainer (who we call Nell.)

"Hello Paul, nice to see you, how are you feeling?" He asked.

"Hi Nell, I feel great" I said (knowing what was coming next).

"When do you think that you'll be back playing again then?"

"Hmm, in about half an hour." I said.

Nell's eyes went wide, and his eyebrows raised, like he was having a prostate exam. This was clearly not the response that he'd been expecting.

He asked, "Have you cleared it with Paul, (Paul Murtagh the club owner)?"

To which I replied, "I didn't know I had to"

"Yes, we need to make sure that you've recovered enough to start playing again"

"Well, I wouldn't be here if I didn't think so" I said.

"Okay, hold on while I call Paul on his mobile"

Nell retreated to a quieter spot and delivered the 'good news' to Paul. This was fair enough I suppose. The club operates to high standards, where player safety has always come first, so I couldn't really complain if they wanted to ensure that I didn't die on them for a second time. That wouldn't be a good day out for any of us.

I did actually think that I'd already told them I would be coming back around this time. But maybe I didn't? Or they had forgotten, or hadn't taken me seriously. Who knows?

Nell returned, "Paul said, that as long as you take it easy, you can play today, then only once a week for the next four weeks."

"Yep, Okay, I'm happy with that," I said nonchalantly, (but secretly thinking) 'there's no way I'm going to sit at home for six days at a time, once I'm back to playing footie again."

But, whatever they said, I would have agreed to, just to get back onto the pitch. I had prepared myself for a couple of weeks of 'bedding back in', but after that (and assuming that there were no ill effects), I planned to 'up the intensity' somewhat, as on the 2nd of January 2019 the trials for the Birmingham County Regional Team were taking place at 'The Oval' in Bedworth, and that date and those trials had always been '**the major target**' that I'd set for my return to competitive football. So now the real work began. I had only four weeks to be fit enough to take part in those trials.

When I broke the news to the rest of the players that I'd be taking part in today's training, there was much surprise.

"Are you sure? Your op was only two months ago."

"What if the ball hits your chest?"

"What if you collapse again?"

"What if, what if..."

Clearly, they had some concerns for my safety, but I also sensed an underlying feeling that some players were maybe a little uncomfortable with having me back on the pitch, especially if I was still vulnerable or a bit fragile. This was quite understandable.

Football (even non-contact football) is always a competitive and physical game, with players wanting to take part and play in the way that they are used to. Nobody wants to be worried, or have to take extra precautions around a player who maybe shouldn't be there (due to ill health or injury.) And nobody wants to be involved in a potential accident with that 'at risk player', which could result in further injury to them.

So, in an attempt to put everyone's mind at ease (and to justify my inclusion), I set about reassuring them how good I was feeling, and how I had built up my training in preparation for this day.

I assured them that I didn't feel at any risk, or in any danger, and I believed that the time was now right for me to return. With this, everyone seemed to relax a bit, but as I got changed I was still feeling a little detached from the group, a bit like the new boy at school. They were obviously a little jittery about my return, but I knew that once the whistle blew and I could show them that I was the 'normal Paul', and not the frail and delicate vision often portrayed of a recovering heart attack victim, then everything would be okay, and that there was nothing to be worried about.

And that's exactly what happened. Once I was out there, it was like I'd never been away.

It was a cold November morning with the sun fighting to clear an overnight mist, and everyone was struggling to coax a scrap of heat into muscles that just wanted to get back into the warm. And as I gradually worked through my usual warm-up routine,

I was acutely aware of being under close observation from the edge of the pitch, where my wife Dawn was watching me like a hawk, and Nell's beady eye was assessing and monitoring my every move, making sure that I was safe and up to the task of taking part. And because of this, I went into best behaviour mode, determined not to give them any reason to pull me from the game. But I was now eager to get things underway.

"Come on Nell, it's bloody freezing, let's get going. I haven't been this cold since I was dead!" Shit! I don't know where that came from, I opened my mouth and it just slipped out.

"Sorry, ready whenever you are Nell" I corrected.

As we kicked off, my lungs instantly demanded a bucket full of air and my heart kicked into overdrive. But this was to be expected. It was only my first training session, and I knew that with each and every session, things would only get easier. Anyway, I had my trusty watch that would be monitoring my heart rate, and would inform me if it were to go irregular or dangerously high. In fact, during the past two months I had become quite an 'Internet expert' on how heart rates increased and decreased as a person progressed through the 'heart rate zones' whilst exercising. And today, this watch would be playing an important part, and I was under strict instruction to check it every few minutes. And if somehow I forgot, then a quick glance to a scowling, wrist tapping wife on the sideline soon reminded me again.

Everything started out well, with a gentle rise in heart rate from a resting 55 beats per minute (bpm) to a steady 110bpm as I'd warmed up, then on to 125bpm as the game started. This was where it remained, stable and level, and at what seemed like a reasonable average. But on my latest 'watch check' (following my first real burst of energy), the needle had moved into the 'red zone', increasing to 160bpm. Not a total surprise, as 150bpm to 170bpm is quite normal following a quick surge of activity.

My heart hadn't beaten that fast since 'the midnight scare', and I'll admit to feeling a little anxious. But I knew that what my heart did next, would be the real indicator. So, I gradually eased down, focussing intently on the dial. And as I watched, relief overcame any worries, as the numbers slowly started to tumble, back down to a more reasonable 100bpm. Phew! All was working as it should. But did anybody notice?

Casually I took a quick glance to the sideline, where my wife gave me a look that could peel an onion. Shit! She doesn't miss a thing. I responded with my best cheesy grin and with two thumbs up. No worries here, all's good I signalled as I re-entered the fray.

The game continued, and I enjoyed five minutes in which I was given a respectfully wide berth by the other players. This was great, I had loads of time on the ball, could do all the fancy tricks and play killer passes like a star. But unfortunately my 'protective shield' was short lived and normal service was resumed, as I was treated with an elbow to the ear and a few raps around the ankles. Don't take advantage Feeney, you are not that vulnerable! I took it all in good spirit, and I wouldn't have had it any other way. I was back, and happy to be treated just like everyone else.

All too soon the session came to an end, and amid the customary handshakes, I was congratulated on how well I had played (and on still being upright.) The hour had passed so quickly, and I was overjoyed to have made it through without incident, and as I walked to the sideline and saw the look of relief on my wife's face, a wave of guilt came over me. I had been so caught-up in my own desire to play football again, that I hadn't given a thought for how Dawn must have been feeling as she looked on, hoping and praying that history didn't repeat itself. Who's to say that what happened before, wasn't going to happen again? It was always a possibility and there had been no guarantees.

It must have been devastating for her, when after my previous game, she had been faced with the awful possibility of having to live the rest of her life alone. And today, I had put her in a position where that possibility could have been there again.

It had been okay for me. I had been aware at all times of how my body was feeling and how it was reacting. I had felt good and I'd played without worry. Taking it for granted that there would be no problems as I raised my heart to levels that were challenging for a 'fit and healthy' person, let alone for a sixty-two-year-old recovering from heart surgery.

Upon reaching her I asked, “Are you okay?”

My reward, a nod and a smile, “As long as you are.” I gave her a kiss, followed by a big hug, and made a promise to never again fail to take other people's feelings into consideration as a result of my actions.

I counted my blessings that I had such an understanding and supportive wife.

Today I turned a real corner in my recovery. It had been a day that I'd planned for, and looked forward to for some time. And I always knew that when it came, it would bring with it, not only the exhilaration of playing football again, but also a good dose of fear and trepidation that would have to be faced and overcome, if I wanted to do the things that I had before. And at the end of the day, everything had turned out well. It had been a good introduction back into football, and I'd come through it without any problems. I had tested out my 'new heart (which had passed with flying colours), and now I could stop sulking around the house like a grumpy old man, and get back to playing regular football again without any worries. I was delighted, but it was just the start. I now had four weeks in which to train hard in preparation for the County Regional Trials.

The Birmingham County Regional Trials

Finally the big day had arrived. The 2nd of January 2019. A date that had been circled in the diary since leaving hospital 83 days ago.

Following my return to training last month, I'd not only been focused on getting some strength back into my leg muscles, but had also stepped up my cardio work, hopeful that my heart and lungs would be able to cope with what was going to be asked of them. And with four good training sessions now behind me, I was starting to feel confident that what had caused my cardiac arrest had now been put right, and I was less likely to end up face down again. Yes, I knew that I was far from 100% fit, but I could only hope that it was going to be enough. I had no more time to prepare anyway.

It is with some irony that these trials and my return to competitive football were to be held at 'The Oval' in Bedworth. The place where in my previous game, it had all gone so horribly wrong. But, here I was, three months on (with heart Mk II), back at 'The Oval'' to take part in the 'best of the region' player trials. It's funny how life seems to go around in circles.

Today would involve the best players from each of the teams in the Birmingham County Walking Football League, taking part in a competitive walking football session, in which our abilities would be assessed. Then, if we were considered good enough, we could be selected to represent the County and the Central Region in games against the best teams, with the best players from the other regions of England and Wales. Plus the team would also represent 'the central region', against the UK's international teams, along with forming a pool of players who would be available for selection into the England Walking Football squad.

I was joined at these trials by my Birmingham teammates Dave Whatmore and Roy (the roadrunner) Williams, and upon our arrival we had hatched a plan, that being: 'If we stayed close together, we would possibly all be selected to play for the same team.' This would give us an advantage, as we play together all the time.

Well, our cunning scheme lasted all of five minutes, as when the warm up started, I became a bit over excited and shot off down the pitch like I'd been fired out of a canon.

Unfortunately, I seemed to have missed the 'we're gonna start out easy' memo, and my enthusiasm to impress, had now caused me to become separated from my mates. A consequence of this, was that I was picked to play in a team of players who were nearby. Players that played for rival teams, and who had been my opponents all year. And to make matters worse, my Birmingham teammates (who had stayed together), were picked in the team to play against me.

The game started with me playing in my preferred position of central midfield. This suited me perfectly, as it put me slap bang in the middle of the all the action, and in a place where I could hopefully be able to have some influence upon the game. Central midfield is a key area of the pitch, and a place where you either control the game, or you lose it to your opponents, who control the game.

Everyone began cautiously, with both teams determined to keep possession of the ball with short safe passing. And neither team looking to push forward in search of a goal, in case it left them exposed at the back. But as the clock ticked on, and players became more relaxed, the game opened up, with our opponents becoming more adventurous and putting our goal under constant pressure. Eventually, their dominance on the ball told, and the deadlock was broken as they slid the ball past our stranded goalkeeper to go 1-0 ahead.

The re-start saw little change, with the confidence of our opponents growing as the game progressed and they continued to push us back, forcing us to defend attack upon attack. And as the opposition dominated the play, I became increasingly frustrated at not being able to control my area of pitch. I didn't feel involved. The game was being played around me rather than through me. And even though I was taking up good positions, the ball just wasn't being given to me. It was as if mates were just passing to mates, instead of playing the ball into areas that would allow us to be a threat to the other team. Maybe it was a case that they felt more comfortable passing the ball to someone who they were more 'familiar' with? I don't know. But one thing was for sure, it would have to change if we were going to break our opponents grip on the game, and I was determined to raise the issue during the half-time break.

The second half started where the first left off, with constant pressure on our goal. But suddenly, during one of their attacks the ball broke free, won by one of our defenders, who, after hearing me screaming for the ball in midfield, played it forward. I was just inside my own half, facing my own goal and with space around me. The player who's job it was to mark me, now caught forward as my team broke out of defence.

As the ball arrived at my feet, I was aware that I still had an opposing defender behind me (who would by now be closing the gap between us), so I swept the ball first time to one of our players wide on the right wing, who pushed it onward into the opponents' half.

Avoiding the now challenging defender, I brushed past him and moved into the empty space beyond, knowing that 'by rights' I should receive the ball back again, and if I did, then I would be through on goal with only their keeper to beat. And to my surprise, no sooner had our wide player moved past their defenders, when he angled the ball straight back across the pitch, back into the middle and right to where I was waiting.

Managing to bring the ball under control, whilst moving it towards goal with a good first touch, I could see the keeper rushing out towards me, making himself bigger and attempting to 'narrow the angle', so I shaped my body to play the ball to his left, and as his weight shifted in that direction, I slipped the ball past him and into the goal on his right. The score was levelled at 1-1 and we were back in the game.

Drawing level seemed to settle us down a little. And as I began to enjoy more possession of the ball, I was able to play to the standard that I'd hoped for my return. Unfortunately though, even though the team's performance did improve, we were unable to add to our solitary goal, whereas our opponents scored another and the game ended with us losing 2-1.

For me, the final score in the game wasn't really that important. Only months ago, had set myself a tough personal challenge of recovering from my surgery and regaining a level of fitness, that would allow me to take part in these Central Regional Trials. Following which, I planned to make a full return to competitive walking football.

Taking part in the trials had been an important step. They had been my constant source of motivation, when at times, I'd needed to 'dig in' and push my boundaries to get fitter and stronger. There were many times, when it would have been a lot easier for me to just sit on the sofa, nurse my wounds and watch TV. But the need to prove to myself that cardiac arrest and heart surgery hadn't 'finished me' either as a person or a footballer, had always been stronger, and taking part in these trials had been my reward.

Once the game had ended, I sat in the dressing room with a big beaming smile. I was proud of myself. All the hard work that I'd put in had been worthwhile. Here I was, three months on from heart surgery, playing at the ground where last time out I had died. And during the trials, I had played well. I'd had a good game and shown that I was still capable of competing against the best of the region, plus I'd topped it all off with scoring my teams only goal. And the icing on the cake: This time I wasn't going to be leaving 'The Oval' in the back of an ambulance.

Several days later I received an email from Russ Watkin (the Central Regional Team Manager), to say that I had been selected to become part of his squad to represent the UK's Central Region.

A Successful Year

As spring rolled into summer, the Birmingham over 60's team had gone from strength to strength. We were playing well, with camaraderie and team spirit at an all-time high. Surely, there was nothing that could stop us from achieving our best season ever.

Health wise, I now felt fully recovered from my bypass op. I had no pain, no aches, no after-effects whatsoever, and considering that I'd been opened up and my heart operated on, I was amazed at how the human body can cope with such trauma and then have the ability to heal itself so completely.

It just goes to prove, that even if you have suffered a cardiac arrest, had a heart attack, or been through heart surgery, it doesn't mean that life has been taken away from you. With achievable goals in place and a positive attitude to reach them, there is no reason why you shouldn't be able to return to a normal life, and participate in, and enjoy the same activities that you did before.

On the football front, six months of training and playing had seen me gradually return to full match fitness, and I was now back to playing close to the same standard that I had before.

Game after game I was an 'ever present' in the team, and proud to have played an integral part of getting us to the lofty league and cup positions that we now found ourselves. On two occasions, I had even surrendered my usual midfield role and 'donned the gloves' to help out in goal, when we didn't have a goalkeeper available.

[During my spell 'between the sticks' I only conceded the one goal. But I have to confess, that on that occasion, the ball was struck past me from the half way line, over 25 yards away. It came as such a surprise, that my feet were rooted to the spot as it flew past me like a rocket.
After that game, I was never asked to play in goal again, I can't imagine why.]

It was now September 2019, and the team only had two games left to play, and they were big ones. Of these games, the first was a Regional Final against our 'old enemy' Hartshill Strollers, with the winners having the right to claim to be the best over 60's WF club in the UK's Central Region. The second game (and the last league game of the season) was a 'winner take all' league decider, against our close neighbours Coleshill Strollers. The outcome of which, would determine who finished in first or second place in the over 60's WF league.

The WFA Regional Final

There is a competition in the UK walking football world called the WFA National Cup And in 2019, there had been a record entry of 198 teams, all hoping to show that they were the best WF team in the country. The format for the competition is: The country is divided into eight regional areas, South West, South East, North West, North East, Central, London, East and South, with teams from each region competing against each other in a knockout scenario, with the winning teams progressing into the next round. Eventually, when each region has only two teams remaining, those two teams will play each other in a 'Regional Final' to determine the best team in the region. These eight 'best teams' will then compete in a one day play-off tournament against each other at a National Finals day, where the top performing team are crowned as the over 60's WF UK National Champions.

The whole occasion of reaching a Regional Final should have been a celebration, but for me, it turned out to be a bittersweet affair. It all started one week prior to the game, when I received an email from the manager confirming that I had been selected to be part of the squad of players who would be taking part.

I was thrilled at the thought of being in a final again, and although I've played in a few before, playing in this one had special meaning for me, given the circumstances of the previous year.

So, with the excitement of a kid at Christmas, I packed my kit bag early (not forgetting my lucky pants) and polished my boots (at least three times) whilst I waited patiently for the big day to arrive. And once it did, and following a long drive to the ground of Hartshill Strollers, I met up with my teammates, who like me, were all in good spirits and eager to get the game underway.

As soon as everyone was present, we made our way on-mass towards the changing rooms. It was at this point that our team manager approached me, stopping me in my tracks.

"Paul, we have too many players today, somebody will have to 'drop out'."

I thought: Why is he telling me? Does he want my opinion? Does he want my support? Or does he want me to deliver the bad news to the unlucky player?

I gave his predicament some thought, knowing that whoever got 'the axe' at this late stage, would be absolutely gutted to be left out. Then I had an idea.

"Tell you what" I said, "I'm prepared to sacrifice my place in today's game, on the understanding that IF we win (and therefore progress to the National Finals), then I would definitely be included in the squad of players to take part in those finals (this was somewhat of a risk, as if we were to lose today, then we wouldn't progress to those finals at all.)

The manager was happy with my solution. And so, my inclusion in a National Football Final, would now depended on the upcoming performance of my teammates (or so I thought).

So, putting any disappointment behind me, I led the team through the pre-game warm up before taking my place on the sideline, where I promptly turned into the stereotypical dad at the school soccer match, and began directing the play, planning the moves, and making every pass, without ever actually touching the ball. In truth, the lads on the pitch played brilliantly, and I also felt that I had played a part from the line, by supporting and encouraging them as best I could. Admittedly, at times, I had to suppress the urge of running onto the pitch and hoofing the ball into the Hartshill goal, before wheeling away with both arms held high (like one of those nutter supporters you see on TV), but I thought better of it. We were deep inside 'the Black Country' (west of Birmingham), and although I'm a Birmingham player, I come from the neighbouring City of Coventry (where we don't speak funny like them), so I stood out like the balls on a bulldog. Who knows what they would have done to me if I had?

As expected, Hartshill were difficult opponents and gave us a tough match, but at the final whistle, Birmingham had proved to be the better side, winning the game 2-0. We had just become the best over 60's WF team in the region, and now we were on our way to the National Finals in Worcester, where we had the chance to become the best in the UK. But first, there was the small matter of a league decider at Coleshill to be taken care of.

Last Game Shootout
Who's The Best In The League?

With the disappointment of not playing in the Regional Final behind me, I arrived at the ground of Coleshill Strollers for the last over 60's league game of the season. A game that would determine the overall league winners.

In the changing room, the manager named his starting line-up, choosing for me not to start and naming me as a substitute. This wasn't any surprise considering how well the team had played when winning the Regional Final against Hartshill. It made perfect sense to continue with the same winning side, and at least being named as a substitute, would mean that at some time, I would get my chance to be involved, and with it, an opportunity to reaffirm my position within the team.

Before the game even started, there was tension in the air. And with the game being a league decider, and with 'the Strollers' already being above us in the table, we were fully aware of what would be required. Basically, if we were going to walk away as league champions, then only an outright Birmingham win was going to be good enough.

Straight from the first whistle, the game proved to be a very physical and unfriendly affair, with 'off the field' friendships counting for nothing, and with a Coleshill team who were prepared to 'put a foot in', and not allow us any space, or any time on the ball (not what you'd expect from a bunch of 'old codgers' playing a non-contact sport.)
And to give credit where it's due, Coleshill's 'robust' approach to the game worked well. We were unsettled, and before long, the ball found it's way into the Birmingham net and we were 1-0 down. This was quickly added to, when the referee awarded Coleshill a second goal, in what was a rather farcical set of circumstances. Those being: A Coleshill player struck a shot from distance, which hit the Birmingham crossbar before rebounding down onto the ground, around the vicinity of the goal line, where it was collected by our goalkeeper. As the Coleshill players celebrated, the referee (who was 20 metres away and unable to seen clearly), then approached a female spectator, who was seated in the stand, 15 metres behind the goal, to ask her if the ball had crossed over the line or not. The female spectator replied "yes, I think that the ball did cross over the line." And with that, the referee allowed the Coleshill goal to stand. We were now 2-0 down, with the game effectively beyond our reach.

The half-time break couldn't come soon enough, and upon the re-start I got my chance to become involved, when the manager sent me onto the pitch in an attempt to get the team back into the game. BUT, no sooner had I adjusted to the frantic pace of the game, when he took me back off again. I had been on the pitch for only 15 minutes. What the hell was going on? In order to win this game (and the league), we now needed to score goals, and there was a possibility that I could do that. So why wasn't I being given that opportunity?

Confused and frustrated, I resumed my position back on the side-line, next to a manager who remained tight lipped regarding his decision.

The clock ticked away.

Then, with 30 seconds remaining in the game (and with three goals required), the manager turned to me,

"do you want to go back on?"

Needless to say, that with so little time left, I felt that this wasn't a tactical decision, but an attempt to appease me.

"No" I said, "what's the point?"

And as I turned away, the final whistle blew. We had lost the game 2-0, and had also lost the league.

After the game, I was approached by several of the Coleshill players, who asked: "Why didn't you start the game Paul?" and "why did your manager take you off, when your team needed goals?"

But I just shrugged, I didn't know the answers. They knew as much as I did. But what I did know, was that something had changed. My standing within the Birmingham team had suddenly gone from being a valued player one minute, to 'not being required' the next. But all wasn't lost. There was still the WF National Final to be played at the weekend, and I had an assurance that I would be included in that game.

Rock Bottom
The WFA National Finals

Taking part in the National Finals Tournament in Worcester was going to be a huge day out for me. Not only did Birmingham WF have the opportunity to become the best over 60's team in England, but the date of these finals was also hugely significant. It was near on, the one year anniversary from the day that I'd had my cardiac arrest whilst playing for the team.

Just being at these finals underlined, that although you may have suffered a major trauma, doesn't mean that you can't go on to recover, or to achieve the goals that you may have thought out of reach.

And personally, just being here to compete in a football final at national level (only one year after heart surgery), was going to be both a celebration and my reward for all the hard work that I had 'put in' during the past 12 months. It was going to be a milestone day.

BUT, little did I know: If my lack of participation in the previous two games had been disappointing, then things were about to get a whole lot worse.

It all started several days ago, when I received a team email, confirming the arrangements for the day and naming the squad of players that would be taking part. But as I eagerly opened it and scanned down the list of players, I couldn't see my name.

Maybe I'd missed it, so I checked again. But no, my name definitely wasn't there. Surely a mistake had been made? So I fired off an email to the manager (and captain), pointing out that they had forgotten to add me to the list of players. I waited for a reply for what seemed like hours, and when it finally came, it wasn't the response that I had been expecting. There hadn't been an error at all. I just wasn't included.

"What about the agreement that I would be in the squad?" I asked.

"What about my contribution in all of our previous games?"

"What about everything I've given to the team?"

"Where is the recognition?"

"Where's the reward?"

"Where is the loyalty for God's sake? One year ago I had even died whilst playing for you."

The answer I got was, "You're not the player you used to be."

I couldn't believe what I was hearing. I was completely devastated. I had given my absolute everything to the team, but now I had been unceremoniously 'dumped' from the squad on the eve of the most significant game of my life. And the reason that I'd been given? No, I wasn't buying that at all, and nobody else would either. How could I be considered good enough to represent the central region, yet no longer be good enough to play for the team that I had played in all year?

It was the worst day in all my 40 years of playing football, and I felt sick to my stomach.

I didn't know what hurt the most. The heartless way in which I'd been left out, (given how much it meant to me), or the thought that I had naively carried on giving everything, whilst all the time, plans had been afoot to remove me from the squad?

The whole episode left a bad taste in my mouth. I felt that I had been betrayed.

Nevertheless, there was nothing that I could do, decisions had been made. And whatever my feelings, they didn't matter. I was no longer a part of it any more, so I had little choice, but to spend the day at home, where all the time I just sat and thought about how my mates were getting on at those finals.

I learned later, that Birmingham had played well, progressing through several games to reach the tournament final, but were unfortunately beaten by a good Blackburn Rovers side, so finished the day as runners-up, with medals to show that they were the second best over 60's team in the country. Who knows? Maybe if I had been there I could have made the difference. I would like to think so.

And, with the sound of that final whistle, an end was signalled to the footballing year.

Taking stock, it had started so well with a speedy recovery, a return to fitness and participation in a successful Regional Trial. Then, following a summer of hard work and with only three games remaining, the team were in a position to achieve multiple honours.

Unfortunately, it wasn't to be, and we ended up as Bridesmaids not Brides.

And for me personally: After being an integral part of the Birmingham team all year, I had missed out playing in a Regional Final. I was only allowed a 'token appearance' in the league decider. And I was left out of the National Finals altogether.

It was a disappointing, emotional and painful end, and far from the celebration that I had been hoping for.

Birmingham WF 'Peaky's On Tour

BUT THEN, a few days later, and just when I thought that everything had gone 'tit's up', I received an email from the Birmingham WF boss and England WF manager Paul Murtagh. It read:

'Birmingham WF have been invited to take part in an exhibition game against Derby WF at Derby County FC's stadium, Pride Park. The game will take place on the 28th September 2019 during the half time interval of the EFL Championship match between Derby County FC and Birmingham City FC. Do you want to play?'

Did I want to play? Too bloody right I did. How many times do you get the chance to play in front of a potential 33,000 people, on the turf of a top class football stadium? An email went straight back with my reply. Yes, count me in.

And so, only a handful of days later I was sat amongst the Birmingham City fans, with the chants of 'Birmingham, Birmingham, Birmingham' echoing from the underside of the Pride Park roof.

Just before 3pm, both teams of professionals

entered the arena, causing the noise level to soar, as both sets of fans showed their appreciation and support by trying to 'out sing' the other. It was a big game, a local derby, a clash between two clubs with intent to show that they were the best in the Midlands.

The match kicked off, with the ball moving end to end as both teams searched for an early goal. But, exciting as the on-field play was, I found myself being unable to concentrate. The reason being: Under my seat and nestled between my legs was my kitbag. And in that bag, were my boots, pads, socks, shorts and the Birmingham shirt that I had played in all year (well, not the actual (No.5) shirt that I had died in twelve months earlier, as that had been cut off in hospital. But my new 'adopted' number 9 shirt (no tempting fate here.)) And with the thought of knowing why I and the bag were here, I could only think of one thing: 'Before long, I'm going to be out there on that same pitch along with my teammates, entertaining the crowd and demonstrating what walking football is all about (that's if the crowd don't all disappear to the toilet in the break.)

With only ten minutes remaining until the half-time whistle, we vacated our seats and made our way down and under the stand, looking for somewhere where we could change into our kit. For me and my mate Dave Whatmore, this turned out to be within the unglamorous confines of the disabled toilet (somewhat unbecoming for those about to star in the half-time entertainment), but we didn't really care. Above us, we could still hear the noise of the crowd reverberating throughout the stadium, and very soon, we would be walking out onto the sacred Derby County turf, to perform in front of that crowd.

It was incredibly exciting, but also a little intimidating. As the visiting team, how would we be received. Will we be mocked, heckled or even abused by the partisan crowd? Who knows, football fans can be pretty ruthless at times. I guess we were just going to have to wait and see.

When we first became aware of this game, one of the lads suggested (just for a bit of fun), wouldn't it be a good idea to all wear flat caps, just like the Birmingham street gang did in the hit TV show Peaky Blinders? It was an idea that was taken up with some enthusiasm, so hats were obtained, and were now being donned proudly atop our greying (and some balding) heads.

So, here we were, the opposing team about to enter the Lion's Den, wearing the colours of a rival team and looking like a bunch of extras from a Hovis ad. What possible reason could they have to abuse us?

Now at pitch level and gathered in a corner of the ground, we awaited the half time whistle and our cue from the security staff.

Phweeeeet, that's it, we were on. And upon that sound, the talented young professionals walked from the pitch, to be replaced by a group of old codgers, who ran (some shuffled) on, like they were about to play in a World Cup Final.

And would you believe it? A ripple of applause broke out from the crowd. The feeling of running on to that lush green, billiard table flat surface whilst being applauded was something quite special. It was a small slice of what it must feel like, to walk in the boots of a professional footballer. What an experience!

As our game was only scheduled to be a short one, the teams were quickly ushered to a specified area of the pitch. But I (being armed with a GoPro), managed to abscond, and 'did a runner' into the centre circle, where I set about recording the full 360 degree scene around me. I was only going to get this opportunity once, so it was a case of just do it and apologise later if scolded, (or rugby tackled to the ground) by the security staff.

Suddenly, a cheer went up. Shit, 'the pitch rozzers' must have spotted me? Are they on their way to apprehend me? But no. As I looked around, there were no burly bouncers bearing down on me. The crowd had been cheering because the automatic pitch sprinkler system had activated, causing both sets of players to scatter, as jets of water cascaded through the air, hunched over as they ran for cover from a good drenching. The crowd were loving it. The sight of a bunch of old fogies trying to escape from beneath the umbrella of water was something to behold.

And did I laugh at the misfortune of my poor teammates? Too bloody right I did!

With the sprinklers now turned off (and with hair plastered to heads) the game got underway, with the crowd enthusiastically cheering every kick of the ball, pass, shot or save. And the more the crowd cheered, the more the players were caught up in the excitement of it all, and the faster the game became. Until, within no time at all, the 'walking' part of walking football had completely fallen by the wayside, and the game changed from a sedate demonstration, into a win at all costs game of life and death. Thus proving: No matter what age you are, or at what level you may play, that competitive football spirit never leaves us!

With such limited pitch time, the teams had gone 'all out attack' straight from the whistle, with both creating chances, and with either capable of taking the lead. But it wasn't until the final minute of the game that the deadlock was broken, when a ball from the Birmingham defence was threaded through midfield, before being coolly slotted into the corner of the net, past a scrambling Derby keeper. Birmingham were 1-0 up. And before the game even had a chance to restart, the referee blew the final whistle, ending all possibility for Derby to redress the balance.

And upon the sound of that whistle, we all stopped kicking lumps out of one another and became best of friends again, shaking hands to the sound of applause, and the chant of Birmingham, Birmingham, Birmingham, which rang out from the Brummie supporters.

Admittedly the game wasn't to the same standard as what the crowd had come here to see, but it was still a game of football. And as lovers of the game, they had enjoyed it all the same, and as such, their applause now rang out as a sign of admiration, and in respect for us still being 'out there' and 'doing it' at our ripe old age.

But sadly, our brief moment of fame and our time on the turf had come to an end, and as the professional players emerged from the tunnel, we were ushered from the pitch and towards the nearest sideline (which happened to be on the half-way line), where we commenced our long walk back to the opposite corner of the ground.

And it was at this point, that the most unexpected thing happened.

As we made our way around the outside of the pitch, supporters of both teams were standing to applaud us. And as we passed by, the applause would then be taken up by the next section of crowd, and so on, all the way around the ground and until we reached our exit point. The scene being somewhat akin to when a team conducts a lap of honour following a big event. I hadn't given a moments' thought to the crowd reacting in this way, and was quite taken aback by their appreciation of our efforts to entertain them. It was completely unexpected and was a wonderful surprise.

And, not being one to let a moment pass without gaining the full experience, I went with it, and was soon waving back (sometimes with both hands raised above my head) as I soaked up the accolades and thanked them in return for their hospitality and kindness.

Walking from the Derby pitch to the sound of that applause was the most incredible feeling, and for me, it was the highlight of the day and a fitting end to what had been a challenging year. It was an experience that I will never forget.

Soon after, and following a quick change back into 'civvies', we returned to the stands where we took our place amongst the Birmingham fans as the second half got underway. Sitting there, couldn't help but look down to the area of the pitch where we had just been playing, and then around the ground at the 28,400 fans who surrounded the scene.

Who would have thought that only 12 months ago, I had left the lowly Bedworth United pitch in the back of an ambulance, and yet today I had just played on, and been applauded from, the pitch of a championship football club. I could only shake my head in disbelief. It didn't seem possible.

Then, the Birmingham fans broke into song with their adopted anthem:

Keep right on to the end of the road
Keep right on to the end
Though the way be long let your heart beat strong
Keep right on to the end
Though you're tired and weary
Still journey on 'till you come to your happy abode
With all our love we'll be dreaming of
We'll be there at the end of the road.

[The song 'Keep Right On to the End of the Road' was written by Sir Harry Lauder in 1917. It's words aimed to

provide inspiration and to encourage perseverance to the troops in WWI.

Not being a 'blues' (Birmingham City) fan, I hadn't paid much attention to this song before, but having heard it sang on this day (and within the context of my circumstances), I can't help but feel that the message it conveys, is not only appropriate to my story, but is also a good positive message to anyone who may need motivation or encouragement, when on the road to recovery or rehabilitation].

The Year In Short

Looking back on what has happened during the past twelve months, it has been one hell of a journey. And, for the benefit of those who may have skipped through the book, or flipped to the back pages for the answer to: "How come he was dead, but he's still writing this book then?" Well, here's a quick summary of what you've missed.

Everything started with an unexpected death. Mine! Quite a surprise and not the best start to the year. Then I was blown into, pummelled and literally shocked back to life by a bunch of strangers armed with an AED, before being whisked off to hospital in an ambulance, where I was put into a coma. In hospital I was 'tied' to a bed for 18 days, shaved bald, turned pink and had a small airship inserted into my penis, which was then stretched up to the ceiling.

Then I was told, "Mr Feeney... You've had a cardiac arrest. You've got a heart defect. You need a triple heart bypass."

So, they stopped my heart (again). Replaced the dodgy arteries with a huge vein from my leg (still not sure how my leg keeps working without it), and nine days later I was sent home to recover (where I couldn't lift a plate, couldn't climb the stairs and couldn't have a wee unless I was holding onto the wall).

Back on the road to regain fitness, I was humbled by 'the Pink Blur' (a spangly grey haired granny and legend in Lycra.) Two months after surgery, I resumed playing football. Had a successful Regional Trial, and watched as my team won a Regional Final, lost a league decider and lost a National Final (all of which I wasn't part of.)

Quitting the team, I walked away, believing that all my efforts and progress were for nothing. BUT, out of the blue (and in the spirit of all stories with happy endings), the day was saved, when I stepped out onto the pitch and played football (with my old teammates) in front of 28,000 people.

Quite a contrast to the scene in which I'd been a participant only 12 months earlier.

Dear reader. As I bring this book to conclusion, I must apologise in advance for the lack of 'funny bits' in the following two chapters. But if you have enjoyed my story, please read on, as these final words are probably the most important that I have written.

Facing Cardiac Events

Whilst I appreciate that not everyone's experience of a cardiac event is going to be the same, one thing is for sure: Whether you survive it (or not), is not only down to luck, but can also be down to you. And there are certain things that you can (and should) do, to give yourself the best chance of survival.

Basically, there are two paths on which to arrive at a cardiac event.

Route 1. The event is preceded by some kind of warning sign or indication. This can be: Pain or a feeling of tightness and constriction in the area of the chest. An irregular heart-beat. Sustained low blood pressure. Swelling in the legs, feet or ankles. A shortness of breath. Dizziness and nausea (and a few more besides). And should you experience any of these, then my best advice would be to do something about it. Tell someone. Don't be alone. Let others know, so that they can offer you advice and support. And then, get an appointment to see your doctor and have it checked out. Doing this one thing early could help to save your life. And if like me, where you don't have any signs, but become aware of a possible hereditary condition within the family (possibly due to deaths relating to cardiac issues), then also let the doctor know. Get it on record Get yourself on the radar!

Route 2. The cardiac event that is unforeseen, happens suddenly and comes without any warning. Unfortunately, there isn't much you can do about this one. You just have to hope, that, if it does happen, you are lucky enough to be in the right place, with the right people, at the right time.

BUT you CAN help to prevent such an event from even happening, by maintaining a healthy lifestyle, eating a good, healthy and balanced diet, by taking regular exercise, and by trying to live a stress free life with a positive mental attitude. And should that cardiac event still occur, then you will have done everything possible to help influence the outcome of it, and will have given yourself the best possible chance of surviving it.

And, whatever 'cardiac path' you were on (Route 1. The prior warning, doctors visit, hospital test route, or Route 2. The no warning, sudden cardiac event scenario), if you get to the point of being told; "You have a heart condition, you will need to have cardiac surgery," the important thing is to then deal with that news (hard as it is), by accepting the situation you are now in. There really is no other option.

Your heart problem isn't going to disappear or magically get better on it's own, so the quicker you can 'come to terms' and can accept that the upcoming surgery is a good and necessary thing (which will save and prolong your life), then the sooner you will be in the best mental state to handle what is to come.

Unfortunately, there is a misguided perception, that once a person has suffered a heart related event, their lives must then alter to avoid the risk of a repeat of their problem. This is far from the truth. Yes, it may be considered that some 'adjustments' may be required, and yes, some form of medication will possibly be prescribed, but with regard to changes in lifestyle (especially an active lifestyle), there is absolutely no reason why a person should not be able to participate in the sports, interests and hobbies that they enjoyed prior to their cardiac event. In fact, it is actively encouraged for them to do so.

To the layperson, the whole scenario of cardiac surgery is the stuff of nightmares. Just the thought of being on the operating table, laying there with your chest opened up, and with everything that should be on the inside, now exposed and being 'messed about with' on the outside is like a scene straight out of a horror film. And with this image at the forefront of our minds, cardiac surgery is often viewed in negative terms, and as the penalty for having a defective and malfunctioning heart. But, through my experience, I am aware that the cardiothoracic specialists see things quite differently, and view cardiac surgery in a much more positive way. Viewing the various procedures that they perform as an opportunity to 'put right' a persons' heart, so that that person will be able to continue with their life and even enjoy a better quality of life.

Without intending to trivialise heart bypass surgery in any way, a cardiothoracic surgeon once told me "we do these operations every single day, and although they are not without risk, they have a very high success rate. These type of operations are 'bread and butter' to us, so there is absolutely nothing for you to worry about. It's just another day at the office".

And once you are able to embrace that same mindset, and accept why you need the surgery and what it is going to do for you, then you will have the situation beaten. And before you know it, the operation will be over, you will be out of hospital, and the 'new and improved you' will be on the road to a better and longer life.

The Importance Of AED's

According to national statistics, it is estimated that approximately 60,000 (out of hospital) cardiac arrests take place in the UK every year, 12,000 of which, will occur in a public place. Of these 60,000 cases, approximately 90% to 95% of those not receiving treatment will sadly die, whereas when a defibrillator is used and effective CPR is performed within 3-5 minutes, then the chance of survival increases significantly from 5% to 75% (that's a potential of 54,000 - 57,000 lives saved each and every year.) Add to this the improbability for the ambulance service to arrive within the first 3-5 minutes, and the need for on-site AED machines becomes even more important in saving lives. And with an average cost of between £1,000 and £2,000 per machine, there is no excuse for AEDs not to be available in public buildings, leisure centres, workplaces, schools and community areas across the UK. It's a small price to pay to save lives!

[Note: Sadly, also included in these yearly statistics are (on average) 270 children, who will die in the UK every year after suffering from sudden cardiac arrest at school.]

In order to safeguard yourself and others: If you belong to a club, a sports team, an exercise class, attend a gym or any other public group or gathering, then ask the organisers if they have an AED available and located close by. If they say 'no', then raise the question why not! And if they don't see a need to have one, or have no plans to install one, or fob you off with some other poor excuse, then my advice would be to play your sport, take your exercise or have your meetings somewhere else. Somewhere that recognises the importance of saving lives. Who knows, that life could be yours!

When I decided to move from Coventry WF and play my football for Birmingham WF, a major consideration in that decision was the fact that BOTH of Birmingham WF's training facilities have AEDs available on-site. In fact, only a short while after my life was saved by the AED at Bedworth, one of the AEDs at Birmingham was called upon, and used to save the life of a player who had suffered a cardiac arrest whilst training there. So, within a handful of days, two lives at two separate clubs (only a few miles apart) had been saved by on-site AEDs. And had it not been for those AEDs, neither of us would have survived.

As a result of my cardiac arrest in 2018 (and following the subsequent media reports), I was told that several amateur sports clubs had contacted Bedworth United, to say that my 'event' had highlighted to them, how essential it was to have an AED available at their facilities, and that as a result, they too, would now take steps to have one put in place. Hopefully, they will never need to use those

AEDs, but if they are needed, and even one life is saved as a result, then the media reporting my 'event' (which I had mixed feelings about at the time) has proved worthwhile.

When a good friend first encouraged me to write this book, my initial reaction was 'why?" To which he replied; "The experience that you've had, how you've dealt with it and your recovery from it, could be of help to others. You've been there, you know what it's like. Tell people your story, it may help to give them some inspiration or motivation should they find themselves in similar circumstances".

OK, I thought, I'll write a book, how hard can it be? Well, to be honest, it's been a lot harder than I ever could have imagined. Not for any emotional or psychological reasons, but just because I wanted my book to be different, and I wanted to say so many things.

I didn't want to write a 'How to avoid a heart attack or cardiac arrest' type book, I'm not an expert, and anyway, there are loads of them on the shelves. I wanted to write a book 'first hand' from the victims perspective. What it's like to have a cardiac event. How did it feel to face heart surgery? How I recovered from it. What life was like afterwards etc. etc.

But it wasn't just about 'my story.' I also wanted the book to be informative. To give a better insight into the processes and procedures involved, and to dispel some of the myths and demystify the medical terms that are used.

Finally, I wanted the book to raise awareness of the importance of AED's, and how (by having them available) over 50,000 lives could be saved in the UK each and every year.

That's the book I wanted to write.

Hopefully, within these pages I have managed to achieve some of that, as well as giving you a few laughs along the way. And if that has been the case, then the writing of this book has all been worthwhile.

Acknowledgements

First and foremost, my heartfelt thanks go out to Stuart Roe.

You once said to me 'on the day that you went down, you were lucky to survive'. Well Stu, you were right, but the real luck I had was to have you there to help me. Even with the minutes ticking by and with no signs of success, you still never gave up. Your determination to revive me and to then keep me alive, is the reason that I am here. Words alone cannot express the thanks, or repay the debt that I owe you, you truly are a special person. Thank you.

To my cardiothoracic surgeon Mr Tom Barker for the use of his incredible skills in 'fixing' me.

To the Bedworth & Birmingham mouth to mouth relay team of Mark Welch (BDWF) and Mark Gibbons (BWF) for keeping my brain alive, and to Karen Peacock for the 100 yard 'defib dash'.

My lovely wife Dawn, who's endless love, support and understanding carried me through. Always there by my side. My family; Jo, Matt, Nik, Jen, Si and Faye who all showed great strength during a difficult time. Nik and Si, for keeping the troops fed and watered between hospital visits, and Jo for the brain teasers and daily puzzles. Don't forget all, I will be having two birthdays each year now!

To my good friends Dave Whatmore and Roy Williams for their contribution to these pages (the cheque's in the post lads).

To Paul Murtagh, the staff and players at Birmingham Walking Football Club. Thanks for taking me in and making me an honorary Brummie. One day I'll learn the language, promise.

To Russ and Kim Watkin and the players of Bedworth and District Walking Football. Good friends since that day. What a way to start a friendship eh?

To my friend Bart O'Shea. The man who gave me the initial push to commit my experience to paper (although I have cursed you for it many times), many thanks, it all came together in the end.

And to Steve Evans for his thoughtful and moving gift of the framed photograph. A version of which proudly graces the cover of this book.

To my long time pal Martin Slevin. Thanks for all the help, advice, guidance and expertise on how to put these words together.

To Atrium Gym for getting me back on the bike (no pun intended).

The walking football community (whether you've played with or against). Thanks for sharing the pitch with me, and giving me so much enjoyment.

And finally, to anyone I may have missed, but who also played a part in my story. Cheers guys.

Printed in Great Britain
by Amazon

61519769R00125